D1152575

Mike Ripley really is an archaeologist as well as an award-winning crime writer. He discovered his first (Iron Age) skeleton in 2001 and named it 'Morse'. Apart from the eleven Angel novels, he has written for radio and television, lectured on crime writing and reviewed for over twelve years, which has involved reading around 2,000 crime novels. He is currently the crime critic for the *Birmingham Post*.

Also by Mike Ripley

ANGEL UNDERGROUND

Mike Ripley

ROBINSON
London

Constable & Robinson Ltd
3 The Lanchesters
162 Fulham Palace Road
London W6 9ER
www.constablerobinson.com

First published in the UK by Constable,
an imprint of Constable & Robinson Ltd, 2002

This paperback edition published by Robinson,
an imprint of Constable & Robinson Ltd, 2003

A copy of the British Library Cataloguing in
Publication Data is available from the British Library

ISBN 1-84119-669-X (pbk)
ISBN 1-84119-459-X (hbk)

Printed and bound in the EU

10 9 8 7 6 5 4 3 2 1

This one is for
Chris and Julie
and, again, Tim Coles
my consultant pilot.

(And also in memory of
The Talented Miss Highsmith)

Author's Note:
This is a work of fiction.
None of the people or practises
described herein bear any resemblance
to actual archaeologists, archaeological
units or archaeological methods
in Britain now or in the past.
Yeah, right.

To the angel of the church at Pergamum write:
'These are the words of the One who has the sharp
two-edged sword: I know where you live; it is
the place where Satan has his throne.'
Revelations 2:12

As in life there are exceptions to every rule . . .
Inland Revenue Tax Calculation Guide SA151W

Archaeology is not a science, it's a vendetta.
Sir Mortimer Wheeler

Chapter One

Base Line

'Elvis is dead!' my mother wailed down the phone.

'I'm glad you've found closure on that one, Mum,' I said as calmly as I could despite my racing pulse and churning stomach.

How had she got my number?

'Not *him*, you idiot. Elvis my darling PBP.'

Now I remembered: Elvis her Vietnamese pot-bellied pig.

'I hope it was swift and painless,' I said.

She could be on a mobile, walking up the drive right now to press the doorbell. That would be just like her.

'Oh it was. The driver never really had a chance. £12,000 in damages.'

'That should buy you a new one,' I said sympathetically.

'Damage *to the car* that hit him, Fitzroy, don't you listen?'

'Sorry, Mummy dearest. Was the driver OK about it?'

'Oh *he'll* be fine. *He'll* be out of hospital in a couple of weeks and walking again in a month. Anyway, that's not why I rang.'

'What do you want?'

'Why should I want anything, Fitzroy?'

'I'll answer that when I've solved the one about why did the dinosaurs die out and why it's always the left shoe you find at the side of motorways.'

Should be a doddle by then.

'A meteor in the Gulf of Mexico and because your right foot's always on the accelerator,' she said calmly.

'You've got an answer for everything, young lady, haven't you? That tongue of yours will get you into serious trouble one of these days.'

'Actually, it's got me *out* of trouble on more occasions than –'

'Mother! Not in front of the children, per-lease!'

'Don't be such a prude, Fitzroy. There is something I want, though, and that's your help. Can you come down here at the weekend?'

'Down where?' I asked cautiously.

'Suffolk, of course.'

She actually meant just across the Suffolk border in Essex, but Suffolk sounded better. She was such a snob, but either way it was a safe distance. I was so relieved, I said yes before I could stop myself.

'Good. Saturday evening then and you can meet everybody.'

'Who's everybody, Mother?'

I was beginning to think that Norman Bates was a much misunderstood character.

'A few friends, that's all. You can bring whatshername, the one you never introduced to anyone.'

'Amy?'

'Yes, her,' said my mother, the way only mothers can. 'And don't forget to bring a bottle. Several bottles.'

I took a deep breath, knowing I was going to regret this.

'Let me guess, you're having a barbecue.'

'Yes, we are!' she said, surprise in her voice. 'How did you know?'

The King was dead. Let's eat the King.

'I didn't know you had a *mother*,' said Amy.

'Ha-ha, very funny, get back in the knife drawer.'

I had told her I had a mother; I must have. It's just the

sort of thing women ask. Her memory must be going. She was probably working too hard.

I wouldn't have gone into too much detail, that was probably a fair bet, but I was sure I hadn't said all those things Amy claimed I had. I think she was just winding me up.

The maximum security retirement home? Well, I might have said something like that but just for a joke. The sailing round the world one-handed because she hadn't understood the meaning of *single*-handed? OK, not a very good joke but actually quite plausible if you knew my mother. The business about applying for Paraguayan citizenship to avoid the War Crimes hearing in The Hague? It had been a good party and it was late and again, not necessarily the realms of fantasy here. The dropping out of a safe middle-class existence to become a really bad painter and sculptress in an artists' community, most of them unreconstructed hippies now with bus passes, on the Essex coast? Ah. That one was true.

True, but not life-threatening. Or so you'd have thought, but then I knew my mother and Amy didn't. And my mother didn't know Amy. It was a low-stress recipe for life – my life – which had worked up until now and, dammit, there was no reason for it not to go on working.

Amy was highly unlikely to sacrifice her weekend for a trip into the backwaters of East Anglia to eat roast Vietnamese pot-bellied pig and drink Argentinian Chardonnay, both served lukewarm knowing my mother. There were no decent shops there for a start and she always got a nosebleed if she was ever more than a mile away from Harvey Nichols (the personal shopping service), Gina's (shoes) or Anya Hindmarch (bags, of which you can't have too many). Mind you, she probably gets discount as she's in the business herself – fashion, that is – to the extent that she doesn't call them shopping trips so much as market research which allows her to write off a fair amount against tax.

In fact, Amy's quite a name in the rag trade, but behind the corporate scenes these days ever since she sold or leased or franchised (I never actually did discover which) her brand-name creation, the TALtop, to a consortium of High Street stores. The TALtop made her; a quality, multi-purpose blouse cut so cleverly that a Size 16 woman could comfortably get into a Size 14, a Size 14 into a Size 12, and so on. I had once suggested she cut out the hassle of fabrics and sewing and packaging and just print a load of labels and she had considered that for a minute or two. The TALtop wasn't the exclusive, short-term, must-be-seen-in item of the sort she now wears, it was smart/practical for the working girl and Amy's initial methods of marketing, using focus groups of smart, practical working girls (usually in the nearest wine bar to their office on Thurs-days – pay day), was way ahead of its time. I had tried to persuade her that TAL stood for That Angel Look but she thought that naff in the extreme, preferring to leave a touch of mystery as to what it actually did mean on the basis that everyone knows what a JCB mechanical digger is but who calls it a Joseph Cyril Bamford? I suppose she has a point. I mean: 'Oh, we're getting a man with a Joseph Cyril to come and dig the new swimming pool' just doesn't cut it, does it? And anyway, having to admit that it really represented the initials of the three founding-mothers of the idea – Amy being the 'A' – would only lead on to why the 'T' was dead and the 'L' was in prison and Amy had been left in sole possession of the company. Some might say that didn't look good on the corporate public relations front, but what the hell, it worked for me.

Thinking about it, which I did for almost a nanosecond, Amy and my mother would probably get on like a house on fire. A house, say, in Pudding Lane in London in 1666, which was a pretty good reason for keeping them apart.

'I'd better humour the old bat and nip down there,' I said to Amy after I'd hung up. I was still wondering how she'd got the number and I noticed my hand was shaking and that reminded me we were out of tequila.

'You could sound a bit more enthusiastic,' Amy said cheerfully, not looking up from the laptop balanced on her knees but holding out an empty wine glass. 'How long is it since you've seen her?'

'Not that long,' I said airily, swooping up the glass and heading for the kitchen. Over my shoulder I added, 'The Visiting Hours will probably have changed by now.'

It had actually been four years – or was it five? – and at times it had got a bit scary. Mass destruction of property had been involved (mostly mine) and violence too; even a death. We were that sort of family, not so much close as in your face. Why couldn't she just stick to Christmas cards like everybody else? Why did she have to storm back unannounced into my life with outrageous demands like: *Come for dinner?*

'For God's sake, she's only asking us to dinner,' said Amy, still focused on her laptop but her hand out for the glass I had refilled. 'Why are you so paranoid?'

Paranoid? Me? I'm the sanest person I know; in fact I'm the only sane person I know. You tell me that dropped toast always lands butter-side down and I'll believe you. You say that cats always land on their feet: I'll go with that, and I've had some experience in that field. But tell those things to my mother and she'll strap a piece of buttered toast to the back of a cat and go looking for a high building.

As for Amy, well she's living with me. I rest my case.

'She's after something, she always is,' I said, flopping down heavily on the sofa next to her so that she bounced.

The laptop almost fell off her knees but the hand holding the wine was as steady as a rock and the level in the glass didn't move.

'No, she's probably not, she just wants you to feel guilty. That's what mothers do,' she said. 'It's their job.'

She held her glass to her face and looked at me over the rim.

'Well, punk, d'you feel guilty?'

'Now you're scaring me,' I admitted.

'Doesn't take much,' she huffed, getting back to her

laptop. 'You've gone on to Scotch, that's a dead giveaway. Is that *all* Scotch, by the way?'

I looked at my glass as if noticing it for the first time.

'It said on the bottle it was twenty-five years old so that must be past its sell-by date. Thought I'd finish it off.'

'We must be out of tequila.'

She knew me too well.

'All right, I'll put my hands up to it. Yes, my mother does scare me.'

'Why?'

'She just *does*.'

'How?'

'In every which way you can think of and then some. When we were kids, she'd take us to the zoo for the day and everything would be fine. Then, as we were leaving through the main gate, she'd grab us by the hand and dash into the car park shouting "Run for your lives, they're loose!" She'd skip rather than walk. For years she maintained that her cafetière was haunted. She developed an unnatural fear of tablespoons. We had Christmas in August one year because she was bored. She would only go on holiday to countries beginning with "I". She is the one sandwich the picnic is short of. She is the part left over in self-assembly furniture. She is the noise in the system.'

I had her full attention now.

'Wow!' she breathed. 'Stress, or what? She kept you on your toes, didn't she? You should be grateful. She's the one who gave you your edge.'

Dammit, she did know me well.

Then she turned back to the laptop screen and delivered the killer punch.

'Can't wait to meet her.'

After that bombshell I needed most of the rest of the whisky in order to get to sleep that night. Even then, I awoke with a start and the bedside clock flashing 02.43.

'She is after something,' I said out loud. 'She said it. She said, *There is something I want, though* . . . And I was so bleeding relieved that she was seventy miles away I never asked her *what* it was she wanted. Bugger, bugger, bugger!'

Amy turned over and forearm-smashed me across the throat without opening her eyes.

That was Wednesday, or rather, early Thursday morning, which left me two days in which to dissuade, decoy or deflect Amy. There was no point in even thinking I could get out of it. A no show by me on Saturday would have Mummy Dearest on the doorstep or smashing through the french windows on the end of a rope preceded by a stun grenade, before sparrowfart on Sunday.

No, I had to go, but there was no reason why Amy should. She'd never shown any interest in my family up until now and, to be fair, I'd never asked about hers although she had volunteered the information that her parents had died in a car crash when she was twenty-one. And I was grateful she'd told me that up front as it was one of the ones I was going to use if she ever asked about mine. I wouldn't now, of course. Even I have some standards.

But people have funny ideas about families. I blame the kids mostly, especially the ones who go to the nearest university so they can live at home. When I went, I never once looked at a course prospectus, I used a road atlas and a mileage chart. Or the ones who get married and buy a house round the corner (with room for a granny annexe extension when the time comes) so they can have a baby-sitter on tap and they let them have a spare set of keys. Now that would have me heading for the top of the London Eye with a high-powered rifle in no time at all.

No, a quick social visit once every four or five years was about as much as anyone should be expected to take, if the family in question was anything like mine. And I am sure I'm not alone in this. Ever wondered why the phone company's 'Friends and Family' promotion never caught on except among spread-betting freaks who had up to six different bookmakers on speed-dial? And I for one never listened to the adverts urging people that it was 'Good to talk' or 'Keep in touch'. Forget it. There is just too much 'communication' these days and all of it between people with nothing to say. It was like the craze for Citizens' Band radios in this country – thankfully as short-lived as a politician's memory – when there was a scramble to get the radio sets installed in trucks and cars, but nobody had anything to say. They had to issue a free booklet called 'How to keep a conversation going'. Pathetic. And it will happen again, with people texting each other (and then calling up the voicemail to make sure they got the text message) to say they'll be in such-and-such a chat room on the Internet that night. Will they have anything to say when they get there? Will they hell. It'll never happen. No text please, we're British.

Mind you, I wouldn't personally be without the Philips mobile Amy had insisted I carry; I just never give out the number to anyone. In fact it was the third mobile she'd assigned me (I'm not counting the pagers), all of which had either been broken or lost somewhere down the line without a tear shed in their passing (except for the vibrating pager, which had its moments).

The latest one was a pay-as-you-go model and Amy kept the calltime topped up from one of her credit cards as she didn't trust me to do it myself. As far as I knew she was the only person who had the number and the only numbers in the memory were: her mobile, the house in Hampstead (hers), the office space she rented on top of one of the flash retail piazzas on Oxford Street and the payphone in the house at Number 9, Stuart Street, Hackney.

Amy didn't know about that one. Well, she knew about the house, which was where I had lived before I met her and one thing had led to another and I'd moved over to Hampstead because she had a widescreen TV and a better sound system and more than one bedroom, and she was paying all the bills anyway so it seemed to make some kind of sense. What she didn't know, though she probably suspected, was that I was still paying the rent on Flat 3 at Number 9, Stuart Street. It wasn't a large outlay due to a long-standing arrangement with the landlord of the property, a certain Naseem Naseem, for whom I had once done a very important favour. I kept it on for sentimental reasons – I'd had some good times there and the other inhabitants were trustworthy, as they had to be because I knew where they lived! – and there were sound practical reasons too. It was a good place to store stuff, a convenient place to crash when revisiting old friends in Hackney took its inevitable toll on the synapses and brain cells, not to mention the liver, and when cohabiting proved too hard, it was a good place to run to. In fact, the old flat enshrined my Rule of Life Number 114: When the going gets tough, run away and hide.

It works for me.

Except when it comes to mothers. Then you can hide, but you can't run away.

I spent most of the Thursday hatching up hare-brained schemes to divert Amy's flight path from Suffolk, or rather the part of north-east Essex which would prefer to be in Suffolk, at the weekend.

This involved about an hour not so much surfing as drowning in the shallows of the Internet on Amy's computer whilst nursing a whisky hangover trying to find a search engine which would come up with something sensible when you fed it with the words 'wife', 'mother-in-law' and 'apart'. It was useless. No wonder only eighteen per cent of everything that's up there ever gets looked at – and I mean *ever* – it's mostly rubbish.

There was nothing for it but to shake out the cobwebs from the old brain and go in search of inspiration, which is exactly what I did. A nice healthy stroll took me to the Tube station and nobody mugged me on the Northern Line, so by noon I was ensconced in the front bar of The Guinea in Bruton Place. It's a pub you have to get to early if you want one of their individual steak pies and I like to be punctual when it matters.

As pubs in central London go, The Guinea is top spot. In fact, it's one of the few 'pub' pubs left in that it's a pub not a bar, a bistro, a gastro-pub, an 'Irish' pub, a café, a theme pub that was once a bank, a Big Steak House (who'd go to a Small Steak House?), a 'family' pub with a 'fun factory' tacked on to it, or simply a chrome and steel crypt not called anything except a series of random numbers where they look at you in a funny way if you ask for a beer.

The Guinea is a proper pub. It sells excellent Young's ales in pints (and one is rarely enough) and it has small partitioned, cramped, smoky bars which are just great for meeting people – actually, you can't help meeting somebody if you fall over them. And it does food, well, steak pies anyway. Admittedly that could be tough on vegetarians, though there is a full-scale restaurant in the back which does loads of stuff. OK, so that's mostly steak and lobster, but it does have a cracking wine list and a great, if secret, stock of brilliant Lebanese wines. Mind you, you have to be in the know to order them and as the restaurant staff seem to have some sort of unofficial job exchange programme with Italian restaurants in New Jersey, it's advisable not to push the matter if at first you don't succeed.

So I was setting myself up for some serious thinking. I was on my second pint of Young's Special, my steak pie frosted with salt in front of me. Alcohol, salt, carbohydrates and protein. All necessary food groups.

I was no wiser when I got to the fifth pint, but by then I had met two advertising executive types from the agency round the corner, a businessman from Nottingham down in town for the day, a guy from a music agency in Soho whom I vaguely recognized, two Danish girls backpacking around England (distance covered to date: two miles) and, best of all, a US Marine sergeant off-duty from the American Embassy who knew fifty-three ways of killing a man bare-handed. Or so she said. I believed her, but by then I was believing anything.

16

At various points in the afternoon, I explained my problem of the coming weekend and the imminent collision of two female worlds and sought their advice. The advertising agency guys were no help at all. I suspected they still lived with their mothers. The Nottingham businessman wanted my mother's phone number. The music agent wanted Amy's phone number. So did one of the backpackers. But the US Marine Corps sergeant – bless her all the way from the Halls of Montezuma – came up trumps.

'Tactical diversion,' she said, lighting a Marlboro with a Zippo engraved with a Harley Davidson Fat Boy bike. 'You need to offer a secondary target that is both achievable and attractive.'

'Go on,' I said, borrowing the lighter for my own cigarette and admiring it. 'I like the cut of your jib so far.'

'OK, so what's she got her sights on at the moment? A weekend in the country meeting your mother, right?'

'More or less,' I agreed. 'Cool lighter.'

'Genuine Zippo. We've got hundreds at the Embassy and nobody's allowed to smoke there any more. Anyways, the country and your mother still gonna be there next week, week after. Yeah?'

'Yeah, absolutely.'

I was warming to her though I couldn't for the life of me remember what she'd said her name was. Maybe she hadn't. Maybe she wasn't allowed to for security reasons.

'So for *this* weekend you need another target for her. Someplace else she can go. Someplace she wants to go to but has never got round to it and now the chance is there, but it has to be this weekend. Could be a band, a concert, a theatre performance. Some hot ticket which is really hot, a see-it-now-or-die kinda hot.'

'Brilliant! I could kiss you!'

'You just did.'

'I know, but I've never said that to a US Marine before.'

'People only get to say it once usually,' she said in a growl hot enough to turn Iwo Jima sand into glass.

But she didn't push my hand away.

'There's a show, a play, she's been dying to see for months and it really is a Hot Ticket job and the last night of the run is Saturday. If I can wangle tickets we can postpone Mother and postponement is just one further step down the yellow brick road to total forgetfulness.'

'Can you get tickets that hot?' said the beautiful sergeant, draining the last of her pint.

'Sure,' I said confidently.

'And even if you don't get them, you'll tell her you've got them and then just before curtain up, when it's too late to go to your mom's, you'll say you lost them or left them in a cab or in your other wallet and whatever she does to you then is easier than –'

'You,' I said sincerely, 'are a tactical genius and deserve another drink. What'll it be?'

'Surprise me.'

I think I did. I certainly surprised the barman. He'd never been asked for Young's chocolate stout mixed half-and-half with champagne before, but he was willing to give it a shot.

It's that sort of pub.

My US Marine sergeant – she said her name was Virginia Richmond, but I didn't believe that – had to leave around six for a dinner date, but said she was really sorry to be going and what a treat it had been meeting me.

What she really said was something about how refreshing it was to go into a pub and not have men hitting on her.

I was still trying to work out if that was an insult when she wrote a phone number on the metal case of her Fat Boy Zippo with a felt-tip pen.

'In case things with Amy don't work out,' she said. 'Or if things do, it just wipes off.'

I waited until she'd gone before I copied the number on

to a beer mat and then wiped the lighter clean, pocketed it and rang Amy on the mobile to see if she was still at the office because I was in serious need of a lift home.

She told me to find a cab, get it to pull up outside her office and then text her and she'd come down. She told me to stay in the cab because they were like gold dust on Thursdays, late night shopping in the West End, and from the sound of me she could do without me going into the office and embarrassing her.

Sir! Yes, sir! I thought, but I didn't say it and maybe it should have been Ma'am! Yes, ma'am! Either way I thought it best not to tell her about my encounter with the US Marine Corps, and just follow orders quietly.

I found a cab easily enough near Bond Street Tube station and told the driver 'Oxford Street,' which he didn't think was funny as we were on it, so I added quickly, 'Pick up one then on to Hampstead.' That cheered him up. Saying 'Hampstead' to a London cabby was usually a safe bet, almost as popular as saying 'Heathrow' in a foreign accent.

We were outside the right piazza in about two minutes flat and I tried to sit upright in the back seat of the cab and focus on the keypad of my mobile whilst listening to the cab driver's Late Night Shopping Night rant.

'It's not what it was, you know, this late night shoppin' lark . . .'

I got NAMES and AMY was the first up, which was good as my fingers felt far too big for those tiny buttons.

'I mean there used to be decent shops along 'ere, but look at it now. You've got these big stainless steel shopping malls or megastores every quarter mile, but what's in between 'em? Bugger all, that's what . . .'

I found MESSAGES and confirmed it was going to the right number and then the tricky bit started: the typing.

'I mean, look at 'em. You've got a Foreign Exchange Bureau every ten yards to swindle the tourists, dodgy leather shops always with a sale on, burger bars or crap souvenir shops. And look at the litter . . .'

I settled on: 'Rdy wn u r. Amgek' which was pretty good for me in the state I was in. Then came the really difficult part: deciding which Icon to send with it.

'Makes you ashamed to be a Londoner, really, dunnit? I mean look at all the boxes and the bottles and the rubbish. People just don't care these days, do they? I remember when we had them bomb scares a few years back. Probably the Irish lot. You're not Irish, are you, mate? Not that they've ever done me any harm, but they started putting bombs in litter bins so they took all the bins away, must've been for a coupla years. But the place wasn't the tip it is today. People took their litter home. Had a bit o' pride in the place . . .'

I settled on the smiley face with its tongue out which my Icon selector told me meant 'Prrffft'. It seemed to make perfect sense.

I pressed SEND, waited through REQUESTING until SENT came up and decided not to save the message for posterity.

'I mean there's no fun in just window shopping any more, is there? Not here on Oxford Street. I mean this is Shopping Central, or it should be. Used to have a bit of class this street did, but it's bloody filthy nowadays.'

I made the occasional grunting noise of agreement, threw in the odd 'Too right, mate' and settled back in the upholstery feeling perfectly at home.

The cab was an Austin Fairway and I felt I knew it intimately. I should, I own one of them and when I need a real one I always make a point of hailing a Fairway or the older model, the 4XS. I used to have one of those too – the perfect vehicle for London if you don't want to be noticed, although the Hackney Carriage authorities frown on deli-censed black cabs being sold off to civilian punters in London itself and they tend to ship most of them out to the provinces.

My 4XS had been called Armstrong so the Fairway replacement was, natch, Armstrong II. A replacement had been necessary as Armstrong (I) had sort of exploded in a field in Suffolk a few years back.

The last time I'd been visiting my mother.

Suffolk.

Time for a reality check. What was that cunning plan I'd cooked up to keep Amy away from Suffolk? Sending the text message had exhausted me and the cab driver droning on and on didn't help. I was trying to concentrate so hard I almost missed it.

It happened so fast it was like a fight, a flashpoint bad temper fight between commuters pushing each other to get on or off a train, or an argument over who was first in the queue for the ice-cream van on a boiling hot day. A fight in public between total strangers, usually men. They don't often result in serious damage, except to bruised egos, and they are really, really quick with lots of badly aimed blows from flailing limbs. (A serious fight is usually with someone you know well; and lasts longer.)

From where I sat – in the back of a black cab on Oxford Street – I could see down the entire length of the shopping arcade (sorry, 'piazza') to the long, wide escalators at the end which took the punters up to the next floor (sorry, 'level') of boutiques and designer-label outlets. I knew that the offices above were served by a lift which came down as far as that upper floor and then staff had to get on the down escalator and walk out through the ground-floor bazaar (sorry, 'atrium') of more shops.

And sure enough, there was Amy on the escalator, a lot sooner than I had anticipated. She must have been already in the lift when I'd texted her but even in my state, I could see that it was her, though she wasn't making it easy. The hat, for example, made her look as if she was going to a funeral and the sunglasses suggested a gangster's funeral. And was that one of her coats? And why was she holding the collar up around her throat? She was well known in the rag trade but this Greta Garbo act seemed a tad over the top.

Then my alcohol-flexed pupils registered the fact that two or three steps down from her on the escalator were a

21

brace of in-house security men dressed in blue uniforms and peaked caps like they were the only people in the world who hadn't seen *The Full Monty*. If Amy thought she needed personal security to go home at night just so the guards could radio back 'Amy has left the building', then the delusions were setting in big time.

But the two guards jumped off the escalator as if they'd rehearsed it and pulled away from her, straight down the arcade towards me and the cab and for a second I lost sight of Amy behind them.

For another second I thought they were coming for me but they veered off to my right and their left and lunged at a tall, thin man holding a carrier bag, bundling him into an alcove between two shop fronts. The poor sod clearly didn't want to go and I saw the arm with the carrier bag flourishing as if he was signalling for help but it was impossible to hear anything. It was like a short silent movie. In fact it probably was, as the incident would have been taped by at least four closed-circuit cameras though none of the late night shoppers in the arcade turned a hair.

And then Amy was full-on in my vision, walking rapidly towards me, having lost the sunglasses and the hat, and for a moment I thought I had imagined them all along.

Then I had the cab door open for her and she was climbing in and I was smiling my best smile.

'Fucking drunks!' she hissed as she bobbed in.

I assumed she was referring to me, so I kept smiling and quiet all the way home.

But for once, I was wrong.

Chapter Two

Definition of Edges

The next morning I woke alone. Amy had left me four messages all saying the same thing: she had gone to Edinburgh and I was to phone her office after 2 p.m.

One message was in text on my mobile, one was on the flashing answerphone and one was left as a screen saver on the computer. The fourth was a hard copy print-out of the screen saver which she had stapled to the front of my T-shirt and which I only saw when I risked having a shave and looked in the bathroom mirror. She'd even printed it out in reverse so I could read it as a mirror image, which really rather spooked me.

Now there was nothing unusual about her nipping off to Edinburgh, or Estonia or Elsinore for that matter, at a moment's notice and I was sure she had given me a moment's notice at some point the previous evening. It was just I couldn't remember her mentioning it. But then I couldn't actually remember very much about the previous evening.

We had arrived home and she had cooked something – I distinctly remembered hearing the microwave go 'ping' – while I struggled to open a bottle of red wine. I knew it had been red from the stain on my T-shirt, but after that I lose the detail. I was pretty sure we hadn't had a row and I certainly couldn't find any bruises, plus I had woken up in the bed, not in the spare room or on the futon sofa, which these days I always count as a bonus.

Bottom line was she was out of town for the day which

gave me plenty of time to put my cunning plan into operation. I made myself some coffee and slipped on a Sarah Vaughan CD to put me in cunning plan mood. It was easy: go to bank, withdraw exorbitant amounts of folding cash money, find Terry the Tout in any one of three pubs around the Haymarket, buy theatre tickets, surprise Amy on her return, avoid seeing Mother.

On the second cup of coffee I realized the fatal flaw in the plan. Finding Terry the Tout wouldn't be a problem, even though these days he called himself an Entertainment Consultant. All I had to do was find one tout sniffing around the box offices for early returns and get his mobile number. All the touts have them to help last minute ticket trading and many have accounts with motorbike messengers who can deliver your tickets (at a premium, of course) even as the curtain is going up. And I had no doubt he could get me two tickets for Saturday evening. He'd look on it as a challenge: last night of a limited-run, sell-out show with the cast returning to America the next day? No problem, sir. That'll be . . . well, you think of a number which bears no relation to the price printed on the ticket, sir, then double it.

No, the tickets weren't the problem. Being in the theatre with Amy when I should be in Suffolk was the problem. I would have to come up with a cast-iron excuse, preferably at the very last minute, to fob off my mother, maybe even negotiate a flying visit one day next week when Amy was at work.

I could do that. I spent most of my teenage life doing that. I should have Certificates in it.

But the best laid plans of mice, men, female US Marines and West End ticket touts are sometimes destined never to get off the ground.

Just after two o'clock I rang Amy's office and asked to be put through to her secretary, Debbie Diamond, as instructed. Now I'd never met Debbie Diamond and, come to think of it, Amy had made sure I never had, saying that she was too valuable an asset to her career to be jeopardized by any sly, underhand remark I might make. As if.

According to Amy, she came across as a shy and retiring, yet somehow ruthless and domineering, spinster ogre. 'You can tell at a distance that she keeps tissues up her sleeve,' Amy once said, 'but I rely on her totally to keep me organized. So on pain of serious death, do not upset her!'

I got the message and when she delivered it there was that don't-mess-with-me look in her eyes. So I had respected her wishes. I've always found fear to be a useful ingredient of successful relationships.

'Miss Diamond? It's Roy Angel, Amy's –'

'Ah yes, I have instructions for you.'

Note that. No 'Good afternoon,' no 'How can I help?' just 'I have *instructions* for you' all cold and impersonal. Mind you, there are people down in Soho who pay good money for phone calls like this.

'You are to meet Amy off the 0955 shuttle tomorrow. That's 0955 landing at Stansted. She told me to stress that.'

'Stansted?'

'No, she told me to stress the landing time.'

'Sorry, that was me stressing Stansted,' I said, apologizing to this anonymous robot. 'Why Stansted? And why tomorrow?'

'Stansted because it's an airport where aeroplanes land and tomorrow at 0955 because that's when hers lands.'

I tightened my grip on the phone, thinking: *best behaviour, best behaviour* . . .

'Just a minute. Let me get this straight. She's in Edinburgh, right?'

'Yes.'

'And she's staying overnight?'

'Yes. She has a reception tonight and a breakfast meeting tomorrow.'

'Saturday?'

'I believe it follows Friday, even in Scotland.'

Sarky cow. *Best behaviour, best* . . .

'And she's flying back to Stansted instead of Heathrow.'

'Yes. Didn't she leave you a note?'

The question hung on the wire. Surely she didn't know about the note stapled to my chest, did she?

'She didn't go into detail. Why Stansted?'

I don't know why I asked, I already knew the answer and dreaded it.

'It's on the way to your mother's,' said Miss Diamond and I couldn't tell if she was smirking or not and usually I'm good at that.

'And you're not to worry about Amy's things,' the robot ploughed on as if she had a script. 'She has all the clothes she'll need with her and all you have to do is remember to . . .'

'Pack my Thomas the Tank Engine pyjamas?' I said before I could bite my tongue.

'. . . buy some wine and collect the car.'

The wine I'd remembered.

'What car?'

'Amy's BMW. It's in the car park here at the back of the building. The security guard has the keys.'

'What's it doing there?'

'I believe you picked Amy up in a taxi last night . . .'

Damn; she was good.

'Can't it stay there?'

'You'll need it to pick Amy up. She specified you must use the BMW and not, I repeat her words, *not* to use your own vehicle.'

'I bet she told you to say "vehicle", didn't she?'

'As a matter of fact, she did. I have no idea why. Just announce yourself to the security man and he'll give you the keys. Any time before five would be fine.'

'Her wish is my command. Anything else?'

'Yes, I've booked you into the Crest Motel, Romanhoe for one night.'

That was that, then. Outflanked totally. I had a car, I had Amy half-way towards the Essex coast and I had a bed booked for the night within walking distance of my mother's house. If I didn't pick up Amy's car I was in trouble. If I left Amy standing at Stansted Airport, I was dead meat. Once at Stansted it was indeed quicker to get to the Essex coast than back to Hampstead. I was hooked, landed and gutted. No escape. It couldn't get any worse.

'I've booked you the Honeymoon Suite,' said the deadly Miss Diamond.

Two strange things happened when I went to pick up Amy's car.

If you go into central London every day it is reckoned that, at a minimum, you are filmed by something like twenty-seven video cameras. I knew that – that wasn't strange – but I'd never been asked to pose for one before.

I took the Northern Line down to Tottenham Court Road, making it two days out of two when there was no trouble on the line and I didn't run into anyone I knew. (Now *that's* pretty strange.) Then I hoofed it down Oxford Street, diverting only to buy a couple of CDs for the journey – the Calle 54 collection of Latino jazz for me, the Buena Vista Social Club for Amy – before nipping down the backstreets to the fenced-off car park behind the shopping piazza and Amy's office.

There was a security guard there, dressed in the same bluey-grey wool uniform they all wore complete with peaked cap, in a hut little bigger than a sentry box but with a split door so he could open the top half and lean on the bottom. From a distance he looked like an aggressive landlord in a really rough pub daring somebody – anybody – to order a drink.

'Hi there,' I said with my second-best smile. 'I've come to pick up a BMW.'

'Yeah, right,' he said, not moving a muscle but implying: *Like I've not heard that before on a Friday afternoon?*

'Serious,' I said meekly, conscious that I was on Amy's turf and better not leave a mess. 'I'm expected. Collecting a car for Amy May on the orders of Miss Diamond in the office.'

He produced a clipboard from behind his back with

such a sleight of hand I thought for a moment that he'd had it wedged in the cleft of his arse.

'Name?'

'Angel.'

'Initials?'

'F.M.'

'It says M.R. here.'

I bit my lower lip.

'That means *Mister* Angel.'

'No, it doesn't say that,' he said slowly. 'Mister Amy, that's what it says.'

'That'd be me,' I said, almost drawing blood now.

'Got to get clearance. Step back from the desk, please.'

'What?'

'Step back from the desk while I phone you through.'

I took a step backwards as he picked up a phone and dialled. Only then did I notice the camera mounted above and behind his head. It had a red light blinking above the lens but that meant nothing. The cheap security cameras bought as a deterrent or to get you into the local Neighbourhood Watch (and thus lower your insurance premiums) have flashing red lights even though they're not connected to anything.

'Debbie? Garage here,' he said with an air of importance. 'Chappie here says he's collecting Miss Amy's Beamer.'

Behind him the camera moved through a ten-degree arc on its motorized mounting, then the lens extended. I smiled into it.

'Could you turn around, please?' said the guard, the phone clamped to his ear.

'Excuse me?'

'Turn around,' he said with a nothing-to-do-with-me-mate shrug.

I gave the lens a killer look then turned and put my hands on my hips. After about fifteen seconds I turned back.

'Satisfied?' I asked.

The guard held up a finger and listened into the phone.

'She says yes,' he said, deadpan.

I looked into the lens, blew a kiss and mouthed: 'Any time, Miss Diamond.'

I hoped she could lip read.

Then there was the curious man with the carrier bags as I drove Amy's BMW out of the car park.

He was tall, thin and pale, almost gaunt, and had his hair cut short to a stubble, though that wasn't unusual. Very few of us males in London had hair any more. He wore a grubby navy blue raincoat tied with the belt and he had a carrier bag in each hand. He stood with his back to the rear wall of the piazza building opposite the entrance to the car park, so I was within ten feet of him as I swung Amy's BMW out on to the road. He seemed interested in the car park, but not in me.

It was strange that I should notice him. We didn't even make eye contact.

Maybe we should have.

Could have saved a lot of trouble.

I hate Stansted. London's third airport? What a joke. Where're they going to put the fourth – Birmingham? Mind you, I'm not too keen on the second, Gatwick. I'm a Heathrow man, always have been. Maybe it's something to do with driving black cabs, which have always floated around Heathrow like bees around a hive, or perhaps because it has a fair choice of bars and you can get real fish and chips at more or less any hour. It also has half-decent bookshops, there's an even money chance of running into somebody famous and, though it's not a facility they advertise much, there's always the chance to buy something at bargain prices, especially if you can pay cash and you have a vehicle with the engine running outside. It's not called Thiefrow for nothing and the lesser-known freight terminal on the southern perimeter road, 'Cargo Village' to the locals, can offer you even bigger bargains, though you might need a truck for some of them.

There are also quite a few legitimate, or semi-legit, items on the go at any one time, just check out the passenger lounges. You'd be amazed how many people leave it to the last minute to realize that they are over the luggage limit, or can't be bothered to lug around those two extra litres of cognac any further, or that they'll never get *that* much dope through Customs back home unless they can put up a good case for it being for personal consumption. The personal consumption of Manchester, say. That's the real plus about Heathrow: there's always someone wanting to sell something and because they're doing it against the clock, it's a buyers' market.

Stansted is just boring. The bar always has travelling football supporters in residence, the bookshop doesn't do the early paperback editions of novels which the grown-up international airports do, the 'long stay' car park means exactly what it says (be prepared for a long stay as it's miles from the terminal), and the planes are so far from the boarding gates that anyone catching the shuttle to Edinburgh feels like they've walked half-way there before they get to snap on their seat-belt. In fact I'm sure I've done an Edinburgh trip where I worked out that the walk from the main entrance took longer than the flight itself.

So maybe I was biased but I really didn't like being there, especially not at nine thirty on a Saturday morning with the prospect of a weekend with my mother staring me in the face like a gun barrel.

Amy's plane landed ten minutes early, something which always happens if I'm late meeting someone off one but never happens if I'm a passenger on one. And, naturally, her luggage was the first off the carousel whereas mine would have been well en route to Baghdad by now.

'You're on time,' she said, shooting me a kiss and slipping the shoulder strap of her overnight case over my arm.

'You're early and this is bloody heavy,' I said, sagging under the weight of the case. 'What's in here?'

'Presents. A twenty-five-year-old malt for your mother and a twelve-year-old one for you.'

'How do you know my mother drinks Scotch?'

'A shot in the dark. You picked up the BMW?'

'Yes, yes, I can follow orders, you know,' I said wearily as we walked towards the machines where you pay off your car-parking fee with a second mortgage.

'No problems?' she asked, but not looking at me.

'No. I had to smile at the video camera for your Miss Diamond, though. Visual identity check said the security man, but I reckon she was just winding me up. How does she know what I look like anyway? Have you described me to her?'

'In a general sort of way,' she said and without looking at her I could tell she was smirking.

'Is that why she made me turn round so the camera could get a good shot of my arse?'

'Maybe that was the bit I described,' she said, stifling a chuckle. 'In a general sort of way.'

In the car – a new Series 7 BMW which Amy had splashed out on because she was worth it – I asked her what she'd been doing in Edinburgh.

'The usual. Two meetings with designers, going through the plans for new shop fittings for one of the stores on Princes Street, and then a reception for some Finnish buyers on a jolly. That went on a bit. Can they drink, or what? Got a light?'

'They probably couldn't believe the prices,' I said as I passed over my Zippo without thinking.

'That's true,' she said, lighting a cigarette and pressing buttons so that the window opened, her seat slid back and the automatic thigh massage unit came on. I'm convinced having that in the passenger seat is the only reason she lets me drive the Beamer.

'They were like kids in a sweet shop. They ordered Scotch by the bottle with the top off. God knows what the price of booze is in Finland.'

'You should have taken them down the Oxford Bar,' I suggested as we turned on to the A120 and, with a heavy heart, headed east.

'Too downmarket,' she came back.

'That's why I like it.'

'You got into a fight with a policeman in there last time we were up there.'

'It wasn't a fight, it was an intellectual argument about the impact of punk and the neo-romantic backlash in popular music. Anyway, he was off duty.'

'Bollocks!' Amy exhaled smoke. 'It was about football.'

'Don't be silly. Do I look depressed enough to argue about football in a Scottish pub? If I get that tired of life, I'll let you shoot me.'

She reached over and stroked my thigh which, unlike hers, remained unmassaged.

'That's a done deal, darling. Did you remember to pick up some wine?'

'Of course. The dreaded Ms Diamond reminded me. There's a case of mixed in the boot, half-and-half Carmenere and Sauvignon Blanc – Chile's finest export.'

'*Chilean*?' she snorted. 'You've pushed the boat out, haven't you? It is your mother, you know, and you don't see her very often. You could have got something with a bit of class.'

'Hey, don't knock the wine, it's good stuff. Anyway, as far as my mother's concerned, if it's wet and it's got alcohol in it, she'll love it.'

She let that one go in silence for about a minute then she said:

'It'll probably be a vintage by the time we get there at this rate.'

'What's the rush? I'm just observing the speed limit,' I countered.

'I didn't pay all that fucking money for this car so it could observe the speed limit!' she snapped. 'Anyone would think you didn't want to get there.'

Anyone who'd met my mother would.

'What's the rush? I thought we might stop off some-where nice for a spot of lunch, maybe.'

'Like where?'

I spotted a road sign up ahead.

'Braintree,' I said quickly.

'What the hell is there in *Braintree*?' she said in her don't-mess-with-me voice. 'Anyway, I thought we were going to a barbecue.'

'I doubt if that'll get going before evening,' I said, having totally forgotten to ask my mother what time she wanted us.

Then again, if she had a whole Vietnamese pot-bellied pig to roast and the prospect of people arriving bearing liquid gifts, she'd probably have started at dawn.

'I thought we might offer to help with things,' Amy said slyly. 'You know, before the other guests arrive.'

'Guests?' I snorted. 'It'll be a bunch of mother's arty-farty friends. This place she lives, Romanhoe, it's a self-appointed artists' colony where anyone who can fight off the arthritis long enough to hold a brush or who can remember which way a potter's wheel spins, calls themselves "creative" and churns out junk which usually ends up – unwanted – in the local Oxfam shop. The whole village is a sort of minimum security prison for geriatric hippies, all bitter and twisted that their art has never been recognized. And for "unrecognized" read: not sold.'

Amy flipped her cigarette out of the window, roughly in the direction of Braintree.

'Your mother's done a few not half bad sculptures.'

'Not half bad? Is that one up from "recyclable"? And how would you know?'

'I checked out her website.'

'*My mother has a website?*'

'You didn't know?'

'No, I sodding didn't, but it just proves my theory about the rubbish up there on the web. But then, that's typical of my mother. She wouldn't know how to turn a computer on, but there she is, secretly putting herself about on the Internet without telling anyone.'

'I think you're missing the point,' said Amy.

'No, she's always been secretive. She always operated on a need-to-know basis, the only person needing to know being her. When we were kids she'd say "See you later"

33

and a week after we'd get a postcard from Nice or Tuscany or somewhere saying "Back Saturday".'

'You're lying.'

'Not much, but you get the drift.'

'Then it must be a family trait.'

'What do you mean by that?'

'You never told me you had a mother.'

'My mother wasn't too keen on telling me!' I paused for effect, as if the mists had lifted from my eyes. 'You could be right, you know. I've inherited her natural secrecy. That's why I never told you. You can't blame me for that – or anything else I haven't told you. It's an inherited condition on my mother's side, like a sort of truth haemophilia, and I am not responsible for it, therefore blameless. Now, in the past and at any time in the future.'

Even though I was watching the road ahead I could tell she was looking at me through narrowed eyes.

'Is there anything else you've genetically forgotten to tell me?'

'No, not a thing. But then, I would say that, wouldn't I? Given my rare medical condition.'

She didn't say anything for a while and when I risked a look at her she was examining the Zippo, admiring the engraved Harley 'Fat Boy'.

'Nice lighter,' she said at last. 'Where d'you get it?'

'Oxford Street,' I said without missing a beat. 'One of the street traders outside the Tube station. It was dirt cheap.'

'Hmm . . .' she said suspiciously, as if there was something to suspect.

As if.

Since my last visit, the Crest Motel had been dumped in a field between the Colchester bypass and the sole access road down into Romanhoe. It was the sort of place which hung large white banners over the fence at the front offering 'surf and turf' specials for less than a fiver, was constantly advertising for bar staff and had a sales conference of one sort or another permanently ensconced in the function suite, which was probably called, with suitable naffness, the Iceni Rooms.

A bored receptionist smiled at us from behind a plastic desk which was bare apart from a computer terminal, a display of leaflets from the East Anglian Tourist Board and a bowl of Mint Imperials. She let her nails scrape over the keyboard and read something off the screen which seemed to give off a smell strong enough to overpower her scent.

'Ah yes, the Honeymoon Suite,' she said snootily as if we were plumbing new depths of tackiness. 'Mr and Mrs May, is it?'

'That'll do,' said Amy cheerfully.

She was eyeing up the receptionist's uniform with a view to redesigning it with extreme prejudice, preferably with the receptionist still in it.

'And how long will you be staying?'

'What's the hourly rate?' I asked innocently.

'Hourly?' Amy rounded on me as if outraged. 'You booked me for an all-nighter.'

It was a routine we'd done before.

'Just the one night, then,' muttered the receptionist concentrating on her keyboard and blushing deeply.

We stood there holding hands and smiling sweetly at her until she handed over our keys.

The village of Romanhoe was still a couple of miles down the road, or rather either side of the road which straggled down the hill towards the river estuary and then the sea. Technically it was a port, but with a concrete 'hard' rather than a harbour and these days that was occupied almost exclusively by sailing boats and yachts, mostly owned by weekend visitors from London. Once upon a time, timber boats from Poland had worked the river and there had been a thriving barter system between the locals and the Polish crews, exchanging Marks & Spencer jeans and underwear for duty-free cigarettes and over-proof vodka. The timber yard had long gone, along with all other gainful employment. Signs which previously had read 'To the Port' now said 'To the Marina' and the last remaining ship's chandler's was now the 'Riverside Boutique'.

There was still a railway station in the old town, though nowadays it took commuters to day jobs in London in about an hour and a half (and not the fifty minutes advertised on the posters) rather than shipped freight from the port. Alongside the railway line ran Station Street, a row of eight late Victorian houses which had been identical two-up, two-downs originally but once home improvement became fashionably trendy they had morphed into residences of 'individual character' sprouting extensions, porches, attic bedrooms and, in one case, a solar panel roof. Every front door was a different colour and I just knew they had been chosen from a swatch-book with names like Sea Mint, Dawn Frost and Turtle Bay.

My mother lived at Number 5 and the plan was to drive round there, drop off the wine, hopefully find her too busy preparing the barbecue to have time for us and then zoom off to find a nice country pub for lunch. I also had a back-up plan to take Amy down to Clacton Pier and make her go on some of the more stomach-churning rides, which she would just love, killing a few more hours until we had to return and face the music.

The door of Number 5, which was painted a shade of red called Crimson Tide or similar, was wide open.

Even in the hermetically sealed, air-conditioned BMW I could hear the thump of the bass line to Eddie Grant's 'Electric Avenue'. I could also smell smoke. The dark blue, almost purple, smoke that was pouring out of the door of Number 5 and drifting down the street like a poison cloud.

Amy looked at me.

I looked at Amy and shrugged.

'Party on,' I said.

Chapter Three

Primary Fill

'Elvis won't be done for hours, so we've started the party without him. You did bring booze, didn't you? Oh, yes, I see. Chilean, eh? Well, you know my rule: drink anything as long as it doesn't come out of a bottle that can be turned into a lamp. The food will be out in the garden in about five hours or so. Meantime, make yourself useful. White in the fridge, red outside on the patio. You must be . . .?'

'Amy.'

'Of course you are.'

'This is for you, Bethany. I'm a great fan of your work.'

'Really?'

'Only from your website, though. I was hoping to see a few pieces . . .'

'My Christ! Twenty-five-year-old malt. This is getting stashed away right now. I don't believe it: presents and you've visited my little website. *You* can stay.'

I disposed of the case of wine as ordered then I went back out into the street and took the two hundred emergency cigarettes I had hidden in the boot of the BMW. I was going to need them.

The car wasn't in anyone's way that I could see, so I locked it for the night.

My watch said it was 12.55 p.m. The first race from Newmarket hadn't started, it was still two hours to kick off in the Premiership and the sun shone overhead.

Whatever happened to normal Saturday afternoons?

*   *   *

I could have taken the Beamer, parked it at the motel and walked back before anyone realized I was missing. Come to think of it, I could have nipped back to London, taken in a show and gone on to a club and still got back before they had stopped talking about Amy.

Amy, not me.

Within fifteen minutes my mother was introducing Amy to her friends as 'a fellow artist'. After half an hour it was 'she's in textiles, big time' and not long after it had moved on to 'that well-known fashion designer'. By the time Mother hit the third bottle it was 'that internationally famous, universally renowned designer' and Amy was pooh-pooing her, going 'Oh, not really . . .' but loving every minute.

'Come on, Bethany,' she said at one point, 'you're embarrassing me.'

'Look,' I whispered in her ear, 'she's not saying you're any fucking *good*, but you are well known . . .'

Not that any of Mother's guests had ever heard of Amy – that was obvious from their collective dress sense on which they were obviously advised by a blind assistant down the Oxfam shop – but they were politely impressed. For most of them the prospect of free booze all day and a roast pork supper at some point in the evening was the best offer they'd had for many a year. They weren't going to blow it by being rude to their hostess's new pet. Still, that meant they left me alone.

At least Elvis, Mother's old pet, was in good hands. Somehow she had persuaded the local butcher to do the necessary on his corpse and provide a barbecue big enough to take him, complete with motorized spit. The only trouble was that the contraption took up virtually the whole of the back yard – Mother's distinction between two slabs of concrete 'patio' and 'garden' being a fine one measured in feet rather than yards.

Elvis had been a big beast in life and had been trimmed in death. The head, thank goodness, was missing and so were the legs – secreted, I suspect, in the local butcher's deep freeze. Even so, the rest of his carcass still made for

a fair-sized roast, turning hypnotically over a pit of glowing charcoal big enough to double for an inside shot of one
of the *Titanic*'s boilers. Fat and juices oozed and dripped,
incinerated in black oily smoke as they dropped into the
fire pit. What breeze there was coming off the estuary
ensured, by some uncanny twist of meteorological fate,
that the smoke invaded the house and consequently the
front door had to be propped open to provide a through-
draught and prevent the guests from choking to death.
I didn't need a TV celebrity chef (and there was almost
certainly one within the county boundary – there always is
these days) to tell me that Elvis was going to take a lot of
cooking and so the door remained open all afternoon
allowing anyone and everyone to wander in. And they
did.

I met all Mother's artist friends and the rest of the
population of Romanhoe as well, making a point of telling
them all who I was. Naturally, they were all shocked and
confided that they *never knew she had a son*. At that point
I would put my finger to my lips and whisper, '*Two* actually, and I'm the youngest . . . *and* there's a daughter – but
none of us talk about *her*.' Then I would drift off to open
more wine or check the CD player before they could think
of a supplementary. If nothing else I was seriously under-
mining Mother's street cred in this town, which was petty,
I know, but somehow satisfying.

I struck up quite a rapport with the local butcher on
barbecue duty. I recognized fairly early on the hunted look
on his face which told me that somehow Mother had
conned him into this, which gave us a brothers-in-arms
mindset. Plus, he had two buckets filled with ice and cans
of Red Stripe lager stashed behind what looked to be the
rusted-out body of an old Ford Prefect but was in fact one
of Mother's pieces from her welding-and-blowtorch
period.

The butcher was big, burly and red-faced with long
sideburns and curly hair and called Alan. Stretched tight
over his barrel chest and revealing arms that looked as if
they could have wrestled Elvis let alone fillet him, he wore

a stained white T-shirt emblazoned with the legend: I WAS MAD BEFORE I ATE BEEF.

'Do a lot of these gigs?' I asked, making conversation, as you do at parties.

'Never done one of these before,' he said, pointing at the rotating, glistening Elvis who, I had to admit, smelled better now than he ever had in life.

'You mean roadkill?' I asked.

'Good one,' he laughed, indicating I should help myself from his ice bucket. 'No, I meant Vietnamese pot-bellied. Bit of a rare breed round here. Done lots of roadkill though.'

'You have?' I asked, though not really wanting to know.

'Venison.' He winked when he said it but I must have looked blank. 'Deer. Up in Suffolk. They're always throwing themselves in front of cars. Bloody suicidal, deer are.'

'They've been depressed ever since they heard about Bambi's mother,' I agreed.

He laughed some more and prodded Elvis with a long two-pronged fork which could have come from one of those German engravings of Hell, though they probably sold them in Homebase.

'How did you get caught?' he said, taking a pull on a can.

'What do you mean?'

'How did she con you into being barman for this lot?'

I hadn't realized that I had automatically followed my main survival rule for parties: find the corkscrew/bottle-opener – and hang on to it.

'Oh, just natural calling, I suppose. You know everybody here?'

'Just about. All bloody loafers. Never come in my shop. They go to the supermarket where it's cheaper or they say they're bloody vegetarians or they only buy orgasmic.'

'Pardon?'

'Organic meat. Organic vegetables. That sort of stuff. Always wanting to know if the beef's been fed on genetically modified grass or some such rubbish. It's a big thing round here. Not that you see them turning down a free meal here, though, do you?'

'Maybe they think Elvis was raised organically – if that's a word.'

'Was he buggery,' said Alan with conviction. 'Elvis ate anything, he wasn't fussy. Tried to eat the vicar's car one day.'

'He tried to eat *me* once.'

'Me too,' said Alan, raising his can to me. 'Did you know him well?'

For a moment we must have looked like two mourners at a Viking funeral, grieving and drinking to a fallen comrade who was slowly and succulently roasting his way to Valhalla. Then I realized what was behind the question.

'Can't say I did. I don't get up here to visit . . . Bethany as much as I'd like.'

'Known her long?'

I guessed he had asked that of other men and they'd taken one look at the muscles on those brawny arms – never mind the lethal toasting fork he was holding – and thought carefully before answering.

'Lifelong family friend,' I said. 'Known her since I was a piglet.'

'She's a fine figure of a woman,' said Alan, probably unaware that he was one of the few people on earth who could get away with a line like that. 'Deserves better than this bunch of so-called artists she hangs about with. Tossers, the lot of them.'

He jabbed at Elvis with the fork, with far more violence than necessary.

I have a Rule of Life which goes something like this: Anyone will tell you anything as long as you ask them in the right way.

The downside is that sometimes they tell you far more than you want to know.

Alan was right. Mother did deserve better than this. But so did he.

I pulled the cork on a bottle of white wine, pushed it half back and stuck the bottle in one of his ice buckets, taking out another can of Red Stripe to make room.

'Save me some crackling,' I said.

I caught up with Amy at that stage in all parties when the initial supplies of wine were starting to run out, the music had moved on to late Motown and the guests had begun to fling themselves about, regardless of the furniture, to 'Armed and Extremely Dangerous', which was a pretty fair description of them. It was only 5 p.m. and there were still four hours of daylight to go. Elvis was about half cooked. New people were arriving all the time. You could tell them because their clothes didn't smell of smoke and pork fat.

Amy was clicking off her mobile phone when I slipped my arm round her waist.

'You're not working, are you?'

'Absolutely,' she said. 'All in a good cause, though.'

'You've just rung the local off-licence, haven't you? Ordered some more wine on your credit card.'

She looked genuinely surprised.

'How did you know that?'

'She's my mother, I know how she operates,' I said smugly. 'Are they going to deliver?'

'Deliver? They're closing the shop and coming to the party!' And then she burst into a fit of giggles.

'I see she has turned you to the dark side,' I growled.

'Didn't take much,' Amy spluttered. 'Just a nudge. Your mother's an absolute sweetie.'

'You're pissed.'

'Of course I am. Aren't you?'

'Only a matter of time,' I said, resigned.

'Well, keep it together for a few more hours, there's someone coming she wants you to meet. Later on, when we eat.'

'She's hardly said two words to me all afternoon. And as for eating, have you noticed that there's no food around except for roast Elvis?'

Amy wrinkled her nose.

'It certainly smells good, but I wish you wouldn't keep calling it Elvis.'

'Whatever. It looks like there's roast pork on offer and nothing else. I hope she hasn't invited any Jews, Muslims or vegetarians.'

'Stress out, Angel, it's all under control. Somebody's bringing bread and salad stuff later.'

'Enough to feed the five thousand, I hope. How many people are there in here?'

'Bethany certainly is popular,' she said over the rim of her glass. 'Can't think why you've been hiding from her all this time. Not ashamed of her, are you? I mean, what's to be ashamed of?'

I looked at her pityingly.

'Just wait, you'll see. There'll be a price to pay for all this niceness. I know her. The Force is strong in her. And as for her popularity, just remember this is a colony of would-be artists. They'd crawl on their knees across broken glass for a sniff of communion wine and a Twiglet if it was free.'

'Cynic.'

'Sucker.'

At that point the wind must have changed direction for a cloud of particularly acrid black smoke invaded the kitchen from the garden. I think it had something to do with Alan the Butcher deciding to baste Elvis with Red Stripe lager by shaking a can, popping the tab and spraying the roast, the charcoal and anyone who was in the way, with the contents.

'I'm going outside to have a smoke in the fresh air,' I coughed. Amy was already being chatted up by a scruffy oik in a Hawaiian shirt whose opening line was: 'And you paint – what?'

Out on Station Road I settled my backside on the bonnet of the BMW, carefully balanced a glass and an open bottle of Chardonnay I had yoinked from the fridge on the way out on the new paintwork and unwrapped a fresh pack of cigarettes. Away from the smoke and the people squashed into the house, it was quite pleasant sitting there on a

43

deserted street next to a railway line, the odd seagull free-falling up in the sky, the metallic chinking of ships' bits as the yachts settled in their mud moorings as the tide went out – clearly audible, between tracks.

Which was when the police arrived, two of them climbing out of the Essex Police Ford Mondeo which pulled into the kerb in front of the BMW. They stood and looked at me, their hands resting on the top of their door frames.

'Not thinking of driving, are we, sir?' asked the uniform from the passenger side.

'Not my car,' I smiled truthfully. 'Just looking for somewhere to take a load off.'

'Crowded inside, is it?' The other uniform nodded towards the house from which smoke and music poured in equal proportions.

'A bit busy,' I admitted.

'Good,' said the two policemen together.

Then they took off their peaked caps, threw them into the car, shut the doors and locked them and headed inside.

I should have known that Mother would have invited the local force in order to cut down on the complaints from neighbours. It's usually good policy. They didn't stay long, but long enough to suss the place for later when they came off shift and could come back as civvies. Good public relations, Mum.

It was after the cop car had gone though that I really took my hat off to her, as the next arrival on Station Street was the vehicle delivering the 'bread and salad' Amy had told me about. I had half expected a vicar on a charity run in a second-hand Volvo or maybe a local baker coming off shift with his Citroën Bellingro (the van that seems to have replaced the old Ford Thames for small traders) stuffed with warm loaves. But then, I had been drinking all afternoon. I hadn't had enough to expect what actually did turn up and park right in front of me, just where the police car had stopped half a bottle before.

The cops hadn't been able to deal with one of my mother's parties, so they'd called in the army.

44

I have to admit I looked at the label of the bottle of wine I'd borrowed just to check the alcohol content because I wasn't sure I was seeing this for real. If it was a hallucinatory by-product of this particular Chardonnay, then I wanted to make sure I remembered to order a case. Or three.

It all happened with the precision of a military operation. Well, it would, wouldn't it? They were soldiers, after all.

The truck, a ten-tonner, stopped right there in front of me and two soldiers jumped out of the cab, double-timed it to the back, pulled back the canvas covers and dropped the rear flap. Two more uniformed men dropped out of the back of the truck, bending their knees like they were practising for a parachute landing. Why should I think of that? Because they were wearing red berets, that's why. They actually were paratroopers – the Airborne Brigade or whatever it was they called themselves these days. The Paras. I had to hand it to Mother; when they sent in the army to quell one of her parties, they had to send the best.

Except that these boys had gone over to the enemy. Instead of unloading the latest in laser-guided weaponry and storming the house there and then, they began to lift plastic trays of bread from the back of the truck. There were bread sticks, French baguettes, bread rolls, even sesame buns, all freshly baked from the smell, and then a tray of bowls with clingfilm stretched across them like drums which I could see contained green salad and tomatoes.

The caterers had arrived.

I poured myself the last of my wine and decided not to speak unless spoken to. These guys were trained to kill after all.

The four of them formed a line on the pavement, ignoring me. Then I saw that a fifth uniform had descended from the cab. This one had pips on his shoulder flashes, but you could have pegged him for the officer by the fact that he was carrying two bottles of champagne.

'Good evening,' he said to me, nodding slightly, showing his teeth.

I showed mine back and grinned inanely. It was either that or salute.

'You're not Fitzroy by any chance, are you?' he said in an accent you could peel figs with.

'Oh, I think chance had a lot to do with it,' I said, conscious that I was slurring the few words I could manage.

'Thought you might be. Bethany described you.'

Of course she did. I'd be the one out in the street with a bottle and a glass, his arse propped up by a new BMW.

He tucked one of the bottles under his arm and held out a hand and as there wasn't a gun in it I decided it was safe to shake it.

'I'm pleased to meet you,' he said, smiling. 'I'm –'

'Rupert!' my mother yelled from the doorway.

'Mother! Behave!' I shouted back.

After all, the man was bringing food. Just because he was an army officer that was no reason to call him a 'Rupert' – the all-purpose other-ranks' term for an officer of breeding, class, natural authority and absolutely no intelligence – in public.

'No, that's right,' said the officer, still gripping my hand. 'It *is* Rupert. Rupert Tyrell. Captain, actually, but don't worry about that. Pleased to meet you. I've heard so much about you.'

Oh shit.

Now what?

'Well, I think he's a sweetie,' said Amy, dabbing at her mouth with a yard of paper towel. However much she'd paid for that kissproof lipstick, it couldn't handle warm pork fat.

'So does Mother,' I said, chewing on an army-issue poppy-seeded baguette, which was really rather good.

'He's totally charming.' She reached over and grabbed a

cherry tomato from my plate, saying 'Yoink!' as she whipped it away.

'Only with older women,' I said.

'He's been charming to me.'

'I rest my case.'

'Bastard. Yoink!' She stole a spring onion. 'You think he's that young?'

'No, it's just that we're that old now.'

At the back of my brain something was telling me that I must have been drunk to have said that. Another part of my brain was pointing out that the fact that Amy hadn't attacked me with the salad tongs meant that so was she.

'I think this is the somebody she wanted you to meet,' Amy said in what she thought was a whisper. She tried to focus on the last olive left on my plate but I yoinked it away before she could.

'Oh bloody hell,' I said, shaking my head.

'Don't take it like that,' she said, reaching out a hand and stroking my knee so that the last of the meat juices on her fingers came off on my jeans. 'A woman as . . . as . . . *vital* as your mother . . .'

Vital?

'. . . is bound to look for someone younger, with energy . . .'

'You don't get it, do you?' I began searching for my cigarettes.

'Get what?'

'She wants me to do something, she said so when she rang. And it'll be something to help out young Rupert there, believe me. Whatever it is, I'm paying back a favour. That's the way she works. I'll be the one picking up the tab for these bread rolls at the end of the day, you'll see.'

'How can you distrust a person so much?' She yoinked one of my cigarettes. 'How can you sit there and be so bloody confident that you're right and there's absolutely no room for doubt? Why are you so bloody sure she's always got an ulterior motive?'

'She's my mother,' I said. ' Which part of "Duuuh?" don't you understand?'

* * *

47

By nine o'clock most of the guests had gone. Most of them hadn't really been guests anyway, just transient observers a bit like you get at road accidents, on their way somewhere else but giving the party a look just in case.

Alan the Butcher was still hanging in there, out in the back garden roasting what was left of Elvis to a frazzle, the charcoals glowing red, giving him an underlit hellish quality. He was singing along to the music (Frank Sinatra by this time – *Only The Lonely*, the good stuff) and talking to himself. He was holding his long-handled fork and a large carving knife, even though there wasn't much left on the roasting spit to prod or carve, but which ensured he would go on talking to himself.

Inside the house there was a hard core of about a dozen still standing, still drinking, in the kitchen and a few couples trying to dance in the front room. To get from the kitchen to the front room you had to step over no more than four bodies. Given the amount of booze and protein that had been consumed, I called that a result.

Rupert was there of course, although his squad of crack catering corps bakery troops had been dismissed and sent back to barracks as soon as they'd delivered the buffet.

We all met on the stairs, as you do at parties. No one said, 'Let's meet on the stairs and have a serious conversation in five minutes' time.' It just happened that way; as it does at parties.

Mother took the high ground, a good tactical move, parking herself on the eighth or ninth step, placing an open bottle of champagne behind her on the tenth. Rupert and Amy took alternate steps down so that their knees almost touched. I sat on the third step, feet on the hall floor, no more than a yard from the open front door. I could do tactics as well.

'You've met Fitzroy, Rupert?' said Mother, automatically chairing the meeting.

'Well, briefly, when we arrived. It's been a bit of a bun fight in here,' said Rupert, smiling at us all in turn.

'Good buns,' said Amy straight-faced. I choked down cigarette smoke.

'New recruits in the catering corps. Gave them the job to do as an exercise. Bit of a challenge. Seemed a shame to waste them,' said Rupert enthusiastically. 'Bit naughty, I suppose, bringing them here.'

'We won't tell,' said Mother. 'Now ask Fitzroy what you wanted to ask him and then we can have a dance. We haven't had a dance yet.'

If she was trying for her seductive kitten look it wasn't working. Hungry hyena sprang to my mind, not that Rupert noticed.

'Well, I know this must sound a bit odd, coming from a complete stranger, I mean, but Bethany has assured me you're the man with the ideas and you might be able to help me with a problem I've got.'

'What sort of problem?' I asked slowly.

'It's my godfather. The problem's with him.'

Rupert looked at me as if that explained it all. Then he looked at Amy, searching for the sympathy vote and, dammit, if she didn't give it to him, nodding wisely and even reaching out and patting his knee. (She withdrew her hand faster than a newly baptised snake-handler in a North Carolina church when she saw my mother's expression.)

'Godfather as in old, fat Italian with a curious sense of honour and the contract to supply olive oil to the British Army?' I tried, knowing it would sink like a stone. 'I'm sorry, Rupert, but I don't *do* godfathers, or godmothers for that matter. I don't have any myself and I don't see why other people –'

'Yes you do,' said The Mother From Hell.

'I didn't know you had *godparents*!' Amy breathed excitedly.

'I thought we didn't speak of them in the family any more,' I said, trying to reassert some sort of moral authority. 'Though of course, with time off for good behaviour and the parole system the way it is these days –'

'No, no,' said Rupert, conscious that he was losing the plot, 'it's not the fact that I have a godfather, it's what he's doing that's the problem.'

'I know I'm going to regret this, Rupert, but what is your

godfather doing which so upsets you and with which I could possibly help?'

Given the amount of booze I'd had I was quite pleased that sounded as sensible as it did. Consequently I was off-guard when the answer came.

'Archaeology,' said Rupert. 'He does archaeology. It's very worrying.'

That was when I should have run screaming from the house. But no, I stayed and looked stupid, waiting for my brain to catch up with events and forgetting the old saying: Those Whom The Gods Find Not Paying Attention Die Young.

'Worrying, yes,' I said reasonably, 'but it's not against the law. Yet. Well, not in Essex.'

'Suffolk, actually,' said Rupert, like I was interested. 'He's digging in Suffolk.'

'I'm sure it's allowed there. What's it got to do with me?'

I didn't really want an answer. I wanted to say why not come back to me one day when I gave a fuck, but it's not the sort of thing you say out loud – not when your mother seemed to be on a promise later that night. I didn't want to offend her.

'Your mother said you were an archaeologist,' Rupert beamed innocently.

That did it, the gloves were off now. She was toast.

'I didn't know you were an *archaeologist*!' squealed Amy, clapping her hands in delight.

Her too.

'But I'm not,' I said, trying for the voice I usually reserve for the magistrates' court.

'You did it at university,' said my mother.

'Did you?' giggled Amy.

'That was a long time ago on a planet far, far away. It was a way of meeting girls, getting out into the fresh air. I was a sickly child.'

'Bollocks,' said mother. 'Well, apart from the bit about girls.'

'It was part of my course, just a passing fad. I only did a couple of terms . . .'

'I seem to remember one summer vacation when you conned your father – not me, I hasten to say – for an all-expenses-paid dig in . . . where was it now? . . . oh yes, the Parish of St Andrews in Kingston. We naturally assumed you meant Kingston-on-Thames, not bloody Jamaica!'

'It's an easy mistake to make,' I said limply.

'We had to get the consul to send you home for the start of term, if I remember right. "What archaeological dig?" he said.'

Amy was going purple trying not to burst out laughing.

'She'll be getting the naked-on-the-rug photographs out next,' I sniped.

'Your baby album?' Amy spluttered.

'Who mentioned babies?'

'Don't change the subject, Fitzroy. Rupert here doesn't want our family history.'

'Well, actually . . .' Rupert started then thought the better of it. He wasn't an officer for nothing.

'Your very expensive education qualifies you to help Rupert in my opinion, so shut up, stop whining and listen to the dear man.'

Her voice swooped down and she gave Rupert the old up-from-under-the-fringe-of-red-hair look which meant he was putty in her hands.

'Now, Bethany, I don't want to impose on Fitzroy. I'm sure he's got lots on his plate,' soothed Rupert.

'I have, I have,' I pleaded.

'Such as?' Amy and my mother said it together, then looked at each other. Then smiled.

Scary.

'Fitzroy was put on this earth to be imposed upon,' said Mother with the confidence of someone who actually had put me on earth before I could think of anything. 'Impose away, Rupert.'

'Well, if you really don't mind . . .'

'Impose, impose,' encouraged Amy.

'As I said, it's my godfather. He's called Arthur Swallow,' Rupert began. 'Long-term family friend, was my father's commanding officer for a while. He was always a bit eccentric in a nice old boy sort of way, but lately he's become quite obsessed.'

'With archaeology,' I said and Rupert looked at me like I was psychic.

'Absolutely so. He went on courses, training digs I think they're called, and read everything he could get hold of. This was long after he'd retired. Then he started digging.'

'So?' I was still expecting a punchline.

'He started digging in his garden. His own garden.'

'You sure we're talking archaeology here and not just enthusiastic horticulture?'

'Oh no, this isn't gardening, this is *digging* as in trenches and wheelbarrows and planking and he's even got a bulldozer now. Look, let me show you something.'

Rupert unbuttoned a breast pocket on his uniform jacket and produced a folded sheet of paper inside which was a smaller piece, obviously something cut from a newspaper. He handed me the sheet first, which was a photocopy of a news item from the *East Anglian Daily Times*, but held on to the real clipping.

'Read that one first,' he urged.

Amy stretched over to try and read it upside down, giving Rupert a direct line of fire down her cleavage. I held the paper so she read it as well without raising his blood pressure, or Mother's.

SUFFOLK SOLDIER TURNS TREASURE HUNTER

A retired soldier and former magistrate is to spend his retirement excavating the grounds of his family home at Woolpack in the hope of finding the official treasury of Queen Boadicea, abandoned nearly two thousand years ago.

Lt-Colonel Arthur Ransome Swallow, 66, is convinced that his Woolpack Hall house is built on or near the site of the official mint of the legendary Boadicea, queen of the Iceni tribe, who led an unsuccessful revolt against the Roman legions in AD60. 'I am convinced the queen had her coins minted in this area,' said Lt-Col Swallow. 'The Iceni are always referred to as coming from Norfolk but in fact they occupied most of what is today north Suffolk and several hoards of Iceni coins have been found nearby.'

Lt-Col Swallow is to conduct his excavation solely within the grounds of Woolpack Hall, near Hadleigh, which he inherited following the death of his brother Gerald last year. 'I am not a rich man,' he said yesterday, 'in fact I am just a pensioner now and I will have to rely on volunteers to help dig the site during the summer. Any coins will, of course, be donated to museums in Ipswich and Norwich.'

A spokesman for Field Archaeology Groups in Suffolk (FAGS) warned that: 'Unsupervised excavations should be treated with caution. An enthusiastic amateur can actually damage sites of archaeological interest.' Dr Simon Roylance, senior lecturer in ancient history at the University of Essex, said he was surprised at the planned excavation as 'there is no documentary or archaeological evidence of a specific Iceni site in the Woolpack area whatsoever.'

Lt-Col Swallow is to appeal for volunteer helpers through youth groups and schools, stressing that facilities will be minimal but camping sites will be available. 'It will be hard, physically demanding work, with no pay,' said Mr Swallow, 'but should be very rewarding educationally.'

'What do you think?' Rupert asked enthusiastically as soon as he judged I was at the bottom of the page.

'First reaction? Who called the poor sod Arthur *Ransome* Swallow? Parents can be so cruel sometimes.'

My mother looked up to the ceiling.

'Er . . . anything else?' Rupert said, blushing because he thought he had stumbled into a family minefield – which he had.

'I'm guessing the dig was a disaster. The old boy probably had detectorists crawling all over the place by the first night. If anything was there, it was nicked in the first week.'

'*Detectorivists*?' slurred Amy, her eyes crossing.

'Detector*ists* – people with metal detectors, who come at night mostly. Sometimes called Nighthawks. They justify themselves by saying that seventy per cent of the metal finds in the British Museum are down to metal detectorists, but don't point out that they trashed ninety per cent of the archaeology to get at them.'

Rupert turned his head as if he'd seen *The Exorcist* once too often and gasped at my mother, 'He *does* know his stuff, Bethany. You were quite right.' Then he swivelled back to look at me.

'Spot on. Absolutely spot on. That's exactly what happened. How did you know?'

'Put the word "treasure" in a headline and they come out of the woodwork. No archaeologist would breathe the word until long after the site was dug and the finds were ready to go on show. These days they track all the archaeological websites. probably have one of their own. Most proper sites employ security guards at night now. Poor old Arthur here can't even afford diggers. But this is dated – what – ten years ago?'

'Absolutely,' Rupert enthused. 'That was then but this is now.'

He handed over the real newspaper cutting which was about four inches square but the bit I had to read had been circled in ballpoint pen. A date had been scribbled on the bottom from eleven days before. It would have been a Wednesday and the newspaper would have been the *Guardian*, which is when and where the archaeological Situations Vacant appear.

Private Excavation Suffolk
Supervisors, site assistants and finds processors needed for late Iron Age site. 1 year contracts. Day rate from £75. Accommodation provided free on site, also transport from

mainline station (Ipswich). Open trowel policy. CVs to Iceni
Rescue Archaeology, Woolpack House, Hadleigh.

'So? Notice the difference?' Rupert quizzed eagerly.

'Well, he seems to be a bit wiser ten years on and a bit more organized,' I said, reading the cutting again. 'Seventy-five quid a day rate plus free accommodation? Most diggers would kill for that. It must be costing him a fortune if it's coming out of his own pocket. What's he done, won the bleedin' Lottery?'

'As a matter of fact,' said Rupert dead serious, 'he has.'

Chapter Four

Surveying

'It wasn't a huge win; I mean not a roll-over double-top jackpot or whatever they call them. Just a modest £840,000 or so,' said Rupert the next morning over breakfast.

We were all in the dining room of the Crest Motel and it was Sunday morning and the last call for breakfast and I could hear the village church bells, which were at least a mile away, as clearly as if they were inside my head. I could hear them even when they stopped.

It hadn't been my idea to meet for breakfast, see my mother for a second day running, or continue the conversation Rupert had started about his eccentric godfather deciding to blow his Lottery winnings digging up his garden looking for Iron Age treasure which almost certainly did not exist. (It was coming back to me slowly, as I slurped coffee and summoned up the strength to tackle a piece of toast.)

I remembered that I had shot myself well and truly in the foot by insisting that Queen Boudica had not been queen long enough to establish an official mint and, as far as I knew, no coins bearing her name had ever been found. She had become queen of the Iceni, the Iron Age Celtic tribe which had lived in north Suffolk and south Norfolk, in about AD60 and almost immediately gone on the rampage against the invading Romans who, after all, had never done anything for us apart from the roads, the wine, the legal system, central heating, sewers and so forth. After turning over Colchester, London and St Albans she then got well and truly stuffed in a battle with the Roman legions on a site never convincingly identified, but which just might be somewhere under the present-day Watford Gap service station on the M1.

Somebody – Amy, I suspect – had interrupted my flow by asking why I called her 'Boudica' and I'd said, all confident, that I thought everyone knew that 'Boadicea' was a spelling mistake in a medieval manuscript which had been picked up by the Victorians when they were looking for a great British heroine to stand alongside Alfred the Great. That had become locked into the public consciousness once that bloody awful statue of 'Boadicea' in her chariot with the big knives coming out of the wheels had been dumped on the Thames Embankment. Her name really was *Boudica* – pronounced Boo-di-ka – which was a Celtic word meaning 'victory'.

At that point Rupert had looked at my mother in adoration and she had given him one of her told-you-so looks in return.

'You *do* know what you're talking about, don't you?' Rupert had said as if he was about to ask for my autograph. 'You're just the chap I need.'

'Told you so,' my mother had added rather gratuitously.

'To do *what*?' I had pleaded.

'To go in there, sort of under cover, and suss the place out. Make sure the old boy's not being ripped off. There's some rum things been happening down at Woolpack House lately, but I'd like to tell you about them tomorrow. You are staying over, aren't you? Excellent. Let's do breakfast, as they say. I've got to call for my transport back to barracks. I'm on call tonight.'

'You mean "on duty"?' Amy had purred, seemingly quite taken with him.

'No, I'm off duty, but still "on call", if you know what I mean.'

He had tapped the side of his nose then, though none of us had a clue as to what he was talking about, and gone to find the phone.

Mother had stood up, realized her bottle of champagne was empty and stomped down the stairs, stepping over me, to get another.

At the foot of the stairs she had tossed her head and said, 'My work here is done' before heading, in more or less a straight line, for the kitchen.

'He's an idiot,' I had said.

'He's nice,' Amy had said.

'I bet he's worried about his place in old Arthur's will. Wants to make sure there's some of that Lottery money left when old Swallow meets the Amazons on the great lake in the sky.'

'You're just jealous.'

'Of what?'

'The fact that he's rather good-looking and extremely fit – did you see his arse of steel? Oh, and that he's younger than you.'

'Is he? I hadn't noticed.'

'Trust me.'

At that point, Rupert had returned to offer us a lift back up the hill to the motel as neither of us were in any fit state to drive. We both agreed at once, Amy just so she could sit next to that tungsten butt and me because I'd never ridden in a Military Police car before.

In the few brief seconds of consciousness after my head hit the pillow of the kingsize honeymoon bed, narrowly missing the one wafer-thin mint that had been left in ambush there, I thought about Rupert.

What sort of an army officer can call up the Redcaps like other people do minicabs? Or con the regimental cooks to cater for a party for my mother, who was old enough to be *his* mother? Or have a godfather who is digging up Suffolk for non-existent 2000-year-old coins? And why was Amy smiling in her sleep?

The phone woke us at just after 9 a.m. It was my mother, telling me that she and Rupert were in the dining room starting breakfast without us and, by the way, she'd brought the BMW up from the village.

I hadn't even noticed that she'd lifted the keys from my pocket.

She might have lost her precious Vietnamese pot-bellied pig, but she hadn't lost her touch.

I could have forgiven Rupert most things, even the fact that he was so freshly clean and close-shaved that he sparkled, that he wore a white shirt and tie on a Sunday morning and that he seemed to regard breakfast as an opportunity for conversation. But even I bridled and joined in when he described £840,000 as 'modest'. Despite falling prices, that was still 16.8 *kilos* of cocaine at street prices, or a fleet of about sixty of the new Minis designed by BMW should you get the urge to remake *The Italian Job* on a grand scale.

'You can buy a modest amount of archaeology for 840K,' I said. 'Why not let him have his fun if that's how he wants to spend his winnings.'

'I've no objection to his little hobby at all, in fact I've helped him with it over the years,' said Rupert reasonably, smiling at Amy whenever he could. 'And once the money's gone, it's gone. Arthur never married and apart from a lump sum to his housekeeper, he's leaving everything to the British Museum.'

He must have caught my look.

'I'm not after his money if that's what you're thinking,' he said.

'He was thinking no such thing!' Amy yelped, patting Rupert's hand.

Oh yes I was, I thought.

'Oh yes he was,' said Mother over the top of a menu card. 'I think I'll have eggs and bacon . . .'

We all looked at her.

'What?'

'Look,' said Rupert earnestly, 'I know exactly what's in my godfather's will because I witnessed it and as such I won't get anything, although he has promised me a couple of things from his military collection for the regimental museum. But any assets he has left on his death are well and truly spoken for and the chances of him making a new will are zero. Not that I would want him to. I'm perfectly happy with my lot.'

I reached for a piece of toast from the rack a waitress had placed in the middle of the table, but then thought the better of it. I was still in no condition to handle the noise, what with the church bells booming in the distance.

'So if you're happy with your lot, and this Arthur Ransome character is happy digging up his garden treasure-hunting, where's the problem?' I managed.

'Arthur *Swallow*,' said Rupert, 'Ransome is just his middle name. I make the same mistake myself sometimes. His parents must have been great fans of the Ransome books. *Swallows and Amazons*, *Peter Duck*, that sort of thing. Did you know that Ransome was a spy for us, in Russia, at the time of the Bolshevik revolution?'

I did actually, but I wasn't going to encourage him so I blank-faced him.

'It's funny what parents call their children, isn't it? Mind you –' I could sense it coming – 'isn't your name Fitzroy Maclean? As in the soldier. Damn fine writer too, from what I remember. Had to read *Eastern Approaches* at staff college. Bloody good.'

'Yeah, my father thought so as well. He was reading it the day I was born. Lucky, really. The week after, he got *Mein Kampf* out of the library.'

'Don't listen to him, Rupert,' said my mother. 'He answers to Fitzroy or Roy, take your pick.'

'He answers to anything except "It's",' said Amy, all innocent, and of course they looked to her for the punchline.

'As in "It's your round" or "It's your turn to do the washing up" or "It's all your fault". You never get a response to any of those.'

'So why can't Mr Swallow have his fun, then?' I said, sticking to my guns.

'Because I don't think it is fun any more,' said Rupert.

'It's certainly not harmless. People have started to get hurt.'

'You mean as in Health and Safety accidents? Diggers falling into trenches, putting a mattock through a foot, sitting on a sharpened trowel, that sort of thing? We always blamed the drink in my day.'

'No, nothing like that. More serious.'

'What, like tetanus? Blood poisoning? Amoebic dysentery? Malaria?'

'Don't be ridiculous, Fitzroy,' snapped mother. 'We're talking about England.'

'So was I,' I said.

'You mean you can get all those doing archaeology?' Amy fell for it.

'Actually I meant by just coming into contact with an archaeologist –'

'Fitzroy!'

'You don't know the conditions these archaeologists have to live in, Mother. You might understand better if you did. Perhaps then you wouldn't be so quick to judge.'

Mother's breakfast arrived then – eggs, bacon, halves of tomatoes resembling giant bloodshot eyeballs and fried bread. The very sight of it diminished my will to live.

'I'm going to eat now,' she said primly, 'and you remember the old family rule. "Mummy's mouth open, Fitzroy's mouth closed." '

'Aw, that's sweet,' smirked Amy. 'Was that from when you were a likkle baby?'

'I think he was twenty-seven before it sank in,' growled my mother.

'And that was only because she was holding a steak knife –'

'Uh-ah,' she said, waving her fork in a menacing way. 'You can carry on, Rupert.'

Rupert swallowed hard and looked around the table, perhaps only now realizing what he had let himself in for. Still, he was a good military man, undaunted by overwhelming odds.

'I meant hurt as in physically hurt, probably by other people,' he said.

'As opposed to what?' I asked. Fair question, I thought. For all I knew he might mean by visiting aliens, supernatural forces or a crack squad of National Insurance inspectors.

'By people not involved in the dig,' Rupert ploughed on. 'There have been, well, frankly there's no other way of saying it . . . *attacks* on some of the diggers. At night. That's why the police think it could be detectorists.'

'Nighthawks?' said Amy, all serious like it wasn't until last night she thought that was somebody who trawled gay bars.

'Exactly!' Rupert was pathetically pleased to find an audience. 'Nobody can prove anything, of course, but there have been a number of incidents. Several diggers have quit and I think two or three had to go to hospital for treatment. That's why Arthur's advertising again, for more staff. There's a bad feeling in the camp. Morale is low and I don't think Arthur can cope.'

'I seem to remember he was offering pretty good pay and conditions,' I said, thinking back through the haze to our conversation on the stairs. 'He should be able to attract some decent people.'

'Can I see that advert again, please?' Amy asked Rupert, as if Rupert could deny her anything. His hand shot to the inside pocket of his snazzy green blazer to produce the cuttings he had shown us last night.

'Funnily enough, he doesn't seem to be able to attract the right sort of staff at all,' said Rupert. 'He has a good – what do you call them? – staff officer type.'

'Project manager?' I offered.

'That's the one. She's called Joss and seems to know what's what. Then there's a chap called Ben and one called . . .'

'Dan?' I suggested.

'How did you know?'

'There always is one called Dan. Go on any dig site and yell "Dan" and you'll get an answer. Bet you there's a token American as well. There'll be at least three paid-up members of the *Buffy the Vampire Slayer* fan club, an ex-Hell's Angel or two, fifty per cent will be vegetarians and the number of left-handers will be twice the national average. If you're lucky, two out of twenty will be able to drive.'

'Have you done some sort of study?' Rupert asked seriously.

'Ignore him,' said Amy, reading the newspaper cuttings, 'he's doing cynicism at night school. What does "open trowel policy" mean?'

'Not a clue,' said Rupert.

'It means your godfather is providing all the tools they'll need right down to personal trowels. Most archaeologists carry the same one around for years and the more worn it is the higher the status. They give them names like Mr Pointy or Excalibur or Gimli, for God's sake.'

'What was yours called?' Amy asked sweetly. 'When you were a student?'

'Bob,' I said.

'As in Marley,' said Rupert. 'When you were digging in Jamaica.'

'Something like that,' I said quickly as Mother choked on a piece of fried bread.

I was impressed that he'd remembered the story. He must have been taking notes.

'You know, I'm more convinced than ever that you're just the man I need,' he gushed as I struggled to keep my hand steady enough to pour more coffee. 'You seem to know all the right stuff.'

'To do *what*, Rupert?'

'To go up to Woolpack House and join the dig for a few days – a week at the most. Keep your head down and see what's what. Tell me where things are going wrong, so I can help old Arthur stop short of making a complete ass of himself.'

'Oh no, Rupert. Sorry, but my digging days are over.'

'It's summer, Fitzroy,' said my mother. 'Think of all those young female students in tight jeans and skimpy T-shirts.

They do a lot of bending over when they're digging, don't they?'

I had nasty feeling that somewhere from the remote past my mother was quoting my own words back at me.

'It could be fun,' said a voice.

Amy?

She held up the newspaper advert and pretended to read it.

'It would be a change to get away from the rat race for a week, do a bit of treasure-hunting. He's throwing in free accommodation.'

'It will be very, very basic,' I said. 'Trust me.'

'You mean like Center Parcs?'

'Much, much more basic, darling, and that £75 rate, that's per *day*, not per hour.'

She flinched at that, but pressed on.

'Oh come on, where's your sense of adventure? It'll be like on that television show where they dig things up against the clock. I love it. What's it called? *Time Bandits*? No, that's a film. It's –'

'Don't ever mention that show in front of a field archae-ologist,' I said sternly.

'You go along and keep an eye on him, Amy,' said my mother. 'It'll be a hoot.'

'No it won't. It'll be hard physical slog and you won't find any treasure because there's none there to be found. You'll get very dirty, break your nails and anyway, you don't have the right clothes.'

This last point, I thought, would be the clincher. Wrong again.

'Are there not shops? Do I not have credit cards?'

'Go, girl, go,' urged The Mother From Hell.

'At least come and have a look at the site while you're here,' said Rupert, leaning in over the table towards Amy, sensing a weakness. 'A quick look. We can be there and back in half an hour.'

'What, to Hadleigh? Half an hour? In a helicopter maybe,' I snapped, feeling that somehow I was losing it.

Rupert looked at me with what I'd swear was admiration.

'Exactly. How did you know?'

If we'd been armed, we could have carpet-bombed Woolpack House and probably saved everyone a lot of trouble in the long run. But then we weren't, and anyway we didn't have speakers strapped to the undercarriage booming out 'Ride of the Valkyries' and it wouldn't have been the same without that.

The helicopter was a big army Westland job, the sort you can identify by the deep, slow chug-chug of its engine long before you see them. In fact they sound more like a turbo-prop plane than a helicopter. This one came complete with pilot and co-pilot and had been parked, along with several others, on a concrete field within the barracks in nearby Colchester, into which Rupert had whisked us in his Range Rover without anyone stopping or questioning us. No one saluted us either, which disappointed me though nobody else seemed to notice.

Once Rupert had mentioned helicopters, Amy was putty in his hands. We had checked out of the motel, letting Mother take our stuff and the BMW back to her house where she had a few domestic duties to attend to. (It seemed that Alan the Butcher had fallen asleep in the back garden rather too close to the dying embers of the barbecue and Mother had promised to change the dressings before he went home.)

I did make one last stab at talking Amy out of it, which she naturally put down to the fact that I must be frightened of flying in a helicopter.

'You can forget that, dear.' Mother had come to my aid. 'Fitzroy had his Private Pilot's Licence before he had a driving licence. Cost us a bloody fortune in flying lessons.'

'I didn't know you could *fly*!' Amy had said in full mock shock mode.

'We could get you on the controls if you like,' Rupert had offered as a further sweetener.

'I'll pass on that,' I had said. 'Light aircraft are easy – and safer than driving on a motorway. Helicopters are difficult. To drive one of them you have to be able to rub your stomach and pat yourself on the head at the same time. Too much co-ordination needed for me, especially this time in the morning.'

What had genuinely worried me was whether what we were doing was, sort of, legal. It might be all right for Rupert to go joy-riding in an army chopper but two hung-over civilians going to suss out a dubious archaeological site on the urging of a mad mother? I didn't fancy spending a week in the garrison's Glasshouse, which is the one thing all ex-servicemen remember about Colchester.

In the Range Rover on the way, Rupert had assured me that it was perfectly normal for him to take up civilians. It was a routine training flight, which was going ahead anyway and was actually going near Woolpack House. Well, quite near, but the diversion would be good navigational practice for the co-pilot. And Rupert was in charge of public relations for the regiment, so it was down to him who got free rides in helicopters, tanks or whatever. There'd be no problem.

'Which is your regiment, Rupert?' I had asked.

'The SAS actually,' he'd said.

After that I didn't worry. Just went with the flow.

Rupert did the guided tour bit, pointing out the sights as we flew over them. Down there was the A12 road which went up to Ipswich and beyond, and that was Dedham Vale – John Constable painting country – so now we were over Suffolk, and sure enough, in the distance the impressive suspension bridge over the River Orwell. Then we were altering course to north-west to bring us in a wide arc around rather than over Hadleigh, which would include the village of Woolpack.

It was a good five years since I had seen Suffolk either

from the ground or the air. For some reason, people think Suffolk is flat, uninteresting and thick because it used to be said that it was the only English county without a university. None of it is true but the local residents do have a habit of encouraging outsiders to believe such stuff, mainly so they stay outsiders. To the west of the small market town of Hadleigh there is a triangle of villages – Kersey, Lindsey and Boxford – which are known, subconsciously, to millions of television viewers as they have appeared as backdrops to endless BBC drama series. Rumour has it that one of the stipulations put on the film crews is that they never reveal their true location. As a consequence, the only 'outsiders' who buy retirement cottages there tend to be BBC executives, actors or television critics and journalists. It might look sleepy and it has the second lowest crime rate in the country, but it also has the highest number of media 'opinion formers' per head of population of anywhere, including London. Even Notting Hill. Suffolk just keeps quiet about it. I like that, and the beer's better too.

'We're coming up on Woolpack now,' said Rupert, straining against his seat-belt to point things out to us. 'There's not much of it. Two pubs, one at each end, a shop and a few houses. Woolpack House is one of the farms off to the north.'

'Isn't there an airstrip around here?' I asked, raising my voice over the noise of the engines, though it wasn't as bad as I had expected it to be.

'Yes, but we'll give that a wide berth so as not to encroach on their space. Got to watch out for those Sunday morning flyboys in their little crates. Oh, sorry, Roy, you were one of those, weren't you?'

'It was a long time ago,' I said.

Amy gave me her I-didn't-know-you . . . look but I ignored it.

'There's Woolpack,' said Rupert as the 'copter banked and began to lose height. 'We'll give Arthur a quick buzz at about two hundred feet. He's quite used to us, so we shouldn't frighten the horses.'

'They have horses?' Amy asked him, dreamy-eyed.

'Er . . . figure of speech,' he said.

'He's got a bulldozer,' I observed.

'What? Where?' Amy pressed her nose to the window.

'Down there. To your left. A big Victorian house, looks like it could have been a rectory, set back from the road. See? There. Stables and outbuildings to the side, a white Transit van parked outside the front door. And just in case you have trouble spotting which house I'm talking about, it's the one where the back garden looks like a World War I battlefield and there's a man mowing the lawn with a bright yellow bulldozer.'

'That'll be Arthur,' Rupert said enthusiastically. 'He likes the hands-on approach and one of the perks of paying for this whole show is that he gets to drive the bulldozer.'

'He's not really mowing the grass, is he?' asked Amy.

'He's stripping,' I said.

'What?'

'He's stripping off the topsoil and the lawn and the flower beds by the look of it, to get at the archaeology underneath.'

Once again Rupert looked at me like you would a talking dog.

'You *do* know your stuff, don't you?'

'More than Arthur seems to. I can see from here he's not going down far enough for anything to show up. The trick is to strip an area at one go, down to the natural, undisturbed surface. If he goes back over what he's done to take more off, the 'dozer will trash anything there. He ought to have somebody machine watching for him, spotting and marking anything which shows up.'

'He's waving at us,' said Amy.

So he was, but a white-shirted arm extending out of the plastic door of the bulldozer's cab was all we could see of him. There was no sign of anyone else around the house or the dig site, though it was difficult to see where one finished and the other started.

Woolpack House had once had a long, rectangular front lawn bisected by a tarmac drive running maybe a hundred yards down to the road and a good acre or so of land at the rear which had what looked like an orchard and had probably contained a vegetable garden and maybe a pond. It was difficult to tell now as most of it had been chewed up. Three trenches each about ten metres long were clearly visible round the back, as were two spoil heaps of recently dug-out soil and a third mound which had been there some time judging by the weeds and grass growing on it.

Then the helicopter was over the house and banking to the left to turn south and south-east back towards Colchester.

'Can't we land and get a closer look?' Amy asked Rupert, giving him the old up-from-under look which had melted far stonier hearts.

'Can't land, I'm afraid,' said Rupert, 'as it's not in the flight plan. But old Arthur would be more than happy to give you the guided tour, maybe even let you dig a bit . . .'

He tailed off as he caught my steely glance.

'You've fixed us up with jobs there, haven't you?' I said.

'Well, your mother . . .' Rupert blustered, but he did have the decency to blush.

'She would, but it's not on. No way, no day. We have a life. We're far too busy to go off on a digging spree at a moment's notice. We have responsibilities. We're too old for that sort of gypsy lifestyle.'

'I realize it was a lot to ask,' said Rupert, blushing deeper. 'I am so sorry for trying to impose on you and I wouldn't have done it but for Bethany being so adamant that you'd both jump at the chance to –'

'She was right. I could do with a break from the business,' Amy said suddenly. 'And archaeology sounds like fun.'

She smiled her best smile. It wowed Rupert; it flattened me.

I didn't say another word until the chopper landed back

in the garrison, I just thought of the horrific prospects of Amy and my mother agreeing on something.

It was my perennial problem with life: always outnumbered, always outgunned.

Rupert drove us back to Romanhoe to pick up the BMW. Along the way he filled us in with a few minor details, such as how we'd got our new jobs and, basically, how we no longer had control over our own lives. I thought it a bit rich that Mother had put Amy in the frame, never having met her before. Me, I was a legitimate target; she knew me. It was probably revenge for not having been introduced before, but what was really spooky was that Amy seemed to be going along with it. Was it some sort of female double-bluff? I knew I was out of my depth on this one.

The recruitment of diggers – 'site assistants' or 'excavators' if you wanted to be posh (the pay doesn't differ) – is a haphazard affair on most archaeological sites at the best of times. Occasionally they ask if you have any experience and, occasionally, they take up references. Rarely do they ask if you can actually stand up unaided, tell the difference between Roman hypercaust tile and a modern sewer outlet (until it's too late), speak English, point to the south when they've told you which way's north, have a drink/drug/allergy problem, know which is the business end of a spade, have previous convictions for running amok with a mattock, or have had a tetanus jab within living memory.

Years ago some disaffected members of the Musicians' Union enrolled their dogs to make the point that anyone could get in. (OK, so I'm a member of the National Rifle Association in the US, but that was done for a bet.) If those musical dogs ever wanted a job on a dig, they'd have no problem.

As most of the work is short-term contract, three months being the norm, six months a luxury, it makes it hardly worth checking up. That used to make it very attractive for the itinerant digger who could traverse the country from site to site keeping one step ahead of the taxman and anyone else he or she wanted to avoid. The trouble was the taxman was getting better and nobody dared pay in cash any more. As the pay rates were rubbish to begin with, and had in no way kept up with inflation, it was becoming less and less worthwhile joining the dig 'circuit' moving from archaeology unit to archaeology unit around the country, grotty hostel to grotty hostel, and the old contract digger was a dying breed. In fact, diggers were in short supply and I had read somewhere that the proposed excavation at Heathrow's Terminal 5 site, which would require around two hundred of them, was having to recruit as far afield as Turkey. The concept of offering a decent wage and better working conditions to attract dedicated diggers seemed totally remote to the powers that ran archaeology in Britain and it had probably ever been thus.

From what Rupert told us, he had had 'a jolly long chat' with Arthur Swallow and told him I had been born and raised in the area (true), took a lively interest in local history (untrue), got a 'cracking degree' in archaeology (dodgy), had tons of experience on rural Roman sites (hardly), and after a few years out couldn't wait to get back in the field and wield a trowel in anger (utter bollocks). Naturally Arthur couldn't refuse to take on someone his godson thought so highly of, even though he'd never actually met me. I would, however, have to fill out an application form when I got there. Joss the Project Manager would sort all that out for me, even though there was another girl actually handling the recruiting of diggers.

I asked if there had been many replies to Arthur's advertisement and Rupert said hundreds, although as the summer season had started, a lot of university students were already fixed up on digs. It seemed that quite a lot of the applications they'd had at Woolpack House were 'simply not up to snuff'.

I knew what that meant. Whoever was doing the recruiting would be going through a pile of one-page CVs on a personal crusade trying to spot people they knew and either offering a job on a whim or turning them down flat, depending on whether they liked them or not, the colour of their eyes, whether they'd got a better degree than they had, whether they were too tall, whether they'd been to a university they had been turned down by, or whether anyone else on the dig knew them and had a bad word to say about them. I've seen it done by star sign before now, but it's only to be expected in a closed and gossipy world such as archaeology. It was highly unlikely that anyone would remember me from my student days as a digger. I was pretty sure that all my contemporaries were now accounted for by spouse, mortgage and 2.4 labradors or Her Majesty's Prison Service.

'Remind me,' I had said to Rupert, 'why are we doing this?'

'Because Bethany said –' he began, flustered.

'No, what are we hoping to achieve by all this? By me – us – going on this dig?' I had rephrased.

'Well, it's as I told you. There's trouble in the camp. It's not a happy camp,' he had said. 'There have been incidents – fights – usually after dark and equipment has gone missing or been destroyed and a couple of diggers have ended up in hospital. No one is saying anything too much about it and I honestly don't think Arthur realizes what's going on, but something is. I want you to dig around – oops, sorry about that! – and see if you can get the full picture and fill me in. Just give it a few days, see what you can see and give me a call.'

He had given me a business card which had nothing on it except a mobile phone number. Nothing else. No name, rank, serial number or address. It was the sort of untraceable card which they give out to potential informers in Northern Ireland. Judging by the way things were going over there, they probably had plenty to spare.

'You never know,' Rupert had said as we pulled up outside my mother's house, 'you might even enjoy it, getting back into the swing of things.'

'We might even find treasure!' Amy had squealed in a little-girl voice I hadn't heard for ages.

'I doubt that,' I had said sternly.

'Not even a single gold doubloon or whatever they're called?'

'On a Roman site it would be a gold *aurens*, but don't get your hopes up.'

I had been going to say something about having a better chance of winning the Lottery than finding one, but then I remembered that Arthur Swallow had.

'Whatever you do, if you find a coin do *not* stick it in the top of your sock and leg it down Portobello Road market with indecent haste. That's considered very bad form. A hanging offence in the archaeological world.'

I had once found a medieval gold coin on a site, a coin known, funnily enough, as a Half Angel. I had stuck it in my sock and hoofed it down to the Portobello Road with indecent haste.

But I didn't mention it.

My mother offered us lunch (cold pork sandwiches), which we declined, and a chance to help clear up the debris of last night's party, which we also declined but for which I volunteered Rupert. It was the least he could do as we had to get back to London to get ready for our new lives as ordained by my mother as diggers at Woolpack House. In any case, there were still two guests from the party who were sitting on the kitchen floor, having just come round, and Alan the Butcher was trying to clear up the back yard despite his heavily bandaged hands, so Rupert would have enough help.

Mother was *so* delighted that we had agreed to join Rupert's crusade to save his dotty godfather and was *so sure* we would have enormous fun doing it that she didn't want to delay us; which was fine by me.

As we prepared to get into the BMW, she gave Amy an elaborate double-cheek kiss whilst saying 'Don't be a stranger' to me, and 'You know where I live' in a vague yet meaningful way to Amy.

Us knowing where she lived wasn't the problem.

On the way back to town down the A12 I tried every-thing I could think of to talk Amy out of coming back up to Suffolk to dig.

'It's hard, physical and dirty work.'

'I'm not afraid of getting my hands dirty.'

'I'm not talking just hands here. There are two sorts of conditions on a dig site: the ground is baked hard as concrete and dust gets into every crevice, or it's raining and you have to move mud, which is heavy as well as . . . muddy.'

'Sounds like it'll get me fit quicker than the gym.'

'You'll be starting work at 7.30 a.m. as it's summer.'

'I'm often at work by then.'

'But in a board room, having coffee and pastries, not in a field where the only comfort is a chemical toilet – if you're lucky.'

'Don't be ridiculous. It's a lovely house and they offer accommodation. It'll be like a camping holiday.'

'When did you last go on a camping trip? Your idea of an expedition to the Lost World is a visit to Brent Cross Shopping Centre.'

'Look who's talking. I never had you pegged for Indiana Jones.'

'And you're no Lara Croft.' Though I wasn't too sure about that, so I thought I'd play one of my trump cards. 'Anyway, you haven't got the right clothes.'

'I could buy some gear if I have to. Hell, I could *design* a new range of archaeological leisure wear. Sell the concept to that TV programme, what's it called? *Time Lock* or something?'

'I told you never to mention that show. Anyway, diggers don't have money to spend on clothes unless they're army surplus – and they're not fussy whose army – and they've got lots of pockets. Every day on a dig site is Dress Down Friday. Think of it like that. You'll hate it. You haven't got any old clothes.'

As soon as I'd said it I knew I had made a tactical blunder.

'Hah!' she shouted. '*All* my clothes are old! Not that

you'd notice. And with your wardrobe, you'll fit right in.'

'How will they cope at work without you?' I said, changing tack.

'Badly, but they will. I'm due some holiday. In fact, I'm due a lot of holiday. When did we last go on holiday? We've *never* been on holiday!'

This was not going well.

'I suppose it *might* be interesting,' I tried, 'just for a few days. It was always fun in the summer. All those young, nubile second-year undergraduates in their tight shorts and V-necked tops, always bending over . . .'

'They were probably watching your tight-fitting jeans when you bent over,' she countered. 'But of course, you were *young* then . . .'

I noticed her long fingernails, painted a shade of blood red called O Positive (the TV ad said it 'Ohhhh – Positive!' in a dead sexy voice), and began to clutch at straws.

'You'll break all your nails within the first half-hour.'

'I was going to book a manicure anyway.'

I gave up and sulked most of the way back to Hampstead, whilst she whistled the *Raiders of the Lost Ark* theme just to annoy me.

As she pulled the BMW up in front of the house, she said:

'Go and open the door and put the kettle on, would you? I've got to check something on my laptop.'

I was putting the key in the lock and deactivating the alarms before I remembered that her laptop was stowed away in the boot of the Beamer and she had made no effort to get out of her seat and get it.

She had also kept the engine running.

Which was odd.

Chapter Five

Diggers

The going was tough. It was time to go shopping.

Amy spent Sunday evening drawing up lists of things she might need 'Windows' shopping on the Internet. Scott heading for the South Pole or Fawcett going up the Amazon would have given their eye teeth for such quality preparation time.

I plugged myself into an old movie on one of the satellite channels and nursed a large brandy, letting her get on with it. I had, foolishly, expected her to actually go shopping herself the next day, which was always a reliable distraction. When she appeared at one point and asked me if I needed a Swiss Army knife (I'd said 'Of course') then I was convinced that was what she was up to. What I hadn't banked on was that she was e-mailing her wish list to the dreaded Debbie Diamond, who would do the shopping for her. I had forgotten that one of the perks of being as high up the pecking order as Amy was that you qualified for a personal shopper. Even on a Sunday Miss Diamond was responding by e-mail saying there would be no problem filling Amy's shopping list. I was tempted to suggest she went and bought a life while she was out there.

'So you can pick everything up at the office at twelve,' Amy told me, 'and we can be off by one.'

'I can? We can?'

I tore myself away from the movies thinking that Steven Segal wasn't really an underrated actor after all. I had counted on Amy rampaging round the shops for at least a week, by which time she would have forgotten all about Woolpack House.

'You have a problem with that?'

'No,' I said carefully, 'but I'll have to pick up a few things for myself.'

'Such as?' she asked suspiciously.

'Boots,' I said quickly. 'I've got an old pair of boots somewhere. You do have some, I take it? You won't be allowed on site without decent work boots. It's Health and Safety rules.'

'I've ordered Timberlands,' she said.

'And Debbie Diamond's going to wear them in for you? OK, that's fine. What about a sleeping bag? You'll need one if we're slumming it with the hired hands.'

'Have you got one?'

'Sure.'

'What's it called?'

'Hemingway,' I said before I could stop myself.

'Thought so,' she said with a smug smile. 'I'll try Harrods.'

'I've also got to dig out my old trowel.'

'Trowels are provided. You said that.'

'Yes, but you look more serious if you turn up with your own personal one. I'll pick up a WHS for you.'

'What's that?'

'Er . . . I don't really know. They're the best trowels for diggers. All archaeologists have WHS ones. It stands for Well-Hard Steel or something.'

I was losing her.

'A WHS is the Gucci of trowels. You can't be seen with anything less,' I tried.

'Oh, right. Good. Get me one, but muss it up a bit or whatever you do. Don't make it look blindingly obviously new, OK?'

'Gotcha,' I said, hiding a smile.

And so – and I was only following orders – first thing

Monday morning I was trundling over to Hackney in Armstrong II, cutting through the rush hour traffic as only a black London cab can. As I drove I thought Armstrong would be just the sort of vehicle a couple of ageing hippy student types recently into archaeology would use. The new BMW and Amy's Freelander were far too flash, given that the average archaeologist's idea of slick personal transport was a bicycle with three gears. Armstrong would have the advantage of being both cute and politically correct, as it was a diesel engine and didn't have the image of conspicuous consumption which the Beamer and the Freelander did. The average digger straight out of university wouldn't have the nous to realize that, environmentally speaking, Armstrong was by far the biggest offender of the three.

Most of the stuff I needed could be retrieved from Number 9, Stuart Street or acquired nearby, and whilst I was there I thought I might as well check up on the inhabitants just in case they'd killed each other in my absence.

Actually I was only worried about one of them. Mr Goodson, from the ground-floor flat, had never been a trouble to anyone. He kept himself to himself and never complained about the noise and/or unruly behaviour of the rest of the house. In return, none of the rest of us had complained about his annoying habits such as paying his rent on time, negotiating politely with the landlord for structural repairs or accepting without question parcels of dubious origin for us when we were out. He would be at work, of that I was sure. He was something in local government, though nobody knew exactly what.

On the top floor, in Flat 4, lived Inverness Doogie and Miranda. She was a local newspaper reporter in Islington, he a rising star in the culinary world of the West End. Not that Doogie had his own restaurant yet. He was still in the twilight world of posh hotel kitchens, though his escalating outbursts of violence towards staff and customers alike were certainly putting him on the road to own-restaurant status if not an entire TV series.

Both of them would be at work on a Monday morning,

which left only Flats 2 and 3, my flat, with possible occupants.

Flat 2 was the lesser of the two evils. I was pretty sure Lisabeth would be out practising alternative medicine at one of Hackney's latest aromatherapy/holistic centres which also doubled as a pulse delicatessen. I had heard she was really enjoying her work, which I believed, and that she had lost weight recently. Yeah, right.

Fenella – Lisabeth's partner – was more difficult to call; in more ways than one. The last I'd heard she was a 'personal customer communication interfacer' which basically meant she worked in a call centre, cold-calling people between the hours of 6 p.m. and 9 p.m. (for some reason they're not allowed to do it at other times) on a spurious market-researching pretext. What Fenella did was the targeting, the hard sell coming in the follow-up phone call a week or so later.

It goes like this. Fenella's posh and expensively educated voice asks you if you can spare twenty seconds – absolute tops, darling – to answer three questions: have you been on holiday yet this year, would you prefer an activity holiday, do you use a travel agent or organize your own holiday? Naturally you answer because Fenella is so polite, says thank you several times and, as promised, doesn't overrun her twenty seconds, although if you wanted to chat to her she'd rabbit for the rest of the day. A week later, one, two or three different cold-callers – professional this time – will call offering you the services of a travel agent with late summer/early winter deals (because you haven't been yet), or membership on special offer of a new local gym and sauna (the 'activity' question), or an insurance company offers you travel/holiday insurance, which you have to think about if only for the sake of the kids after you've selfishly decided not to use a travel agent (Question 3). Fenella's quite good at it and the call centre must love her because they don't often get someone so well-spoken who is also so thick she doesn't know what she's doing half the time. Normally they're in Public Relations.

Whatever, she wasn't at home either or she would surely have jumped out of ambush as I crept up the stairs and passed her door. Drunk or sober, I'd never made it up those stairs unmolested when Fenella had an ear open for me, and to be honest if it looked as if I was going to I would start whistling, or do a quick tap step just to let her know I was home. (I once resorted to the opening bars of 'West End Blues' in the days when I played the trumpet for a living, but only the once. Lisabeth opened the door that time.)

So, empty house. Nobody home. Be afraid. Be very afraid.

At the door of my old flat I put the key in the lock and turned it, then flattened myself back against the landing wall before pushing until the door creaked open to its full extent.

Nothing happened. It was quiet. Too quiet.

I risked showing my right eyeball around the door frame. The hallway seemed clear, the doors to the bedroom and bathroom open. Check. I could smell fresh air from the open window. Check. That was a good sign although I am regarded as something of an eccentric in leaving windows (even two floors up) permanently open in London. But then, unlike all other Londoners – and I include the Queen – I'm not frightened of burglars.

For a start, I've got very little to pinch – that they'd find – which wasn't well over-insured and anyway, I've got an alarm system. Technically, I suppose it's more a defence mechanism than an alarm system, because quite often it kills in total silence. And indiscriminately, which is why I was being careful.

'There you are, old fella,' I said to him when I poked my head around the bedroom door.

Springsteen opened one eye, then closed it again and yawned so that his pink mouth and white fangs stood out like some hellish archway against the mass of black hair which had elongated itself across the full width of my old bed. He stretched front and back legs to their clawpoints, exhaled down his nose and went back to sleep.

'Putting on weight,' I said, but very quietly, as I tiptoed by him to get into the wardrobe on the other side of the room.

'Not stopping,' I said, as he might look asleep but I knew he was listening, 'just collecting a few things. Going away for a few days with Amy. You remember Amy? You liked her.'

Well, he hadn't attacked her. Yet.

'You're not going to believe this, but I'm taking her digging. Archaeology, would you believe? Got to look the part, of course, so I've come to dig out my old boots and – ah, here it is – faithful old Hemingway.'

My old green padded double-zipper sleeping bag was on top of the wardrobe, rolled up and secured by an old leather belt with one of those Confederate flag buckles which had been quite fashionable years ago. I decided it was a nice touch. Archaeologists would think it trendy.

'Now, the boots.'

The wardrobe door was slightly open but I thought nothing of it as it had never closed properly. In the bottom, amidst an assortment of old clothes (most of them mine), bent clothes hangers and trainers well past their smell-by date, were a pair of Transporters, fine work boots made in China with steel toes, leather uppers and thick plastic soles.

Stuffed into the left boot was a freshly killed pigeon with half its feathers missing. It couldn't have been dead for more than twenty-four hours, just about the time Amy was deciding to go treasure hunting.

'Springsteen! How did you know?' I shouted as I swung round.

But he was gone.

From under the sink in the kitchen I retrieved my old tool box and emptied it of everything except a five-metre retracting metal tape measure, a few two-inch nails and four six-inch ones, a claw hammer with a rubber grip and,

81

of course, Bob, my trusty trowel, the blade of which was worn down to a triangle about three inches long.

'Are you the plumber?'

I shot backwards and upwards out from under the sink, managing to limit the damage to a glancing blow on the back of my skull.

'Fair play, Fenella, fair play. You could give someone a heart attack creeping up on them like that in your . . . your pyjamas . . .'

Fenella stretched her arms down by her side and flexed her fingers like a cat, then made a fist and stifled a yawn. She was barefooted and wearing blue pyjama shorts and top decorated with gold moons and stars. I instantly thought of an American TV weatherman who used to say that the evening would be 'starry and moony'. Well, perhaps that wasn't my first thought, but it came a close second.

'Oh, it's you. I've been working nights,' she said, yawning again, 'so I volunteered to stay in for when the plumber comes to fix our shower.'

'When's he due?'

'Last Wednesday.'

'Sounds about right. What are you doing working nights?'

'Oh, just answering phones. It's only temporary.'

'What sort of work is it?'

'Just conversation, really. I talk to people about my schooldays. I'm a sort of storyteller. They get five minutes and then I have to think up something different for the next time they ring.'

'And they do ring back, do they?' Why was I getting a bad feeling about this?

'Oh yes, they do, some of them three or four times a night.'

'And they're mostly men, are they?'

'Not exclusively.'

'Do gym slips and playing hockey feature at all . . . No, never mind. It's best I don't know.'

'Don't know what?' she mewed sleepily.

'Nothing, nothing at all. Did I wake you?'

'You must have done. Were you shouting at Springsteen?'

'I may have been,' I said defensively, picking up my tool kit and kicking the door to the sink unit.

'You might as well collect your mail now you're here. Why *are* you here?'

'Bringing my trusty Bob out of retirement,' I said.

'That sounds faintly rude,' she said primly, which was rich considering her idea of a night shift. 'Who's Bob?'

I held up my trowel proudly.

'You're going gardening?'

'No,' I said patiently, 'I'm off on an archaeological dig.'

Her eyes opened wide at that.

'Wow, like on the television . . . that programme on the telly where they do makeovers on the faces of dead people?'

'Not quite. This is just a small-scale Iron Age dig in Suffolk.'

'Is it a henge? I've read about henges. Ancient sources of Druidic power . . .'

I had forgotten Fenella was still in the New Age.

'And they're not just made of stone, you know. There's a wooden henge in the sea somewhere – a seahenge they call it. That's in Suffolk.'

'Norfolk actually, but I know what you mean. No, nothing so esoteric. This will be just a few holes in the ground in the middle of Suffolk.'

'Sutton Hoo!' she whooped suddenly. 'That was the other place I was trying to think of. That's in Suffolk.'

I was quite taken aback at Fenella thinking of two things at once.

'Yes, it is, but I'm digging at a place called Woolpack, twenty or thirty miles away.'

'There was treasure at Sutton Hoo, you know. I saw a programme on the History Zone about it. A Viking ship sank with all its treasure.'

'It was Saxon and it was buried there.'

She looked at me as if I had taken leave of my senses.

'Why on earth,' she said cockily, 'would anybody bury a ship?'

I shrugged my shoulders.

'They got tired of waiting for the plumber?'

Hackney, being one of the many villages which make up the sprawling mass that is London, is one of the few places left where you can still find a genuine ironmonger's rather than a DIY superstore. I got personal service and my purchases in brown paper bags when I bought a ball of nylon string, a line level, a couple of indelible black marker pens, a Stanley knife and a brand new WHS trowel for Amy. I was tempted to ask the very nice man in the brown coat behind the counter if he would take the edge off the trowel with his grinder, but in this neck of the woods that would make him an accessory to going equipped for burglary.

So my next stop was Duncan the Drunken's garage down the road. Duncan is probably the finest car mechanic in the world. He keeps your vehicle on the road, doesn't ask questions and gives you as many VAT receipts as you need. He also has the longest surviving Yorkshire accent of anyone who has lived in London for twenty years. Indeed, he's probably one of the longest surviving Yorkshiremen in London as he's never made any secret of the fact that he thinks all Chelsea supporters are hairdressers and women shouldn't drink pints.

''Ey up, Angel, long time no see,' he greeted me as I walked in through the double doors of his side-street garage.

He had room to work on about three cars at a time. The waiting list, and he always seemed to have one, would be parked up and down the street much to the annoyance of the local residents, but each would have a 'Residents Permit' or a 'Disabled' sticker in the windscreen for the benefit of the wardens.

He was working on a new Volvo S70, connecting terminals to a box near the battery.

'Fitting alarm systems now, Dunc?' I asked just for the hell of it.

'Aye. Good trade.'

'What happened to the one it came with?' I nodded at the car, which from the registration was less than a year old.

'It got nicked, didn't it? Fancy a cuppa? Simone's got the kettle on.'

'Who's Simone?'

'Lovely girl. Makes a big impression on you.'

He stuck his screwdriver in a pocket of his overalls and held both his hands, fingers like curled claws, about six inches away from his chest and then weighed them up and down.

'That's a nasty case of arthritis, Dunc, you wanna watch that.'

'Ha-bloody-ha. You're getting to be a real old fart now you're mar –'

'Now, now,' I wagged a finger at him. 'We don't mention the "m" word, do we? It's not good customer relations. But I will have that cuppa.'

'Thought you might,' he grinned, then he shouted towards the partitioned office section at the back of the garage: 'Simone! Two teas, love, but hide the biscuits!'

There was a muffled shout of acknowledgement from inside the office.

'So what you after, young Angel?'

'Two things. First off, the use of an angle-grinder for a coupla minutes.'

'It's over there on the bench, help yourself. There's even some goggles somewhere. What's up? Bodywork job? Nothing wrong with Armstrong, is there?'

'No, he's fine. It's this.' I held up the new trowel still in its vacuum pack. 'I want to take the edge off it, make it look like it's been used in anger.'

'You going bricklaying or summat?'

'Digging – archaeology, up in Suffolk. The trowel is the tool of the trade.'

'Bloody hell. You mean like on the telly, that programme . . . *Time Tunnel*, is it?'

'Not quite like that, this is a real dig.'

'In Suffolk? What the hell is there up there? You should stay round here, stick to what you know. There's talk of them restarting the Smithfield excavation and there's always stuff in the papers about the Museum lot.'

I presumed he meant MOLAS, the archaeological unit of the Museum of London.

'This is a private dig as far as I can make out,' I said.

'In Suffolk?' he repeated, shaking his head. 'You're not playing away from home, are you?'

I knew exactly what he meant.

'Amy's coming with me actually. She's getting all excited, thinking it's going to be a treasure hunt.'

'Treasure, like hoards of coins? Wanna borrow a metal detector?'

'There's no buried . . . you've got a metal detector?'

'Tool of the trade, lad, tool of the trade.'

That worried me for a minute as I began to think why on earth a motor mechanic would need a metal detector.

'All right, sometimes when I've had a few, not all the screws go back in the right place so I do a quick sweep with the detector to pick them up off the floor.'

'After they've fallen out,' I said.

'Well, yeah. I call it quality control.'

'Fair enough. The other thing is where can I get some rolling tobacco, the "imported" variety?'

By that I meant the sort that didn't come with a health warning in English or the legend 'UK Duty Paid'.

'No problem,' said Duncan. 'How much?'

'Just a couple of pouches. Golden Virginia rather than Old Holborn.'

'Three quid a go, compared to seven-fifty in the shops do yer?'

'Sounds good. Where?'

'Number 27 up the street, just knock on the back door

and tell them I sent you. But Simone'll get it for you if you give her the money.'

He nodded over my shoulder as his face squelched into a lascivious grin. I turned to see Simone coming out of the office holding two mugs of tea carefully in front of her. A considerable way in front of her.

She was probably just sixteen, taller than I was, her blonde hair done up on top of her head with what looked to be a pair of black lacquered chopsticks, making her look even taller. She wore a blue denim shirt tied under her breasts and rip-cut denim shorts of a darker blue, leaving a midriff showing off a triple-pierced belly button. Her legs ended in backless high-heeled sandals and her toe and fingernails were painted green and black alternately. She had bangle earrings the size of the hoops you used to get at fairgrounds and a gold nose stud. Her mouth was outlined with silver lip gloss and her tongue protruded ever so slightly as she concentrated on carrying the two steaming mugs. Apart from that, I hardly noticed her.

'Work Experience,' breathed Duncan. 'A different one every two weeks. Bet you don't get nothing like that in . . . Suffolk.'

At Mrs Patel's shop round the corner (it was now part of a chain called At The Shopper's Convenience or something but it would always be Patel's to us locals) I stocked up on vital supplies: a white sliced loaf of bread, a tub of some-thing which spread like butter but had never seen a cow in its life, a jar of Marmite, the biggest vacuum-pack of Cheddar cheese there was, six packs of Jaffa Cakes, a bunch of bananas and ten packets of Green Rizla cigarette papers.

All the delicacies a young archaeologist could dream of; all vegetarian and I even made sure the bananas were from a politically correct source.

As an afterthought, I nipped back into the off-licence section and added a bottle of vodka. Just to be sure.

When I had everything stashed in Armstrong I called

Amy's office on my mobile and asked for Debbie Diamond. She picked up with an annoyingly primptious 'Good morning, how can I be of help?' and I said:

'Hi there, you old voyeur you. It's me, the guy you like to watch on your security camera.'

I hadn't for one minute expected the reaction I got.

First there was a sharp and very audible intake of breath, then:

'Listen, *toerag*, any more shit from you and you won't be on the street, you'll be *off* it and enjoying hospital food if you catch my drift. One more –'

'Hello?' I interrupted, thinking one of us must have got a crossed line. 'Reality check, please. I'm supposed to be picking up stuff for Amy. Amy May, like the boss lady. Am I getting through here?'

'Oh, it's *you*, isn't it?'

'Who the bloody hell did you think it was?'

'Never you mind,' she snapped, recovering her natural bad attitude. 'Everything's ready and it's all downstairs in the piazza at the security desk, so you don't have to come up to the office.'

'I thought at least you'd offer to put the kettle on for me, or even the cappuccino machine. After all, the boss isn't in today and I was hoping we could finally meet face to –'

'Let me see if I can fit you in,' she said, now fully recovered and in battle mode. 'Oh wait, I've got a three o'clock . . . Ah yes, hell's freezing over then. You can come up after that.'

'Tell me, Miss Diamond, what was it *like* in the Waffen SS . . .?'

But she had cut me off.

What had I said? I had long ago realized that Amy had poisoned the old bat against me but this was going large on the animosity front and perilously close to being well out of order. I worried about it for – well, for about as long as it took for me to remember I had the Ian Dury tribute album, *Brand New Boots and Panties*, in the CD player I'd had fitted where real cabs have the fare meter. Sir Paul McCartney, bless, making a decent fist of 'I'm Partial To

Your Abracadabra' took my mind off things as I pointed Armstrong up West.

The security office in the Oxford Street piazza was a glass-fronted box with a young black guy sitting behind a console of twelve-inch closed-circuit TV screens. Even though he'd probably seen me park Armstrong on the kerb right outside, he still made me press the voice-box button and identify myself and say what I wanted before he made the glass doors swish open and pop together behind me with a *Star Trek* shooshing noise. I was impressed. Even the security on the security office was tight.

'Collecting for Amy May,' I said, just to see if the name struck fear into his heart.

'Can you manage it all?' he said, not looking up from a clipboard where he was ticking me off some list.

I peered over his bank of TV screens and let out a low whistle. There was a fat cylinder of something green wrapped in plastic no bigger than a domestic hot water tank, which I guessed was a sleeping bag, five Harrods carrier bags, a giant one from Louis Vuitton, one Burberry, one from Waterstone's bookshop and two from Selfridges' Food Hall. Miss Diamond had been busy this morning.

'Birthday presents?' asked the security guy, passing over the sleeping bag.

'Archaeology,' I said foolishly, then made light of it. 'Don't ask me, mate, I'm just the bloody cab driver. Go here, pick up this, drop off that, so forth, so fifth.'

'Oh yeah, right,' he sympathized and began to hand over the carrier bags.

The Selfridges bags were the heaviest, but they clinked when they moved so I didn't mind that, but I had to lean over the console to take them from the security man's hands. As I did so, I noticed the photographs taped to the edge of the left-hand column of CCTV screens.

There were three of them, grotty black-and-white prints taken from videotape from the security cameras, all with time codes in the bottom right corners. They all showed the same man, two head-on from above, one in a thin, gaunt close-up profile. The haircut, the raincoat and the carrier bag in his hand were all the same as the man I had seen hanging around the car park at the rear of the piazza when I'd collected Amy's Beamer.

'Who's he?'

'Some perv we've got a watching brief on,' said the guard, disinterested. 'Bit of a flasher, I believe. Somebody here will have complained about him, so we keep an eye out.'

I wondered if Debbie Diamond had a flashing stalker and my earlier call had tripped a nerve ending.

'You'd be amazed the sorts we get hanging around here,' said the guard.

'No I wouldn't,' I said deadpan. 'I'm a cab driver.'

Amy sat in the back of Armstrong reading as we rattled up the A12 and into East Anglia, only occasionally deigning to speak to me. She was still sulking about my insistence on using Armstrong, although she said she accepted my twisted logic that it would fit our archaeologist image better.

And to improve that image, she was giving herself a crash course in the late Iron Age/early Roman period from the bag of books Debbie Diamond had picked up for her. In the mirror I had spotted her flicking through three or four Shire Archaeology titles – booklets on individual topics – as well as *The Handbook of British Archaeology* by Lesley and Roy Adkins, which has pretty-much Biblical status on most sites in this country.

'Was this a Roman road?' she asked me suddenly, somewhere near Chelmsford.

'At one time, yeah. Main road between Colchester and London.'

'And Colchester was the Roman capital of Britain, right? Not London.'

'To begin with. The reason the Romans went there was because it was the nearest thing to a British capital at the time, home of one of the big tribes.'

'The Iceni, right?'

'No, they came from north Suffolk. The local tribe round here were the Trinovantes, although at the time of the Roman invasion they were under the thumb of another tribe, the Catuvellauni. Most of their territory was to the west around what is now St Albans and the Romans settled them back there, giving Essex back to the Trinovantes. They liked to keep the natives apart.'

'You make it sound like the Wild West.'

'It was. Britain was the frontier of the Roman Empire and London was its Dodge City, a real rough, tough place, with taverns and whorehouses and lots of dodgy traders selling shoddy goods to the tribes.' .

'Tribes, as in Indians, like in the movies?'

'Sort of. There were no "British" as such and some of the tribes hated the other tribes more than the Romans, actively helped them divide and conquer. It must have been the Roman nightmare when the Iceni started the rebellion and the Trinovantes and the Catuvellauni joined them. And they almost did it. They burned Colchester, beat the shit out of a Roman legion, then turned over London and St Albans. The Romans were seriously thinking of pulling out permanently.'

'And *Boo-di-ka* led the rebellion, right? In AD60 or thereabouts?'

'Yes, as queen of the Iceni, after the death of her husband, King Prasutagus.'

She was quiet almost for a minute, then she let out a disdainful snort.

'Huh! It took a woman.'

'It usually does,' I said under my breath.

Half-way between Colchester and Ipswich I turned on to the back road for Hadleigh, the nearest town of any size to Woolpack. I wanted to arrive at Arthur Swallow's backyard dig whilst there was plenty of light for a look around but not time enough to have to do any work. Visiting Hackney and collecting Amy's shopping had provided quite enough stress for one day.

I was working on the theory that the dig would pack in around five o'clock, though being summer, it was not unheard of to go on until seven or eight if there was overtime in the offing. I remembered finishing off a training dig on an Iron Age barrow in Dorset by car headlights once, but that was because we'd been in the pub all afternoon. That was back in the good old days when if you had to dig out a ditch, the dig supervisor would mark it out in metre lengths with bottles of beer as an incentive to get to the other side. These days it's all Health and Safety legislation and stupid, petty rules like no alcohol on site, no loud music (in case you don't hear the bulldozer coming up behind you) and having to wear hard hats and luminous 'viz vests' in fluorescent yellow. Some sites even insist on a no smoking policy, though not many as an archaeological dig is about the only workplace left where the non-smokers are in the minority and they have to go outside and stand in the rain during tea-breaks. The only time the rule is usually enforced is if you had to take samples of, say, soil or burned mortar or charcoal or the ash in a cremation urn burial, which was fair enough. I have witnessed more than one Iron Age cremation where the dearly departed appeared to have put on weight in the two thousand years since they were planted in the ground.

The other strand to my game plan was to catch the diggers off duty and down the pub, where they would surely be after a hard day's work. On site they would talk about the archaeology and little else. Off site, with a pint of cider inside them (it didn't take much), they would still talk about the archaeology but with all the added gossip they'd been storing up about how badly the site was run, who was digging which feature wrong, who was sleeping with whom, why there wasn't more money in the geophysics budget, why the previous site they were on was always better, why the project manager was always a congenital idiot. They could always be relied upon to bitch and be indiscreet. Any group of archaeologists in a pub anywhere can come up with more grievances than the

International War Crimes Tribunal in The Hague, and quicker. I was relying on it.

'Nice town,' Amy said as we drove through the middle of Hadleigh, but I knew she was thinking she was glad she'd done her shopping in London.

'Make the most of it, that's the last bit of civilization you'll see. Next stop is Woolpack.'

'Hey, come off it. I like the countryside. You're always dissing me as a Zone One Warrior, but I can appreciate this landscape, it's really beautiful.'

'I wasn't talking about the countryside being the end of civilization. I was talking about the archaeologists. They're just not your sort of people. They have no fashion sense, care little for personal hygiene, have no small talk other than the novels of Terry Pratchett – which they know off by heart – and whilst they can spot a buried bronze coin at fifty yards, they can't hit a waste bin with a used tea bag from six inches.'

'I can put up with you, I can put up with them,' she said.

That seemed to settle it, so I stopped arguing. To my surprise, I felt Amy's fingers caress the back of my neck through the open passenger screen.

'Come on, it'll be a break for us, away from it all,' she purred. 'It'll be *fun*.'

I should have known then that it would end in tears, but there was a signpost pointing down an even smaller road to Woolpack and suddenly we were rumbling down a leafy lane flanked by fields of barley, back into Suffolk's bloody past, in more ways than one.

The village of Woolpack looked on the ground very much as it did from the air and in both cases if you blinked, you missed it. As Rupert had said, there was a pub at each end and very little in between, so I gave the pubs my full attention.

The Drovers' Arms was the first, at the southern end of the village, and it looked to have been created from a pair of cottages at some time before World War I and not painted since. It had a hanging sign above the front door which showed a be-smocked shepherd and a column of sheep, although the paintwork was so faded and chipped, it could have been Napoleon leading his troops back from Moscow. There was absolutely nothing to show it was open or even in business.

The pub at the far end of the village was called The Chequers and was a smaller version of the brick-built roadhouses which had been dotted across East Anglia in the 1930s and then again in the early 1960s with little regard for local architectural style. It looked antiseptically clean, advertised that it had a restaurant, letting bedrooms and car park, and had a newly painted sign showing a black and white chequerboard, which probably belied its origins as a pub of the long-defunct Bullard's Brewery of Norwich. Just the sort of place the archaeologists wouldn't be seen dead in.

Woolpack House, on the other hand, looked much worse on the ground than it did from the air.

Some of Arthur Swallow's Lottery winnings had obviously gone on a tarmac surface for the track which ran from the road to the house. The rest seemed to have been dedicated to ripping up surfaces.

The bulldozer we had seen from the air wasn't in sight as we chugged up the drive but we could see where it had been, stripping off the turf and topsoil from one half of the lawn, leaving a thirty-yard-long barrow-shaped spoil heap alongside the driveway. From the air, the spoil heap itself would have looked more like an archaeological feature than anything the bulldozer had uncovered.

'So that's archaeology, is it?' Amy said in my ear.

'I'd call it aggressive gardening,' I said.

'What's the point?'

'I don't know. I'll need to have a good look around, see how the land lies, find out if old Arthur had any reason for ripping up his lawn or whether he's just digging at random.'

'He left the rose beds intact,' Amy observed.

There were half-moon rose beds on either side of the drive, which were so thick and overgrown that they looked more like barbed wire entanglements than floral features. They only added to the overall impression of a Flanders battlefield and a couple of days of heavy rain would complete the picture.

'We should have packed our wellies,' I said as I parked Armstrong outside the open front door of the house. 'If it rains, it's going to get very muddy out there.'

'I checked the weather forecast on the Net,' said Amy as we climbed out, 'and it said bright and sunny all week.'

'Damn'was good thinking. Archaeologists are obsessed with the weather. It's either too wet and you're digging slop or it's too hot and the ground has turned to concrete.'

'There's just no pleasing us, is there?' she said straight-faced.

'Gangway! Coming through!' somebody shouted.

In the doorway, and filling it, was a large white-haired elderly lady with arms like ham hocks and legs which looked as if they had been planted in a pair of outsize trainers. She wore a butcher's apron which had been liberally smeared with muddy handprints and she was holding a round plastic washing-up bowl filled with the filthiest water north of the Orinoco.

She took two steps towards us as we took three steps to the side and then she launched the bowl of water in the general direction of one of the rose beds. Some of it made it, but most of it splashed on to the tarmac drive, running off in a brown, muddy stain, apart from the pint or so which splashed the bottoms of my jeans.

'You must be in charge of pot-washing,' I said, putting on my best smile.

'Finds Assessment,' said the woman, who wouldn't see seventy-five again, in a voice which dared me to comment.

'You missed a bit,' I said, bending over the miniature mud slide she had just created on the drive to pick out a curved shard of red-glazed pottery about two inches long. 'Samian ware. Nice piece.' I showed it to Amy.

'Imported? First century?' she said, looking at it closely.

I was impressed. She hadn't wasted her revision time in the back of the cab.

'Could be. They did make it in this country, in Colchester I think, but the posh stuff was imported.'

'Mostly from southern Gaul, around Narbonne,' said the beefy woman. 'It's much shinier than the copied stuff they made in Britain. You must be the new diggers.'

'We are,' I said politely. 'Is Mr Swallow expecting us?'

'He is, but I doubt if Joss is. She's the project manager, so nobody tells her anything.'

Amy flashed me an anxious glance but I nodded understandingly at the woman as if this was only par for the course in archaeology, which it was. I was determined to strike up some empathy with her. She may have been old enough to have been my grandmother but she was big enough to play for England at any one of a number of contact sports.

'Always the way, isn't it? You must be . . .?'

'Oi musn't be anything,' she said, letting slip her Suffolk accent, 'but I happen to be Mrs Hawksbee. I'm Mr Swallow's housekeeper when it suits me and in charge of "finds processing" when it suits him, which means I get to wash and clean all the rubbish he digs up instead of just the mess he leaves around the house. Sorry about your trousers, by the way. When it dries it'll brush off. I have to throw the pot-wash . . . the *processing* water out here. We've blocked the sinks twice this month and had to get a plumber out from Stowmarket.'

I refrained from saying anything about how easy it was to get a plumber in London and tried to look sympathetic.

'I'm Roy and this is Amy. Is Mr Swallow around?'

'No, thank heavens. He's been in Hadleigh all afternoon at the police station. If he's out of my hair for an afternoon I count it a blessing.'

'There's no trouble, is there?' Amy asked and I groaned inwardly.

We hadn't even unpacked and here she was cross-examining the faithful family retainer who was highly unlikely to reveal any scandal or juicy gossip to two complete strangers she'd only laid eyes on seconds before.

'There's *always* trouble where Arthur is, moi dear. I reckon they've given him a parking space down at Hadleigh station the amount of times he's been there. If he's not down there demanding more police patrols because of these Nighthawk folk who come with their mine detectors after dark, then he's pushing them to find out why they haven't caught the tearaways who beat up two of our diggers. And if he's not down there banging on the desk and saying how he's a ratepayer and how he used to be a magistrate, then they've hauled *him* in 'cos he's started a fight with the local farmers or that time when he chased the bloke from English Heritage off with a shotgun. Then there was the anonymous letters sent to that professor at the university, though they never proved that. And there was the time he drove the bulldozer on the road without a proper licence, but that was fair enough, he did do that.'

She paused for breath, taking enough into that massive ribcage to keep a deep sea diver going for hours.

'Of course, he's no stranger to it. They had him in and out of there like a rabbit in a hole for months when his brother died. Mind you, that was serious. Nobody ever did fathom why Mr Gerald blew his own head off like that. Him just finishing Sunday lunch then walking out of the french windows into the garden and putting that gun in his mouth. Terrible thing to happen, after such a nice bit of roast pork as well.

'Anyway, you'd better go round the back and report to Joss. She's the pretty one who looks like she knows what she's doing. You can't miss her. She stands out a mile amongst the others.'

Of course, sometimes you can totally misread people.

Chapter Six

Field Walking

As we walked round the side of Woolpack House on a Yorkstone paving path which seemed to be the only firm footing left in the area, Amy could hardly contain herself.

'Hey, if we want to know what's going on around here, let's just ask Mrs Hawksbee. The old battleaxe is busting to dish the dirt. Probably doesn't get out much.'

'If you think she's a gossip, wait till you meet some diggers,' I said as we turned the corner.

To the side of the house, whatever had grown there had long been stripped away as far as a distant hedge which ran alongside a field of barley or wheat. The naked sandy surface of the ground – what archaeologists call the 'natural' – was pitted with holes and slashed by ditch sections, and the piles of 'spoil' which had been dug out of them had been dumped in no discernible pattern or order.

'Jesus!' Amy sighed. 'He won't get on *Gardeners' World* with this, will he?'

'He's got the digging bug big time by the looks of it,' I agreed.

'Isn't there a law about uncontrolled digging? Some sort of Crimes Against the Landscape Act?'

'There should be, but if it's his land I don't think they can touch him. If he wants the dig accredited and given any sort of legitimacy then I suppose he'll have to be monitored by someone. The County Council maybe, or English Heritage.'

'Didn't the old gasbag say he'd chased one of them off with a shotgun?'

'She might have mentioned something of the sort.'

We turned the corner to the back of the house where the devastation stretched out, it seemed, for as far as we could see. If what had been the side garden or lawn now resembled an abandoned building site, then the land to the rear including what was left of an orchard now looked like Omaha Beach without the welcoming slap of the incoming tide.

It was a battlefield of trenches and mounds of earth and shell holes and of slouched figures in platoon strength moving slowly across the scarred landscape, all of them dark and grey against the sinking afternoon sun. Some held picks or shovels over their shoulders like rifles at port. Some pushed wheelbarrows wearily towards a spoil heap and in silhouette looked for all the world like stretcher bearers on the Ghost Road. They mostly wore camouflage combat trousers with bulging cargo pockets, and baseball caps seemed to be regulation issue. They all moved in silence and slowly, as if walking through heavy mud although the ground was quite dry, towards a green metal lock-up tool shed. It was a sombre and, for me, a rather moving sight. I remembered the feeling at the end of the first day's work after the weekend when you'd try to work through to the other side of your hangover. By knocking-off time you still had the hangover but you were too knackered to care about it.

The only person not trudging in from the digging fields was opening the driver's door of a filthy white Transit minibus when she saw us.

The van was so dirty people had written in the grime with their fingertips. There was the usual 'Also available in white' comment but also one which said 'If my wife was as dirty as this I'd stay home more' in quite a flowing script. The driver was a young female dressed in black vest, black jeans and black combat boots. Her long black hair was in a ponytail strained through the hole at the back of a black baseball cap which bore the legend 'X-Wing Fighter Pilot'.

She had big round eyes, a snub nose and a broad smile which she turned on automatically to reveal teeth as good as mine.

'Actually, it might not be a bad idea to get Mrs Hawksbee talking after all, especially if Arthur's not around. See what else she can tell us,' I suggested.

'Later,' said Amy, linking her arm through mine. 'Let's go and meet Joss.'

I could have sworn she'd never even glanced towards the van but somehow she'd seen Joss before I had.

'You must be Joss.'

'And you must be the friends of the godson,' she said with just a trace of a northern accent, showing us the smile again. It was a very nice smile.

'I'm Amy, he's Roy,' said Amy. 'We're the new recruits.'

'Arthur told me to expect you – and here you are!' She clapped her hands to show pleasure and surprise. 'Which is about the only thing that's gone to plan so far today.'

'You're the project manager, you're supposed to have problems,' I smiled back at her.

'You've been on a dig before, haven't you?'

'It's been a while,' I admitted.

'Can you read a level?'

'Sure.'

'Know how to put in a base line?'

'Yeah.'

'Can you do planning?'

'As long as the pencil has an eraser at one end.'

'Ever taken soil samples?'

'Tons.'

'Do you know which end of a mattock you don't shove up your arse?'

'The sharp one.'

'Do you want to be site supervisor?'

She was still smiling, so perhaps I hadn't been paying enough attention.

'Excuse me? Was that a job interview? And I passed?'

'Actually, if you'd only got the question about the mattock right you would have got the job,' said Joss. Then she seemed to notice Amy. 'Unless you'd – '

'No, carry on. I'm new at this game. It's all a learning curve for me, but Roy – he's been at it for years, he's only being modest. Quite a few years, actually, probably since before you . . .'

She let it hang for ten seconds, just to wind me up.

'. . . before you went to university . . .'

Joss didn't seem to notice the sub-text.

'That's my trouble,' she said. 'Seven years and three degrees in archaeology but I've never actually been on a dig before, other than a two-week summer school training session. In Wales.'

She added the 'in Wales' as an afterthought and with a shudder.

'University of Lampeter?' I tried, as it was famous for two things: being in one of the smallest university towns in the country (way out in the country) and archaeology.

''Fraid so. Good course but very theoretical,' she mused.

'Is it true that when it was rumoured that Lampeter was to get a McDonald's, they put it in the prospectus to boost applications?'

Joss laughed. She had a nice laugh.

'Probably. They say that you turn to either the Bible or the beer if you go there.'

'Which did you choose?'

'Both. Look, it's knocking-off time here and I've got to drive some of the volunteers back into Ipswich in about twenty minutes, but I could give you a quick site tour. Mr Swallow usually does that himself but he's not back yet. You up for it?'

'Lead on,' I said.

'Absolutely,' said Amy. 'We're all eyes. I mean ears.'

I tried not to flinch as her fingernails dug into my forearm.

Most of the diggers were congregated around the green

metal tool store, a mobile lock-up rectangular box of the type hired in to every building site, packing away their tools for the night and making quite a racket as every mattock and shovel clanged when it hit the metal floor. A pair of diggers eyed us suspiciously as they rolled cigarettes and waited to stack the wheelbarrows in there on the last in, first out in the morning basis.

Joss led us away from them, though, out on to the site proper.

'How many diggers have you got?' I asked her.

'Site assistants,' she said. 'Mr Swallow prefers site assistant and we should have sixteen plus two supervisors, but we don't. We've got eight full-time diggers – site assistants – though another two are supposed to arrive this week as well as you two, which was a surprise, but a pleasant one. So if we don't lose anyone else, then we'll have twelve, plus me, plus Dan the Man the finds officer and an assistant finds officer. Plus, Mondays and Fridays, we get volunteer pot-washers –'

'You mean finds processors,' I said.

'I see you've met Mrs Hawksbee,' Joss said, pausing to raise her eyebrows. 'She's been here longer than the archaeology, but she keeps the volunteers in line and she is quite knowledgeable after all these years. Though Dan says she's not as knowledgeable as she thinks she is.'

'You said there'd be a "Dan",' Amy whispered to me, but Joss overheard and misunderstood.

'We'd be lost without Dan the Man,' she said defensively. 'He does know what he's doing. Dan Gilpen – you must have heard of him if you're on the diggers' circuit.'

'I've been out of the field for a while . . .' I said lamely.

'He's the ex-London cab driver who took up archaeology when he retired and put himself through college when he was sixty-five. Swears like a trooper and specializes in Roman pottery and is particularly shit-hot on Samian ware. Sounds like a right East End geezer, the sort you wouldn't buy a second-hand car from.'

For me, that didn't narrow it down, but I knew what she

meant and the name did ring a bell somewhere in the back of my memory.

'Didn't he turn up a hoard of coins in the City last year? It was in the papers.'

'That was him, on a dig for the Museum of London. Mind you, he wears more gold rings and medallions than the average hoard. His sense of fashion is timewarped to the early Eighties.'

I could sense Amy biting her tongue.

'Why are you short-staffed? I saw the advert and the day rate is good, plus the free accommodation. I would have thought you'd have had diggers biting your hand off.'

'Well, I bit when I saw the project manager's job come up, but then I'm desperate for field work experience. Anyone wanting a serious career in archaeology probably got put off by the rumours about Arthur.'

'What rumours?' Amy asked bluntly.

'That he runs a cowboy outfit and that this isn't a serious dig. He's made a lot of enemies over the last ten years, has Arthur. In the world of archaeology that is. But then, we advertised late in the season and most university students would have already been fixed up for the summer. There aren't that many professional diggers left on the circuit and they tend to go for year-long contracts which will see them through the winter.'

We had reached the first of a line of grid-pegs marking off the dig into ten-metre squares, twelve grid boxes in total. Even I could see that some of the squares were not exactly – square.

Joss saw me eyeing the line.

'Yes, I know. I'm afraid we're getting careless out here. I wasn't kidding, there is a supervisor's job going and somebody's got to pull things together or this excavation will become a joke like the last one.'

'You were still at school then!' Amy blurted out, but Joss wasn't fazed in the slightest.

'I've had to read all the evaluations and dig reports for the area, including Arthur's report which he had printed privately ten years ago. You might say that Arthur's was very much a minority opinion.'

'He didn't find anything?'

'Let's just say he lives in hope,' she said diplomatically, 'but he hasn't found what he's looking for.'

'That would be some connection with Boudica,' said Amy, pronouncing it right just to remind me, not that it was necessary, that she was a quick learner.

'In his dreams. We've got some first-century Roman finds, but we've also got bits of Iron Age and Anglo-Saxon, though that's pretty much what you would expect in this part of the world. We're certainly inside Iceni territory as was, even if only just on the edge, there's an Iron Age barrow at Rougham a few miles away and we're between two possible Roman roads to the west and east of us running up to Ixworth. Plus, the Sutton Hoo burial is not that far away towards the coast.'

'So you've got Iron Age, Roman and Anglo-Saxon finds but have you got any dateable features?'

'Have we got any features at all? This is the question. I think we have a couple of ditches and there are some possible post-holes but not enough to make much sense. No sign of any definite buildings or industrial use as yet, but we've only had a couple of weeks on the area. Half the problem is sorting out where Arthur's already dug. He's been at it off and on for nearly ten years.'

'No plans?' I asked and she shook her head. 'Geophys? Aerial photographs?'

Joss's head just kept on shaking.

'Surely there's a pre-ex plan of the site, isn't there?'

'Don't laugh, but the pre-ex-plan is a blown-up photograph of the gardens taken about five years ago for *Country Life*.'

Now I was shaking my head and when in doubt did what all archaeologists do: sink down on my haunches and look closely at the earth, then scan the horizon, then look back down at the ground, waiting for an answer to scream itself at me.

'So where's the archaeology then?' said Amy.

'You're looking at it,' Joss and I said together.

'Duh-uh?'

'Those black stains in the ground, in the sandy "natural" sub-soil,' I said, 'that's what we're looking at. See, here and there,' I pointed. 'Those are where somebody at some time in the past has cut through the topsoil and made a mark. Maybe they were digging a ditch or cutting a foundation trench for something, or burying rubbish in a pit or they were digging a hole for a post to hold up a roof or for a stake which was part of a fence. The dark bits are where the man-made hole has silted up over the years. Dig that out and you can have a good guess from the shape of the hole as to what had been there, and what it was used for.'

'But they're just blobs,' said Amy, not trying to hide her disappointment.

'And when you've dug them out they're just holes in the ground,' I said. 'But that's archaeology.'

Joss smiled down at me. I think she was warming to me.

'Remind me,' she said, 'why do we do this?'

'Beats me. You never see Indiana Jones or Lara Croft digging out a medieval cesspit.'

'So what's that, then?' asked Amy, pointing at a straight dark line where the earth undulated like corduroy. 'And look, there's another one over there.'

'Sorry to disappoint you, but those are bulldozer tracks,' I said. 'Whoever did the stripping wasn't very good at it. You can't strip an area and then drive over it without trashing it.'

'That was Arthur, I'm afraid,' said Joss.

'He should have used a JCB or a 360,' I said smugly, showing off my tactical experience.

'A what?' Amy snapped at me.

'One of those big mechanical diggers that turns through three hundred and sixty degrees. You know, you've seen them on building sites or where they're widening the motorway. They can take up the topsoil with a bucket without driving over what they've just cleaned.'

I mimed the action of a mechanical bucket reaching out and scooping up the earth with my arm and hand. To anyone watching us from a distance it would have looked like we were playing charades and I was doing *Jurassic Park*.

'Problem,' said Joss. 'Arthur doesn't know how to drive a 360 but he has bought himself a bulldozer, so that's what we use. We'll just have to get everybody hoeing the grid squares tomorrow; see if we can see anything.'

Unless things had changed radically, that would go down like a lead balloon with the diggers. Diggers hate hoeing as it is physically exhausting – sometimes, literally, back-breaking – and the least satisfying part of the job in terms of seeing a clear end result. You could spend an entire day hoeing back a ten-metre square and be left with nothing but a ten-metre square of clean, undisturbed 'natural' where no human being had been bothered to make a mark in the previous ten thousand years.

Joss began walking again and we followed her along the bulldozed strip towards what was now clearly an orchard of healthy, fruit-laden trees, mostly apple but I spotted pear, damson and greengage as well. Judging by the underbrush and the suckers sprouting from the ground, the orchard had been left to its own devices for a few years and one of the trees on the edge had been snapped in half quite recently.

'Arthur forgot how to stop the bulldozer,' Joss explained.

'They're tricky things,' I sympathized. 'You have to remember it's a *de*celerator, not an accelerator, so you have to put your foot down, so to speak, to stop.'

'You know how to drive one?'

'Sure.'

'Thank God,' she breathed. 'Anyway, this is the limit of the excavation as planned so far, though Arthur has said he'll take the orchard out if we don't find anything in this strip between here and the house.'

'How big's the area altogether?'

'Woolpack House in total covers four-and-a-half acres,

but Arthur's worked his way round the other sides over the last ten years. This strip here, which is about three hundred metres by thirty is the last undug patch unless you count the front lawns and the rose beds.'

'He seemed to be having a go at them yesterday,' said Amy.

Fortunately she didn't say how we knew and Joss didn't pick up on it. I didn't think it would do our simple digger image much good if we let it slip that we'd had a freebie overflight in an army helicopter.

'I think he gets bored at the weekends,' Joss said. 'And he's only had the bulldozer a few weeks so it's still quite a new toy for him. Digging up the front lawn was definitely not on the original action plan but it wouldn't surprise me if he ended up knocking down the house if he can't find what he's after.'

'Did anyone do a proper evaluation on the place? I mean way back, when he first started?'

'There was some field walking done by local volunteers and a chap from the university but the result was pretty negative and it didn't recommend any further evaluation. And that was mostly over there, in those fields.'

She pointed through the orchard to where the land rose up a gentle slope and a field of wheat or barley trailed off over the horizon.

'They're owned by the local farming mafia, a family called the Scrivenour-Lindleys, and they don't get on with Arthur.' She paused then added thoughtfully, 'Not many people do, actually.'

'But Arthur didn't accept this, I presume?'

'No way. He was, and is, convinced there's something here on his land, but until he won the Lottery – I take it you know about that – he never had the money to mount a full-scale excavation. Nobody would sponsor him so he taught himself the rudiments of archaeology and started to do it himself. There was also something about a family trust which had a mortgage on the place and it wasn't until he could clear his mortgage with his winnings that he owned the place outright. Now he can do exactly what he wants.'

'And he wants to find the place where Boudica turned out her gold coins, right?' said Amy.

'He can dream,' said Joss.

'So you don't rate his chances?'

'On a scale of one to ten, I'd say minus five. You can't find something which didn't exist.'

Amy was confused and so instinctively glared at me.

'Boudica never minted any coinage,' I said. I remembered telling Rupert that at my mother's party but Amy had been too busy checking out the bulges in his uniform to listen properly. 'She wasn't around long enough. She could only have been queen for a year, tops. After her rebellion went belly up, the Romans made sure she wasn't around to stick her face on the coinage.'

'They killed her?' She sounded genuinely surprised.

'It's said she took poison, but nobody knows for sure. The Iceni were pretty much wiped out. We'd say "ethnically-cleansed" today. Finding genuine Boudican coins – you might as well start looking for the Holy Grail.'

'I think it is Arthur's Holy Grail,' said Joss seriously.

'And why not?' I asked. 'Everyone should have one.'

'Some of us have to settle for driving a van full of volunteers home. Come on, I'll show you the accommodation and let you introduce yourselves to the others. Arthur should be back by now, so you should meet him too.'

As we walked back towards the house I managed to get some idea of the scale of the place.

Woolpack House itself was a mid-Victorian country pile built of grey stone and slate tile, neither of which were natural building materials for Suffolk. Whoever had built it wanted Victorian rectory respectability and solidity rather than the thatched roof and painted plaster of the cottages in the village. These days of course it would be the thatched cottages which attracted the premium price.

From the front it had looked normal enough, but somebody had been busy round the back. There was a large dark wooden barn structure which, from the tracks leading up to the double doors, was where Arthur garaged his new bulldozer. There was a single-storey building, recently renovated, with three doors and curtains at the windows, but it was still obvious that it had been one long pigsty at some point. Opposite that was a square building made of brick and blackened weatherboarding shaped like a Swiss chalet, not big enough to be a house and with long windows built into the slanting roof. In amongst the outbuildings had been dropped the lock-up metal tool shed and that other stand-by of the archaeological site, a bank of chemical toilets. But these were no ordinary Portaloos, the sort which could blow over in a stiff breeze. These were, as a sign said, 'Mobile Thrones' – top of the range gear – and had a tasteful wooden screen around them and their accompanying water bowser which probably meant they had shower facilities. I was impressed. Arthur had got one priority right at least.

'It shouldn't be possible to get lost,' Joss was saying, 'although at least one digger's managed it, but that's The Studio –' she indicated the Swiss chalet building – 'which is a meeting room and tea room and there's a TV with video in there. One rule: no muddy boots. We use the tool shed as a boot room. All cooking is done in the kitchen of the main house, so the back door's usually left open. There are fridges in there too, but make sure all your supplies are labelled. There's the toilet and communal shower block. There is hot water but not much of it and you have to wait sometimes if you're way down the queue. And this is The Stables, which is the sleeping accommodation.'

'It's a pigsty,' said Amy, her face dangerously blank.

'It was a pigsty, you're quite right, but now it's partitioned off into ten sleeping units each with two beds. There's not enough room to swing a cat, I admit, but it's clean and warm enough in the summer. You can have a room each if you want, we've got space to spare.'

'It might come to that,' Amy growled softly.

I said nothing. I knew exactly how much room was needed to swing a cat.

'Anyways, make yourselves at home, just find a cubicle that hasn't got stuff in it and settle in. I've got to take the volunteer pot-washers home, but I'll check in with you when I get back and sort out where you go on the tea-making roster and the cleaning rota.'

She flashed her teeth and I flashed mine. Amy smiled weakly. She was still trying to get her head around words like 'communal', 'roster' and 'cleaning' when the words she had really been wanting to hear were 'en suite' and 'room service'.

'I suppose we should be grateful for running water,' she hissed as Joss fired up the Transit and tooted the horn.

'Compared to some sites I've seen, this already gets five stars and two crossed-knives-and-forks,' I hissed back. 'Running water – luxury. Them diggers'll be expecting electricity next.'

'You are joking, aren't you?' she said. 'Either tell me you're joking or call the police on your mobile right now.'

'I haven't done anything,' I protested.

'I meant call them to come and arrest *me*.'

'Joke.'

She relaxed and so did I when I scoped the area and spotted the electricity cables hanging from the house to the pigsty. Sorry, The Stables.

Half a dozen little old ladies trooped out of the house in answer to Joss's tooting on the horn. When they saw us they all smiled and said things like 'Just arrived?' and 'Can't wait to get digging, eh?' and 'See you on Friday' to which one of them added, 'If you're still here!' and they all laughed.

We smiled politely and watched them climb aboard the Transit. Their combined age put them down as post-medieval, but only just. One of them handed Joss a cassette tape as she climbed in the back and Joss, making a 'Here we go' face at us, pushed it into the dashboard player. Someone shouted, 'Turn it up, Joss, luv,' and even when the doors slammed shut we could hear the opening riffs of 'Motherless Children' – Eric Clapton circa 1974.

'My God, why doesn't she just paint "Age Concern" on the door and be done with it?' said Amy.

'Now, now, don't be ageist. Just because we have the suicide pact arranged for when we hit sixty-five.'

'That's the one where you go first, right? Show me what to do.'

'I just love it when you talk dirty.'

She elbowed me playfully in the ribs and when I'd got my breath back I saw that the old dears in the Transit were waving enthusiastically in our direction. Amy even waved back, but I realized it wasn't from us that the little old ladies were taking a fond farewell.

Standing in the doorway of the kitchen was a little old gentleman, thinning a bit on top but still mighty slim and trim. His face and hands carried a deep bronze tan, the sort Amy would buy out of a bottle before going on holiday, and so did his chest. We could see because his white shirt was open almost to the navel, revealing a thick pelt of hair and a gold medallion slung round his neck. He had chunky gold rings on most of his fingers and he was smoking a roll-up cigarette so thin and perfectly formed it could have been H.M. Prison issue. Best of all, he wore a white suit. On an archaeological dig, this guy was wearing a white suit. Tarantulas stuck on slices of angel cake would pay for camouflage as good as that.

'Bloody hell,' breathed Amy. 'Bring on the mirror ball and cue the Bee Gees.'

'I told you flares were coming back.'

'Is that Arthur?'

'I don't think so, but if it is it explains why he spends so much time down the police station.'

The old man, super-cool and leaning on the door frame, drew on his roll-up and blew a perfect smoke ring in the direction of the Transit as Joss steered it around the corner of the house. Her passengers probably wet themselves.

'You must be Dan Gilpen,' I said, extending my hand, 'the Finds Supremo.'

'My reputation precedes me,' he said, taking my hand

with his which was incredibly soft and smooth, though the grip was tough enough.

I was about to introduce Amy when he said, 'And so does yours.'

'Excuse me?'

'Angel, is it?'

'Might be,' I said automatically and perhaps a tad defensively.

'I've heard of you. Hackney, innit?'

'Used to be. Gone up in the world a bit since.'

'What? Stepney?' But he smiled when he said it.

'Hampstead. And I don't mean North Kilburn but-we-call-it-Hampstead.'

At that, he grinned broadly to show that he still had, if only a few, teeth of his own.

'Helllllooo!' Amy shouted. 'I'm here too. Can we plug in the translator?'

'Sorry. Amy, meet Dan the Man. He used to be a cab driver. I'd forgotten.'

Mistakes like that could be fatal in some postcodes beginning with 'E' in London.

'But I don't know how he knows me or where from.'

'K258 GPU,' he said and touched a forefinger to his nose.

'And in English?' Amy demanded.

'Armstrong's registration number,' I explained. 'How . . .?'

'I seen you parked out front, clocked the plate. Used to be owned by a musher called Braindead Brian Stewart, worked out of East Ham. Had to sell it because of gambling debts, word was. Feller called Big Mac McCandy was involved somehow . . .'

'Er . . . yes, right, you've got a good memory for numberplates. It's delicensed of course. I've never done the Knowledge and got the plate.'

'I didn't know Armstrong had a *history*,' Amy said in a sing-song voice to remind us she was still there.

'I used to see it around Hackney way, say to myself: There goes Braindead. 'Course it wasn't. Asked about, your name came up, just in case you were trying it on, pretending to have the plate. Anyways, that was when I was still a musher. I've got a life now.'

'Archaeology?'

'Too right. Keeps me off the streets.' We both laughed at that. 'But I just do the finds. This digging lark is for the birds.'

'The birds seem to find you,' Amy said.

'What, the pot-washers? Yeah well, I'm an eligible widower, ain't I? Look after meself, dress well, like a good time. Bound to attract 'em, ain't I? One of these days I'll let the two richest ones fight over me.'

'You're a Roman pottery man, aren't you? So Joss said.' I tried to get him back on track.

His leathered face creased into a grin again.

'If only that Joss was thirty years older . . . Always dresses in black, you know. Says she's shy and it helps her blend in the background. Likes to go unnoticed.'

'It's not working, is it?' Amy said with an ever-so-sweet smile.

'How would you know, darling?' Dan said to her and I thought a fight was on the cards. 'You've never needed to blend. Looks like yours don't need a background.'

I could see why Dan was a killer down the Darby and Joan Club.

'But you are a bit of a Roman pot specialist, aren't you?' I tried again.

'I do my best. Self-taught mostly, but all the big names come to me now if they find any Samian, though my real speciality is Gallia Narbonensis first century.'

'Haven't I seen you on *The Time Detectives* or whatever it's called? You know, on TV?' Amy suddenly warmed to him.

'Oh, I know the programme you mean,' said Dan proudly. 'I've done most of them 'istory shows. I turn up regular on the Discovery Channel. But I'm handicapped you see, as I don't have letters after my name. A lot of them telly producers are right tossers, you know.'

'And Arthur Swallow brought you in to oversee the finds, right?'

'Not really. I just saw the dig advertised and I turned up; offered my services. I don't take pay for what I do, this is my hobby and if it's interesting, I do it. If it ain't, I piss off somewhere else.'

I knew of people like Dan who followed digs around the country like demented groupies, looking for that one coin, that one pot, that one Saxon sword, that perfect prehistoric flint – the one specimen they hadn't so far encountered. Not that they wanted to keep them, just spot them, maybe even hold them for a second. They would check them off their own private lists like birdwatchers. Some of them claimed to be world experts – on clay pipes (any number of *them*), or bell-foundry mouldings, even tegulated Roman roof tiles – and would give you an hour-long lecture at the drop of a hat. But a few, like Dan, really did know what they were talking about.

'So what are you hoping to find? A good piece of Samian with the maker's mark intact?'

'Been there, done that. I've ticked off most of the known names. No, what I'm after is a piece of bog-standard Roman army issue cookware that's stamped something like "Quartermaster's Stores, XXth Legion". That'd be in Latin, of course.'

'Just that? An army cooking pot?'

'If it's stamped, yeah. Pretty rare, you know.'

'Are you going to find one here?'

Dan shook his head.

'Not a fookin' chance on the basis of what they've pulled out so far.'

He began to roll himself another needle cigarette.

'So they're not finding any . . .' I think Amy had been about to say 'coins' but thought the better of it. '. . . Much stuff?'

'Oh, they're finding *stuff* all right, but there's no sense to any of it. Bits of first century, bits of fourth century. Anglo-Saxon pot, Iron Age pot. You'd have thought old Arthur had bought it job lot at a jumble sale. No pattern to the finds at all.'

Dan took a light from my Zippo and grunted his thanks.

'There again, there's no pattern to this dig. I've seen better organized piss-ups in Temperance tea rooms. Don't take my word for it, though, you talk to the so-called diggers. Wankers, all of 'em. Wouldn't employ them to dig my garden, an' I've got a ninth-floor council flat.'

'You going to stay the course?'

'I'll give it to the end of the week.' He waved his cigarette hand in an aw-shucks movement. 'I suppose some of them are decent kids. That Fifi, who's working with me on the finds, she's OK even if she has some funny friends. And there's Ben, her boyfriend. He seems to know one end of a trowel from the other but the rest I wouldn't give you tuppence for. The accommodation's shite as well.'

'Yes, we're in The Stables too,' said Amy absent-mindedly.

Dan snorted.

'That place there? That's a fooking pigsty, that is.'

'It *used* to be a pigsty,' Amy corrected.

'I don't care what it used to be, it's a fooking pigsty now it's got diggers living in it. Right messy bunch of bleeders. You wouldn't catch me bunking down with them. I'm staying in the village at The Drovers but it's a bit primitive for my taste and the beer's crap. I might see if the other pub does bed and breakfast. Speaking of which, they'll be open now.'

He consulted his watch, a gigantic gold and silver disc which could blind someone if the sun hit it right.

'Can I give you a lift?' I offered, if only to put off the awful moment when Amy and I had to fight over who got the top bunk.

'In an Austin Fairway? Per-lease. I'm retired and I don't have to sit in a black cab ever again. I'll walk. Keep myself in trim. You never know when some of the widows in the village might need a right good seeing-to, do you?'

115

He saw me wince at that and, being an ex-cabby, couldn't resist having a debate about it.

'Don't you turn up your nose at some of the elderly ladies,' he said, prodding me in the chest with a bony forefinger. 'They're discreet, know how to cook, usually have a few bob of their own and – above all – they're *grateful*.'

His face slid into a leer and he cackled, he positively cackled.

He tipped a finger in mock salute and set off towards the driveway with a spring in his step.

As we watched him go, Amy, very quietly, started singing.

'*Staying alive, staying alive . . .*'

Chapter Seven

Trial Trenching

'Hi there, you must be the new diggers.'

I was thankful for the interruption and delighted that this solid, handsome product of a public school was willing to talk to me. I was happy that anyone would talk to me. Amy wouldn't.

'That's us. Amy and Roy.'

'Settling in, are you? I'm Ben, by the way.'

He was taller than me, younger than me and much fitter. Square-jawed and with innocent blue eyes, dressed in a plain black T-shirt with the sleeves ripped off and Gortex combat trousers in camouflage green, and there was a trowel stuffed into the cargo pocket on his right thigh. He had blond hair cropped short and neat rather than in the drastic Number One shaved style favoured by professional footballers and a healthy tan. He had been standing in the entrance to the 'room' we had appropriated for about ten seconds before Amy noticed him.

'Hello, Ben,' she said throatily.

'I know what you're thinking,' he said with a schoolboy grin, like it was the start of a joke.

'You couldn't possibly,' said Amy.

You're too young, I thought but didn't say.

'You're thinking there isn't room to swing a cat in here, aren't you?' Ben pressed on regardless.

'Oh, I don't know . . .' I said, turning my head as if I was calculating the cubic capacity.

'It is a bit cramped for two,' said Amy, which could have

been a hint to me that she was going to claim her own living space. 'But I suppose it's rather clever how they've partitioned it all off.'

The turnaround in her attitude was remarkable. Only seconds before she had been cursing the builder – poor, mentally retarded orphaned son of a female dog that he was – who had carried out the renovation work.

The Stables had been converted with the same feeling for personal space shared by the designers of the honeycomb hotels in Tokyo. It was in fact three pigsties knocked into one, retaining the three farmhouse-style doors where the top could open without the bottom half, all of which opened into a narrow corridor running the length of the building like the corridor of an old steam train. In fact I bet that was where the idea came from as the ten rooms, or 'cubicles' as Amy insisted ('They give sperm donors more room than this,' she'd said and I'd pointed out, just to lighten the mood, that they got magazines as well), all had sliding doors. It was the most sensible use of space given that doors opening inward would be potentially lethal to anyone in the room and if they opened outward, they'd block the corridor. As it was there was just enough space for two army issue camp beds and one narrow chest of drawers with an Anglepoise lamp plugged into the single electric socket. Even with Ben standing in the corridor looking in, I was having flashes of the Marx Brothers' cruise liner scene.

'Trick is, don't spend too much time in there or you'll go stir crazy. People'll be cooking their dinners in the house now but afterwards we watch TV in The Studio or some nights go down to the pub in the village.'

'That sounds . . . nice,' said Amy, managing a smile.

'Oh – cooking,' said Ben as if he'd just remembered something. 'Should tell you, vegetarians go first and they'll take their meals over to The Studio while the meat-eaters get stuck in. Sorry, but we voted on it on Day One. Same goes for Sandwich Patrol.'

'For what?'

'When you do your sandwiches for lunch tomorrow.

Most people do them before they go to bed and leave them in the fridge. Veggies go first.'

'What about bacon and eggs for breakfast, or some fried Suffolk ham or devilled kidneys?' I suggested.

His brow creased in a frown.

'Nobody thought of that one. Will it be a problem?'

'I'll survive,' I said.

'You have got food in, haven't you? The local shop's probably closed by now.'

'We've got supplies for tomorrow,' I said.

'And we'll probably eat down the pub tonight,' said Amy. 'Be nice to meet people if anyone's about.'

'I'll tell the troops,' Ben nodded his head, 'when they've finished stuffing their faces. They don't usually need asking twice. And I'm sure Fifi will come. You haven't seen her around, have you?'

'Sorry,' I said. 'We've met Joss and Dan the Man so far, that's it.'

'Well, she's hiding then, because Arthur's Jeep is parked out front and she was driving him back from Hadleigh. I think he might have lost his licence again. Is that your taxi out there, by the way?'

'Yes,' Amy and I said together, but I said it proudly.

'Cool,' said Ben. 'I saw Arthur giving it the once-over. He'll be asking for a drive of it, you watch. Mind you, I don't know why they let him buy that Jeep, not with his track record of driving offences. And those personalized numberplates! Oh, but you haven't met Arthur yet, have you?'

'We can't wait,' I said.

'It's an experience, that's for sure. And by the way, one more thing. A delicate thing, really.' He blushed ever so slightly and so Amy cocked her head to one side and made him keep eye-contact. I've seen stoats do the same with their prey.

'It's just that you two . . . being together . . . you should know that these internal walls between . . . between the rooms, well, they're really, really thin, I mean, like paper.

119

You can hear everything that goes on. And I mean everything.'

'Don't worry,' said Amy, 'that won't be a problem for us.'

Ben blushed even deeper, but I think he'd misunderstood.

I was the one who had misunderstood when Ben had said Arthur Swallow drove a Jeep.

I'd thought he meant a Jeep.

As in I've-just-won-the-Lottery, therefore I'm going to rush out and buy one of those big shiny four-wheel drive Jeeps like the Wrangler or the Cherokee or even, now that I had pots of money, one of the brand spanking new models, the Liberty off-roader. It must be a common enough dream among punters as they line up at the newsagent's for their Wednesday and Saturday gambling fix. Get those six lucky numbers coming up and it's straight down the garage to buy something big enough and powerful enough to invade Poland in.

But old Arthur just had to be different. Parked next to Armstrong was a Jeep. A jeep Jeep. One of the six hundred thousand or so Jeeps produced by Ford and Willys in America during World War II and named after either 'GP' for General Purpose (vehicle) or the character 'Eugene the Jeep' from the old Popeye cartoons, depending on who you believed.

It was painted regulation green, had the canvas top down and the windscreen folded forward for maximum air conditioning and had an army pick and shovel clipped to the driver's side of the bodywork for authenticity. Naturally, it was left-hand drive.

I knew it would have a 2.2 litre engine and the fuel tank was under the driver's seat, which must have been a comfort to drivers when they were under fire. The first Jeeps supplied to the US Army had ignition keys, but the drivers kept losing them so later models, such as Arthur's, were fitted with a starter button on the floor. They switched from rear-wheel to four-wheel drive by means of a lever in the passenger footwell, could manage somewhere between 50 and 60 m.p.h., had a three-speed gearbox and the brakes, by universal consent, were a joke. The driving position was such that anyone over six foot tall risked sexually assaulting themselves.

I have to admit I stood there and admired it, not having seen one in such good condition before. Amy was admiring it too, but with a jaw-dropping expression of horror rather than my boyish enthusiasm.

And then I realized she was looking at the numberplates.

Arthur's personalized numberplates, for which he probably paid a small fortune though it beggars me why they would have been in demand.

Arthur Ransome Swallow's personalized numberplates.

ARS 1.

'Piss off, you bastard!'

If I hadn't been staring at the Jeep I'm sure I would have noticed the drone of the light aircraft above us, but then probably not. My senses were still tuned to west London values which accept ground and air traffic noise as simply background and that includes jumbo jets unless their landing wheels are actually tugging at the tree tops in Hyde Park.

Amy realized what Arthur was shouting at a fraction before I did, but couldn't resist saying later that she thought he had been talking to me.

Arthur Ransome Swallow shook his fist at the still bright sky and the small propeller-driven plane heading southeast. I screwed up my eyes but couldn't tell at that distance what sort of plane it was though I guessed either a Piper Cub or a Cessna 140 from the outline.

'Not talking to you, of course, just that nosy bugger up there. Comes over twice a day to snoop. I reckon he's taking pictures of the site. Arthur Swallow. You must be Rupert's friends.'

From what I recalled of the newspaper cutting Rupert had shown us, Arthur must have been at least seventy-six by now, but he wore it well despite a slight limp in his left leg as he stepped out of the doorway of Woolpack House to greet us. He had the ramrod back of military bearing and a clipped white moustache to match what hair he had left. His bald pate and face were shiny pink like a baby's, the cheeks and nose hinting betrayal of a liking for good claret.

'I'm Roy, this is Amy,' I said as we all shook hands.

'Of course you are. You're the one who knows all about this digging business,' he said to me, 'and you must be the enthusiastic amateur just dying to have a go? Am I right? I must say you made quite an impression on Rupert. He sounded very taken with you. And I can see why. The boy has taste, I'll give him that.'

'Oh, I don't . . .' Amy started, and I do believe she was tongue-tied.

'No, he was. Sang your praises more than fulsome, he did,' said the old smoothie.

'I'm just happy to be given a chance to come and dig. It's something I've always wanted to do, but I'm afraid I might not be very good at it.'

I hadn't heard her be this deferential since she got investigated by the VAT Inspectors.

'Nonsense, my dear. I can call you "my dear" because I'm an old man and I don't care any more, so you'll have to put with that. As for the archaeology, we'll have you digging with the best of them. Rupert said on the phone that you were fit, very fit in fact, and he's a good judge of people.'

I suspected that Rupert hadn't been referring to Amy's ability to push a wheelbarrow when he'd said she was 'fit' but I couldn't work out whether or not Arthur was in the loop on that one.

Arthur was still holding Amy's hand, patting it, and

not particularly interested in letting her get a word in edgewise.

'Are you settling in, my dear? Have you met the rest of my crew?'

'Only Dan and Ben so far,' said Amy demurely.

'And Joss,' I added.

'My key players,' said Arthur proudly, 'plus Fifi – who's around here somewhere – couldn't manage without those four, not now Sebastian has gone home hurt. Foolish boy. Still, you must have things to do. I know I do. Why don't we have dinner together tomorrow night? I don't like to show favouritism towards some diggers rather than others but I think I can get away with it as you're sort of friends of the family. Seven o'clock? I'll get Mrs Hawksbee to leave me one of her casseroles. She's ever so good, you know. She plays that microwave like a concert pianist whilst I don't know what half the buttons are for.'

'Well, if you're sure it won't upset the status quo . . .'

My opinion was irrelevant. There was no way Amy was going to fight a bunch of veggies for use of a communal kitchen if there was a chance of eating out.

'Settled then. Now if you'll excuse me I've got paperwork to catch up on after spending the whole day answering damn fool questions from our local constabulary. I'll see you on site in the morning. Joss'll find something for you to get your teeth into.'

'Shouldn't we sign on or something somewhere?' I asked, but Arthur looked blank. 'You know, give references, names and addresses, get put on the payroll, that sort of thing?'

A cog turned in Arthur's brain and his eyes lit up like lamps, albeit ones with very low wattage.

'Ah yes, of course, that sort of admin stuff. Paperwork. Can't run a site without paperwork. Fifi seems to be doing most of that now but I'm blowed if I know where she's got to. Must say she got quite excited when she saw your taxi there. I think she might be asking if she can take it for a spin. Loves driving the Jeep. Damned good driver for a woman.'

He caught Amy's eye.

'I *can* say that, my dear, because I'm old and eccentric. You can get away with a lot when you're old, it's one of the few advantages. Probably the only one come to think of it. Anyway, Fifi will sort all that out. Take it from me you're on the payroll as from today. Now I really must be off. I've an evaluation to do; for Rupert as a matter of fact.'

'An archaeological evaluation?'

I almost laughed as I said it. From what I'd seen of the Woolpack House site, he'd had trouble evaluating which way was up. The thought of him doing a commercial evaluation for someone else was bizarre.

'Have to be competitive these days, you know. There are lots of units out there touting for work. Iceni Rescue has to put itself about if it's to be taken seriously. This is not a cabbage patch digging operation, we're in the archaeology business and we mean business. We've got our own website you know. I'll show it to you tomorrow. Till then, take care. Charmed, absolutely charmed.'

This last was to Amy, then he turned on his good heel and limped back inside the house. I suspected that by the time the door closed behind him he had forgotten our very existence.

'Isn't he a panic?' she said, reaching for Armstrong's door handle. 'Come on, I'm starving and it must be time to start drinking heavily by now.'

She looked down at the Jeep again and shook her head.

'ARS 1. Can you credit it?'

'I think Arthur's got a problem with initials,' I said, 'maybe it's some sort of dyslexia. I can't believe anyone can be naturally that dim.'

'What do you mean? The Jeep? He probably did that for a joke.'

'Not just that. The unit, his business name: Iceni Rescue Archaeology.'

Amy's mouth formed a perfect O.

'See what you mean. Bet he gets lots of interesting e-mail.'

*   *   *

124

On the way to the village Amy said, 'They're all a bit weird, aren't they?'

'You haven't met the diggers yet,' I said honestly. 'Welcome to the wacky world of archaeology.'

I pulled up alongside The Chequers and put full lock on to swing Armstrong to a halt facing back to Woolpack House. I've found it always helps to park facing the line of your fastest exit.

'This pub?' Amy said. 'I thought the other one – The Drovers – would be the place the diggers went. This place is modern and ugly, the other one has character and real ale and probably Morris Dancers.'

'Exactly,' I said. 'This one has a restaurant and looks clean, so it won't be the diggers' local.'

'But I thought the whole point was to bond with them?'

'Per-lease. Not until we've eaten. Anyway, they'll see Armstrong out front and come in here if they think there's a chance we're buying. Trust me.'

As I held the door to the Lounge Bar open for her, I said:

'Anyway, you know I'm frightened of Morris Dancers.'

'And white-faced clowns,' she said as if suddenly remembering.

'Why do Morris Dancers wear bells?' I tried.

'So they can annoy blind people as well.'

She'd heard it before.

The bar was spotlessly clean, furnished with comfortable mis-matching chairs which looked as if they had been bought from antique shops rather than ordered from a brewer's catalogue and sturdy iron-framed tables. There was no jukebox, fruit machine or intrusive background music, no idiotic signs about not asking for credit and no stuffed donkeys brought back from Spanish holidays. There were also no customers.

But there was somebody behind the bar, a genial white-haired old cove with a Wing Commander's handlebar moustache, wearing a check shirt and tie and sipping genteelly from a silver half-pint tankard.

'Good evening, sir, madam,' he greeted us in a voice which made me look over my shoulder to see if respectable people had come in behind us. 'What's your pleasure?'

'Can't we have a drink first?' I said before I could stop myself.

He raised his tankard in a toasting gesture to me before putting it down and then placing his hands flat on the bar.

'Very good, sir, very droll. It's going to be a pleasure serving you.'

'But we'll still have drinks first, yeah?'

He laughed out loud this time then Amy, who hadn't had this sort of attention for at least fifteen minutes, nudged me in the ribs.

'And some food.'

'Oh yes, we'd like to eat as well, so . . .'

'G and T,' said Amy.

'A large gin and tonic and . . . let me think . . . is the beer on form?'

'It's Adnam's, sir. Need I say more? The Broadside is the strongest.'

'I know – to my cost. Is that what you're drinking?'

'Eventually, sir. For the moment I'm refreshing the gums with a small gin-and-it. Would you . . .?'

'Pint of Broadside, please.'

He poured and pulled our drinks and said he would get us a menu. This involved walking to the other end of the bar where there was a side door, presumably into the kitchen, and yelling 'Stephen!' in a voice which would have – probably had – carried across a parade ground.

Amy was mouthing the words 'Who the hell drinks gin-and-it any more?' when a younger guy, half the Wing Commander's age, appeared wearing chequered chef's trousers and a white coat. He had an angelic, rosy red baby face and a lock of hair falling over one eye. When he saw we were customers, he beamed.

'Yes, Ray?'

'Diners,' said the older one and flapped a hand in our general direction. There was still no one else in the bar.

'We don't have a menu,' said Stephen, putting his hands on his hips, 'I just stand here and shout at you, but I have to ask first if there are any special dietary requirements or pet hates.'

'I'm very hungry,' said Amy, 'so how about a big juicy steak?'

I knew what she was thinking: pub food in the back of beyond – go for something they can't microwave.

'That's not a problem at all, madam,' said Stephen, pronouncing it 'modom' but doing it so sweetly you couldn't possibly take offence. 'And for sir?'

'The same, but bigger and juicier.'

That got a smile and a distinct twinkle in the eye.

'And to start? I can offer you: home-made potted shrimps with wholemeal toast, a slice or two of *boudin noir* with a creamed celeriac sauce, deep-fried Camembert with home-made gooseberry jam, some smoked wild boar cut like Parma ham wrapped around fresh grapefruit segments, smoked haddock from Southwold with a poached egg perhaps and a little creamed stock, or the soup of the day which is chilled gazpacho.'

Amy broke the silence.

'Yes please. All of them, forget the steak.'

Stephen beamed proudly. Behind the bar the old boy beamed proudly.

'No, won't be greedy. Smoked haddock and the steak,' she said.

'Me too.'

'A wise choice.' Stephen bowed slightly. 'I'll get things going in the kitchen and come back so you can choose your steaks.'

Amy and I carried our drinks to a table near the window and as we sat down she lowered her voice.

'You don't half attract them.'

'No I don't.'

'That old one would be over you like a rash given half a chance, but I didn't mean gays, I meant weirdos.'

'What do you mean, weirdos?'

'Arthur, for one. That John Travolta wannabe Dan for another, not to mention Mrs Hawksbee, now these two. How do you do it?'

'You haven't met the diggers yet.'

'So you keep saying. It can't get any stranger.'

'Hey, you were the one who wanted to come here, not me. I'd be very happy to be back in London loafing about among normal people.'

'Like your old chums in Hackney? Yeah, I was forgetting. This lot must seem fairly normal compared to the circles you move in. And anyway, what's this about choosing our steaks?'

'I don't know. Just go with the flow.'

'Is that one of your Rules of Life?'

'It should be.'

Choosing our steaks turned out to be exactly that. Stephen appeared next to us carrying a large wooden chopping board on which were nine goodly sized pieces of raw red meat, three each of sirloin, rump and fillet cuts. Just standing there with them was probably in contravention of at least a dozen European Community rules about food hygiene. I was impressed and prepared to recommend the place to all my friends.

'The sirloin, please,' I said, 'that one in the middle. Medium rare.'

'Rump for me,' said Amy. 'The biggest. Rare, but not blue.'

'Excellent choices,' said Stephen and swung on his heels back towards the kitchen.

'Do you think he'd leave the board out for the diggers?' I said. 'Half of them won't have seen so much meat in one place before and the veggy half will die of shock.'

'Can't we pretend it's tofu?' Amy giggled.

'Tofu doesn't bleed,' I said.

'May I have a name?' Ray, the older one, asked as he came round the bar and over to us. 'For the order, so Stephen can shout when it's ready. First names will do.'

Amy was about to make some crack about in case we

128

got lost among all the other customers, but I headed her off at the pass.

'Roy or Amy would be fine.'

I had seen the technique before. If any other customers did turn up it would impress the hell out of them that the proprietors were on first-name terms with the early evening diners.

Ray smiled and walked over to the kitchen door and yelled:

'Stephen! The steaks are for Roy and . . . er . . . Angela!'

Then he turned and beamed at us again.

'Passing through or are you staying around here?' he asked politely.

'Bit of both,' I said. 'We've come to work on the excavation at Woolpack House.'

'Ah,' he breathed, rolling his eyeballs until the whites showed. 'The Sainted Arthur . . .'

'He's one of your regulars, is he?' Amy said innocently.

'I wouldn't say that exactly. He used to pop in occasionally, but not since he became a millionaire. Too busy digging, looking for the Holy Grail.'

'I don't think it was actually a million he won . . .' I started, giving Ray just the right amount of encouragement to pull up a chair and join us.

'He could have done with it,' Ray said conspiratorially. 'Most of the Lottery money went on buying the house outright so he could dig it up.'

'I thought he owned it, inherited it from his brother,' said Amy, remembering the newspaper cutting better than I had.

'He did, but he mortgaged the place up to the hilt to pay for all this archaeology rubbish.' He stopped at that and flashed a look between us. 'Oh, I do apologize. I don't mean to denigrate your jobs. Are you archaeologists?'

'We are,' I said, 'so denigrate away, we're used to it.'

'I've nothing against archaeologists *per se* – there are some lovely young boys working up the road who scrub

129

up quite nicely when they come in here. And I always watch that programme on the telly when it's on. *Time Trench* or something . . .'

'So do I,' squealed Amy.

'. . . and that professor from the university, Simon something-or-other, he comes here for a meal with his wife occasionally. It's just that Arthur hasn't made many friends in this village. In fact none. If he had any before, he lost them after that Lottery win.'

'Why's that?'

'Because he hasn't spent a penny in the village. He won't employ any of the locals on his excavation and one or two were expecting some casual work to see them through the winter.'

'Isn't Mrs Hawksbee local?'

'Eileen Hawksbee? Oh yes, but you can't count her. I think they built that house around her, or at least around her mother. She's been there forever. Some would say that Arthur only kept her on to relieve his bachelorhood – if you know what I mean.'

Ray leered at me as he said it then quickly turned to Amy.

'I'm sorry, Amanda, I'm such a gossip. That was just the sort of bitchy remark you'd expect from an ageing queen, isn't it? Doesn't mean to say it's not true, though.'

'So Arthur's not the kind-hearted Squire, then? I figured him as the Lord of the Manor at least.'

Ray put both his lips together and blew; but it wasn't a whistle.

'Good God, no. The Scrivenour-Lindleys are the local aristos. Not that they're very aristocratic – as aristocratic as muck, you might say – but they do own most of the farmland round here and they keep the local peasants in work. There's no love lost between them and Arthur, though. There's a history of boundary disputes and arguments over shooting rights and, you name it. The families have never got on.'

'This is the Scribbler-Who?' I played dumb in order to get the name right.

'Robert and James Scrivenour-Lindley. They're brothers and bigwigs in Suffolk farming. They've always had the land and the money, both married well and both have loads of kids. The Swallows were of an older generation and, let's face it, they were both a bit nutty. Especially that Gerald, blowing his head off like that. But then the Swallows always did have a habit of hogging the limelight. Ah, here's Stephen with your starters, I'll leave you in peace.'

Amy reached out a hand and caught his arm.

'Will you have a drink with us, Ray?' Amy said, all sweetness and light. 'And Stephen too, of course.'

'Why, thank you, Alison, my dear. I don't mind if we do.'

'We must have a chat later so you can fill us in on who's who in the village. You must have lived here quite a while.'

Ray shook his head.

'Just the four months. We get most of the locals in the back bar and all I have to do is keep the flappers flapping.' He put his tankard down on our table and placed both hands behind his ears, flipping them to and fro. 'You hear the most outrageous things!'

He gave us a little back kick with his right leg, grabbed his drink and shot off to the bar as Stephen shimmied into view with our order.

'He is gay, right?' whispered Amy.

'You think?'

We had polished off some excellent smoked haddock and poached egg, using chunks of bread to mop up the bright orange yolks, and then Stephen had served us our steaks complete with tomato-and-onion salad and a bowl of *frites* for us to fight over. Amy had wanted wine and I'd said that might not fit our image as ordinary diggers just trying to blend in. She'd given me one of her looks and I'd ordered a bottle of Malbec.

It was on maybe our third forkful of steak when we

131

noticed there were faces at the window, noses pressed to the glass, breath frosting the pane. At least three pairs of eyes were fixed on Amy's plate, watching as intently as if it was an England v. Germany match. I would swear I saw one of the mouths say 'So much blood . . .' but I couldn't actually hear a thing.

'I wonder what the poor people are eating tonight?' said Amy, her face down just in case they could lip-read from outside.

'I dunno. Shall we ask them in?'

Chapter Eight

Bench Mark

Jason was nice; we agreed on that. Just out of university in Belfast, which I could tell from his blurred accent, he had arrived on site only the day before and this was his first job outside of training digs on the Isle of Man. And didn't this look like a good pub? He'd have a pint, thanks.

Cornell was the obligatory American. When Amy had asked me why I had insisted there would be one, I had just said, 'Because there always is,' although Cornell wasn't quite what I'd expected. He was our age for a start; tall, receding hair at the front, long at the back in a ponytail. Leather jacket, faded blue jeans and the only one to wear rigger boots instead of the uniform trainers. He helped himself to my rolling tobacco and papers, rolling very impressively one-handed, and the only thing he said was yeah, OK, he'd have a pint of Guinness.

Then there was Kali. Not 'Carly' as in Carly Simon, as I had suggested, but Kali as in Kali, wife of Shiva, the dark goddess of destruction. Right. She wore camouflage combat trousers, with a mobile phone in one of the cargo pockets, and a green US Army style vest all the better to show off very muscular arms and the tattoos on her shoulders and neck. They included a single rose wrapped in barbed wire, a spider's web and what could have been a badly drawn woodpecker. When she saw me looking, she fixed me with a 200-watt glare from behind her round, metal-rimmed glasses and I stopped looking. Had we really eaten all that meat? Still, she'd have a pint of cider if we insisted, though she didn't have the money to buy us one back.

Jude and Rory seemed to be an item from the way they stuck together as if they only had the one pair of underpants. For the entire evening I doubted I could have got a cigarette paper between them. They'd been there for three weeks, having heard about the dig from a friend. When I asked if they'd found anything, they looked blank. Amy said later that if they'd said 'True love' she would have thrown up. Jude went for an orange juice with ice, Rory asked if he could have a half of lager.

Gregory was the one on his own. Tall, thin and deeply miserable. Yeah, he'd been on digs before. It was a job. It paid off the student loans. He supposed he'd have a pint, but if I'd brought him a tin of paint stripper he'd probably just have shrugged and drank it. He sat leaning forward with his forearms along his thighs, bringing his chin down to only six or seven inches above his knees in some sort of compensation for his inferiority complex about his height. It wasn't the only thing he should feel inferior about.

Joss couldn't make it as she'd had to go see Arthur to discuss progress, which was a shame, I said. And Ben couldn't make it either – now *that* was a shame, said Amy – because Fifi was in the same meeting and so was Shona, who was supposed to be in charge of planning the excavation, though we all knew what she was planning really, somebody said.

And Amy bought another round, having discreetly stashed her platinum American Express card behind the bar, which ensured rapid and cheerful service from a delighted Ray.

The dig itself? Oh, just like all other digs: badly managed, understaffed, totally disorganized. Oh sure, the free accommodation helped as did the use of the Transit van to and from Ipswich station so at least they could get away at weekends. And the pay was good, in comparison to other units – it was even above the £7.40 per hour rate of the European Union Decency Threshold. (Wouldn't you just know they'd have a Decency Threshold?) And Arthur wasn't that bad an employer. He'd been quite reasonable when they'd demanded an afternoon, as well as a morning, tea-break and they did get the full half-hour for lunch.

At that point, Amy began to roll herself a cigarette.

So what was wrong with the Woolpack site?

Wrong with it? What was right? For a start – *what* site? It seemed that Arthur had simply declared open season on every bit of dirt he owned – which wasn't as much as we might think from the way he lorded it over the village. Some of it he'd dug up once already, about ten years ago; some of it he'd had a go at himself, then got bored and left it. He would say things like 'Let's dig the back garden today' and he meant it, but not in a vegetable-growing way. There didn't seem to be any plans of what he'd done or pre-ex(cavation) plans of what he wanted to do: what he thought *might* be there. In fact no one was quite sure if there was anything there at all. It was all somewhat disorganized. The words 'cock-up', 'dog's breakfast', 'pants' and 'utter pants' were also used.

The general consensus seemed to be that this dig would not go down on anyone's CV as a recommendation for future employers. Kali even went so far as to say that if Arthur had actually won a contract to dig a site somewhere other than in his own back garden (or what was left of it), then the independent monitor appointed by the County Council or English Heritage or whoever, would have closed him down on Day One. Strong words indeed, as everybody knew that most independent monitors have the eyesight of a football referee and the attention span of a dyslexic goldfish and it wasn't difficult to blindside them.

Had he won an outside contract? I wanted to know, but Amy wanted to know what I was talking about. So I explained that for the last ten years archaeology had been gradually 'privatized' and commercialized so that digging units had to compete for work from house builders, land developers, highway authorities and the like with, naturally, the lowest bid getting the job. Smaller units had

135

gone under, others had combined to form 'superunits' in the belief that big was better and the only efficient way forward. It was a philosophy we'd seen work so well in Britain in cars, motorbikes and breweries among other industries. Trouble was it tended in the end to work best for German cars, Japanese motorbikes, Belgian beer and so on.

The archaeologists nodded solemnly at the wisdom which I spoke. I had always found that a bit of global pessimism about the future of their subject goes down well with them.

Kali said she'd never heard of Iceni Rescue actually getting an outside job and she'd searched the Net for any published papers or reports, but they all agreed that Arthur was busy putting together tenders for jobs. That's what Fifi and Shona were doing right now in their meeting with Arthur; trying to put together a bid for a job which had come up in Colchester. And that produced a snort from tall Gregory who suggested that we all knew what Shona really wanted to do with Fifi.

As neither Amy nor I knew who they were talking about, this went over our heads until Jude, who had appeared the shyest and most baby-faced of them all, snapped at him to grow up as it wasn't true except in his sick schoolboy fantasies and even if it was they wouldn't let Gregory watch. Which drew support from her other half, Rory, who advised Gregory not to let Ben hear him say things like that. He'd given up the chance of a dig in Pompeii to follow Fifi to Woolpack House. Which drew a startled double-take of surprise from Jason and a snort from Kali to the effect that he was an idiot too.

This was getting *gooood*, Amy had whispered in my ear as she stood to get another round of drinks in; a round Ray was already pouring at the bar.

I asked what sort of recording system Arthur used on the site, just to bring the conversation back to archaeology, and the answers ranged from 'What's a recording system?' (Gregory) to 'Not one I've seen before' (Rory) to 'Fuck knows' (Kali).

All archaeological digs should keep some form of written record for the archives, although there is plenty of squabbling about which system is best. (And there are those who argue that we shouldn't dig at all, merely 'interpret'.) The old-fashioned way is a central record where the site supervisor keeps a running log – or is supposed to – of every feature, layer or cut uncovered on a site, giving it a number and constructing an overall 'matrix' (an almost holy word in some quarters) which basically tells you what happened on the site and in the order in which it happened. A Context Sheet system has the same end result except the sheets are filled in by the diggers as they dig individual cuts or features or discover things like floor layers, graves, cremation pots, buildings, foundation trenches, whatever. All the sheets are collated, or data inputted these days, and the 'matrix' is worked out on a computer. As even a small dig could have maybe a thousand different context numbers, a site matrix could end up resembling the DNA chain for re-creating dinosaurs out of amber.

The gist of what the diggers were saying was that if Arthur was keeping a central context register, then they hadn't seen it. They certainly hadn't been asked to fill in context sheets, not that any of them had actually dug any decent features yet.

At this point, Jude thought she should defend the two post-holes she'd found that day – *possible* post-holes, grunted Gregory – and Rory said he was pretty sure he had the edge of a ditch. That was typical, wasn't it? Diggers were always getting asked 'What have you found?' and where the enthusiastic volunteer will start going on about bits of pottery, pieces of charcoal (I've even heard 'burnt charcoal' when they get carried away), worked flints and bits of animal bone, the hardened digger who does it for a living will be happiest when they find an *edge* and they have some idea of what they're digging.

So – I wanted to get this straight – Joss was the project manager, who organized things, virtually doing everything except the actual archaeology? Yes, I'd got that right.

This Fifi character and Shona – they were into planning and also working for Arthur on the tender side of the business of Iceni Rescue Archaeology, although there didn't actually seem to be much of a business. That was fair enough, they agreed, and they had done a couple of watching briefs, hadn't they? Yes, they had, they agreed amongst themselves, Colchester Garrison for instance, even if it was only digging a hole for a new electricity junction box.

OK then, what about Ben? What did he do? Apart from sniffing after Fifi's spoor? (Kali). Oh, that was so unfair. He'd met Fifi when he was supervising a training dig on Hadrian's Wall and followed her here just as a digger. He could get a supervisor's job anywhere. Did I know he'd turned down a dig in Pompeii? Did I need more proof that he was a total tosser? (Gregory).

So why isn't he supervisor, as there doesn't seem to be one? Dead man's shoes. (Gregory, of course.) No, that was being ridiculous. (Jude). Shut the fuck up, Gregory. (Kali). It had nothing to do with what happened to Sebastian. Ben had always said he just wanted to do some digging, not take on extra responsibility.

So what had happened to this Sebastian? But it wasn't me asking, it was Jason, who I remembered was also a new boy, but showing the digger's inbred appetite for gossip.

It appeared that Sebastian had disturbed some of the Nighthawks who had plagued the site, the metal detectorists looking for coins. Not that he'd seen anything, just heard a funny noise and gone out to investigate one Saturday night. He'd come back early from visiting his girlfriend and knew something funny was going on because everyone else was away for the weekend. He wandered out to investigate and got whacked with a spade somebody had left out on site. Ended up with a mild concussion and a broken arm. Old Arthur had found him and driven him to hospital in the Jeep. The police had been around but nobody had seen anything and that included Sebastian.

And the others? (This from Jason again.) That was just a stupid fight with some of the locals after the pub shut, seemed to be the common opinion. Two diggers called Dan (both called Dan!) had got into a ruck with some farm workers after a night on the beer. Not here of course, this seemed a nice pub even though it was a bit posh, but down The Drovers. They'd quit the next day – hence the advert which Amy and I responded to.

I bet that there had been a lot of responses to come on such a generous dig, but that was met with an odd silence from the assembled throng except for a muttered 'Fifi looks after recruiting' from Jude.

Amy had announced she was going to the loo and went.

When she'd returned she'd said, 'Where have they all gone?'

'They've gone home to bed,' I said.

'It's not even half-past nine!'

'They have to get up early in the morning.'

'It was their round!' she said desperately.

'There was that, too. But that's archaeologists for you. Deal with it. We have to get up early as well, remember? We're supposed to be diggers.'

'I haven't had any coffee yet,' she sulked.

'And we haven't paid the bill. Plus, we really should tap up Ray to find out a bit more about Arthur's standing round here. He seems to be the local grapevine.'

'Yes, we should,' she said, suddenly enthusiastic. 'We might find out something useful for Rupert as well as it being good background for us. Help us with our cover stories.'

I hadn't the heart to tell her that our cover had been blown the second she had flashed the Amex card. Well, not at least while she had a tab still running.

'Good thinking,' I said.

'Brandy with the coffee?'

That's my girl.

'Don't mind if I do, Annabelle,' said Ray, pushing a third

brandy glass twice against the optic before leaning on the bar so we were face-to-face. 'Now what was it you wanted to know?'

'All the dirt,' said Amy before I could get a word in.

Ray beamed wolfishly across the top of his brandy balloon.

'*Where oh where* shall I begin?' He hammed it up something rotten.

'How about with Arthur Swallow?' I suggested.

'Well . . .' Ray leaned forward close enough for us to smell his aftershave. 'The local feeling is that he was doolally to start with, but really went barking mad when his brother topped himself ten years ago.'

Amy kept a dead straight face.

'Yeah, we'd heard that,' she said. Then she sipped her brandy and pointedly looked at her watch.

God, she was good at this.

'That was what tipped him over the edge,' said Ray, trying to recover the gossip high ground. 'It was after that he started ripping out the house and digging up the grounds. Of course he couldn't before because the brother owned it, but once it was his, he just started digging holes everywhere and called it archaeology. He's spent ten years looking for buried treasure according to the locals and then he goes and wins the Lottery. What does he do? He digs more holes! Is he one sandwich short of a picnic or what?'

'The brother – Gerald? – any ideas as to why he killed himself? It's usually money or – women.'

I didn't like the way she'd paused and looked at me before she'd said 'women', but Ray didn't seem to notice anything.

'Well, money certainly, by all accounts. The Swallows always were impoverished gentry only good for the army or the clergy. But you're quite right, Angela dear, there was a woman. You've met their Mrs Danvers, so there has to be a Rebecca.'

'A long-lost love of Arthur's?'

'Oh no, not Arthur,' Ray confided in her, 'the brother,

Gerald. She was his wife, I believe, a child bride or something during the war. I can't remember her name but she died towards the end of the war in an air raid on Ipswich – so the locals say, of course. It was well before my time let alone yours. Can't think that Arthur would be very old himself at the time. Anyway this young wife of Gerald's gets herself blitzed by the Luftwaffe and Gerald never gets over it. Turns the house into a bit of a shrine and himself into a recluse. Some say Arthur stayed at home to look after him. But this, mind you, was fifty, sixty years ago and it must be ten years since Gerald blew his head off.'

'It was quite sudden, I understand,' I said.

'Well it would be,' snapped Ray. 'You put a twelve-bore in your gob and pull the trigger, it usually is quite quick.'

'No, I meant his decision to do it. It was over Sunday lunch. He got up, walked out through the french windows and did it. They'd had a nice piece of roast pork,' I ended lamely.

'Maybe there was no crackling,' said Amy drily and Ray giggled into his balloon glass.

'You've been talking to Mrs Danvers, haven't you?' he said.

'Mrs Hawksbee may have mentioned something, as you do – to two complete strangers who have just turned up on the doorstep.'

'Yes, well, that's Eileen Hawksbee for you, the uncrowned queen of village gossip and scandal. Until I moved here, that is.' He twinkled. He positively twinkled. 'She's dying for Arthur to find some buried treasure so she can have a new Woolpack House story to trade on. Gerald's suicide was the last big thing to happen in the village.'

'Until you moved here,' Amy said sweetly.

Ray beamed at her.

'Ah, dear . . . dear . . . er . . . dear lady, how kind.'

'Don't the locals take an interest in the dig?' I tried.

'Not really, not if there's no work going there or no loot to share out. They just let Arthur get on with it.'

141

'I heard he'd been hit by metal detectorists, ripping the place up after dark.'

'Pah! Don't believe a word of it. That sounds like Arthur trying to make himself important or giving him an excuse for another run-in with the police. They pop in here from time to time and they're all heartily sick of him. Anyway, if there really had been a gang of rough and ready characters up to no good, roaming the countryside after dark – you don't think *I* would have noticed them? God knows, I've been on the look-out for long enough!'

Whilst we had been downloading Ray's personal website of village gossip I had been vaguely aware that there was a back bar to the pub which had, over the evening, filled up with customers. It wasn't until we had staggered out front and were climbing into Armstrong that I noticed the Public Bar entrance down the side of the pub's frontage, and only then because three men chose that moment to emerge from it.

I heard them even before they were properly out of the pub, their voices raised to just the right pitch of drunken bravado to suggest trouble might not be too far away.

'Oi there, taxi!' one of them shouted, which in London would be something I would automatically ignore – just as a real cab would.

Out here in darkest Suffolk – and I do mean dark as the only light around spilled from the pub – it sounded mildly threatening. I shut my door, flicked on the central locking and fired up the engine, not for the first time regretting the fact that as a getaway vehicle from a standing start, Armstrong was as effective as a brick.

'I'm sure I ordered a taxi, didn't I?'

The voice was nearer and louder, with a Suffolk accent which made 'I'm' sound like 'Oim' and 'I' like 'Oi' and 'taxi' like 'taarksi'.

'Maybe it was a pizza you ordered,' said one of the others and they all laughed.

'No, it was a taxi just like this one.'

142

I was about to release the handbrake when Amy did what I had been dreading and pulled down her window.

'This one's taken,' she said in her don't-mess-with-me-sonny voice. (The one that usually gets us into trouble.)

I turned to see Loudmouth put his hands on the window and level his face with Amy's. He was blond and had a ruddy, weather-beaten face and hands like bunches of sausages. He was also young, pissed and with his mates. Not good.

'This is a London taxi, innit?' It came out as 'Lunnun'. 'Bit out your way, ain't you?'

'Well,' said Amy, eyeballing him, 'if I can't pay what's on the meter I guess I'll just have to sleep with the driver. It's the law now, you know. In London.'

I dropped first gear and was about to let up on the clutch when the front door of The Chequers opened and there stood Ray, hands on hips.

'Why, if it isn't young Mr Scrivenour-Lindley. I thought you'd been avoiding me all night and yet here I find you sneaking down my back passage without so much as a goodnight kiss.'

At this, Loudmouth's mates cracked up – 'Whoa, Jimbo, your luck's turned' – and he disappeared from Amy's window frame to turn to Ray.

'Is that you saying there's free beer, then?'

'Oh, I'm sure we can run to a nightcap,' Ray said sweetly, bowing flamboyantly and waving his right arm towards the door.

'Fair play if you're paying. We'll certainly have one for the road, won't we?'

Loudmouth's friends agreed, in fact they thought it was the best idea they'd ever heard and by the time they had taken two steps back into the pub, we were forgotten.

'I hope they weren't bothering you, Amelia,' said Ray.

'Not at all,' said Amy, slumping back in her seat. 'I'm specially trained to talk down to people like that.'

I caught the weather forecast on Radio 4 as we drove back

143

to Woolpack House: fine and dry, temperatures at least average, could this be the start of summer?

There was one exterior light on over the front door of the house itself and several others shining from round the side which led to the archaeologists' encampment. There was no sign of Arthur's embarrassingly numbered Jeep but the Iceni Rescue white Transit van was parked behind the outbuilding they called The Studio.

'Listen,' hissed Amy after I had turned off Armstrong's engine.

'What? I can't hear anything.'

'Exactly. Abso-fucking-lutely nothing.'

'Amy, it's called the countryside,' I said patiently.

She cuffed me lightly on the back of the head and I made a note to keep the sliding glass partition shut in future when she was in a mood.

'I don't care if we're on the moon. Whenever you have more than two students together after dark, there will be music, drug-fuelled dancing or raucous drinking or uninhibited – albeit brief – sexual coupling. That's the natural order of things. But, Hark! Not a bleedin' sound.'

'You don't know many archaeologists, do you?'

'I didn't know you were an archaeologist –'

'Yeah, yeah, whatever.' Was she ever going to let that one lie? 'Point is, they're all in bed by now.'

'But it's only eleven o'clock!' she protested.

'And they'll be up and around at six, making their sandwiches and pulling their boots on. It's the price they pay for doing a job they love, never seeing a TV programme shown after nine thirty, never seeing the end of an evening kick-off football match, never having heard the words "Time, gentlemen, please!"'

'That's sad,' she said wistfully, then forgot all about it. 'You take our stuff in. I'm going to have a shower.'

'Fair enough. I'll make us some sandwiches for tea-break tomorrow and stick them in the fridge.'

'My, what domestication, but don't let me stop you. There's a bag of foody things in the boot.'

'I know. I picked up your personal shopping, remember? Anyway, I brought some stuff myself.'

'I noticed. Bring the bottle of vodka inside when you come.'

I had noticed when we arrived that the sliding doors on the individual rooms in The Stables didn't have proper locks, only deadbolts on the inside.

That would probably spook Amy when she realized but it didn't surprise me. A gaggle of archaeologists (or whatever the collective term is) living together is usually a safe environment. They are either basically very honest or they have nothing worth nicking, so most personal possessions are fairly safe. That, of course, did not apply to the kitchen and the contents of the communal fridge which, unless clearly labelled with an owner's initials, tended to be treated like Red Cross parcels for any digger with a case of the munchies.

As Amy disappeared into the Mobile Thrones shower with a towel and two bottles – one of shampoo and the vodka – I began to ferry things in from Armstrong, starting with our sleeping bags. The night was clear with a slight nip in the air and, as Amy had said, as quiet as the grave. Even the The Stables themselves were quiet, too quiet, considering that there must have been ten or so people sleeping there in a relatively confined space with thin walls. Maybe they were having a party elsewhere and we hadn't been invited. Maybe they had perfected totally silent sex. Not a whisper, not a snore, not a fart disturbed the night.

Caught up in the silence, I tiptoed across the yard where at least I could hear the sound of running water from the Mobile Thrones block. I had one hand full of carrier bags and the other on the kitchen door knob when I heard the scream and I knew at once it was Amy.

I dropped the bags and sprinted down the side of the chalet building they called The Studio and took the steps to the Mobile Thrones block in one bound. There were only two steps so it wasn't that dramatic a gesture and I was glad there was no one else around as I bounced off the door. Rubbing my shoulder, I noticed the sign saying PULL and did as it commanded, then pushed open the inside door marked FEMALES.

Amy was standing on the slatted wood floor, naked except for a towel bunched up in each hand with which she was violently rubbing her body like a demented cheerleader with a pair of wet pom-poms. Her hair was plastered across her face.

'There – is – no – hot – water,' she said through chattering teeth.

'And this is my fault?'

'Yes,' she snapped.

'Blue suits you,' I said, letting the door swing closed on her.

I recovered our shopping bags and found the lights in the kitchen. My loaf of bread, tub of something which wasn't butter and jar of Marmite didn't take up much shelf space and I decided to keep the Jaffa Cakes in our room for added security, not wanting to put temptation in the way of the other diggers.

Amy's stuff was another matter. The croissants, the Brie, the rillettes, the Orkney crab pâté, the wholefood yoghurt and the fresh figs were all safe enough, the diggers wouldn't know what they were, but the freshly squeezed orange juice, the Dorset organic honey and the soft set blueberry jam might go communal given half a chance. I used one of the indelible markers I had bought to write Amy's name on them all and then stuffed them in the fridge between half a dozen plastic tubs of what looked like humus which had 'Fifi' in red ink scrawled over them. For a moment I puzzled over the 'Fifi' in small but flowery script, the dots over the 'i' being small circles. It struck a chord somewhere. Who did I know who used to write like that, sometimes making smiley or sad faces of the circles?

And then I thought about how Amy had screamed loud enough for me to hear her thirty or more yards away and yet nobody had emerged from The Stables – a few feet from the toilet block – to see what the problem was. Maybe they were just all tired out, the poor dears.

Amy certainly was. Back in our room she had already climbed into a sleeping bag and was laid out on one of the beds, only a few wet strands of hair showing out of the mouth of the bag.

My bag. She had climbed into Hemingway.

I was touched by the gesture and the thought that my luck was in.

Then I realized she had climbed into her sleeping bag and somehow wriggled into Hemingway as well. Now there was a signal that a woman wanted to be left alone if ever there was one, cocooned inside two sleeping bags.

It took me a good ten minutes to wrestle Hemingway from her.

Chapter Nine

Machine Watching

We may not have heard our fellow diggers during the night, but they made up for it in the morning. The first alarm clock went off at 0550 and was a fairly acceptable buzzing sound if you didn't mind it being so early. Five minutes later there was an old–fashioned tinny bell ringing somewhere down the corridor; a minute after that a radio playing classical music. Then one which played the theme from *Thunderbirds*, another buzzer and then a talk radio station.

I unzipped Hemingway and rolled off the camp bed and on to the floor having forgotten I was only a few inches above it. From Amy's bag only her hair protruded. The alarms and the increasing sounds of footsteps and of doors opening and closing produced no response. She remained as inert as a futon abandoned in a hedge.

From the backpack I had brought in from Armstrong the night before, I pulled out my wardrobe for the day – actually, for the whole week – and dressed in a green ex-Dutch army work shirt, Gortex camouflage combat trousers which were waterproof but breathable so your legs didn't sweat – also ex-Dutch army, thick 'rotproof' Commando socks and my Transporter boots. I made a mental note to e-mail NATO and tell them not to rely on the Dutch contingent as all their clothing was being worn by British archaeologists.

With Bob the trowel stuffed into the right cargo pocket, mobile phone clipped on to the left, tobacco and papers in the breast pocket, I felt I looked the part and I set out to do what all professional archaeologists do as a prerequisite to a successful day's digging: put the kettle on.

Neither Amy nor I had remembered to bring coffee, so my first task would be to scrounge some, but I needed to avail myself of a Mobile Throne first.

In the MALES section, two of the shower units were in use and by one of the washbasins Ben was wet shaving.

''Morning,' I said as I squared up to one of the urinals.

'Oh, hi,' said Ben between razor strokes. 'Sorry we didn't make it to the pub last night. Good time had by all, I hear.'

'Yeah, they seem like a good bunch. No stamina, though.'

'Early to bed, early to rise and all that.'

I ran water into the basin next to his and began to splash my face.

'I should have warned you,' he said. 'The hot water comes on at five and goes off at nine in the evening.'

'So we discovered. Didn't you hear the screaming?'

He paused, the razor just on the tip of his chin.

'Sorry?'

'Amy tried to have a shower late last night. I think she found it refreshed the parts she hadn't meant it to reach.'

'Oh, I see.' The razor continued upwards. 'Didn't hear a thing.'

'Then you must have a clear conscience,' I said, reaching for the paper towels.

When he said nothing I turned to find him staring at me, the razor again in freeze-frame.

'To sleep so soundly.'

'Oh yeah, right.'

He went back to looking in the mirror, but I swear I saw him blushing under the shaving foam.

As I strode towards the kitchen, feeling my way into the boots I hadn't worn for so long, it struck me as odd that Ben was shaving and at least two of the guys were shower-ing. Most archaeologists take a shower at the end of the day not the start and a healthy stubble cuts down on the sunburn and weather-beating of the face, unless you have a secret tube of Norwegian trawlermen's moisturising cream, as I did.

I had expected the kitchen to be a hive of activity but there was a solitary female there, spreading peanut butter on to a slice of toasted granary bread.

She was no more than five feet tall, even in her black work boots with inch-thick plastic soles (probably Dutch). She wore a Greenpeace T-shirt and faded blue denim bootlegs which had had the back pockets ripped off leaving two even more faded patches, one over each buttock. Her hair was short, boyish and white, not blonde and she wore small square glasses in those irritating wire frames that are supposed to bend back into shape, but never quite do.

'You must be Fifi,' I said cheerfully, flashing my second-best smile.

'No I mustn't,' she said in a Scottish accent, but it was a posh Scottish accent, maybe Fife if not Edinburgh.

That seemed to be all she was going to offer so I said:
'Then you must be Shona.'

'And you'll be Fitzroy.' She said it with all the natural superiority of a barrister.

'I was wondering if I could scrounge a cup – two cups – of coffee?'

I didn't bother wasting my best smile on her. I knew when I was beaten, even at this ungodly hour of the day.

'No scrounging necessary. Mr Swallow provides tea, coffee, sugar and milk free gratis and for nothing. Help yourself.'

'That's cool. I was expecting to contribute to a kitty or something, like they have on most sites,' I said, just to be chatty as I began opening cupboards and drawers to find things. But then I realized I was talking to myself.

Shona and her slice of toast had gone. Oh well, not everyone can be a morning person.

I filled the kettle and continued to rummage around

150

until I found a glass and two cups. I poured myself some of Amy's freshly squeezed orange juice and while I drank it I located a jar of instant coffee but, even better, a tin of ground coffee which looked and smelled like a strong Mocha blend. At the back of a cupboard I found a dusty Melita plastic filter and an open pack of filter papers. Excellent.

By the time the water boiled I had found a tray and had croissants in the oven.

The kitchen door opened and Kali entered and stopped dead, staring accusingly at the coffee filtering through into a Pyrex jug I had found on the sink. She sniffed the air.

'That's a coffee filter,' she said in a voice you wouldn't argue with.

'Yes?' I said hesitantly.

'We've been wondering what it was since we got here.'

I placed the tray on the floor near the mouth of Amy's sleeping bag. Juice, fresh coffee and hot croissants. What more could a girl want?

'Good morning,' I said gently, pulling down the zipper of the bag.

The bottle of vodka, half empty, rolled out but I caught it before it hit the concrete floor.

'Let's go to work,' I said loudly, yanking the zip all the way and jumping backwards to avoid the foot that shot out, aimed at my crotch.

Just for that I grabbed one of the croissants as I ran for it.

To my surprise, given the banging and crashing that had been going on since dawn, I was the first on site. There was just me, the dew and a wisp or two of morning mist shading a slow-burning rising sun. It promised to be a nice day and the air was fresh and sweet and clean. I rolled myself a cigarette.

I had a good reason for strolling out there apart from the fact that it was far safer than staying in our cubicle in The Stables with Amy. Before the sun got up and dried the ground it should be possible to see if Arthur had uncovered any genuine features as he stripped off the topsoil with his bulldozer, though if he had it would have been by dumb luck. A bulldozer should be used for moving piles of spoil, not stripping. The 'dozer blade can shave off the topsoil quite accurately, taking it down in centimetre layers if the driver knows what he's doing. The trouble is as seventeen tons of 'dozer moves forward on its caterpillar tracks, it totally mashes anything it might have uncovered. On most sites – proper sites – they use a JCB digger which can stand at the side of an area and scoop up topsoil with its bucket or, preferably, one of the big Volvo 360s which can stand back and lean over a site with its long mechanical arm. They're used so much now for putting in evaluation trenches – to judge the extent of any archaeology – that the width of their scooping bucket is taken almost as the standard industry width of a trench.

Machine watching is an art in itself and an all too common publicity shot is the one of a disgruntled archaeologist wrapped up against the cold and wearing a bright yellow viz (visibility) vest and a hard hat standing, hands in pockets, nuts frozen off, beside a huge mechanical digger in a sea of mud. Occasionally they spot something – a patch of darker earth or the edge of a feature – and then they rush forward, dodging the teeth of the mechanical bucket scoop, to mark it before it dries out and disappears or the sun goes over and you can't see it without shadow. Machine watchers will use anything to mark the uncovered features: grid-pegs, six-inch nails, meat skewers – I've even seen a set of the flags of all nations like you would buy for kids at the beach pressed into use. Good ones will then go over the ground immediately with a Total Station Theodolite, zapping in key points of features with the aid of a laser, which can then print out a computerized plan of what has been uncovered.

It was fairly obvious that the Woolpack House site didn't

run to a TST system. In fact a pack of the flags of all nations seemed beyond it, although an attempt had been made to lay out a grid of ten-metre squares using twisted iron rods with painted wooden blocks jammed on the tops, uncapped grid-pegs being probably the most dangerous thing on an excavation site apart from other diggers.

Arthur had stripped – badly – an area about thirty metres wide running due south for at least a hundred metres into an apple orchard, though at least four trees had sacrificed themselves in the cause of archaeology. He'd obviously had several goes at it as some areas were dried out and encrusted whilst there were patches of lighter, sandy soil – the 'natural' he should have been trying to get down to – though not as many as there should have been. The whole area needed several more inches taking off, but not with a bulldozer. As Joss had said, it was now a hoeing job to clean up a decent surface to see if there was anything there to dig and I knew that hoeing big areas ranked only just above cleaning out cesspits with a toothbrush among the digging fraternity.

I walked over one of the marked-out squares, took out my trusty Bob and crouched down to have a quick scrape at the dark topsoil. It needed some vigorous trowelling to get through the top two inches but then an orangey sandy clay dotted with small chalk nodules began to show through. That was what we should be looking for, the 'natural' subsoil into which the Romans or the Iceni or whoever had dug pits, ditches, stake-holes or foundation slots for structures – basically, a load of holes in the ground. Those holes would have filled up with a (to use a technical term) 'fill' of darker soil and, if you were very lucky, fragments of pottery, nails, bits of tile or mortar, maybe the occasional coin which could give you a date. The digger's job was to dig out the holes someone else had dug two thousand or more years before and to guess from the shape of the hole why it had been dug in the first place. That was all there was to it on a site like this which had no obvious structures above ground level. A castle, for instance, would have been nice. All we had, if we had anything, were holes in the ground; if we could find them.

Running along the side of the cleared strip was a spoil heap about five feet high. Arthur would have taken off the turf or grass first so that would be at the bottom of the pile, fermenting away nicely. I hope he waited until winter to move it as the smell in the height of summer would be indescribable.

I climbed up the heap just to get a better perspective of the site and with my first step my boot dislodged a piece of pot from the spoil. I picked it up and gently scraped the worst of the mud from it with the point of my trowel. It was part of the base of a small bowl, about two inches across, grey-black and relatively fine. It looked like Black Burnished ware to me, but I was no pottery nerd. I slipped it into one of my pockets and hoped I remembered to show it to Dan the Man before I sat on it.

From the top of the heap I estimated that behind the house itself, Arthur had about three acres of land, assuming that his boundary was just beyond the orchard where a field of something shone a golden yellow in the morning light – that strange East Anglian light so valued by painters for the last two hundred years. The house and grounds were in a shallow depression, surrounded by fields which gave a false horizon. I knew the village and The Chequers couldn't be far away as the crow flew, but I couldn't see them.

I tried to think why someone in the late Iron Age or the early Roman period would settle here and could see no obvious natural advantages. Joss had said there was an Iron Age barrow not far away and we were supposed to be between two Roman roads running north/south, though neither of them ran here. Not that there had to be an obvious reason. If Arthur was right about having something from the Boudican period here, then the most likely thing would be the remains of a small Roman settlement, no more than a single farmstead. In the mid-first century, this would have the settlers' frontier. As veterans from the Roman legions retired, they would be given chunks of land

and a few slaves and they'd claim that stake on land out beyond their fortress in Colchester, whether the local tribes minded or not. In western movies they were 'sodbusters' or 'homesteaders' and would have been played with sympathy by Van Heflin. In real life they were probably the last people you wanted as neighbours as they were the invaders who had been trying to exterminate you a few years before, and when the tribes went on the warpath under Boudica they were the first to get the chop. Such isolated farmsteads must have been dotted all over north Essex and Suffolk but few substantial ones have been found as Boudica made a pretty good job of torching them.

'So what's the plan, then?'

It was Gregory and he had got up close without me hearing him. He carried a blue metal hoe over his shoulder.

'How should I know?'

Gregory slid his hand down the handle of the hoe and began to turn it so that it swung like a propeller, making swishing noises in the air. It was standard operating procedure for diggers waiting for something to do. In fact, there were two sorts of bored diggers: those who twirled hoes and those who flipped their trowel over and over, catching it by the handle.

'I thought you were taking over from Sebastian?' he said.

'As supervisor? News to me.'

'That's what they said.'

'Who did?'

'That's what everybody thinks,' he said sulkily.

I stomped out the remains of my cigarette in the spoil heap, noticing another piece of pot and an oyster shell near my boot.

'Joss said we'd be hoeing today so I presume we make a start with one of these squares,' I said. 'I'll grab myself a hoe and come and join you. Bring some shovels too.'

'That'd be cool,' he said but he made no move as

I walked by him, just stood there staring intently into the distance, still twirling his hoe.

Half-way back to the outbuildings I met Rory and Jude pushing wheelbarrows containing shovels, hoes, buckets and green foam kneeling mats. They walked side-by-side as if they couldn't bear to be more than a yard apart.

'Good morning,' we all said together as soon as we were in smiling range.

'Thanks for all the drinks last night, Fitzroy,' said Jude.

'Don't thank me, thank Amy.'

'We will,' they said together.

'What do you want us to do?' asked Rory, peering over my shoulder. 'I see you've got Gregory hoeing already.'

'Well, I just suggested we start cleaning back in ten-metre squares, but it was Joss's idea really.'

'Sounds good,' said Jude, looking at Rory and he looked at her and they nodded to each other and smiled at me and they pushed their wheelbarrows around me and headed on to site.

By the time I got back to the outbuildings, Jason, Kali and Ben were hovering outside the tool shed, loading up wheelbarrows with tools being passed out to them by the long-haired American, Cornell, who had half a roll-up cigarette stuck to his bottom lip.

We grunted greetings at each other and Cornell, still handing out spades and hoes and finds trays (which were really the plastic boxes you buy seedlings in at a garden centre), said:

'You the gang boss then?'

He kept his back to me as he spoke, leaning back into the metal shed to pass out more tools. I took the next hoe he handed out. The others just looked at me.

'Nobody told me I'd been elected,' I said, picking up a shovel as well. 'And if I was nominated, I wouldn't vote for me.'

'Joss said that Arthur had told her that he'd been told you were very experienced,' said Kali as if she was opening for the prosecution.

'And he thought that meant in archaeology? Must have been a crossed wire somewhere. I'm here as a humble digger.'

'Well, somebody's got to be supervisor now Sebastian's gone,' she muttered.

'Why? Let's have a democratic collective with policy meetings every hour,' I suggested cheerfully.

'Now you'd be taking the piss, there, wouldn't you?' said Jason with a smile.

'So who's got the most experience?' Kali persisted. 'Gregory and the two love-birds out there are straight out of university.'

We all looked automatically to where the three figures in the distance were hoeing a line from east to west. With a blue background they could have been figures on Chinese porcelain.

'Me too,' said Jason.

'Hey, count me out,' growled Cornell. 'I flunked sixth grade. I'm just a grunt and proud of it. Until something better comes along.'

'OK then,' said Kali, pointing fingers at both Ben and me. 'How many professional digs have you been on, say six-month contract minimum? I've done four.'

'Three for me,' said Ben, almost relieved. 'Roy?'

I did some quick calculating. I had been the first out on site and assessed how far they'd got so far, which was basically nowhere. That, as far as I was concerned, was a good day's work already done. I hadn't met anyone yet who seemed to know as much as I'd forgotten about digging, except this Ben character, who clearly didn't want the job. I didn't think there was anything I could screw up on this site, as I wasn't convinced there was anything to screw up and, biggest plus of all, being supervisor would mean I got to boss Amy about.

'Not including this one, six,' I lied. 'But that's just in this country. Do you want abroad as well?'

'I'm impressed.'

There was a metallic ring to the voice now the tool shed was half empty and I had to turn to see that it was Joss standing in the doorway, with the diminutive Shona behind her left shoulder. Shona wasn't looking at me, she was looking anywhere but, scanning the horizon to her right and then the house to her left. She looked like an American Secret Service man protecting a Presidential candidate.

'With what?'

'Leadership qualities, motivational and communication skills, man-management techniques, a charismatic management culture . . .'

'I bribed them,' I said, holding my arms out from my sides. 'Promised them Jaffa Cakes at tea-break.'

'Whatever it takes,' she said, touching a finger to the peak of her baseball cap in salute. 'They seem to know what they're doing for once.'

'It was your idea to start hoeing, I just passed it on.'

She wrinkled her nose in embarrassment, which was rather cute.

'What are you looking for?' Shona butted in. I had forgotten she was there.

'For a level, a tripod, a staff and a planning board. We do have such things, don't we?'

'We keep the level in the house,' said Joss, 'along with a set of cameras. Don't tell me you were thinking of doing a pre-ex plan of the area?'

'Somebody has to,' I said.

'I'll get the level for you,' offered Shona and set off towards the house.

'It's looking dangerously like an archaeological site out there,' said Joss.

'And I'm afraid I seem to have been elected supervisor.'

'You mean I'm in the presence of The Chosen One?'

'Hey, be fair. It wasn't my idea.'

'I bet it wasn't Kali's either.'

'Oooh, you're sharp, you can be in the shower scene.'

She smiled at that and it really was a very charming smile.

'But you're right. What surprised me was that Ben didn't put himself in the frame more.'

'Ben's here for true love, not the archaeology.'

'So I hear.'

Joss stuck out a thumb, turned it downward like a Roman emperor and pressed the air.

'Fifi has him right there. Ben's only here to persuade her to go to Italy with him.'

'And what about Shona?' I asked, and then remembered something. 'Oh bugger, she was supposed to be doing the planning, wasn't she?'

'Well yes,' Joss said diplomatically, 'but she needs to be asked, or rather, told when she's needed, if you see the difference. Does that make sense?'

'To a man with my managerial skills? Perfectly.'

It was still only eight o'clock – the in crowd in London were just coming home from a good night's clubbing – when Arthur joined us on site, dressed in green wellies, a Barbour and a tweed flat cap. I did a double-take to see if he had a broken shotgun over his arm and a pair of labradors sniffing out the hedgerows.

'And how's my new supervisor getting on?' he beamed.

'Well, I'm not sure I should –'

'Nonsense, dear boy, nonsense. Joss has filled me in, told me you were the unanimous choice of the troops. That's good enough for me. Got everything you need?'

'I need a back sight,' I said, patting the Nikon level I had set up on its tripod.

A known height above sea level was needed as a bench mark or back sight in order to take readings of the relative heights of anything we dug. You placed the measuring staff on the known bench mark and took a reading which gave you the height of the actual level machine. Add those two together and then take away the reading you got when you placed the staff on whatever you were digging.

'Got one somewhere,' said Arthur. 'Had a surveyor chappie put one in when we converted the pigsty. Over here somewhere.'

I followed him as he strode towards the orchard.

'Found anything yet?'

'No features as such, but we're still cleaning back. One or two bits of pot have come up in the cleaning layer.'

'Excellent. Get them in to Dan, see if he can spot date them for us.'

'But they're unstratified,' I said, meaning that they had come from no definite archaeological feature and could have got where they were by centuries of ploughing or on the bottom of somebody's muddy boot.

'There's no such thing on this site, Fitzroy, everything is part of one basic feature if my theory is correct. We are dealing with an isolated settlement here, a one-off uncontaminated by any development. Well, until they built the house, of course. Ah, here's your bench mark.'

Near the bole of an apple tree was a short pinewood stake driven into the ground but so overgrown with grass and weeds that I wouldn't have known it was there without Arthur. He stamped the grass around it flat with his wellingtons until we could see that there was a small plastic bag nailed to it, the bag containing a piece of white card on which had been written a height in metres above sea level.

'There you go. All set now?'

'I suppose so. I thought we should have a pre-ex plan of the whole area as a priority – unless, that is, you've had geophysics done or there are evaluation reports I should see . . .'

'Let's discuss that tonight, shall we? You are coming to dinner and bringing the delightful Amy with you, aren't you?'

'Of course.'

'Good for you. Now don't let me get in the way. You carry on. Splendid work. Splendid.'

I watched him walk back towards the house, nodding and smiling to the digging crew who all responded with polite greetings and then grinned broadly once he was gone.

They were all thinking: what a harmless old nutter.

I was thinking that he was the third person so far this morning to have called me Fitzroy, yet I couldn't for the life of me remember telling anyone that was my name.

Although we didn't really need it, I set up the level on its tripod and asked Shona to balance the extendible staff on the bench mark so I could take a reading. Then I realized I had nothing to write it down with. Shona sighed and produced a flip-over policeman's notebook and a biro from her cargo pocket. I said she should keep a note of today's reading and make sure the level wasn't moved or, if it was, take another back sight. Before she could say anything, I added that I thought she should be in charge of the level as she would be in charge of planning.

The change in her demeanour was instantaneous: I distinctly saw an eyebrow move and there was a definite spring in her step as she walked back to the house to make up a planning board and fetch her drawing kit. There at least was one happy digger and I thought I had better check on the rest, so I picked up my hoe and joined the end of the line cleaning back the first ten-metre square.

'Anything coming up?' I asked Jason, who was nearest to me.

'Could be. Jude's got something,' he said.

Down the line, Jude leaned forward enthusiastically.

'We think we've got a linear and a couple of post-holes,' she said proudly.

That was a good enough excuse to stop hoeing before I had actually started, so I walked the long way round to avoid treading on anyone's cleaned area. Jude was right, she had uncovered a dark linear stain in the sandy natural, about half a metre wide and running east-west across the square, the west end disappearing under the spoil heap, the east end running into an uncleaned neighbouring square. It was about half a metre wide and relatively straight, probably a drainage gully, and nearby were three circular dark blobs about twenty centimetres across which could possibly be post-holes – or, there again, they could have been made by tree roots or by burrowing animals or maybe they were just blobs.

'Right then,' I said professionally, 'can you put a section across it, Jude? Make it a metre wide. Rory, chase it and see if you can define the edges back to the spoil heap. We'll pick up the other end when we do that square. Kali? Can you half-section those blobs, see if they are post-holes?'

They all nodded eagerly. Even poking at a dark stain in the ground was preferable to hoeing.

I walked down the line to where Ben and Cornell were scratching at the dirt.

'Anything?'

I crouched down on my haunches and shielded my eyes with my hand. The sun was quite bright now and it was shaping up to be a really nice day.

'No features,' said Ben, 'but various bits of pot.'

He was using one of the seed trays for his finds and he pushed it towards me with his hoe as a croupier would distribute betting chips. About a dozen shards of pottery covered the bottom of the tray, all of it basic bog-standard cooking pot quality. Several pieces had been snapped into two or more pieces and, from the absence of mud on the broken edges, fairly recently.

'I didn't do that,' said Ben, reading my thoughts. 'That's how it came up.'

He knew I had been thinking of the old digger's maxim: how do you tell the difference between a piece of pot and a piece of stone? You hit it with the edge of your trowel. If it doesn't break, it's stone. If it does, you've got *two* pieces of pot.

'Ploughing?' I suggested.

'Arthur's bulldozer more likely,' he said and I agreed with him.

I stood up and began to roll myself another cigarette. Cornell and Kali didn't need a written invitation to down tools and start roll-ups of their own.

'You don't mind smoking on site?' Ben asked me, leaning on his hoe.

'I once knew a supervisor who tried to ban it,' I said, firing up my Zippo. 'It took the surgeons three hours to remove the trowel handle from him. Unless you're taking samples for analysis, I can't see it does much harm and it keeps the troops happy.'

I waited a minute, so he didn't think that 'keeping the troops happy' had made me think of her before I asked where Fifi was.

'I think she's helping Dan with the finds this morning,' Ben said, 'as we don't have any volunteer pot-washers today.'

'Finds processors,' I corrected him.

'Yeah, right. All Fifi does really is keep Dan the Man from strangling Mrs Hawksbee. We call her Frau Blucher round here.'

'I got that impression too. Still, if you want to know what's going on around here, she seems to be the one to ask.'

'Maybe we should ask her about the archaeology,' he said, keeping his voice down so only I could hear.

'What do you mean?' I lowered my voice as well. People forget how far voices can carry out in the wide open spaces in all that fresh air.

'Come on, be honest, you've been around. Have you ever seen a site as ballsed-up as this one? No planning, no pre-ex, no geophys, no direction, no checking up on people's experience or references. It's a shambles.'

'You mean the sort of site where any idiot can walk in and be made supervisor?'

'Well, yes.' Then he added, 'No offence.'

'None taken,' I said. 'It *is* a complete balls-up.'

I was playing around with the level, spying on the house, which was always good for a laugh. The Nikon telescope lens inside it had a range of about six miles on a clear day and more than one young archaeologist working an urban site had been accused of being a peeping tom, sometimes totally unjustly; often not. Bringing the cross-hair sights to bear on the back of a supervisor's head was also a popular pastime for the bored digger.

I had the back of Woolpack House in the cross-hairs and I could see Dan the Man in a crisp white T-shirt pottering about in the kitchen, but that was about as exciting as it got.

Until a green blur fogged the lens and then disappeared until I turned the level a few degrees north-west and readjusted the focus.

It was Amy, dressed in a lime green TALtop, khaki shorts rolled up a good nine inches above the knee, her new designer work boots and, peeping over the top of them, lurid pink socks. She had her hair tied back, her Armani sunglasses on and she carried a spade at a jaunty angle across her shoulder. In her haste to get to work while there was still daylight, she had forgotten to put a bra on.

By the time she was within thirty metres of our grid-squares, Jason, Cornell, Gregory, Ben and even Rory had stopped digging or hoeing and were openly watching her every step. She hadn't had an audience this young and this innocent for a long time, but she stuck her tongue out at me through the level telescope to let me know she knew I was there.

I let her get right on to site, to within two metres of the level, before I looked up and shouted:

'Tea-break! Back to the house!'

Somebody had thoughtfully put the kettle on and it turned out that Jude was on tea duty so while she busied herself in the kitchen, the rest of us knocked our boots clean or scraped them with trowels and piled into The Studio.

'Have they stopped looking at my bum yet?' Amy asked me, not caring that Ben, Jason, Cornell and Gregory were still within earshot having followed us off site.

'Hey, they don't get out much, OK?'

164

It was a one-storey, one-room building with no windows except in the steep sloping roof, where there were six large skylights, three either side. The furniture consisted of two long trestle tables with benches either side, and a battered leather sofa with three non-matching armchairs in a semi-circle around a big screen TV which was connected to a video recorder and a DVD player. The tops from jars of instant coffee, pressed into service as ash-trays and all full, were balanced on just about every flat surface.

Jude appeared with a tray of mugs – teas on the left, coffees on the right, sugar in a tin in the middle along with the solitary spoon. I nipped back into The Stables and collected three of the packets of Jaffa Cakes I had brought as emergency iron rations. As I walked back across the yard, Joss appeared from the kitchen and spotted them, making a big show of rubbing her hands together and running her tongue around her lips. It was a curiously long tongue, quite hypnotic in some ways.

'That's bribery and corruption,' she grinned.

'Told you I was bribing them,' I said. 'But the corruption comes later.'

The diggers were bent over the tray of mugs like sea-gulls over a dead fish on a beach. All except Amy that is, who had commandeered one of the armchairs, crossed her legs and was allowing Jason to spoon sugar into her coffee mug. It was cruel of her to lead him on like that. She didn't take sugar.

I tossed the Jaffa Cakes on to the table and told them to help themselves. As a swarm they moved in on them.

'So what did this place use to be?' I asked Joss, handing her one of the remaining cups of instant sludge.

'The Studio? It used to be a studio, as in painting.'

'Arthur's a painter?'

'No, not Arthur, his brother, Gerald. The one who –'

'Boom!'

We both jumped. Gregory had crept up to the side of us and put two fingers up against his temple as he'd shouted it and then stood there grinning.

Joss and I simply looked at him. After about five seconds

he broke eye contact and slouched off muttering, 'Be like that, then . . .'

'He gives me the creeps, that one,' she said.

'Me too.'

'I think he fancies me.' she shuddered.

'Me too,' I said. 'I mean I think he –'

'I understood. Quit now, whilst you're ahead.' But she blushed as she said it.

'Was Gerald any good as a painter?' I tried.

'I'm no artist, don't ask me. Have a look around the house. Arthur's got his stuff hanging everywhere, but if you want an uninformed opinion, he stank. Arthur's got all his paintings because he couldn't sell any. The one above the stairs isn't bad, if a bit kitsch. It's like that film *Rebecca*, you know, the mysterious young bride jilted – or was she murdered? – by the mad Mr Manderley.'

'I know exactly what you mean,' I said.

That was twice somebody had mentioned *Rebecca* and I was about to ask Joss if she had any idea of this mysterious woman's name as Ray down at The Chequers had already proved himself congenitally incapable of remembering the names of females in the same room. But Dan the Man interrupted my train of thought, or at least one of them.

He entered carrying a big white mug which had a map of the London underground on it and headed straight for me. His crisp white T-shirt bore the legend: ARCHAE-OLOGISTS DO IT IN HOLES.

When he was close enough to let me count the gaps in his teeth he began to chuckle.

'Are you the owner of vehicle K258 GPU?'

'You know I am, Dan,' I said.

His grin widened.

'You've got one hell of a flat tyre. Offside rear. Looks like somebody's taken a knife to it. Thought you'd want to know.'

They had made a good job of it too. The tyre was as flat as

a pancake and I could see at least two, maybe three, slits where a knife – double-edged by the look of it – had been forced in.

There was a time and place for mindless vandalism and I couldn't work out why this should be it and me the victim. It seemed a totally pointless crime. If I'd had a good reason to do such a thing I would have done *two* tyres at least, leaving Armstrong stuck in the middle of Suffolk. That would really have pissed me off. Didn't they realize that taxis carried a spare in the boot?

Maybe they did.

I resigned myself to shifting all the stuff Amy had crammed in the boot space to get at the spare and the jack and the wheelbrace and to getting my hands dirty when I had so far managed to keep them clean that morning. It was as I was inserting the key into the handle of the boot that I noticed, carved into the paintwork just below in letters about an inch high, the single word: 'GO'.

Now that was annoying. That was spiteful and vicious and would be a bugger to remove, yet in a way it was oddly reassuring.

This wasn't mindless vandalism after all.

This was personal.

Back out on site, they all came up to me at some point in the morning and said how awful it was about my car and I couldn't possibly think one of them had done it, could I? I'd said no, of course not, and restrained myself from pointing out that not one of the sods had offered to help me change the wheel.

I had made a point – though nobody seemed to notice – of moving Armstrong a few yards out from behind The Studio where he'd been parked overnight. Now I could see him from any part of the site and, using the telescope in the level, I could read his numberplate quite clearly. I couldn't actually make out the inscribed 'GO' instruction, I just thought I could.

After about half an hour's hoeing, Amy sidled over to me.

I was kneeling on one of the foam 'prayer mats' and cleaning a patch of ground with my trowel. She planted her boots wide apart, making sure they were in my eye-line, and leaned over me.

'Whatchyerdoing?'

I looked up through the inverted V of her legs. Ten metres away the faces of Jason, Ben and Cornell all met mine, then they all looked away, eyes to the ground in concentration.

'Don't bend over like that in front of the troops,' I said.

'Why not? Is it bad for morale?' She was all innocence. It was not an act she'd ever really made convincing.

'No, it's bloody good for morale, but it's shit for productivity. Broken any nails yet?'

I felt a tingle of triumph as she had to look to check, but her blood red nail polish was intact.

'You reckon one of them did it?' she said quietly.

'Too bloody right I do, just can't guess which one – or why – or when – or how. Keep your ears open.'

'Yes sir, Mr Supervisor. Is that what I have to call you now?'

'"Master" or "Wise One" is customary.'

'Get stuffed. Anyway, what are you doing?'

I trowelled away some more dirt.

'Look at this patch of natural. It's different to what you've been hoeing, see? It's dirtier, there's a greyish tinge to it and the odd fleck of charcoal and less chalk nodules. It's just not as clean as your stuff only a few metres away. I reckon it's a change.'

'A change of what?'

'A change in the natural which might just be a redeposit and I want to see if it's just a patch or if it extends into the next grid square.'

'A redeposit? Of what?'

'Of the natural. I think maybe somebody disturbed this

168

ground but only briefly. We need to know why they did it and whether there's anything under it.'

'Can't see a thing myself,' she said and stretched her arms above her head, holding her hoe like a weight-lifter going for Gold.

Through her legs I saw Jason sneak another crafty glance.

'Could it have been these cowboy metal-detectorists who shivved Armstrong?' she said through a yawn. 'God, this is boring.'

'There's no sign we've been visited in the night and anyway, why would they? And I told you you'd be bored. Want to go home yet?'

'No,' she said quickly. 'It's just I wanted to *find* something.'

'We are finding things – features, things we can dig. I know it might not . . . hang on, you've just had a brilliant idea.'

'I have?'

I fished Armstrong's keys out of my trouser pocket and handed them to her.

'In the boot there's a metal detector I borrowed from Duncan. Get it out and see if it works and you can go treasure-hunting on the spoil heaps.'

'Yes!' she said, clenching a fist in the air. 'Now *that's* archaeology.'

By lunchtime we had two ten-metre squares cleaned to billiard-table standard. Ben had agreed with me that there seemed to be a change in the natural on the border of the two squares and we had then uncovered what appeared to be a pit – a circular dark blob which wasn't a ditch or a gully and therefore had to be a pit. It made a sort of sense: the ground had been dug or disturbed at some point in history and later on somebody, wanting to get rid of some rubbish, had dug a hole in which to bury it. Any gardener will tell you that it's easier to dig a hole where the earth has already been dug.

I told Ben to get Shona to draw it in on the pre-ex plan (she was now on to Sheet 2 and going like the clappers) and then to half-section it. He asked if I had a preference for which way it should be sectioned and I told him to make his section south-facing as it was easier to draw a profile from west to east that way. In terms of the archaeology it didn't matter in the slightest, it just made the plans look neater.

Ben nodded in agreement, bisected the circular blob with a length of string stretched between two nails and began to dig out the southern semicircle with his trowel.

The first square had shown up a gully and five post-holes or maybe they were stake-holes and maybe only three of them were real. Kali asked me if and how I wanted them recorded, which was a good question. I said I'd get back to her on that. Jude and Rory had almost finished their section across the gully and asked the same thing. Cornell asked if I wanted him to leapfrog Ben and start on a third square. Jason asked what I thought of leaving a baulk, on which we could run the wheelbarrows, between squares on this side of the site and the ones he assumed we would do on the east side.

So many questions. They were all looking at me. I had to take an executive decision.

'Clean up any loose!' I shouted. 'Lunchtime!'

We were almost back at the tool shed when we all heard something which made us turn and look back down the site.

I had totally forgotten about Amy, who was half-way up the side of the spoil heap way down the other end. She had the headphones on whilst she was using the metal detector and so hadn't heard me call time on lunch.

We could hear her, however, just as anyone singing along to a personal stereo is twice as loud as they would normally be.

She was waving the detector – which looked like a mine-detector, basically a lollipop on a stick attached to you by a prosthetic arm. She was waving it almost as if she was conducting a band with it and she was doing a very energetic jig, or as energetic as the mud on her boots would allow, flinging out first one leg then the other like a Cossack practising under water. The pink socks rolled over the tops of her boots flashed in the sunlight.

'Treasure!' she was shouting, or perhaps singing. 'Treasure!'

We all watched her in silence then I said:

'Who's on tea duty?'

And we all turned back towards the house.

Amazingly, Amy had found treasure of a sort. Well, a coin to be precise. Not a gold doubloon or anything, but a copper alloy coin nonetheless, heavily greened with oxidization.

She had clumped into The Studio where the rest of us were sitting down to eat, drawing disapproving looks because her boots were double their natural size with mud. I pointed at them.

'I know,' she said breathlessly. 'It's a bugger to run in these with all this mud on them. Still, it's good for the thighs.'

No one seemed to want to argue further and we all stood around admiring her green coin saying 'Nice one' and 'Fair play' and then getting back to our sandwiches. I offered Amy one of mine.

'What the fuck is this?' she said loudly, spraying me with white bread crumbs.

'Marmite and cheese,' I said defensively. 'I made them last night.'

'Christ, do you hate me that much? I've put some strange things in my mouth in my time, but . . .'

I let her rant on. The others were staring drop-jawed but I reckoned it was good policy to have them just a tad scared of Amy.

It had always worked for me.

The sun came out in the afternoon and most of the digging

171

crew stripped off at least one layer of clothing. Fortunately Amy did not as she was by now obsessed with the metal detector and had covered the site twice and was on her third sweep of the spoil heaps. I had seen it get to people like that before. In fact I'd once seen a digger stabbing at the ground with his trowel until he had a hole almost a metre deep, far beyond the actual range of his detector. He would have been digging still if I hadn't taken pity on him and pointed out that the signal he was picking up was from the steel toecaps in his own boots.

Ben called me over to where he had finished half-sectioning his pit. It had turned out to be a decent enough fifty centimetres deep and had been filled with just one single layer of dark deposit. Conclusion: a rubbish pit; or at least a hole cut in the ground for the sole purpose (as far as we could ascertain) of taking a man-made deposit of crap, either domestic or industrial, in the days before Suffolk County Council provided you with wheelie-bins and weekly visits from those cheerful dustbin-men who can whistle and sing at the same time so loudly, so early.

'Any finds?' I asked Ben.

'Yeah, a goodly few. Domestic stuff, indicating occupation of the area. Animal bones – and teeth – pig, cow, deer maybe, plus oyster shells, bits of tile and some good bits of pot.'

'Roman?'

Oyster shells and tile were good indicators of the Roman period, but then they ate oysters in the Middle Ages and they reused tiles (and nails, and foundation stone) which they found on old Roman sites. They probably called it recycling.

'The pot isn't,' Ben said, holding out a chunky piece to me.

It was the handle, or part of the handle, of a jug and even though it was encrusted with muck I could see that the pottery had a green glaze sheen, a green which resembled mucus so uncannily that it is commonly known as 'snot-pot', though it's not a term you'll hear on the *Antiques Roadshow.*

'That's medieval,' I said as I handed it back.

'Absolutely. I've got more bits of it too.' He pointed at his finds tray with his trowel. 'Along with some bog-standard cooking ware. But that green-glaze stuff is definitely thirteenth/fourteenth century. Very datable.'

'Well, like they say on television: It's Day One and we've already found evidence of medieval habitation.'

'It's not what Arthur is looking for,' he said.

'You might have a point there. Tell you what, I'll go and get a camera and we'll photograph it. Get Shona to put it on a plan and then take out the other half, see if there's any more datable pot.'

'You're not thinking something might happen to it, like it might disappear overnight?'

'Stranger things have happened,' I said.

But I wished I hadn't because stranger things started to happen before I was half-way back to the house.

My phone rang. It wasn't the 'jazz' ring I had programmed in for calls, but rather the bleepety-bleep signal which told me I had a text message. (Now that it was possible to download special rings from the Internet and 'send them to a friend' it was a favourite game among the laddish crowd to change somebody's ringing tone to, say, the James Bond theme or *Mission Impossible*, to embarrass them when their phones went off just as they were chatting up a sophisticated piece of totty in some expensive wine bar in the West End.)

I unclipped the phone from my trousers and pressed the OK button as I walked. The message just said: 'REV 2:12'.

It could have been a numberplate, it could have been the instructions on an outboard motor. It could have been a wrong number.

I pressed the OK button again until it asked me if I wanted to reply to the sender's number. It was another mobile number, which meant nothing to me. I clicked back to the main menu without texting back. The phone would store the message and the number.

I continued towards the house and spotted Dan the Man lurking in the kitchen doorway smoking a roll-up. I remembered the piece of pottery in my pocket. I would ask him about that.

Then I'd tell him to go and have a look at the pottery Ben had found in his pit.

And, whilst I had his attention, I could ask him where they kept the cameras.

And he just might know where I could lay my hands on a Bible.

Chapter 10

Grave Fill

When I called time on the day's digging, some of them actually looked disappointed and for a moment I thought they would argue that there was plenty of light left and they didn't mind working unpaid overtime, as diggers are wont to do. But Cornell was already trudging back towards the house pushing his wheelbarrow and the others gradually followed.

I had to climb the spoil heap and grab Amy by the shoulder to attract her attention. Since lunchtime she had found six square-headed nails and no more coins, but she had stuck at it like an addict. Reluctantly she pulled the headphones down around her neck and switched the detector off. I told her to come and help me take down the level.

I unscrewed the Nikon and placed it in its foam-protected box then began to dismantle the tripod, taking my time and filling her in on my strange text message, recalling it from the phone's archive to prove I wasn't making it up.

'And did Dan have a Bible?'

'He didn't need one,' I said, 'he knew the passage: *To the angel of the church at Pergamum write: "These are the words of the one who has the sharp two-edged sword: I know where you live."* Book of Revelations, chapter 2, verse 12.'

'Bloody hell. He knew that off the top of his head? Is he a church-goer?'

'Only to meet widows. Thing is, who would want to threaten me?'

'You want a list?' she said with a raised eyebrow. 'Anyway, who says it's a threat?'

'Oh, come on. *I know where you live*? What else could it be? A reminder from the Census Office that we should register to vote?'

'You must have upset somebody, difficult as that is to believe.'

'Somebody who has my mobile phone number.'

'Good point. Did you try texting back?'

'I'm not looking for a penfriend. I tried to ring it but just got a cut-out messaging service.'

She grabbed the phone from me and checked the number I had stored in the archive.

'Nobody I know,' she said, handing it back. 'Could be somebody back in London, somebody you've upset. Somebody with a room temperature IQ and no sense of humour. You know loads of people like that.'

'Well, I hope Arthur's got a sense of humour,' I said, pulling in the extended legs of the tripod and locking them off. I took the piece of pottery I had found early from my pocket and showed it to her.

'This is known as BB2 – Black Burnished ware, second phase. Wheel-thrown and fired in a furnace rather than on a bonfire.'

'Roman?'

'Roman period, from mid-first century onwards. Made in Colchester, north Kent and eventually all over. But Roman period, just like your coin and your nails and all the other pot scattered on the spoil heap.'

She waved the flat of her right hand over her forehead and made a 'Whoosh' sound. 'And your point is?'

'*On the spoil heap*. Everything Dan has been asked to pot-wash – sorry, process – so far has been Roman period, but it's all come from the top cleaning layer which has ended up on the spoil heap. The only proper feature we've dug today was Ben's rubbish pit and everything in *there* is medieval, seven or eight hundred years later yet *below* the Roman finds. Unless Arthur has been digging features and not telling anyone, or leaving any noticeable trace, then . . .'

'The finds have been planted.'

She might not know much about archaeology, but she could smell a con when the wind was right.

'Don't say anything until we can sound him out over dinner.'

'Christ, I'd forgotten! I'm a mess!'

She was. She had slipped on the spoil heap and landed on her backside at least twice during the afternoon, but the diggers had politely refrained from laughing out loud. (Realizing she had the earphones on and couldn't hear me, I had.) The back of her shorts, her boots and her knees were caked in dried mud and there were smears all over her TALtop where she had wiped her hands, which were smeared black with charcoal. I couldn't blame her for that. It was me who had told her the test for charcoal was to crush it between your fingers. I had just forgotten to tell her about its staining properties.

I was slinging the tripod harness over my shoulder when she said, 'That won't improve Arthur's mood either.'

She had noticed the approaching hum of a light aircraft before I had and I turned to look.

'Probably the same one he yelled at yesterday,' she said. 'He's convinced it's spying on him. The diggers say he's obsessed with it because it comes round about this time every day, though sometimes first thing in the morning as well. Don't look at me like that. You told me to keep my ears open.'

I bent over and let the tripod strap slide off my shoulder as I took the Nikon level out of its box.

'So let's spy on him, shall we?'

I used the metal sights on the level as an initial guide and then put the telescope to my eye and fiddled the focus knob until I caught the outline of the plane and could track it and sharpen the view.

It was a Piper Super Cub, a hardy two-seater built up

until the 1990s on a design used by the Americans during World War II for spotter planes. They were docile enough to fly, could work a short, rough airstrip and were high-winged, so good for taking photographs from.

On a clear day they reckon that a normal-sighted person can read the registration letters on the wing from about four hundred feet. When I was taught to fly my instructor always said that if somebody could do that, you were too fucking low.

This Super Cub was well above that but with the Nikon lens, it wasn't a problem.

'Remember this,' I said to Amy. 'Golf – Alpha, X-ray, Romeo, Victor.'

'Damn!' she squealed. 'I *have* broken a nail! Sorry, what were you saying?'

After we'd showered, we dressed for dinner. I exchanged my boots for trainers but kept the combat trousers as they were still clean, in fact totally mud-free – only to be expected as I was a supervisor – and chose a plain white T-shirt with a discreet D&G logo.

'Is that it then?' Amy said. She had just returned from the Mobile Thrones block and was wearing a towelling robe and her work boots. 'I thought you were going to make an effort.'

'I've got my leather jacket in Armstrong,' I said defensively. 'It's a MaxMara.'

'No it isn't. The label might be, but the jacket isn't. Have you got any wine to take with us? Didn't think so. Pick up some decent cigarettes while you're out and don't take too long. I'll be ready in twenty minutes.'

I reckoned that gave me at least an hour.

The diggers were forming a queue to use the kitchen, the veggies elbowing their way to the top of the food chain. One of them wolf-whistled at me as I walked across the courtyard to Armstrong and I distinctly heard Gregory say, 'What's he all dressed up for?' Wait till they saw Amy.

I drove down to the village where Ray was just opening up The Chequers.

'Roy, dear boy, how lovely to see you. Is . . . er . . . Alice . . . not with you?'

'No, she's getting changed. We've been invited to dine with Mr Swallow tonight,' I said, camping it up.

'You'll be wanting a bottle of claret, then,' he said. 'Better make it two.'

'I'm in your hands,' I said without thinking.

'I wish, dear boy, I wish.'

Ray insisted I had one while he went to get 'the good stuff' from the cellar, so I stood at the bar, sucked on a bottle of Beck's, unwrapped the last surviving packet of cigarettes from Mother's party and cranked my Zippo into life. The front bar was empty and so was the whole pub as far as I could tell, though a radio played fuzzily somewhere in a back room and a clock ticked loudly behind the bar. I thought of all the pubs I knew in the West End which, by this time, would be bursting at the seams with office workers, drunks who'd been there all afternoon, pimps, tarts, touts and phoney charity workers rattling collecting cans, all trying to make themselves heard over the background music which in turn was drowned out by the enormous screen and stereo speakers of a TV showing BSkyB. It was enough to make you feel homesick.

When another vehicle drew up outside, alongside Armstrong, I naturally took an interest as it broke the monotony.

It was one of the bigger Land Rovers, a Defender, with a Go-Faster stripe of dried mud all down the side as if someone had been seriously testing its off-road capabilities, although the only ones you see in London are used on the school run in the mornings. The driver's door opened and closed and a tall figure with close-cropped blond hair walked around Armstrong, giving him a good once-over before coming into the bar.

In London I would have ignored him completely, but here in this quiet rural backwater I thought it only polite to nod at him.

He nodded back.

He was about my age, slim and fit and wore octagonal steel-rimmed glasses. Most bizarrely, he wore a Hugo Boss double-breasted suit, the trousers of which were tucked into green Hunter wellingtons. And I'd been worried about being over-dressed.

'Is Ray around?' he asked me. His accent was North American but I couldn't quite place where.

'Just getting something for me,' I said. 'Won't be a minute.'

He nodded again and remained standing about a foot inside the door, watching me. Not looking at me: watching me.

'Find anything?'

'Excuse me?'

I had an immediate guilty conscience which may have come from being discovered alone in the well-stocked bar of an empty pub on other occasions before this.

'On your little dig up at Woolpack House,' he said, hardly concealing a sneer.

'Oh, shedloads,' I said.

It was his turn to say: 'Excuse me?'

'Shedloads,' I repeated. 'It's a technical term in archaeology when you find lots of finds, especially finds you were hoping to find.'

I could almost feel the static as the hairs on the back of his neck went up, but he didn't show any emotion, just quietly said, 'I see,' as if he was talking to himself.

'Mr Jankel! What can I do for you this lovely evening?'

Ray appeared behind the bar, a dusty bottle in each hand and the remains of what must have been an awesome cobweb at some point across his forehead.

'I'll be working late tonight, very late,' said steel-rims, 'so I'll need a key.'

'Of course, my dear sir, of course.'

Ray put the bottles on the bar and rummaged underneath it until he came up with a Yale key which he tossed across the bar and which steel-rims caught one-handed without seeming to extend his arm.

'Thank you. Goodnight.'

He slipped the key into his jacket pocket and turned and left without another word.

I started to pry some notes from my wallet as Ray wiped the wine bottles with a drying cloth.

'Is he with the local Gestapo?' I asked, hoping for some more local gossip instead of change.

'He's a cold fish is that one,' Ray confided with indecent haste. 'Name's Hans Jankel. Oh don't worry, he's a Canadian not a Kraut. Works for the Scrivenour-Lindleys. Rents a room here two or three nights a week.'

'So if you rent a room here, you get a key to the bar? Cool.'

'Thought you looked impressed,' he smiled.

'Then again, if farmhands round here can afford Hugo Boss suits, maybe I'm in the wrong profession.'

Ray made a playful swipe at me, slapping the back of my hand.

'Foolish boy! Jankel's not a farmhand, he's their game-keeper.'

Most of the diggers were still cooking or eating while watching TV in The Studio when Amy and I walked round to the front door of Woolpack House, which was a pity. Only Dan the Man – showered and changed into his white suit, a clean shirt and a Maverick bootlace tie – was around to see us.

He was coming out of Mobile Thrones, slotting gold rings on to virtually all of his fingers whilst rolling a cigarette, which was a pretty neat trick. When he saw us, he stopped dead and gawped and shreds of tobacco began to fall like snow from his cigarette paper.

Or rather, when he saw Amy.

Her dress was something she'd been working on for the last few months, her Next Big Thing after the TALtop which had gone through just about all the variations and relaunches possible including a 'comeback' phase. If it worked, and if it sold, we would never have to worry

181

about a personal pension plan or where the next BMW was coming from.

She had code-named it the 'FF' for Fake Fortuny and I had played a small part in its development. The original Fortuny dresses, designed over ninety years ago, were famous for their batwing sleeves, their figure-hugging wet-look silk and, of course, the Delphos pleat which enabled them to be scrunched up into a ball and carried in a handbag. The magic of the pleat was that however long it remained scrunched up, it came out perfect and fitted like a wet T-shirt. I think the record for keeping an original in its bag was forty years and it still hung like sex on a stick. Amy's design had dispensed with the batwing sleeves – in fact, dispensed with sleeves entirely – and cut the length to just above the knee to save on material, even though the pleats still took up three or four times as much as you needed for the average (and universal) short, black party frock. Amy's theory was that if you could fit a mobile phone in your handbag, you could fit one of her Fake Fortunys, which could be whipped out at the slightest hint there was a party in the offing.

For the prototype she had brought with her she had used silk, though she was experimenting with synthetic mixes, which she had tie-dyed blood red at home in the kitchen. This was where I came in. I had been mooching around the bookshops in the Charing Cross Road one afternoon when she had called on the mobile and told me she was staying in that night and could I pick up a pair of stockings for her on the way back? Now that seemed like a plan to me and it took me less than two hours to select a pair of long-fit sheer black nylons with a seam running up the back. (I also picked up a decent Chardonnay and a bottle of Johnson's Baby Oil just in case.)

When I got home, the kitchen could have been the set of *The Hampstead Chain Saw Massacre*. Amy was wearing white overalls splattered with red dye, had a plastic showercap over her hair, rubber washing-up gloves on her hands and a cigarette drooping from the corner of her mouth. She grunted a thanks and took the stockings from me, ripping open the packet with her teeth and yanking one out. With kitchen scissors, she cut the foot off the stocking and then began to cram it with blood red and dripping twisted silk which she took from a pan on the cooker. She had become The Sausage-Maker From Hell.

I lost interest in the rest of the process but I do know it involved putting the dress-in-the-stocking in the micro-wave, then tumble-drying for a couple of hours in with three large fluffy bath towels. The end result, however, was spectacular. Out of the bag and over the head and Amy was sheathed in a continuous creamy ripple of material which shone as if she had just stepped out of the surf. I pointed out that it worked even better without under-wear and she agreed. Thus my second, vital, contribution to the British fashion industry.

Dan the Man seemed to agree that the end product was impressive, though he didn't say so. He didn't say any-thing as we walked by him and round the corner of the house. He just stood there, rooted, an empty cigarette paper between his fingers.

Of course he could have been a purist and have noted that steel-capped calfskin work boots don't actually go with a Fortuny, even a fake one. But Amy was damned if she was going to risk her Jimmy Choo shoes in the mud or on the gravel, so she carried them until we reached the front door where she balanced herself with a hand on my shoulder to toe-and-heel the boots off and squeeze into her Jimmys.

The door was open an inch or so but I knocked anyway and when Arthur appeared we saw that he'd made an effort as well. He had clipped on a bright yellow bow tie which did little except highlight the soup stains on a faded white cotton shirt.

His moustache positively bristled when he saw us.

'I say!' He said it like Leslie Phillips used to say 'Hello' in a deep, upper-class lounge lizard voice. 'There was no need to go to all that trouble, but I must say it is appre-ciated. Oh yes, fair play.'

Then he reached out and took the two bottles of claret from me.

'And you look simply stunning, my dear,' he added, over his shoulder, already disappearing with the booze. 'Do come in. Go through and sit down while I get a corkscrew.'

Woolpack House wasn't a big house as country piles go. I mean it wasn't one of those country house detective story places where there are thirteen windows but only twelve rooms. But even so the entrance hall was big enough to have been rented out as a spacious, self-contained apartment for three or four hundred squids a week if it had been in Knightsbridge. Then again, they would have had to get rid of the staircase complete with oak banister which ran up the left wall then doglegged across a balcony-like landing and ended in a passageway leading, presumably, to the bedrooms.

On the wall on the landing, facing the door (but you had to look up) and dominating the hallway, was a single painting lit by a single brass lamp hanging from the top of the frame. It was a life-size painting of a young woman in military uniform standing straight, but not at attention, a half-smile across thin lips, her hands together just to the side of where her navel would be under the square-cut tunic and the slim tailored skirt which came down to below the knee. She wore some sort of a cap with a peak, a shirt and tie and sensible shoes. Even from where we stood it was obvious that the painter had tried to emphasize her shiny black hair and rosy-cheeked fresh face, but hadn't got the balance right so that her complexion was washed out, almost ghostly. Then again, the painting could have faded over the years as the woman wore the uniform of a corporal in the ATS, the women's army service of World War II.

'Is that *her*?' Amy hissed. 'You know, that *Rebecca* character Ray was telling us about last night. Oh God, I've seen this movie. Arthur will become obsessed with me, convinced I'm her come back to life.'

'Don't be ridiculous, she looks nothing like you,' I hissed

back. 'And in any case, you're thinking of *Dracula*, not *Rebecca*.'

'Well, that's a relief. It's a crap painting, too.'

The first door off the hall was the dining room, which at one time had probably been quite impressive but was now crying out for a make-over or at least a good scrub down and some paint. There was a plain pine table with five chairs around it, though only three matched, facing french windows where the paint was peeling and at least two of the glass squares had cracks running across them. The sunlight coming in from the west picked out a hailstorm of dust motes in the air. At least the view was good, down the side of the driveway sighting directly between two long beds of roses which had been allowed to grow and fall over creating a tunnel effect of pink and white flowers, even though they were probably past their best for the year.

'It's so airless in here,' Amy said, taking charge.

She stomped over the threadbare carpet towards the windows – and I noticed in passing that either her Jimmy Choos were of different sizes or the floorboards were uneven – and grasped the handles of the windows. Nothing happened, so she automatically looked for a deadlock bolt at the top and then the bottom.

'I'm afraid they don't open,' said Arthur behind us, making us both jump. 'Nothing sinister, it's just that I lost the key some years ago and never got around to doing anything about it.'

He was carrying a tray which he placed on the table. On the tray were forks and spoons, a plastic tub of table salt, a squeezy bottle of ketchup, a bottle of HP Sauce and an opened loaf of thick sliced white bread. I was glad I'd brought the claret now I knew we were dining in style.

'But in case you're wondering . . .' he started.

'No I wasn't,' Amy said too quickly.

'. . . those are the very windows which my brother Gerald went out of. He just got up from the table, picked up his shotgun, which always used to stand over there in the corner, and went out into the garden to his rose bushes to do the deed. Don't look so aghast, my dear young girl. Everyone knows the story. Now, what's missing? Ah yes, glasses. And the wine. Where did I put it?'

'You kept a loaded shotgun in the dining room?' Amy said desperately.

'Yes, yes, I know,' Arthur conceded. 'Bloody stupid thing to do. I keep it in the office these days. Much safer. Back in a moment.'

As soon as he had gone, Amy put her head on one side and said:

'He is not of this planet, is he?'

'Just visiting.'

Arthur came back with the wine clutched under his arm and five glasses intertwined in his fingers.

'I asked Fifi and her friend Ben to join us, hope you don't mind. Mrs Hawksbee has left us a huge casserole. Now you pour some wine, Fitzroy, while I make sure I haven't set fire to the kitchen.'

He bobbed out again.

'At last I get to meet the mysterious Fifi,' I said, handing Amy a glass.

'What's mysterious about her? She's really nice. Reminds me of a much younger version of your mother.'

'You've seen her? That's more than I have.'

'It was in the showers this morning,' Amy said between sips of wine. 'She was quite charming. She knew who I was.'

'Oh, that's all right then. I was beginning to think she didn't actually exist.'

'I think you might like her. I do.'

But I wasn't going to get the chance.

Ben turned up but he had Shona with him, not the mysterious Fifi. At least he had the decency to look embarrassed.

'I'm sorry, but Fifi has an absolutely crippling migraine and just wouldn't be the life and soul of the party. Arthur said it would be OK to bring Shona here to make up the boy/girl/boy/girl thing.'

He ended with a smile but it was a limp one. Shona, meanwhile, hadn't said a word but hadn't taken her eyes off Amy.

'Is that *a dress*?' she asked her and immediately realized what a stupid question it was.

I wasn't worried. Amy was specially trained to talk down to people like her.

'It was field walking which turned me on to archaeology,' said Arthur, although no one had asked him.

I wanted to ask really interesting questions. Such as: Having gone through life with initials spelling 'arse', which must have been hard enough, why get a personalized numberplate?

Or: What's it like to win the Lottery? And: Where did the money go?

He could have warmed up with a couple of easy ones, for instance: Is this beef or lamb in the casserole? Surely it's not pork? And we would have liked to have heard the answer to that one.

We were pretty sure it was meat of some sort from the way Shona reacted – as if surprised by an enema in church – when Arthur staggered in bearing the huge cast iron pot, his hands enveloped in oven gloves in the shape of lobsters. He wouldn't let a guest go hungry, though, and Shona was presented with a pound of Co-Op Cheddar (extra mature) still in its vacuum packaging.

And another one: Where were those very expensive bottles of claret I had brought? They had not reappeared since Arthur took them into the kitchen. Instead, we were drinking a Bulgarian Cabernet that hadn't been told the Cold War was over.

'And the funny thing was, that was exactly what I was doing – walking a field.'

He mopped up gravy with a folded slice of bread.

'They'd retired me out of the army years before and they were talking of retiring me off the Bench to make way for younger magistrates who were more "in tune" whatever

187

that means. Well, two retirements were quite enough for me. I wasn't going to let it happen again. As the philosopher said: "Once is happenstance, twice is coincidence, third time is enemy action."'

'Goldfinger,' I said automatically.

'What?'

'Goldfinger said that.'

'Chappie in the James Bond book?'

'Yes.' I winced as Amy scraped one of her Jimmys down my shin.

'I'll be damned,' said Arthur. 'Anyway, I was looking for something to keep the old brain cells moving and every morning I would take the dog for a walk around the estate, across the fields. Of course it wasn't our estate and they weren't our fields but nobody minded in those days.

'I toyed with the idea of becoming a naturalist for a while. Don't worry, ladies, I didn't say "naturist" – I knew I was too old for that! But there were all these local wildlife experts popping up on the television in those days and I thought I could do that. So there I was, walking the fields every morning trying to spot badger spoor or vole droppings, that sort of thing, and one day I noticed something where the ground had just been ploughed and I thought – pardon my French, ladies – blow me to buggery, that doesn't belong here.'

I fought to keep the giggles down. Arthur was perfect casting for the old joke about the retired Wing Commander presenting the prizes at Speech Day at a posh girls' school. When recalling his exploits flying Spitfires in the Battle of Britain, he says, 'Suddenly these three Fokkers came at me out of the sun.' The girls all start to giggle so the prim headmistress interjects and points out that a Fokker was a type of German aircraft. The old buffer turns to her and says, 'Quite right, madam, but these fokkers were flying Messerschmidts.'

'Do you know what it was?'

'A piece of tile?' (Ben).

'Heavily degraded burnt daub?' (Shona the killjoy).

'Pottery?' (Me).

'A coin?' (Amy).

'Even better as it turns out – a clay coin mould. Naturally I had no idea what the thing was but a chap in the museum in Colchester Castle looked it up for me, said it was early first century, and British not Roman. So I started thinking as to who was minting coins in this neck of the woods before the Romans came and it came to me – Boadicea!'

I started to say another word beginning with 'b' but Ben, diplomatically, got there first.

'Bit of a leap of faith, that, isn't it, Arthur?'

'Got to do that in archaeology, my boy, otherwise you'll never get anywhere. Old Mortimer Wheeler used to say that and he was an old soldier. You can gather as much evidence as you like but if you haven't got the imagination to think how it might have got there, then it's next to useless.'

'So you started to gather evidence?' Amy said sweetly, as if to a child.

'No, first I went back to school and read everything I could about Boadicea. And don't tell me, I can see it on your faces. When I was a lad we called her Boadicea, not this New Age Boo-di-ka rubbish. Dammit, if it was good enough for Queen Victoria, it's good enough for me.

'Not that there are many good books to read about her. Mostly it's romantic nonsense written by middle-aged women about a sorely wronged noble savage who really just wanted to be a good mother. Nothing about what she actually did.'

'Which was . . .?' I prompted.

'Leading the native tribes in a rebellion against a barbaric and repressive imperialist superpower, that's what,' said Shona, though I felt Boudica needed less defending than Arthur probably did.

'Not all of the native tribes,' I said majestically, 'just the Iceni, the Trinovantes from Essex and the Catuvellauni from Hertfordshire. Tribes in other places were quite happy with the Romans. Some had even encouraged them to invade. Maybe they liked the idea of decent roads, centrally heated houses, law and order, cheap wine, a single European currency . . . I mean, what did the Iceni ever do for us?'

Ben laughed out loud and even Arthur chortled.

'She almost succeeded in throwing the Romans out!' Shona blurted.

'No she didn't. If she hadn't started a ruck the odds were the Romans might have pulled out because dear old Britannia hadn't turned out to be quite the profit-making investment they thought it would be.' I was on a roll now; time to throw in a few statistics. 'They had four legions here – four. Out of a total of twenty-four. Twenty legions to rule the rest of the world, four for this poxy little island. It didn't make sense. Seneca, the key adviser to Emperor Nero, was into Britannia for sixty million sesterces personally and he was wanting to cut his losses. But once Boudica comes thundering out of the backwoods like some Iron Age Delia Smith with attitude, there was no way the Romans were going to leave.'

'Fitzroy's got a point,' Arthur conceded. 'Couldn't let a more primitive technology triumph or let the Roman gods be defeated by the old Druidic ones.'

'No, he meant they couldn't be seen to be beaten by a woman,' said Amy.

'Got it in one,' I smiled at her.

'But . . . so . . . what exactly are you trying to find here?' Ben tried to steer us back on course and give Shona time to finish fuming.

'I thought I had made it clear.' He seemed genuinely concerned that we'd all missed the point. 'I'm looking for evidence of what Boadicea *did*. What do you do when you become queen? You start minting your own coins, show you're the boss. When your subjects can't read or write, you put your face on the coinage. Impresses the hell out of the taxpayers!'

'And you think the Iceni mint was *here*?' Ben tried to keep his voice politely curious but he was verging on the patronizing.

'Well, one of them. There were probably two or three.'

'Four, I think,' said Ben showing off outrageously, 'including one at West Stow here in Suffolk. But none of them ever turned up coins showing Boudica's head.'

'There has to be one somewhere, dear boy. Why not here?'

'But your only evidence is a clay coin mould.'

'It was a start.'

Arthur was starting to colour around the cheeks. Much more of this and he would match Amy's dress.

'And that was – what? – ten years ago?' Ben wouldn't let it go.

'More like twelve, actually.'

'And how many coins have you found?'

'Quite a few. Fifi tells me that Amy found one only today.'

'That was Roman. What about Iceni coins?'

'Well, er . . . none, actually. But now we have the bulldozer, we can strip the topsoil and get down to business.'

'So we are treasure-hunting after all,' Amy said to me accusingly.

'Oh no, my dear, we are looking for evidence. One coin would do. Yes, I'd be happy with just one, as long as it had Boadicea's head on it.'

Shona remained stony-faced. Ben looked like a rabbit in headlights, seeing his archaeological reputation crumbling before him.

'Leave it to me,' Amy said to Arthur, patting his hand. 'I'll find you your gold coin. Today wasn't just beginner's luck.'

'It would be silver, actually, my dear, but thank you for your faith. You have to have faith in this archaeology business.'

There was an embarrassed silence and I hoped Arthur might take it as an opportunity to notice that our glasses had been empty for some time.

We would probably have died of thirst if my phone hadn't gone off.

*　　*　　*

It was only the trill which said I had a text message, but I excused myself saying I just 'have to take this one' – as you do – so I could sneak into the hall, open the front door and light up a cigarette, blowing smoke into the clear night air before fiddling with the buttons on the phone.

I read the message and finished the cigarette. Back in the dining room, Arthur was stacking plates. No one was objecting to the fact that the meal seemed to be over, although Shona was still nibbling chunks of cheese. Ben, Amy and I had had quite enough of Mrs Hawksbee's inedible and unidentifiable casserole and nothing else seemed to be on offer.

'Ah, Fitzroy,' Arthur beamed. 'You're back with us. I was negotiating a move into the library next door. I have whisky there and I'm sure we can rustle up some coffee if anyone wants any.'

'Does your library have a Bible?' I asked.

'Yet a third angel followed, crying out loud, "Whoever worships the beast and its image and receives its mark on his forehead or hand, he shall drink the wine of God's wrath, poured undiluted into the cup of his vengeance."'

'What the fuck does that mean?' whispered Amy.

'I've got a stalker with a good reference book?'

The text message had just said: 'REV 14:9'. As Dan the Man wasn't around, we had to consult Arthur's schoolboy-issue copy of the New English Bible (Popular Edition). We found it on a high shelf in the library, as he directed, in between an illustrated guide to lawn mower maintenance and a Margery Allingham detective story.

Arthur had gone to boil water for Shona who was insisting on lemon balm tea instead of Scotch. She and Ben pretended to check out the shelves of the library until Amy and I finished our little confab and I replaced the Bible on the shelf.

'Sorry,' I said sheepishly. 'A crossword clue that's been bugging us for days.'

Ben nodded as if he didn't believe us but it didn't

matter. Shona just looked like she didn't believe we existed.

'Arthur's not going to find anything, is he?' Amy said, moving closer to Ben so that he could get a better look at the dress.

Ben smiled his rugged, public schoolboy smile which had no doubt taken him far in life.

'Not what he wants to find, that's for sure. He's got more chance of –'

'Winning the Lottery,' Amy and I said together.

'Again,' said Ben. 'Speaking of which, he doesn't seem to have lashed out, does he? I mean you can't argue about the pay and conditions but I would have hired a couple of 360s to clear the area first, or done some proper geophysics, if I'd had that sort of money.'

'He certainly didn't spend it on cooking lessons for Mrs Hawksbee,' said Amy. 'What in God's name was in that casserole?'

'It was *meat*,' said Shona with conviction.

'Are you *sure*?' Amy asked her sweetly.

'So he bought himself some archaeology and a bulldozer and a Jeep,' I said. 'Fair enough. Everyone needs a hobby and boys like toys, but where did the rest go? He sure as hell didn't spend it on the house, it's falling to bits.'

'You've noticed the floorboards too?' said Ben, easing a foot up and down and watching the carpet give under his weight. 'I think the whole place needs underpinning, or a damp course or something.'

'He did so spend it on the house.'

We all looked at Shona. Eventually Amy shot out her red nails in a 'Go on' gesture.

'Fifi told me. She's seen some papers or other. Arthur and his brother Gerald were left the house in a weird joint trust on condition they didn't alter the aspect, whatever that means, in any way, unless one of them bought the other out while they both lived. Neither of them sought to do that and they lived quite happily off the trust for years, even though the trust mortgaged and then remortgaged the property to some mega capitalist bank or other, assuming that property prices would continue to rise. Which they did, but not quite enough.

'When Gerald – Arthur's brother – dies, Arthur can stay here as long as he wants but can't do anything to the place unless he buys out the trust, who inherited Gerald's share. They can't give him any cash because there isn't any and the mortgages now total £600,000 which is far more than the place is worth.'

'So he bought the place at a vastly inflated price, basically so he could dig it up?' Amy shook her head in disbelief and a fair proportion of the Fake Fortuny shook with her.

'What would you have done?' Shona snapped.

'Hired a good lawyer,' said Amy, reaching a hand out and snapping her fingers for a cigarette.

'So most of the money's gone, then?' I asked.

'He's set some aside for this excavation and he bought the computer and the van and he's trying to make Iceni Rescue a viable business, but essentially, yes.'

'Should have known,' Amy inhaled, 'when I saw the white sliced bread.'

'You bitch,' I said, before Shona could. 'But has he done any contract work for anyone?'

Shona shrugged. It was obvious she thought she'd already said too much.

'Fifi tells me he has a couple of watching briefs for the County Council and he's done a few evaluations in the past,' Ben offered. 'She's working on one for him at the moment. Colchester Garrison.'

'The garrison . . .?' I started but at that moment, Arthur reappeared with a tray on which was a steaming mug of something made out of a tea bag and four glasses of the sort you used to get free with petrol at garages each containing a disgustingly large measure of what looked like whisky.

Judging by the expression on Shona's face, though, it could have been meat.

'Here we are,' Arthur announced chirpily. 'The cup that

cheers and better bloody well intoxicate at these prices. Cheers, my dears.'

Whatever else, he had a good eye for a single malt.

'Did I hear somebody mention the garrison?' he said affably.

'I was just wondering if you were doing a job for Rupert,' I said, playing the family card.

'An evaluation at the moment, that's all. When it comes off it'll be a big job, probably too big for this little unit, but Rupert asked me to give it the once-over. Come up to the office and I'll show you if you've finished in here.'

We followed him out into the hall and up the staircase and it was impossible not to notice the life-size painting of the woman in uniform. Close up we could see just how bad a portrait it was. Not only did it look absolutely nothing like Amy, it probably didn't look anything like the woman who was posing for it.

'Impressive picture,' said Amy, but she was probably talking about the ornate gold-leaf frame.

'My late brother Gerald's favourite,' said Arthur, pausing to look at it as if for the first time. 'And mine too, I suppose. Gerald rather fancied himself as a painter, that's why we built The Studio for him out in the yard, but after he died I tried to sell some of his landscapes and, frankly, couldn't get tuppence for them. So they're all packed away up in the attic.'

He pointed down the corridor to a trapdoor in the ceiling with one of those fold-down ladders bolted to it, just to make sure we knew what an attic was.

'But this one I wanted to display for sentimental reasons. She meant a lot to Gerald, and to me.'

'Who was she?' Amy asked as she peered even closer at the woman's face.

'Octavia, my brother's wife. Childhood sweetheart, local lass, wartime bride. Never a good thing to marry when there's a war on. They only had about a year together before she was killed. Tragic and pointless, of course, as these things always are. It happened in just about the last air raid on Ipswich of the war: 18th September 1944.'

'Sad,' I said.

'Gerald took it very badly,' Arthur continued. 'Never recovered, not *mentally*. Clinically depressed from then until the time he killed himself. Still, he's found a sort of peace now.'

'What's she wearing round her neck?' asked Amy, squinting at the picture.

'I've no idea, my dear. It could be a pendant, it could be dirt. I've been meaning to have it cleaned for years. Anyway, that's quite enough of my depressing family history. Let's not be downhearted. Come in the office and I'll show you the plans. The secret plans!'

The office was a tip. It was a converted bedroom, probably the smallest one, and squeezed into it were a designer's drawing frame, a desk with a PC, scanner and printer, two chairs and about a hundred cardboard boxes which contained papers, rolls of plans and maps, and samples of roof tile, brick and pottery. The screen saver on the PC showed a field of golden wheat as if waving in the breeze with the initials 'GS' at the top right of the picture. I wondered if it was a Gerald Swallow original scanned in. If it was, the old manic-depressive had been a damn sight better at doing landscapes than portraits.

Arthur began to unroll one of the large acetate plans and spread it over the sloping drawing frame but Amy and I were looking at the corner of the room by the window, where a twelve-bore shotgun was propped on its butt, wondering if that was the one . . .

'Now gather round and look at this,' Arthur ordered.

The plan was a drawing of Colchester Garrison and was headed 'Proposed Development Subject to Planning Permission for Residential Dwellings'. Even without knowing the scale of the plan it was obvious it covered a huge area of the town.

'The army's new-look garrison,' Arthur said proudly, waving a hand across the plan. 'This is where they will relocate the military stuff, but all this lot will be sold off for residential housing. Point of interest to us is that virtually all of the garrison was built on archaeology-rich sites.

Can't move for the stuff. Stick a spade in and you're bound to hit something. Wait till you see the overlay.'

As he rummaged through another box for a roll of clear plastic, I scanned down the plan, concentrating on the new army site rather than the area earmarked for housing. Quite clearly marked were the proposed sites for a new Communications Centre, an Air Traffic Control post and, most disturbingly, the relocated Armoury.

'Ooh look, they're going to have a swimming pool,' said Amy.

Ben was shaking his head but not for the same reason I was.

'This is a huge area, Arthur,' he said, 'if it all comes up for tender at one go. I would have thought only the larger units would be capable of doing this.'

He added 'properly' under his breath so that only I could hear.

'It would be a challenge, that's for certain. Look at this.'

I moved aside to let Arthur slide a plastic overlay over the plan. This one was not professionally drawn and had dotted outlines in red ink. Arthur lined it up so that the corners matched.

'This should be an *under*lay of course. Everything in red is a known Roman or Saxon feature and there is much medieval archaeology still in situ on the surface. Look, at the eastern corner, a Roman military cemetery which we know is there, but no more than ten per cent has ever been excavated.'

Ben was right about the size of the undertaking if Arthur's plan was anywhere near accurate. There was hardly a square inch on the development plan which didn't cut across a dotted red line.

'And you're tendering for the excavation?' I said. Somebody would have to dig such a site before planning permission was granted and a job like this could run into millions.

'Iceni Rescue are doing a few preliminary evaluations,'

he said formally. 'I thought you chaps would be straining at the leash at a prospect like this.'

'This is too much to take in after a hard day's digging and all this whisky,' Ben said affably. 'I really ought to be hitting the hay. Our new supervisor's very strict about early starts.'

Amy raised an eyebrow at him and his face crumpled. Of course, he didn't mean *her*.

'You keep them in line, Fitzroy. But come on, Ben, let me get you another.'

Ben pulled his glass out of Arthur's reach.

'No, no thank you. I've still got plenty left.'

'I haven't,' said Amy holding out her glass. Now she could get away with that, I couldn't.

'Well then, all those for a nightcap follow me.'

Ben said he would head back to his room and Shona said she would too.

I had almost forgotten she was there. She had not shown any interest in Arthur's grand plans for the British military, preferring to poke about in a box of pottery shards on the floor by the computer desk. I noticed that the screen saver had gone and had been replaced by a standard Windows 2000 design, which gave me an idea.

'Can Amy possibly borrow your computer?' I asked Arthur.

'Of course. Is there anything. . .?'

'She just needs to check her e-mails at home,' I lied. 'Can't live without them, can she?'

Amy was mouthing 'I do?' at me.

'Won't take long, will it, darling?'

'No, just a couple of minutes,' Amy caught on.

'Right then, see you downstairs.'

We waited until they had gone and I told her what I wanted her to do.

'Find the Civil Aviation Authority site – it'll be caa something – and go to Aircraft Registration. See who owns a private plane registered G-AXRV. It should be listed. The "G" at the front means Great Britain. Just type in Alpha, X-ray, Romeo, Victor and see who pops up.'

'Do I need to know why I'm doing this?'

'No.'

We saw Ben and Shona out of the front door and Arthur produced two more mega scotches and we wandered back into the library.

'Can I ask you something, Arthur?'

'Certainly, dear boy, as long as it's not for money. There's none left, you know, but nobody believes me.'

'It's not about money,' I reassured him. 'It's those plans you've got upstairs.'

'Ah, so you are interested. You can see the possibilities too, can't you?'

'Sort of,' I said cautiously. 'I was just worried about whether you should actually have those plans here.'

'What on earth do you mean?'

'They are rather sensitive, aren't they? I mean, military secrets and all that . . . in the wrong hands . . .?'

He looked blank.

'I mean, have you had any sort of security clearance? An SC or gone through DV?'

'What are you talking about, my boy?'

'An SC is your basic Security Check – criminal record, security record and a credit check, of all things. That's for access to anything classed Secret. For Top Secret you go through DV – Developed Vetting, usually involves an interview with a couple of heavies from that building on the Thames you always see in the James Bond films. Those plans must have some sort of classification.'

I didn't think it necessary to go into CTCs – Counter Terrorist Checks – the next phase up. Arthur was befuddled enough.

'Good Lord, we don't bother about that sort of non-sense!' he snorted. 'Got the job from Rupert. He's my godson. I'm his godfather. If you can't keep things in the family, what sort of a state are we in?'

Chapter Eleven

Worm Action

By nine o'clock on the next bright, fine morning, we had cleaned another ten-metre square and had found a line of four stake-holes. I use the term 'we' in the royal sense of a supervisor. Things were going well. Joss looked as if she was pleased with me, so I looked pleased with myself.

'You're actually finding something,' she said. 'I'm not sure that's allowed. I might have to get my trusty trowel out and have a dig.'

'It's not what Arthur wants,' I said. 'From what Ben found yesterday, this is dating medieval, thirteenth or fourteenth century.'

'Is it anything substantial?'

'Doubt it. Looks like an isolated agricultural building, a few drainage gullies and this morning we've spotted these stake-holes – which look as if it might have been a sheep-pen, something like that. No Iceni silver coins, no Roman stuff.'

'But nearly all the finds so far have been Roman period.'

'Yeeees,' I drawled. 'Strange that, isn't it? Do you keep a context register to identify the various layers as they come off?'

'Sort of,' she said coyly. 'What I mean to say is: no. We keep notes but until yesterday we really only had two contexts: the cleaning layer from those squares you've hoed and a general Unstratified one, which could be things people picked up anywhere.'

'Like the spoil heap,' I said.

'Are you thinking what I think you're implying?'

She went all coy again as if I was making an improper suggestion. She was dressed all in black as she always seemed to be, the only variation was that her X-Wing Fighter Pilot baseball cap was back-to-front. It suited her. Coy suited her.

'Roman finds in the spoil heap, which is loose and on the surface. Roman finds in the cleaning layer of topsoil, which is loose and on the surface. Dig down under the surface – medieval finds. Go figure.'

'He's seeding the site?'

She was doing well to keep her voice down, conscious of the bat-like hearing abilities of the average digger when scandal is in the air.

'He has a big stash of pottery and assorted finds in his office,' I said with a smile, so that any digger watching us would think I was chatting her up, however far-fetched the very idea.

'But all that's washed stuff,' she said, thinking hard and tapping a forefinger against her chin. 'Some of it's even marked. Just stuff he's collected over the years. All the finds we've had have had to be washed. You can't fake two thousand years of encrusted mud.'

She had a point.

'Damn it, Holmes, that's positively elementary. Should have thought of that meself,' I said in what I thought was a fair imitation of Arthur. 'But hang on, has anyone really seeded the site?'

'What, you mean against Nighthawks? I don't think so.'

If there's any chance of a dig site being raided by treasure-hunters with metal detectors – and these days there's every chance now that they sell metal detectors for kids aged seven up – then the last job at the end of the day is seeding. This involves an unsuspecting volunteer staggering around with a box of small metal washers, casting them out by the handful like seed and looking like an illustration from a children's Book of the Holy Land. At night, the metal washers drive the illegal detectors crazy, giving off false signals. During the day, when they've sunk into the mud, they drive the legal detector operator crazy.'

'Yet wasn't my predecessor, Sebastian, put in hospital by a Nighthawk? Surely the first thing to do would be seed the site?'

'Nobody thought of it. As to what happened to Sebastian, you could always ask him.'

'I could?'

'He's out of hospital now and staying with his girlfriend at the university in Colchester. I've got her address somewhere, in one of the student residences.'

'I might just do that. I'll get the address from you at tea-break.'

'OK. Did you have a good time dining with Arthur last night?' she asked innocently.

'It was very interesting. Especially the food. Yes, that was – interesting. No, I'd go so far as to say a unique dining experience.'

Joss grinned, then started to flush slightly.

'I know I probably shouldn't mention it, but I am supposed to be the project manager,' she started heavily, 'and you may not have realized how thin the walls are in The Stables.'

I waited for her, my polite silence adding to her discomfort.

'It's just that . . . noise carries and . . . er . . . after you got back last night . . . Well, one or two people say they were woken up by noises coming from your room.'

She was looking at her boots by now and squirming. She was cute when she squirmed.

'I'm so sorry, we had no idea,' I said.

All we had actually been doing was re-scrunching Amy's dress, pulling it between us and twisting it as tight as we could to keep the fake Fortuny pleats in shape. Honest.

'I'll tell Amy she has to restrain herself. For the sake of the neighbours.'

*   *   *

202

Amy waltzed on to site wearing a white DKNY vest over a sports bra, the shorts and the pink socks again. She had the metal detector over her shoulder at a jaunty angle.

It was 9.45 a.m.

She was improving.

Throughout the day I mentioned in passing that I would have to go to Colchester or Ipswich to buy a few supplies. Ben agreed to keep an eye on things, though he seemed perfectly happy teaching Amy how to do a section drawing. I've seen Amy with a sketch pad and a pencil and she didn't need *that* much hands-on tuition.

Around three o'clock I slipped away from site and back to our room in The Stables, collecting a road atlas from Armstrong on the way.

Amy had printed off a page of the CAA's website which showed that the registered owner of Piper Super Cub G-AXRV was one Murray Hooper, with an address in Halstead, Suffolk. From the map there were three possible airfields at which he could be based, to the north-east, the east and the south-west of Woolpack. My plan was to see if he did his regular overfly this afternoon and note which way he headed home, trusting to luck that he wasn't on a training flight or going on to another job. That way I could catch him at his flying club or airfield, if not I could try his home. People are much happier to answer questions if you show an interest in their place of work.

I ran across Joss in the courtyard and asked her for Sebastian's address – and his surname, something rarely used among diggers. She said she had it written down in her room, so I followed her and stood in the sliding doorway as she flipped through an old Filofax.

Her room was spartan and organized. A pile of clothes – all black – were neatly folded on a chair, a pile of archaeology books stacked neatly next to the camp bed on which was a rolled-up sleeping bag, also black. The only really personal item was a poster sellotaped to the wall above the bed. It was a two-year-old events list showing a tour of Astral Reich, one of the least talented, but loudest, bands on the thrash-metal circuit. That and the Filofax left me with a mild sense of disappointment.

'Here we are,' she said, proffering a scrap of paper. 'He wrote it down. His surname is Smith but he's staying with Meryl Peters, a PhD student, in Flat 4 of Fleming House at the uni.'

'Thanks.' I pocketed the address. 'Have you seen Fifi today? I was wondering if she was feeling better.'

'No, I haven't. She seems to be keeping a low profile these days. Try her room, hers and Ben's, two doors down.'

I walked down the corridor and rapped on the door with my knuckles. There was no answer but as Joss was still in her room, I put my fingers to the door panel and slid it open.

Fifi and Ben had put their camp beds together, bless. (Amy and I had already discovered that it was impossible to roll from one to the other without tipping one of us on to the floor.) There were clothes everywhere and half-empty packets of Jaffa Cakes, even a couple of used tea bags staining the concrete floor. This was more like it, though there was no sign of the mysterious Fifi.

I was about to slide the door closed when my eye caught sight of a book which had fallen on to the floor and then had got kicked under one of the beds. I didn't have to go into the room, only bend at the knees slightly to see what it was.

Not many archaeologists carry a copy of the New Testament in their knapsacks, but it's probably not unknown.

I heard the Piper Super Cub before I saw it and had Armstrong throbbing with life by the time it was overhead. Once again he cruised the southern end of the site where the orchard disappeared into the fields of wheat, did one pass and then headed south-west.

That made it, if my guess was right, the airfield at a place called Wickfield Tye, about eight miles as the Piper Club flew, more like twelve by twisty country road. But it was a fine, warm, sunny day for a drive in the leafy lanes with the windows open and some hot samba/jazz fusion belting out at full volume.

The pilot didn't seem in a hurry to land as I caught sight of him at one point, flying a wide circle over where I judged Hadleigh to be. Maybe he was waving to the wife, or phoning her, telling her to put the kettle on. I've known it happen.

As it was we both timed our arrivals as if we'd planned them. I had found the gate in a hedge which had a board nailed to it reading: Wickfield Tye Flying Club (Private: No Unauthorized Admittance), and driven straight in, bouncing over the grass. G-AXRV had landed and taxied to a halt at the end of a rough runway, a few yards from the single hangar and a small prefabricated building which was probably the club house. There didn't seem to be anybody else around and, oddly, no vehicles. The pilot was kneeling by the starboard wheel, a hand on one of the wing struts, checking the tyre pressure or something. It was only when Armstrong was about ten yards from him that he looked up and a frown ploughed across his face. He was in his early fifties, thinning on top, and the fur-lined leather bomber jacket made him bulkier than he was.

'Murray Hooper?' I said as I killed Armstrong's engine and climbed out.

'Yes?' he said uncertainly, which was only to be expected after you've seen a black London cab bounce across a field in the middle of nowhere heading straight for you in broad daylight and you hadn't yet had a drink today.

'I wanted a word about aerial photography.'

If I had thought that would put him at ease, I was wrong.

'How did you get my name?'

'You are the Murray Hooper with the CPL, aren't you?'

It was a bluff, but a way of showing I knew what I was talking about. You need a Commercial Pilot's Licence these days if you are taking aerial photographs or glider-towing

205

or dropping parachutists. Gone are the days when your basic Private Pilot's Licence would do.

'Yes,' he said but he still wasn't pleased to see me.

'I checked you out with Civil Aviation after I saw your plane. Good little flyer those Super Cubs even though they've got a reputation as a tail-dragger.'

'It's only a problem in a cross wind.'

Now he was relaxing.

'You hiring?'

'Depends on the rate.'

'Between £80 and £120 an hour for the Cub depending on distance, plus my time. What's the job?'

'I need some overviews of an archaeological site and the surrounding area. You know, crop mark stuff. I'm sure –'

'Is this over at Woolpack?'

'Why yes, it would be.'

'Then go fuck yourself.'

'Do I take it you don't actually need the work at this point in time?'

'Just fuck off.'

He wasn't squaring up to me, just dismissing me. He turned his back on me and leaned inside the cockpit to retrieve something and I instinctively took a step backwards towards Armstrong, but when he emerged he held something shiny, metallic and square.

'You still here?' he said. 'Thought I told you to fuck off.'

'Is that your absolutely final offer?' I said.

He didn't bother to reply because he had seen what I was just hearing, another vehicle coming through the hedge and across the field towards the airstrip.

It was a Land Rover, the big Defender I had seen outside The Chequers, and it had the same driver, Hans Jankel. But if he was a gamekeeper, then I was Mortimer Wheeler and Hooper was Amy Johnson.

Jankel parked the Defender right across the front of Armstrong. Unless he moved first, I would have to reverse. I had forgotten one of my basic rules of life: always park pointing in the direction of the fastest getaway.

206

'Mr Hooper,' said Jankel as he climbed down from the driving seat.

He had a different suit on, a light grey pinstripe, possibly a Paul Smith, and brown brogues instead of wellingtons.

'What does our digger friend want?' he asked the pilot.

'Him? He's one of the arkies?' Hooper said in disbelief.

'Yes, amazing isn't it,' drawled Jankel, 'at his age. You'd have thought he would have known better.'

'Said he was after some aerial photography.'

Hooper handed over the shiny metal box and Jankel tucked it under his arm. Then he patted it.

'You should have offered him some of ours,' he said without a sliver of a grin. 'We've probably got one of you on here.'

'That's funny, I thought I specified no publicity. Who's "we"?'

'Please don't insult my intelligence,' said Jankel.

'Is there a queue for that?'

'Just go back and dig your little holes in the mud and remember that we are watching and waiting for you this time.'

'Is that a threat?'

'Yeah,' said Hooper, 'and what you gonna do about it? Call the police?'

He laughed, and for the first and only time that I saw, Hans Jankel smiled.

It was about six o'clock when I cut off the Colchester ring road and headed for the university, following the signs for 'Residences' and 'Overflow Car Park' though as we were now into the summer vacation, neither were doing what you might call gangbuster business.

I locked Armstrong and headed for where the car park ended and a concrete walkway with permanently-on overhead lighting began, snaking away into the distance into a honeycomb of concrete buildings dominated by the six main high-rise tower blocks which had been the future of student accommodation about forty years ago. Following the direction of the signposts, Fleming House was a fairly recent addition to the campus, away from the claustro-phobic central cluster and only two storeys high. Like most things at Essex, you could see them long before you got to them. Except, that is, for large white Transit vans with muddy wheels and UEFAU painted in large red letters along the side. Those, you find yourself walking by, inches away. Then you stop, walk six paces backwards and read, in smaller, official lettering on the back door: 'University of Essex Field Archaeology Unit.'

Having more or less tripped over the damn thing, I thought I might as well look it over but I didn't learn much. The mud on the wheels was still damp and the bonnet over the engine warm, so it had been out today. The inside was as filthy as you would expect a unit van to be but apart from a pair of socks writhing on the floor behind the driver's seat and a half-empty packet of Polo mints on the dashboard, there were no clues as to where it had been.

Not that I was in any way sure what I was looking for, or why I was even looking.

Flat 4 was on the second floor of Fleming House, through a glass fire door and up a flight of open-tread stairs. There was no name on the door, but from inside I could hear a radio playing a station ident commercial for SGR Colchester. When I knocked the volume was turned down before the door opened.

'Hi there. You'll be wanting Meryl, I suppose. What's she forgotten this time?'

I presumed this was Sebastian. He didn't look much like an archaeologist, more like an impoverished country vicar who was probably no more than twenty-five but looked to have been born at the age of forty-two. He had curly light brown hair, but what there was of it was disappearing over the top of his head and down his neck, a wisp of a Catweazle beard and he wore John Lennon glasses right down on the end of his nose. He had his right arm in a splint and tied across his chest with grubby white bandage cloth.

'Nothing as far as I know,' I said pleasantly. 'If you're Sebastian, it's you I've come to see.'

Sebastian gave me the once-over, checking out my regulation combats and boots.

'But you're a digger, right?'

'Yes, but not with the university unit. I'm up at Woolpack House in Suffolk.'

He curled a lip at that but I think on his thin, cadaverous face that was what passed for a smile.

'That's a fun dig, that one. Good luck.'

Sebastian made no attempt to invite me in but with his arm in a sling there was little he could do to stop me leaning against the door frame, casually of course, so that I got a good look at the flat.

Student accommodation had certainly changed since my day, when large screen televisions with satellite boxes, a DVD player and a VCR, not to mention a Bang & Olufsen midi-tower system definitely did not come as standard. The computer probably did these days, but maybe not the laser printer combined with scanner and fax modem. A good square yard of the carpeted floor was stacked knee-high with DVD movies, some of them still in their cellophane wrapping, and there was a separate pile, almost thigh-high, of videotapes including boxed sets of *Star Trek Voyager*, *Farscape* and *Aliens*. Even with a broken arm, Sebastian ought to get out more.

'Who is it, Seb?'

A short, but very wide, girl with streaks of wet black hair plastered to her face and shoulders loomed into view behind Sebastian. She was wearing an enormous white beach towel which was held in place by a tuck-and-fold over her ferocious bosom, but just to be safe she kept her elbows in to clamp the towel to her midriff.

'Another outcast from Woolpack, I think,' he said.

'Name's Roy. You must be Meryl.'

'And . . .?'

Sebastian spoke in the kind of sarcastic tone which would have earned him a second broken arm in some of the pubs I knew in Hackney.

'And I've sort of taken over your job there and as I was in Colchester, I said I would pop round and see how you were. People were asking how you were. Joss, Arthur, some of the diggers.'

'Hah! That lot!' He almost spat it out.

'Seb, dearest, where are the chocolates?' Meryl asked, seemingly oblivious to my presence in the doorway.

'I thought you took them into the shower, dearest,' Seb said without taking his eyes off me.

'Oh, here they are.'

She lumbered over to the PC and picked up a large open box of Belgian chocolates, cramming one into her mouth and agonizing over which one would follow it.

'Tell them I'm fine, very well, thank you. Not that any of them care. They probably had a good laugh about it.'

'You know what diggers are like,' I said.

'I wouldn't call any of them proper diggers. Strangest bunch I've ever met. Tell you the truth, I'm well out of it.' He paused and thought something over, then the tic in the corner of his mouth, which was probably a smile strangled at birth, reappeared. 'In fact I'm very *well* off out of it.'

'I understand you disturbed some Nighthawks. Is that right?'

His left hand went instinctively to his bandaged arm.

'Yes, that was probably it. I don't remember much before they hit me.'

'You were *vewy, vewy, bwave*, Sebby,' said Meryl. Most of her had managed to fit on the swivel chair in front of the PC console and it creaked alarmingly as she turned it to and fro through about sixty degrees while she perused the innards of the chocolate box. It was probably her version of aerobics.

'I was just wondering because I hear two diggers got into some sort of altercation about the same time and –'

'You mean the two Dans? They were idiots. We called them Dan B and Dan F to distinguish them. I don't know

210

what their surnames were. They'd only been on site about two days when they got pissed up in the pub and picked a fight with some local hardmen. Next day they legged it.'

'Nighthawk-type hardmen?'

'No, locals. Farmers. Those two thugs who own all the land in Woolpack. Double-barrelled name.'

'Scrivenour-Lindley?'

'Yeah, them. Anyway, what's all this got to do with the price of fish?'

'Did you tell the police about the attack on you?'

He bristled at that.

'Not that it's any of your business, but yes, I made a full statement.'

His voice had risen a half-octave, but I couldn't work out which nerve I'd hit.

'It's just that there doesn't seem to have been any Nighthawk activity since then and not much sign that they got anything. They always leave traces . . .'

'Yeah, well, maybe I scared them off. Now I've got dinner to cook.'

'Ooh, goody!' squealed Meryl.

'So even if you've nothing better to do, I have. Goodbye.'

He swung the door at me with a dramatic flourish, using his left hand. I just had time to put a steel-capped boot an inch or so in front of me and the door hit it and bounced back, smacking into his bandaged arm.

Sebastian let out a very satisfying howl.

I may not be much good at standing up to gamekeepers in flash suits or middle-aged pilots, but with half-crippled snotty supervisors I was wicked.

Instead of going straight back to Armstrong, I headed into the main university complex on a hunch and followed the signs saying 'Information' until I found a glass-fronted office with two uniformed security men sitting on plastic chairs, both reading the same evening paper.

I asked if they knew where the Archaeology Department was and one of them said yes, he did, but there wouldn't be anyone there now, it being seven o'clock in the evening, out of term time and the doors being locked at half-past six.

The other one, who did look up from his paper, noticed how I was dressed and asked if it would be Professor Roylance I was looking for.

I glazed over at that one, trying to remember where I'd heard that name before, until the guard clarified it by saying the Professor Roylance who was doing the dig down at the Hythe, whatever that was.

'Oh yeah, Simon, that's right,' I said, remembering the old newspaper cutting about Arthur.

'He'll be in the bar.'

'The university bar . . . ?' I said vaguely, putting out for more help.

'No way. The Students' Union. Beer's cheaper.'

The student bar was everything a student bar ought to be, except full of customers. It was below ground level, suitably dark and dingy, the carpets were sticky underfoot and the ash-trays smelled of stale beer. There were about a dozen customers in there and I checked them out after ordering a bottle of lager and no glass, although it was so gloomy in there I wouldn't have been able to see how grimy the glasses were.

I reckoned that at least three of them could have been professors, who seem to be getting younger every year, but only one was wearing rigger boots and 'Desert Storm' combat trousers. He was also the only one going through a fat ring-binder file of pre-printed sheets of paper – context sheets for a dig. That was the give-away, along with the fact that he had two pints of beer, one still full, and three packets of crisps on the table in front of him, even though he was alone.

'Professor Roylance?'

He looked up from his ring-binder, a biro poised in one hand, his other reaching for his beer. He was putting a series of ticks in the box marked 'Checks' on the context sheets.

'We're not hiring, I'm afraid,' he said. 'It's a summer school training dig for my undergraduates.'

'I'm not looking for work, I've got a job,' I said, feeling rather surprised to hear myself saying something like that. 'Is this the Hythe dig I've heard about?'

I pointed to the file with my bottle.

'Yes, we go down there every year. You know the area?'

'I'm not too sure what a Hythe is, let alone where it is.'

'It's the old dock area from when Colchester was a working port. Hythe, or rather "Hithe" with an "i", is Anglo-Saxon for a small "haven" – safe place to tie up on a tidal river. The Romans were there first of course, so there's plenty to find even if none of it is very spectacular.'

By this time I had sat down at his table and was on the point of helping myself to a packet of his crisps. Get an archaeologist talking about archaeology and you can almost steal their clothes. There is only one thing they like better and that is slagging off somebody else's dig or unit. That was the second part of my plan.

'Is Meryl digging with you?'

'Yes, she's supervising as she's one of my PhD students. You know her?'

'Only in passing. I've just taken her boyfriend's old job.'

He reached for his full pint. He was probably in his mid-forties with a long thin face and a neatly trimmed beard, but the beard couldn't hide the sallow complexion or curtain off his horribly stained and twisted teeth, which had come from a diet of crisps and beer and the fear of dentists which is endemic among diggers.

'Sebastian? Talk about falling on your feet! So you're at Woolpack House, are you?'

I had a feeling he'd forgotten the words 'You poor sod'.

'Can I get you more drinks?' I asked politely.

'Sure. Two pints of cooking bitter and some nuts would go down well,' he said reasonably without a trace of embarrassment.

When I returned with a tray, both his glasses were empty and the three crisp packets had been ripped open, flattened and weighed down by the ash-tray.

'So you're digging for Arthur Swallow, are you? You poor sod.'

'It's a temporary thing, not a serious career move.'

'Keep it that way. That man is a danger to himself and a disaster to archaeology.'

I wasn't surprised at Roylance's bitchiness, that was fairly par for the course in the digging business, but I had forgotten how secluded a world archaeology was, how cut off from the niceties and subtleties of real life it was. Academics, of course, are always slagging each other off but only an archaeologist, without an ounce of political skill, could have got to professorial level and still be willing to start in on a colleague to a complete stranger for the price of two pints of bitter and a packet of nuts.

'That's a bit harsh, isn't it? I'd have said harmless.'

The professor snorted into his beer.

'Stick around,' he said, 'and watch your back. How long have you known Arthur?'

'About three days,' I said.

'Ten years.' He pointed a finger at his own chest. 'No, more, maybe twelve. Jesus! And the fact that I haven't strangled him in that time shows what a wonderful human being I am.'

'I didn't realize he'd been in the business for so long.'

'He hasn't really. I first met him when he asked us to do some field walking around Woolpack. That was when his brother was still alive, so that dates me. Anyway, we didn't find much . . .'

'Was that when he found his famous coin mould?'

'Oh, that fucking thing! No, he'd already found that by pure dumb luck though you'd have thought he'd tripped over the Sutton Hoo burial from the way he went on about it. Needless to say, we didn't find anything to match Arthur's bloody coin mould, in fact we didn't find anything worth writing home about for the very good reason that there's nothing there.

'But that wasn't half the story. It turns out that these fields Arthur had us walking were actually owned by somebody else and Arthur hadn't bothered to ask permission. We got chased off by a bunch of thugs with shotguns and dogs and the university received an official complaint.'

He paused to drink half of one of his beers and pop open a pack of dry roasted.

'If I never saw the old fool again it would have been too soon,' he continued without prompting, 'but the bastard then turns up in my undergraduate class the next year. It was like he was haunting me.'

'Arthur was one of your students?' I had to suppress a laugh at the thought of Arthur being anyone's student.

'Twice,' said the professor with a sigh. 'When he failed his first year exams it was like the staff had got a pay rise here. Trouble was, about two years later, he comes back on the Diploma course in the Centre of Life-Long Learning and as far as I know he's still here. We just can't get rid of him, though we don't see him very much now he's got his own unit.'

Roylance finished his beer and slammed the glass down.

'What's it like working for the IRA?'

'Yeah, I had noticed that,' I said. 'Arthur has a thing about initials. Not always a good thing. But he actually leaves us alone pretty much on the dig.'

'That's because there's nothing to find there, or, to be more specific, nothing that Arthur wants to find.'

'He seems a tad obsessed by Boudica and a royal mint which probably never existed.'

'And if it did, what are the chances that it was there in his back garden all the time?'

'Same as winning the Lottery?' I couldn't resist it.

'Ha ha, very good. I was seriously worried when I heard

about his win, thinking he'd put it all into Iceni Rescue and start competing for jobs locally. Not knowing what the hell you're doing is no hindrance to putting in a silly bid for a job. The developers just go for the lowest figure, not the quality of the archaeology.'

'But has Iceni Rescue ever threatened your unit?'

'Not seriously, except for giving us all a bad name. I would say that, though, wouldn't I? But it's true. In fact I don't think Arthur has ever actually won a commercial job, thank God. If he's going to dig, he ought to stick to his own back yard.'

'He seems to be doing just that. No sign of any Boudican mint though.'

'You surprise me. Peanut?' He offered the packet but I waved it away and just sucked on my first beer, making it last.

'I don't think Arthur really thinks he's going to find a late Iron Age mint,' the professor said, staring into his glass.

'You mean even Arthur's not that stupid?' I prompted.

'Oh no, I mean he's *even more* stupid than that.' He leaned forward as if about to impart a deadly secret, but instead he belched loudly. 'Pardon. No, I think he has a hidden agenda.

'In all his time as a so-called student here, he was obsessed with the Boudica story. You know how that ended?'

'Badly,' I said automatically.

'For the Iceni, yes. Boudica wasn't captured – and surely the Roman historians would have mentioned it if she had been – she just disappeared after the last battle with the legions. The story goes that she took poison – her and her daughters – and were buried in a secret grave, the location of which remains unknown to this day. Not even those tossers on that *Time Trash* programme, or whatever it's called, would take on finding that grave as a challenge.'

'But Arthur has?'

'Even worse. He's determined to find it in his own back garden, but he'll never admit publicly that that's what he's looking for. Even Arthur realizes he'd be laughed out of court on that one. Finding that coin mould all those years ago, though, that gave him a cover story, didn't it? I mean, there might, just might, be some Iceni coins around that area – it's possible, though not with Boudica's face on them. Enough have been found in the area to make it almost plausible.'

'But the chances of finding Boudica's grave would be . . .'

'Exactly. Same as winning the Lottery *twice*. If Arthur Swallow ever said that was what he was looking for, he'd be a laughing stock.'

'But what makes you think he is?'

Roylance moved in on the fourth pint, before it got warm.

'Look, I've been pestered by Arthur Swallow off and on for over ten years. I've had to get him out of scrapes with the planning authorities, give a character witness statement once when he took a potshot at an aeroplane and I've had to talk to the press when he's made ridiculous statements. Now all that pales into insignificance compared to the pestering he gave me when he was a student here. But even that was nothing to his nagging when he'd won all that fucking money and was setting up his own unit.'

'He tried to pick your brains, did he?' I sympathized, all the time wondering if I could get away before I had to buy another round. I didn't mind that so much but his diet was beginning to work its way through his gastric system and the bar wasn't air-conditioned.

'With bare-faced cheek. He wanted to know everything from pay scales to Health and Safety legislation, planning regulations, even who our best customers were among the developers, but most of all he was desperate to get his Home Office Licence. In the end I helped him out just to see the back of him. The university never saw a penny of all that money, not a consultancy fee, not a grant, not a gift, nothing.'

'That would be a licence to excavate graves, right?'

'That's right. Arthur didn't really care about much else,

217

that was what he really wanted. I saw through it, of course. I knew he had convinced himself he'd got Boudica's grave somewhere under his cabbage patch, the daft old sod.'

'Ah well,' I said cheerfully, 'there's a first for archaeology. I'm working for a nutter. Who'd have thought it?'

'You should have talked to Sebastian before you took the job,' he said, swirling the remains of the beer in his glass. 'He'd have told you what a nutter Arthur is. Could have been killed. Oooh, excuse me.'

He had levered his buttocks off his plastic chair in order to let rip.

I lit a cigarette up quickly, a ready-made one. There wasn't time to roll one.

'You can't blame Arthur for some loony Nighthawk, though, can you?'

Roylance laughed at that. He laughed a lot. In fact he laughed so much he forgot to eat or drink anything for almost a minute.

'Nighthawks? At Woolpack House? They wouldn't lower themselves. All the regular detectorists know there's nothing there worth finding. Good God, man, check out their websites; they think the site's a joke and most of them know more about archaeology than Arthur Swallow ever will.'

'So who broke Sebastian's arm, then?'

He giggled some more and shook his head from side to side.

'Arthur did!'

It was dark by the time I hiked across campus to Armstrong and my stomach was telling me to stop ignoring it. I was in the process of pacifying it with thoughts of a quick Indian or Chinese meal or maybe fish and chips and then my brain reminded me that Amy was probably waiting back at Woolpack House feeling just as hungry and twice as mean. Although I wouldn't have put it past her to have rung our local pizza delivery service with an order, forgetting that it would take the guy on the scooter the better part of two hours to get to Woolpack, if he ever found it. Still, if it wasn't piping hot we got our money back.

I punched her name up on the memory of my phone, half expecting to see another message from my religious stalker, and it rang about ten times before she answered.

'Where the hell are you?' she shouted. She had to as something was playing what sounded like a medley of Slade's greatest hits in the background.

'On my way back. Where are you?' I shouted back.

'I'm in the pub. We couldn't wait for you.'

'We? You're with the diggers?'

'Certainly not. Me and my good friend Mrs Hawksbee are enjoying Ladies' Night down at the local. That's the local pub for local people.'

'Have you eaten?'

'Yes I have. Splendid country fayre cooked by local people in a traditional village local. Come and join us down at The Drovers' Arms. This is where the real people are.' She was speaking loudly for her audience, not me.

'You're in The Drovers?'

'Well, Mrs Hawksbee wouldn't be seen dead in that poof's parlour up the road, now would she?'

'If you say so. I'm on my way.'

Somebody said something to her and laughed and she laughed, then she came back on much quieter as if she had her hand over her mouth.

'Oh, and Angel . . .'

'Yes?'

'Punch it, will you. I can't take much more of this.'

I could hear the music from The Drovers before I turned the bend into the village, even above the throb of Armstrong. The lights were on and a blackboard was propped up against the open front door announcing 'Lady's Night All Drinks Half-Price Before 10 p.m.'

I checked my watch: 10.03.

Amy was at the bar and I was relieved to see she'd left the Fake Fortuny scrunched up in its bag. As it was she stuck out like a sore thumb in her Armand Basi butterfly-print shirt tucked into Dolce & Gabbana check trousers and wide leather belt. Even her work boots seemed to fit the ensemble and I wondered who she had got to clean them; but then I could hardly expect her to walk all the way down from Woolpack House in her Jimmy Choos, could I?

'Just in time,' she said, pecking me on the cheek, 'it's your round.'

'I thought it was Ladies' Night?'

'It is. And your point is what?'

I reached for my wallet. 'Is there anything to eat here?'

'Absolutely. The finest home-made country fayre. I saved you something. Fred!'

An elderly barman struggling with about three orders at once from the howling mob, who were mostly women and mostly over fifty, raised a finger at Amy and winked once.

'So what's everyone having?'

'I'm afraid I'm in with a bit of a crowd, well Mrs Hawksbee's crowd actually, but believe me it's been worth it. You think archaeologists gossip? Fucking amateurs. Try tapping in to the jam-making syndicate. Their combined age is about a thousand, and Christ does that make me feel young again!'

The white-haired Fred hobbled up to our end of the bar. You didn't have to ask to know that his feet were killing him.

'Yes, Amy? Same again?'

'Thanks, Fred love.'

'Right, that's a large brandy, two . . .' From somewhere behind him came the loud and unmistakable 'ping' of an industrial microwave. 'Oops, your dinner'll be ready.'

'Home-made country fayre, right?' I whispered in Amy's ear, though I didn't have to whisper as the jukebox was now on to Queen's greatest hits.

'It's what the locals eat,' she said with one of her dangerous smiles.

Fred reappeared in front of us holding a plate with a grubby bar towel. A raised rectangle of pastry sat in the middle of it oozing a watery brown liquid. At least he'd remembered to take it out of its tinfoil container.

'What's that?' I asked.

'It's a pie,' said Fred, pronouncing it 'poi'.

'What sort?'

'Meat flavour,' he said. 'It's a poi. But don't touch it for a bit, the plate's hot. Now, what about them drinks?'

'Elderflower wine all round? Or do the locals drink rough cider round here?'

'Get real,' said Amy. 'Two tequilas with orange, one with lime, two rum and Cokes, the large brandy – that's for Mrs Thurloe, she's got a cold – two bottles of Rolling Rock, an Ice Beer and a Bacardi Breezer.'

'You're not on the Bacardi Breezers, are you?'

'Not me,' Amy said, 'that's for Mrs Hawksbee.'

'Mrs Hawksbee drinks Breezers?'

'This'll be her sixth.' She saw I was surprised, so she corrected me.

'Not *our* Mrs Hawksbee. Mrs Hawksbee senior. Her mother.'

This I had to see.

We provided Mrs Hawksbee senior with a taxi home, even though she lived in the cottage exactly across the road from the pub, close enough for Armstrong to reach in a turning circle. I think she appreciated it, though, especially as it was a real black cab and, at the age of ninety-five with only the alcohol holding you up, you need all the help you can get.

The surviving Ladies' Night crew made sure she was inside safely before waving to us and disappearing unsteadily into the village night.

I turned Armstrong again and headed towards Woolpack House. It was after midnight and even though I wished for it very hard, Ray and Stephen's pub was shut, so I faced the prospect of a Marmite sandwich to fill my still complaining stomach.

'So what's the story?' I said over my shoulder.

Amy was lying across the back seat, her boots up against the window.

'Well, where do I begin? It's a cracker. Talk about scandal out in the sticks. Whooo! This could make a telly series.'

'How did you hook up with that mob anyway?'

'I was waiting for you to get back. Where the hell have you been anyway?'

'You tell me yours and I'll tell you mine.'

'Good, me first. I was hanging around the house, as you do, minding my own business, and anyway the door was open, looking at that ghastly painting of Octavia.'

'Who?'

'Octavia. Brother Gerald's wife. The bird in the uniform above the staircase. And I was trying to work out what she was wearing round her neck . . . I noticed it last night.'

'What, jewellery?'

'No it isn't, that was my point. Anyways, I was trying to get a closer look when Mrs Hawksbee caught me. She was packing in for the day and on her way down to this piss-up and we got chatting and she invited me along to meet her old mum, who knew *exactly* what it was, and you'll never guess. It was a –'

'Hang on a minute,' I said, squeezing the brake.

Ahead of us a set of headlights had just pulled out of the entrance to Woolpack House and were coming towards us. It definitely wasn't the Iceni Rescue Transit van, I could tell that from the shape of the headlights which were more round and lower. It had to be Arthur's personalized Jeep.

I slowed as it went by us, heading into the village. It was the Jeep with the canvas top up and I was as sure as I could be that it was Arthur driving.

Tracking his rear lights in the mirror, I slowed and did yet another U-turn and started to follow him.

'That was Arthur,' I said through the sliding partition.

'I want to see where he's going this time of night. Keep talking.'

Amy did so, and I kept following Arthur all the way back down the road to Colchester, the road I had driven up only a couple of hours before. Fortunately there were few other cars and no witnesses to see us. Then again, the sight of a World War II American Jeep being followed by a black London taxi was probably a regular event in the dark lanes of Suffolk.

Amy was still talking when he turned on to the Colchester ring road and for a minute or two I thought he was heading for the university.

Then he turned off at a roundabout following a sign saying 'Hythe' and I knew exactly where he was going, and why.

Chapter Twelve

Cut

Octavia Scrivenour had grown up in Woolpack with the Swallow brothers, playing the younger sister to Gerald, the older sister to Arthur. They were both in love with her and it came as no surprise when she married one of them.

Well, no surprise to the two Mrs Hawksbees who between them had been seeing to and doing for Woolpack House for something like three-quarters of a century. (Of course Mrs Hawksbee senior was not actually called Hawksbee, she was Mrs Tolley, it was her daughter who had married a Hawksbee, but Amy was trying to keep it simple for me.)

But 1944 wasn't a good year for a wedding. For a start there was a war on and both Gerald and Arthur Swallow were in it, Gerald already a serving officer, Arthur soon to be one. Their parents had died in 1942 within months of each other, leaving just enough money to bury them decently, and Woolpack House even then was in need of repair. Both brothers faced postings overseas, which both of them duly received: Gerald to Normandy and eventually Germany, Arthur to India and then Burma.

Octavia too was in the army, but stationed nearby on one of the staggering number of military airfields which dotted East Anglia. And there was the problem, for while she had only a few miles to bicycle from her native village to report for duty, it was as if she was entering a different universe. The shy, innocent and simple country girl was getting a taste of a faster, wider world of responsibility, danger and, above all, Americans.

It was the Americans who were to blame for 'turning her head' according to Mrs Hawksbee senior. They and their movies and their cigarettes and their chocolate and their nylons and their money and their dances and their flattery and their sheer energy. No sheltered country girl, bright as she was, could resist that sort of charm offensive.

Not that Octavia was a tart. Not a bit of it. Plenty were, but not Octavia. In a way it was a pity she did not become a tart because what she did do was infinitely worse.

She fell in love.

Gerald must have proposed to her by post. Whatever she was thinking, she agreed and the wedding took place in February 1944 while Gerald was home on forty-eight hours' leave. The reception had taken place in the very bar of The Drovers' Arms in which Amy heard the story. Arthur did not know about the wedding until afterwards and had never been known to set foot in the pub.

The village gossips were, later, divided on the issue of whether Octavia had struck up another relationship before or after the wedding. Whichever it was, with Gerald away she soon began to see far more than was seemly of a young American infantryman called Oscar B. Rivero, who compounded the sin of being American by being a Catholic as well.

For six months they were the talk of Woolpack, in fact the gossip spread as far as Groton and Kersey and, as is the way with such things, as the affair progressed they became more careless.

There was no doubt in Mrs Hawksbee senior's mind (or what was left of it, as Amy observed) that word somehow got back to Gerald. He returned on leave in September and after seven months of marriage, began to negotiate a divorce, or at least a formal separation.

It never happened. Octavia agreed to move away from Woolpack and took a posting in Ipswich, attached to an anti-aircraft battery. The day she took up the posting, Ipswich suffered one of the last air raids of the war.

The one they really felt sorry for, of course, was Arthur.

He returned to Woolpack in October 1944 for the first time since the wedding, to attend the memorial service in the local church – a memorial service for there was not enough left of Octavia for a proper burial. You couldn't help but feel for Arthur, as he'd been betrayed twice.

But then Mrs Hawksbee senior had also felt sorry for somebody else.

She never thought she would have, but she did. The sight of that poor young American, Oscar B. Rivero, standing at the church gates, not daring to go inside and certainly not invited, during that service. Well, that touched even her heartstrings.

Gerald and Arthur had grown up with Octavia – they had had a life with her, even if it was a child's life. Oscar had had only a few months, but they had burned him deep. As she had said, Octavia wasn't a tart. He must have meant something to her. It was all so sad, him standing there, climbing into a Jeep and driving away as the congregation filed out.

And Mrs Hawksbee senior was sure that the Swallow brothers bore him no malice.

Why else would Gerald have painted that picture which Arthur still had on display?

The painting of Octavia in her ATS uniform and wearing, round her neck, the metal dog-tag of one Oscar B. Rivero.

Serial Number: 37362818. Blood Group: A. Religion: Catholic.

'If you think about it,' I said as I eased off the accelerator so as not to dazzle the Jeep with Armstrong's lights, 'Arthur was betrayed three times.'

'He was?' said Amy dreamily.

'Once by Octavia, for choosing Gerald instead of him; once by his brother for moving in quick and marrying her when he wasn't around; and once again by Octavia when she left his brother for somebody else entirely.'

'It's still quite a lovely story in its way. All that wartime passion . . .'

'That's more or less what Arthur said, wasn't it? About a war not being a good time to get married.'

'I don't know why they say that. Seems like good training for marriage if you ask me.'

'Now, now, don't be cynical. Still, she must have been some sort of girl to have that effect on them all.'

'You're not wrong there, partner. She was a girl, not much over nineteen when she died. Mind you, none of them were that old.'

'And Arthur never married and I presume Gerald never remarried. Quite a knock-on effect. I wonder if Oscar B. Rivero ever found true love again?'

'They'll always have Woolpack . . .' she said, trying for an Ingrid Bergman voice and failing spectacularly.

'Per-lease,' I objected. 'That was one of the great movies. Let's not get carried away with this little hill of beans.'

'*This gun is aimed right at your heart*,' she said, segueing into her Humphrey Bogart which wasn't actually that dissimilar to her Ingrid Bergman.

'*My least vulnerable spot*,' I answered, making a pretty fair fist of a Claude Rains.

Up ahead, Arthur's Jeep turned off the A12, without signalling, towards Colchester.

'I've just bloody come from here,' I complained.

'Hey, yeah,' she remembered. 'Where have you been?'

So I told her how I had paid a social call on the pilot Murray Hooper and how we'd been joined by the Gestapo gamekeeper Hans Jankel, whom I *had* told her about but she'd forgotten. And, basically, how I had been politely asked to leave the airfield without finding out very much except that Hooper had a camera on board his plane and Jankel was paying for the film, or rather the Scrivenour-Lindleys who employed him.

'So, bit of a result there, eh?' she said sarcastically.

I ignored that and was about to continue when something struck me.

'Didn't you say that Octavia's maiden name was Scrivenour?'

'Oh yes, they're all related in Woolpack. It must be the country air. One of her sisters married a Lindley and they went all posh and double-barrelled.'

'So she was related to the local farmers?'

'Only vaguely. Maybe it was a half-sister or something. Mrs Hawksbee's explanation of the village's family tree was longer than a DNA chain and I switched off after a while. I think the current Scrivenour-Lindleys are great-nephews-in-law or something. It's a pretty tenuous link.'

'Could it explain why they don't like Arthur? A family feud over the long-lost Octavia?'

'Oh no. This generation have probably no idea who Octavia was or what she did. It's only of interest to us oldies in the provisional wing of the Women's Institute. Anyway, they've got it in for Arthur because he keeps straying on to their land looking for bits of Boadicea.'

'Roylance mentioned that. Said Arthur acted as if he owned the land around the house.'

'Roylance who?'

So I carried on, telling her first about my visit to Sebastian and Meryl which had resulted in me getting the door slammed in my face – although to be accurate, Sebastian slammed it on to his own arm.

'Not doing so well, so far,' Amy observed drily.

'Hang in there, because I'll be asking questions later. Just remember what I said about all that new audio-visual and hi-fi stuff in their flat. On their pay, most archaeologists don't get nearer to that level of equipment than the shop window of Dixon's on a Saturday afternoon.'

Then I told her what Roylance had been happy to tell me for the price of a couple of beers and a packet of nuts. About how Arthur had been a thorn in his flesh for over a decade, about how he seemed obsessed not with archaeology as such, but with archaeology *at Woolpack House* despite being repeatedly told there was nothing there.

And how, if any more proof were needed that he was one square short of a mosaic, he had clouted Sebastian with a spade.

'Sebastian had gone back to the site on a Saturday night after a row with girlfriend Meryl – probably over who ate the last Mars bar or something. Anyway, all the other diggers were away home for the weekend and it was dark when Sebastian turns up on his push bike which he'd taken on the train as far as Stowmarket.

'So he's fumbling around in the dark trying to get into The Stables when he sees somebody down on the site with a torch, poking around. Like an idiot he goes to investigate. It's not that he's brave, it's just that archaeologists are incredibly nosy. Even if it's a Nighthawk doing some illegal detecting, well, he might have found something interesting, mightn't he?

'Anyway, either the torch is turned off or Sebastian loses sight of it, because the next thing he knows is he's down on site being whacked around the head and shoulders with the business end of a spade. When he comes round, he's in the back of Arthur's Jeep being driven hell for leather into Ipswich and the hospital.

'Arthur had had the same idea he'd had – that there were Nighthawks around. Bit of luck that he'd picked up a spade and not his shotgun, really. Of course, Arthur's all over him saying how sorry he is and if it had to be reported to the police – which the hospital probably would anyway – couldn't they pretend it really had been unidentified Nighthawks who had given him a right good spading? Otherwise it would be very bad publicity for Iceni Rescue, make them a total joke.'

'So Arthur offered to pay Sebastian's medical expenses, right?' said Amy.

'Spot on. Five grand's worth. How did you guess?'

'That's what I would have done. How did this Roylance bloke know all this though?'

'The girlfriend, Meryl, is digging with him here in Colchester. All that loot to spend on new gear was too much for her. I told you, diggers just can't keep their mouths shut when the gossip is juicy enough. Probably the only diggers in the country who don't know by now are the ones at Woolpack House.'

We were coming up to a roundabout and the road sign saying 'Hythe'.

'I know where he's going,' I said.

The Jeep negotiated the roundabout, one of those double mini-roundabouts that the planners think will slow down traffic, and disappeared down a hill. We followed, turning through one of the older quarters of the town until we were running along the dock quay, the river somewhere on our left and, with the tide out, well below us. The Jeep continued even after the street lights had ended, passing a scrap yard and a boarded-up pub until it stopped by a tall aluminium fence.

I had Armstrong's lights off before the Jeep's, flipped him into neutral and coasted to a halt in the shadows. There was enough moonlight to see Arthur climb out, sling a rucksack over his shoulder and turn on a torch. As my eyes adjusted, I could make out signs tied to the fence at intervals of about ten feet. They warned: 'DEEP EXCAVA-TIONS – KEEP OUT'.

But as with most digs, the fence panel which acted as a gate was held together with just a piece of rope. Arthur was inside within seconds and his torch beam flashed like a light sabre in the dark, then disappeared.

'You going in after him?' Amy whispered in my ear.

'No need,' I said.

'What's he up to?'

'He's Nighthawking. This is Professor Roylance's site and Arthur is lifting whatever he can carry.'

'Why?'

'So he can plant it out at Woolpack House. That was what he must have been doing when Sebastian disturbed him.'

'I'll be damned,' she breathed on my neck.

'Oh, I should think so,' I said.

* * *

We left Arthur to it and headed back up the road to Suffolk. Amy was snoring quietly before we left Colchester and didn't wake until I had parked Armstrong behind The Studio.

We tiptoed across the gravel to The Stables and grabbed toothbrushes and towels then tiptoed back to the Mobile Thrones block. When we were back in our room and struggling into sleeping bags, Amy whispered:

'It's very quiet, isn't it?'

'It's very late. We'll be expected to be up and about in four hours.'

'Bugger that,' she said, but kept her voice down. 'I mean, it's *too* quiet. It's like they're not here. There's no snoring, no farting, no sex sounds.'

'Most of them sleep alone,' I hissed.

'So what's your point?'

'Where would they go? Clubbing?'

She whispered something else, something about the van not being where it was usually parked, but by then I was drifting off to sleep, whatever the others were doing.

I had it all sussed out. I would get hold of Rupert and arrange a meeting. Better still, Rupert would ask us out to dinner. There was a Ghurka restaurant in Colchester; that would be nice. Even better, Rupert wouldn't bring Mother along. I would tell him about Arthur's little scam, importing his own 'finds' and the almost certainly accidental clobbering of Sebastian. Rupert would know what to do: take the old boy on one side and give him the for-the-good-of-the-family-name speech, suggesting in no uncertain terms that it was now time to hang up his trowel and tend to his rose bushes. Whilst he was at it, Rupert ought to get the plans of the new garrison back before they fell into the wrong hands. Arthur, realizing his guilty secret was out, would of course go quietly. Rupert would pay for the meal, tell us how grateful he was, and I would make him promise to keep Mother happy and, above all, at least fifty miles from London.

Cue happy ending as Amy and I fly back to civilization to the tune of 'Ride of the Valkyries' in one of Rupert's army helicopters.

Then I woke up; but somebody was playing 'Ride of the Valkyries'.

Or rather some thing: Amy's phone on the charger which she'd plugged in and left on the floor between our two camp beds.

She was struggling with the zip on her sleeping bag but I thought, hey, it's her phone and I ducked back down inside Hemingway. The phone stopped ringing before she got to it but I knew that in about five minutes it would ring again to tell her she had a message.

Before it did something heavy hit me in the kidneys, then something landed next to my head. I risked a peek.

'I said it's half-past seven, you slug, you,' said Amy.

She was still lying in her bag on her bed but she'd managed to reach both my boots to throw at me and now she was reaching for hers.

I checked my watch and found she was right. I was up and dressed before her message service called back. All she had done was stretch her arms and yawn and that seemed a bit of an effort. Still, she hadn't had her coffee yet. Bless.

I half expected the digging crew to be out and digging or standing around in a surly mood threatening mutiny. In fact they all seemed to be running as late as I was, fighting over kitchen space to make cups of tea and queuing in Mobile Thrones for the showers and the washbasins. Only Jason and Cornell, the long-haired and strangely quiet American, were actually ready to go on site, standing by the metal tool shed, loading wheelbarrows with hoes, mattocks, buckets and kneeling mats.

Jason threw me a mock salute, Cornell merely glanced briefly in my direction. Rory and Gregory grunted a 'Good morning' each as they shuffled by, Kali just grunted at me. Shona didn't even grunt. At least sweet little Jude managed a smile.

232

She was in the kitchen with Ben, pouring muesli into a bowl from a large square plastic tub.

'I think we've all had trouble waking up this morning,' she said.

'Too many late nights,' I said, reaching for the coffee.

Jude blushed, snapped the lid on the tub and squeezed it back into the fridge.

'You had one yourself,' said Ben. He was making himself a Marmite sandwich and avoiding eye contact, which made me think that the jungle gossip drums had already started beating about what Amy and I had been up to.

'You can say that again,' I said, laying it on thick. 'It was Ladies' Night down at The Drovers and Mrs Hawksbee was leading the community singing.'

'Really?' He seemed rather relieved.

'I kid you not. God knows how Amy got roped into that one. I don't recommend them, in fact I think they should come with a health warning.'

'I'll take your word for it,' he smiled around the corners of his sandwich.

'Is Fifi around?' I asked casually and I was sure I saw him bristle.

'She's up and about somewhere. Probably in with Arthur.'

I suspected that Arthur was more likely to be catching up on his beauty sleep, but I didn't say anything.

'Joss?'

Ben visibly relaxed when I changed the subject. He *had* been bristling when I had mentioned the mysterious Fifi.

'Haven't seen her this morning,' he said.

'Me neither,' said Jude through a mouthful of seeds. 'The van's gone though, so she's probably gone to pick something up somewhere.'

'You're being summoned,' said Ben.

'Huh?'

I swung round to look out of the window. On the steps of The Stables, Amy was waving at me like she

233

was guiding a plane down on to the deck of an aircraft carrier.

'It's coming, it's coming,' I grumbled, sloshing coffee into two mugs.

Jude reached into the fridge she had been leaning against and handed me a plastic litre bottle of milk.

'Thanks,' I said, passing it back to her. 'Got to run. She's unbearable until she's had her caffeine fix.'

'Has she tried raspberry leaf tea?'

'Not at this time in the morning.'

Amy made no move to come towards me as I carried two mugs across the courtyard, she just stood in the doorway of The Stables, weighing her phone up and down in her right hand.

'What's up?' I asked. Something clearly was, as she slopped coffee over her bare feet when she took the mug I offered her. She held up her phone.

'That was West Hampstead police station. The house was broken into during the night. Somebody has to go and see what's missing. You'll have to go.'

'Why not you? It's your house.'

It came out harsher than I had intended. All I meant was it really was Amy's house and she had a far better idea than I had what was in there. When I'd moved in I had come with a supermarket carrier bag – and I'd had trouble filling that.

'I can't handle this sort of thing. It's a violation, somebody crawling all over my things . . .'

Her lower lip started to quiver so I slipped an arm around her waist.

'OK, I'll go. It won't be as bad as you think, trust me.'

That got a smile.

'Trust *you*?'

'Hey, I'm good at insurance claims.'

She hit me gently with her phone.

'Ring me soon as you get there. Promise?'

'Sure. You'll be OK here?'

'Find me something to dig. It'll take my mind off things. Check the computer as well.'

'How do I do that?'
'Check that it's still *there*, Dimmo.'

I asked Ben to take charge for the day and to tell Joss when she turned up. I did try to tell Arthur that I would be disappearing for the day, but Mrs Hawksbee (junior) seemed to be the only one up and about in Woolpack House.

After taxiing her mother home last night I was flavour of the month, so she was full of sympathy when I explained what had happened and promised to tell Arthur as soon as he surfaced. She bit her lip and strangled a tea-towel in an effort not to tell me that that's what you get for living in a big, bad city like London.

It took me nearly three hours to get back to that big, bad city, or at least Hampstead.

From the outside of the house, nothing looked amiss. Amy had told me that the alarms had gone off around 2 a.m. and with the system we have, which has a built-in time delay to allow for accidental setting-offs, a few minutes later an alarm would have sounded in West Hampstead police station. The cops had admitted, after Amy pressed them, that it had been forty minutes before a patrol car had stopped by.

There were some good reasons for this. For a start, 2 a.m. would be just about the time the police changed shifts, so it was a good time to catch them on the hop. Then there was standard operating procedure when it came to alarms going off in the night. Usually the cops will wait until they get at least three complaint calls from neighbours before they act. (With car alarms it's ten.) They didn't get them from our neighbours for the simple reason that the alarm boxes on the side of the house and the garage had been injected with large polymer foam filler, the stuff which you squirt out of a long tube which expands and hardens to fill large cracks in a wall or a foundation.

The boxes were not difficult to get at because they themselves were alarmed and anyone trying to open and disconnect them would have triggered a high-pitched electronic screaming. Unless they were muffled by foam filler which then set as hard as concrete, that is.

So our burglar could have had at least half an hour undisturbed in the house and had even had the decency to close the doors on his way out, which was only fair as he'd broken both of them.

The front door of Amy's house works on an airlock system of a double door with keypad locks and closed-circuit camera to vet visitors. Our burglar had taken out the alarm and then gone in fast and hard, jamming something sharp into the door frames then inserting a car jack or pressure pad and levering the locks until they snapped.

When the police had finally turned up, they had done a brief sweep of the house just to make sure our guest had gone. They had also noted that the CCTV did not have a recording facility so our intruder did not appear on videotape. As this was clearly an oversight on our part, we had only ourselves to blame. It hadn't occurred to them that a thief bright enough to disable the alarms and get through double doors so quickly, would have the security videotape at the top of his shopping list.

The investigating officers had left strips of Police Aware white and blue tape across the locks (virtually an open invitation to passing schoolkids or dishonest milkmen) and gone back to the station to try and track down Amy through the office number she had left with them. Eventually they had found a security guard there, probably an ex-copper, who was prepared to give out her mobile number. In a way it was quite impressive: six hours, roughly, from being burgled to knowing you've been burgled. That was Hampstead for you. In Hackney, people can go for months without realizing they've been turned over.

I was almost grateful for the Police Aware tape because it reminded me that there had been a break-in. Nothing else did. For the life of me I couldn't see anything missing or even disturbed. I checked the obvious first – the wine rack, then the TV, VCR, PC and the other usual sets of initials – and they were all in place. So was the fridge, the dishwasher, the washing machine and the tumble-dryer and I felt foolish for even going to look.

Upstairs – and by now I was acting like a burglar, checking behind doors, measuring every step – I examined Amy's jewellery collection in some detail but was honestly no wiser. I hadn't a clue if anything had been taken, although I knew there was nothing there which could not be replaced. Neither of us had any family heirlooms or really expensive trinkets and neither of us kept large amounts of cash in the house (well, not this one in my case).

Getting desperate now I checked the dirty laundry basket and Amy's two underwear drawers, just in case we had a pervert burglar on our hands. Then I checked my own underwear collection, which took up the corner of one drawer, just in case we had a really sick pervert prowling the neighbourhood. Nothing. Or nothing missing that I could see.

There was nothing left to check except the one place I had been naturally avoiding; the richest part of the house, the most costly per square foot of space, the mother lode. Amy's wardrobe.

I took a deep breath and pulled open the doors and my mobile rang, scaring me half to death.

'Are you home yet?'

'Just.' I sat down on the bed to recover, still scanning the contents of the wardrobe to see if I could see anything missing, a tell-tale space where a hanger should have been, an Armani label where there should have been a Lacroix, a MaxMara out of place.

'And?'

'The bad news is we're going to need a new front door. The good news is nothing seems to be missing.'

'Nothing?'

'Nothing I can spot. Can you remember what was in your wardrobe, going from left to right?'

'Don't be ridiculous. Check everything again before you ring the West Hampstead station. Ask for an Inspector

Hood and get an incident number off him for the insurance just in case.'

'Goodness, I'd never have thought of that,' I said drily, but it bounced off her.

'Is there any mess, have they done anything unspeakable on the floor or in the bed?'

I stood up quickly at that and looked around.

'No, we seem to be OK on that score.'

'No graffiti or damage?'

'Not that I didn't do,' I said honestly. I heard her sigh with relief. 'How's the dig going?'

'Fine, fine. Ben's showing me how to find an edge. It's another pit, we think.'

'You're getting into this, aren't you?' I said, relaxing back on to the bed. 'That's how you tell the professionals from the amateurs. Ask an amateur what they've found and they'll say: pottery, charcoal, flints . . . '

'. . . but a real digger will say an edge, yeah, I know. You staying up there?'

'Only to talk to the Plod and get somebody in to secure the door.'

'Get somebody decent, will you, not one of your mates from the back bar of a Hackney boozer.'

'Of course,' I lied, knowing I had Duncan the Drunken's number memorized.

'And you're sure nothing's missing?'

I lay back on to the pillows, making sure my Transporter boots hung over the edge of the duvet cover.

'Positive. Maybe he was spooked or just took one look at our record collection and decided to have an early night. Apart from the doors being forced there doesn't seem to be a single thing out of place.'

She said something else, but I missed it, because there *was* something out of place.

'What?'

'I said don't forget to get a report number off the cops. And call me when you're on your way.'

'Sure thing. Will do. See yer.'

I fumbled, distracted, for the END button.

It's always the little things, isn't it?

When I had gone to Stuart Street Fenella had given me a pile of mostly junk mail which had arrived since my last visit. There was a credit card bill addressed to 'Mr M. Angel', a bank statement for a 'Mr R. Maclean' and several mail order offers of credit or insurance for 'A.M. Fitzroy' – the usual stuff, most of which would be destined for the recycling bin.

In the haste to collect Amy's shopping and trek off to darkest Suffolk, I had just put the whole pile down on top of the bedside chest of drawers, which I was raiding for clean socks, and then forgotten about them.

They had been moved. Not far, but they had been picked up and put down and, if I needed confirmation, one of the envelopes had slipped down between the drawers and the bed.

How could I be so sure? Because there was no way I would have left Mr R. Maclean's bank statement on top of the pile where Amy could find it. Absolutely no way, drunk or drugged would I have done that. There are limits.

But there it was, on top of the pile.

It was still unopened, but the name was clearly visible in the plastic window of the envelope.

And the address at Stuart Street.

We hadn't been burgled.

I was being stalked.

Downstairs I rang Duncan the Drunken from the house phone and got him at his garage.

I asked him if he could come over to Hampstead right away and fit a padlock to the front door. He said it would cost. I said I expected nothing less. He said 'right away' would cost more, so would 'Hampstead'. I told him not to push it or I'd tell his wife Doreen about the Work Experience girls. He said he was on his way.

I had to look up the number for West Hampstead nick, although Amy probably thought I knew it off by heart, dialled and asked for Inspector Hood.

While I was waiting to be connected I noticed that the answerphone had no messages. None. Zero. Nada. Now that was a first. Four days away and no messages? And I hadn't noticed Amy using her mobile in Suffolk. Had she been fired, excommunicated or, worst of all, gone out of fashion?

'DI Hood,' said the voice in my ear.

I explained who I was, where I was phoning from and what I had found, which was, basically, nothing.

'So, nothing stolen, no damage apart from the doors and no vandalism?'

'That about sums it up,' I said. 'Strange, isn't it?'

'But you'd still like an incident number for the insurance claim?' he said. He knew the game.

'For the doors. Forced entry, new alarms, that sort of thing.'

'Of course, sir. Has anything like this happened to you in the last twelve months?'

I'm not sure why they do, but it's a question they always ask these days. So I'm told.

'No, nothing at all.'

'And your wi . . . partner . . . Miss May? Anything similar happened to her?'

Where was he going with this?

'No, absolutely not.'

She hadn't been making dodgy insurance claims, had she? No, she'd have told me; wouldn't have been able to keep it to herself.

I wasn't nervous, I just felt like a cigarette.

'So this has nothing to do with the Restraining Order?'

What fucking Restraining Order?

'She's taken out a Restraining Order?' I tried to keep my voice calm.

'I have a cross-reference on my computer for an Order

taken out on behalf of Beadle Properties of Oxford Street, but also including your address in Hampstead.'

Beadle Properties owned her offices, I knew that, but what the hell was going on?

'This Restraining Order,' I said carefully, 'it's not on *me*, is it?'

There was a silence long enough for me to drag deeply until my cigarette was finished.

'You are in contact with Miss May, aren't you, Mr Angel?' he said in his best 'I'm on duty' voice.

'Of course I am. I was with her this morning when you rang and told us about the alarms going off. She couldn't face coming so I did and I'm here now, ringing you like you asked her.'

'And where exactly is Miss May at the moment?'

I heard him tapping into a keyboard, taking notes.

'She's at a place called Woolpack House in the village of Woolpack in Suffolk. You've got her mobile number, call her.'

'Is she there on holiday, sir?'

'We're *both* there, together. On an archaeological dig if you must know.'

'What, like that thing on the telly, the *Time Travellers*?'

'Yes, exactly like that. Now who's this Restraining Order against?'

He paused long enough for me to light another cigarette.

'I'm not sure I should say, sir, as you're not directly involved with the case.'

I breathed deeply and exhaled slowly.

'Look, when you spoke to Amy this morning did she tell you it would be me coming back to London and checking in with you?'

'Yes, she did.'

'And you accept that I live here with her?'

'Well, yes.'

'And this property is specifically mentioned on the Order?'

241

'So it says on the computer, that's why it was flagged up when the alarms went off.'

'So why can't you tell me who the Order is against?'

'There could be civil liberty issues here, sir.'

'Yes – *my* civil liberties!' I lowered my voice. 'Look, the Order was granted by a court, right?'

'Of course.'

'So it must be in the public domain and therefore you can tell me.'

'I'm not sure about this, sir. I might have to take advice –'

'And I might have to look up the number of the *Hampstead & Highgate Express* so I can tell them how long it took your lot to respond to the alarm and how you left the scene unsecured with the doors busted open.'

'We don't have the manpower . . . Oh, fuck it. It's somebody called Keith Flowers.'

That stopped me in my tracks.

'I've never heard of anybody called Keith Flowers.'

'Well, that's the name on the Order,' said Hood, then added belatedly, 'sir.'

'It means nothing to me,' I said honestly. 'Where does he live?'

'Now *that* I really can't tell you. Look, sir, can I suggest you have a serious talk with your –'

But I had hung up.

I needed time to think, to plan, to consider my options, to put myself in the right frame of mind to take cool, calm decisions.

'Who the fuck is Keith Flowers?' I screamed down the phone.

'Oh, shit,' said Debbie Diamond.

As I was driving through Camden Town I saw Duncan the Drunken driving his flat-back tow truck on the other side of the road, heading for Hampstead. I tooted the horn and waved at him but he didn't see me. Why should he? I was driving a cab.

Debbie Diamond had told me that Keith Flowers was the 'toerag' she'd referred to when I had called and caught her off guard a few days before. He was 'some low-life' who had been haunting the offices on Oxford Street and had tried to get in to see Amy more than once. He had even tried to have a go at her when she was leaving one night.

Now I remembered. I had been sitting in the back of a real cab playing with my newly acquired Zippo lighter and had watched as the shopping plaza's security guys had manhandled a tall, gaunt figure in an overcoat out of Amy's way. An Amy who had been trying very hard not to look like Amy.

And I had seen him round the back of the offices when I had gone to collect Amy's BMW.

Why hadn't she said anything?

'She didn't want to upset you,' Debbie Diamond had said. 'Thought it would sound really *weak*, you know, dead *girlie*, if she complained about some weirdo in a trench coat following her around. Actually, she thought you might laugh.'

'As if I would,' I had protested.

Actually, the Dreaded Debbie seemed more concerned about the fact that she'd ratted on Amy after solemn promises to keep me out of the picture than she was about our break-in. I had told her I would keep quiet if she did. Maybe the two things weren't connected. I was sure Amy would have told me in her own time, just needed an opportunity. Amy had quite enough on her mind at the moment. It wouldn't be fair to upset her, would it?

Not before I had a chance to strangle her.

I did one run down Stuart Street – just another taxi on the cruise – and nothing out of the ordinary, so I turned round and parked right outside Number 9.

From Armstrong's boot I took a long, four-battery rubber torch and tucked it into the right cargo pocket of my trousers, just in case. I doubted very much if our

Hampstead intruder was hanging around inside, but it was better to be safe than in hospital.

There again, I might need the torch to find the bits of him Springsteen had left under the furniture.

No sign of forced entry on the front door: good sign. No noises inside, house empty: so far, so good.

Up the stairs and still nothing. Outside the door of my flat, which still looked intact: time to exhale.

'Talk of the devil.'

'Jesus!'

Fenella was on the landing outside her flat, wearing pyjamas again (frogs this time), her head on one side looking at me quizzically.

'Why are you holding that torch like that?' she asked.

I lowered it slowly, trying to think of a good answer.

'Just checking the . . . er . . . the . . .' I stumbled.

'Don't worry, I've fed Springsteen this morning.'

'Oh, right. Thanks. Good. Won't need this then, will I?'

I put the torch away sheepishly.

'You haven't had any visitors or any odd callers this morning by any chance, have you?' I tried to make it light.

'No,' she said huffily. 'Some of us have been trying to catch up on some sleep, those of us who work for a living on night –'

'You said "Talk of the devil,"' I shot at her. 'When you saw me. Why did you say that?'

'Because, Mr Me-Me-Me, I actually was talking about you, but half an hour ago, on the telephone.'

'Who to?'

'Shouldn't that be "To whom?" Don't look at me like that. I don't know his name, he didn't say. At least I don't think he did. Just wanted to know if you were around. And Amy.'

'Amy?'

'Yes, Amy. He specifically asked if she was with you. Why are you looking at me like that?'

'And you told him we'd gone on an archaeological dig in Suffolk, didn't you?'

'In Woolpack, right? I got it right? Don't bang your head against the wall like that, you'll hurt yourself. And why are you dressed like a stormtrooper anyway?'

'This is what diggers . . . Oh, sod that. He rang *here*, right?'

'Yes.'

'Have you used the phone since? Has anyone else rung?'

'No, I've been trying to sleep since . . . What are you doing?'

I was jumping down the staircase and diving for the phone on the wall by the door before it could ring. I made it and yelled at Fenella to get me a pen. She moves quite quickly when you shout at her.

When I had the top off and my cigarette packet ready to write on, I dialled 1471. The disembodied voice told me that an 0207 number had called at 1234 hours. I scratched the number down and pressed 3 for redial.

'Hello? St Chad's.'

Well, that was what it sounded like.

'Excuse me?'

'St Chad's Hostel. Who is this?'

It was a man's voice, clipped and businesslike.

'Could you tell me your location, please?' I waffled.

'St Chad's Hostel, Chadwell Heath. What do you want?'

'I'm trying to speak to Keith Flowers,' I said, crossing my fingers.

'I'm sorry, but you'll have to leave a message. There are no direct lines to our residents.'

'Is Keith there?'

'I'm sorry but we cannot give out that sort of information. Who is this, please?'

What sort of hostel was it that wouldn't . . . Oh, bugger.

'This is Inspector Hood, CID at West Hampstead,' I said, slapping a hand across Fenella's mouth which had just fallen open. 'I'm trying to trace Keith Flowers' movements over the last few days.'

245

'I'm sorry, Inspector, you should have said. We have to be careful, you know.'

'That's quite understandable. If you'd like to ring me back, the number is –'

'No, no, that's fine. My name's Roberts, I'm Warden here. It was Keith Flowers you wanted to check on, was it?'

'That's correct, it's just routine.'

Fenella was biting me gently to indicate that I could take my hand away.

'Yes, of course it would be. Today is the day, isn't it?'

'It is?'

'The end of his month with us. He was discharged today at noon.'

'He's gone? Where?'

'Well, of course he's gone. He hung around for half an hour or so saying goodbye to people then he left. He's got a job down in Cardiff, I understand, with some company that backs books for libraries. He was no trouble while he was with us. Few rehab prisoners are, but he didn't strike me as the sort who was looking to go back inside.'

I let all this sink in slowly. Warden Roberts must have thought I was taking notes.

'So Flowers has gone to Cardiff? Today?'

'That's what he said and all his paperwork seemed to be in order. Social Services down there have found him a place to live and have a copy of his offer of employment.'

'I see. Can I get back to you if I have to, Mr Roberts? I don't have the file in front of me at the moment.'

'Of course you can. Happy to help. It's not about that car, is it?'

'Which car would this be?' I asked lightly.

'That bright red thing he turned up in this morning. A BMW it was. Looked fairly new. Said it was a present from a friend, but of course you never really know, do you?'

After I had said goodbye and broken the connection,

I smacked the earpiece of the house phone into my forehead. More than once.

'Bugger, bugger, bugger, *bugger!*'

'What's wrong now?' asked Fenella, exasperated.

'I forgot to check the fucking garage.'

Chapter Thirteen

Skelly

I stopped at a garage to fill Armstrong with diesel and my stomach with a cold sausage roll, a Mars bar and a can of 7-Up and headed over to Wanstead to join the A12 for another charge up into East Anglia.

At a set of traffic lights my mobile bleeped at me: a message not a call. It was time for my Bible class.

The text display just said: 'REV. 2:20'.

I didn't even bother trying to reply, I just threw the phone on to the dashboard.

I had a stalker with a religious bent, or at least somebody who had looked up all the angel references in the Book of Revelations just to niggle me. I didn't think that knowing where I lived or worshipping the beast had any direct relevance to me or was any sort of coded message. Not one that made sense anyway. It was just that the Book of Revelations has got loads of angels in it. Wait until they got to the bit where the seven angels all blow their trumpets. Surely they could find something suitably apt there.

Amy had a stalker, but she'd refused to show me hers when I'd shown her mine. This one was serious enough to go to court over, with justification if the guy could find out where Amy lived, break in there, find my address and then calmly drive off in Amy's BMW. Finding the phone number of Stuart Street would have been easy. I'm not in the residential phone book and I'm not on the Register of Electors for North Hackney (or anywhere else) but anyone can look up Number 9 on the electoral roll in the local post office and find the names of the other residents, two of whom are listed in the phone book. A bit of blag on someone as easy as Fenella and he knew exactly where we were and what we were doing.

Which was, in truth, messing about on a pointless dig for a sad old man who didn't even have more money than sense any more, hadn't got a clue what he was looking for and had no scruples about forging the archaeological evidence when he couldn't find any of his own.

At least things couldn't get any worse.

The phone rang and this time it was a call. The display showed that it was Amy calling me and I guessed that Debbie Diamond's nerve had cracked and she'd told Amy that I knew about Keith Flowers, so I steeled myself to whatever pathetic excuses she was going to come up with.

'Angel, whereabouts are you?'

She didn't sound at all apologetic and not in the least pathetic.

'On the A12, heading back,' I said.

'Get a move on, would you? You might be needed.'

I was about to point out that it was she who had sent me up to London but I could tell from the tone of her voice that now wasn't the time.

'What's up?'

'We've found a body and Arthur's gone totally apeshit over it.'

I was on a straight patch of the A12 south of Chelmsford – on the route the Emperor Claudius had marched with his invading legions and, going the other way, the road Boudica and her war party had taken to torch London – when the phone rang again.

It was Amy again. No doubt she'd forgotten something she had to tell me.

'And another thing,' she started straight in, 'your friend Joss. She's gone missing.'

*   *   *

My imagination had plenty of time to run riot over what I might find waiting for me at Woolpack House. I even tuned in to the local radio stations for warnings of Suffolk being cordoned off, incidents of civil disobedience, riot or war. At the very least, from what Amy had told me, I expected a scene of armed camps, dug in and glaring at each other across the site, and I wasn't far wrong. But they couldn't even do that seriously at Woolpack House.

By mid-afternoon the sun had really got out, and if we had been digging, it would have been T-shirts and sun-glasses weather. But nobody was digging.

In the courtyard at the back of the house outside the kitchen it looked like a party was in full swing, all that was missing was a smoking barbecue although after my last barbecue experience I counted that a plus. A variety of chairs had been dragged out of the house and The Studio, even two faded and slightly mouldy deck-chairs, and placed in a rough semicircle. This home-made amphi-theatre was dominated by Dan the finds man sitting in the middle on one of the deck-chairs. He had sunglasses on and a Panama hat and at his feet was an open case of cans of Stella Artois, on top of an unopened case, both covered with a large bag of melting ice cubes. To either side of him, most of them sipping from beer cans, were Jason, Kali, Jude and Rory, Gregory and Cornell, who was pulling on a large joint. The only thing that was missing was some loud music.

My arrival was greeted with comments ranging from 'Watch it, the boss is back' to 'You've missed all the fun' to 'Nice of you to join us.' The usual stuff.

'I thought there was no alcohol on site,' I said to Dan the Man.

'Not on site,' said Dan with a big smile.

'Fair point,' I said and knelt down to rip a can out of the case for myself. 'So what's happening?'

'We've been given the day off,' said Jude defensively.

'So we can watch the show,' Cornell drawled, not look-ing at me.

The 'show' was taking place way down on the site,

beyond the Mobile Thrones block and the tool shed, beyond the old barn or whatever it had been which had been converted into a garage for Arthur's bulldozer and Jeep. Between there and the edge of the first area we had cleaned stood Amy, Ben and Shona with their backs to us.

Beyond them, a good forty metres beyond them, Arthur's Jeep was parked across another of the cleaned squares and as I shielded my eyes against the sun I could pick out the tyre tracks where he had driven across the site more than once. Using the Jeep as one wall, he had erected three panels of blue perspex to form a box, just like the police would to shield a nasty road accident or a juicy crime scene from the rubber-necking public. If he really had found a body, that's what the textbooks tell you to do before you start to excavate or 'lift' it, though only if you are in a place where there is likely to be a passing public. I didn't think the bottom of Arthur's garden, near a wheat-field in the middle of the countryside, qualified, but Arthur was taking no chances.

Amy turned as I approached, smiled weakly, saw the beer I was carrying and held out her hand. Ben nodded a greeting, pointed towards the Jeep and the plastic screens and circulated a finger near his right temple. Shona just glared at me.

'So, anything interesting turn up while I was away?' I offered them a big cheesy grin.

'We discover this body – well, Ben does,' said Amy, indicating that she wanted a cigarette to go with my beer, 'and Arthur goes mental.'

'I presume you mean a skelly, not a body,' I said.

'Huh?'

'A skeleton, as in: been in the ground a long time and therefore archaeology. Not a body as in: flashing blue lights and sirens going da-da, da-da, let's call all the suspects together in the library.'

'Whatever.' She concentrated on drinking my beer.

'You know that patch of redeposited natural you spotted, near the pit I was taking out, well, I followed that

251

back this morning and the edge of something started to come up,' said Ben.

'A grave cut?'

'I worked that out when I saw the first rib bones.'

'It's not lying supine and it's been placed north/south,' said Shona and I had the distinct feeling she was testing me.

'Two good indicators that it's a pagan burial,' I said, scoring maximum points. 'A Christian would most likely be on his back and east/west,' I pointed out to Amy.

'I knew that. How do you know it's a "he"?' she shot back.

Shona's face shimmered into a smirk.

'Do we?' I turned to Ben.

'I didn't get enough uncovered to be able to tell. Once it was clear it was a skelly, we thought we'd tell Arthur. We thought he'd be interested . . . want to come and help . . .'

'He went bloody mental,' said Amy. 'He started shouting at us to get away from it, leave it alone and stop digging immediately. He charged out here and made us all go back to the house. Said we had to stay clear as he was the one with some licence or other.'

'Home Office,' Ben prompted. 'A Home Office licence to excavate bodies. But it should cover everybody working on the site, not just one person. It's a permit, not like you have to pass a driving test or anything.'

'Well, Arthur had it so Arthur was going to do the skelly.' Amy crushed my beer can with her hand then put the remains of her cigarette in it. 'Told us we could have the rest of the day off or leave the dig and he'd give us all a week's pay in lieu of notice. He was that serious. There was no arguing with him. He just shouted at us to keep away.'

'Where did the screens come from?'

'He had them in the garage where the bulldozer's parked,' answered Ben. 'He got the Jeep and loaded it up and just drove over here. Didn't give a monkey's about driving over the area we'd cleaned back. He drove all the

252

gear out there and set the screen up himself. He's been in there ever since.'

'If we go any nearer than this, he starts screaming at us,' said Amy.

'He's probably got his shotgun out there,' breathed Shona, showing some animation for the first time.

We all looked at her.

'Probably. I only said probably.'

'Has anyone checked the house to see if his gun's still in his office?'

They all looked a little sheepish.

'Right. Amy, you go and do that now. Whilst you're there ask Mrs Hawksbee if Arthur's on any sort of medication.'

'She's not here,' said Shona. 'It's her half-day.'

'O-kaaay, then, Plan B. Find a bottle of his Scotch and bring it out here. Shona, go with her.'

'Why?'

''Cos I don't want you here.'

'What are you going to do?' said Amy.

'Talk to him.'

'He won't let you get close enough. Ben tried and Arthur threw a mattock at him. Said he'd got plenty more ammunition as well.'

'Has he?'

'We left all our tools out there,' Ben said, splaying his palms.

'Look, there are two of us and he's older than both of us put together,' I reasoned.

'He threw a shovel at me,' said Shona.

Amy cracked a grin waiting for my comeback but I didn't bother. It would have been too easy.

'Right then, think like he does. He's a military man and he knows he's outnumbered but he has a strong defensive position and plenty of ammo. We have no cover and can't take him by surprise.'

'So?' Amy said, looking at the ground to hide a sly smile. I think she was beginning to enjoy this.

'So, in the immortal words of that great general Julius Caesar, we outgun the son-of-a-bitch.'

'Caesar said that?' Even Ben was lightening up.

'It may have lost something in the translation. Now where are the keys to the bulldozer?'

'I didn't know you could drive a bulldozer!' Amy had squealed afterwards.

I'd given her my frostiest cool shrug of the shoulders and said that if it had wheels, I could drive it. Then she'd pointed out that it had caterpillar tracks not wheels, which had rather spoiled the moment.

The keys to the small, bright yellow CAT 'dozer were kept on a bent nail in the wall just inside the old barn which doubled as a garage. There was other stuff in there as well. A work bench with a vice, electric drill and angle-grinder and spice-racks on the wall holding screwdrivers, hammers and the like, including some grisly old agricultural tools which were once used for God only knew what.

The 'dozer was easy enough to drive, with a button-push system of three gears and reverse on the left-hand joystick and the blade controlled by the right-hand joystick. She started first time and I took off the brake and she rolled forward and out into the yard to a round of applause from the diggers still sitting drinking beer, now really enjoying the show.

The only thing you have to remember is that the one pedal you have is a decelerator, not an accelerator. Even the most experienced drivers forget from time to time which is why you see all that stop-start action on building sites. There really is nothing much else to worry about, except that in the soundproof cab it's impossible to hear what's going on outside, or for anyone to hear you shouting 'Get out of the way,' which is why they have sirens and flashing yellow lights, as well as headlights for night work. I switched the whole lot on and I must have been quite a sight as I trundled across the site towards Arthur's encampment. All I had to do was remember to decelerate. Fifteen miles an hour doesn't sound a very high top speed, but eighteen tons of metal moving that fast hasn't got the manoeuvring abilities of, say, a house brick.

I judged it perfectly to within ten feet of the Jeep, put the CAT in neutral and engaged the brake then opened the cabin door and stepped out on to the footholds which ran up and over the engine cowling.

'Arthur!' I shouted. 'Come out of there now or I'll sit this thing on top of your Jeep until you can fit it through your letter-box.'

I had actually been amazed that he hadn't stuck his head above the parapet, so to speak, if only to see what the infernal racket was as I beetled down the site (making a right mess of it in the process) towards him in my new yellow Tonka toy.

'Arthur! I mean it! This foolishness has gone on long enough. Get a grip. Act your age, man!'

I thought that was a nice line in psychological reasoning, the sort a hostage negotiator might use. Then again I was relying on basic facts of life. He could throw a shovel at me, but I could squash his pet Jeep into chewing-gum wrapper.

He saw the light, or perhaps realized how silly we both looked, and stood up behind the bonnet of the Jeep. He raised an arm and waved for me to come over in a single, weary movement, then sank out of sight behind the plastic sheeting.

I cut the engine of the 'dozer and jumped down.

I found him sitting on a kneeling mat on the edge of what was indeed a grave cut about five feet long and two feet wide. He had excavated it to a depth of about eight inches, exposing the ribs, an arm and the badly damaged skull of a skeleton lying on its left side. The pelvis, legs and right side were still buried in the yellow silty clay soil.

Arthur had his arms across his knees, a trowel dangling loosely from his right hand. His shirt and trousers were stained with sweat, his shoes – brown brogues, not work boots – scuffed and covered in dust.

'It's not . . .' he started slowly. '. . . not what I thought.'

Then he stood up and straightened his back into ramrod stiffness.

'Can you . . .?'

'Sure, I'll take it from here,' I said. 'We'll get it done. There's plenty of light left.'

He nodded, turned on his heel and walked back towards the house, passing Ben, then Amy and Shona on their way back, without a word to any of them.

As he got to the tool shed and the toilet block, I assumed he would cut round The Studio to the side of the house and then the front door, but he kept going, walking right through the diggers, who had fallen silent, and into the kitchen. When he disappeared into the house he seemed a much smaller figure and it wasn't just a matter of perspective.

Ben was the first to reach me, or rather the screens, pulling them free where Arthur had knotted them to the bumper of the Jeep. No word of thanks or congratulations to me. All he wanted to do was get at the archaeology.

'It's a skelly,' he said, as if accusing me of something.

'All those years at – where was it? – they weren't wasted, were they?'

'It was Dublin actually,' he said testily, 'and what I meant was why all this fuss over a skelly?'

'I don't know. It wasn't what Arthur wanted, that was all he said.'

Amy and Shona were approaching, Amy clutching a bottle. Behind them the rest of the diggers were walking on to site. Everyone would want a look. It was always the way with skellies.

'So you scared an old man shitless with a bulldozer,' said Amy. 'Happy now?'

'Didn't need to as it turned out. In fact I don't think he even noticed the 'dozer, he'd already given up.'

Amy edged nearer to get a good look herself, unscrewed the top of the bottle and took a swig, then handed it to me.

'So what was the big scene about? He didn't think this was Boudica, did he?'

Shona, crouched over the grave cut, snorted at that.

'If he did,' I said, 'it wasn't for long. Unless Boudica changed sex somewhere down the line.'

'It is a man? How can you tell?'

'Os coxae,' said Shona quietly.

'The pelvis,' I said. 'If you want to be sure, look at the pelvic bones.'

'Arthur didn't even bother to uncover them,' said Ben, bending down and brushing soil from the lower ribs.

'Just didn't get around to it. There are good indicators in the skull. There, above the eye-socket where the eyebrow would have been. That's the supraorbital margin and if it's thick and rounded – feels like a pencil – it's usually male. Then you can look at the prominence of the glabella, the ridge here above the eyes.'

I traced a line on Amy's forehead with my finger.

'If it's a smooth contour line, it's female. If it's larger and projecting, it's male. Think Neanderthal and you've got a bloke.'

'You're not wrong there,' she said. Then to Ben: 'Is he bullshitting me?'

'No, he's right on the button,' said Ben. 'If we had the skull out we could look at the mental eminence on the chin –' he used his own head to demonstrate – 'or the mastoid process here under the ear or the neuchal crest at the base of the skull at the back. They're all sex indicators.'

'So it's male.'

'A white male, thirty-five years old, about five foot four inches tall, probably from the Hamburg region,' I said. 'Apart from that, Watson, we know absolutely nothing about him.'

'Now he is bullshitting you,' said Ben.

'He could be Saxon,' murmured Shona. 'The grave cut is under that medieval pit, therefore earlier, and pre-Christian Saxon burials are like this; just a shallow grave and the body dumped in, maybe in a bag.'

'No, I was bullshitting,' I said. 'Can you see it's lifted tonight?' I asked Ben.

'Sure thing. We seem to have plenty of volunteers.' The rest of the crew were almost on us. 'I've got some fine tools, leaf trowels, brushes and stuff back in The Stables. I've even got a dental kit. Never used it before.'

'Go for it. Clean it up as much as you can and see if we can photograph it in situ with a scale then bag him and tag him.'

'What's with the dental kit?' Amy asked, suspiciously.

'A set of second-hand dentist's picks and scrapers. They're great for cleaning up a skelly. Archaeologists scour the car boot sales looking for them.'

She didn't look convinced. Maybe I should have told her we were going to check his fillings.

'Come on, let the dog see the rabbit.'

Dan the Man pushed us gently aside so he could get a look at the skelly. The rest of the diggers were forming a circle around the grave.

'Any grave goods?' Dan asked. 'Pot, buckles, pins, hobnails?'

'Nothing by the looks of it.'

'Bugger it then, I'm off. I've had enough of this place. There's a dig started up near Worcester could be a Roman cemetery. They might have something decent up there.'

He took a thin roll-up from behind his ear and I lit it for him with my Zippo.

'Time to move on, anyway,' he said, blowing smoke. 'After Ladies' Night at The Drovers last night.'

'I didn't see you there,' I said.

'Oh, I saw your missus and her mates, but I left a bit early.' He grinned – pure evil. 'Important engagement.'

'So you pulled then?' Amy was never one to mince words.

'Could be,' he said coyly. 'So it might be best to get out of town. Anyways, there's not much going to be happening here, is there? The boss has gone doolally and you've chewed up most of the site.'

I looked back down the squares we had cleaned and the

dug and half-dug features now obliterated by the bull-dozer's tracks.

'I'll set them on hoeing again tomorrow,' I said.

'There's a thankless bloody task.'

'That's what diggers are for, isn't it?'

The keys were still in Arthur's Jeep and I asked Amy to drive it back to the house while I put the bulldozer away. She pouted a bit, fancying herself 'with the Panzer' but then agreed that a Jeep, a real one, was pretty cool too.

'By the way,' she said quietly, 'there's still no sign of Joss, or the unit Transit van.'

'Give me a minute,' I pleaded, 'I can't think of everything. One step at a time, as they say at your meetings.'

'Arthur's shotgun's missing as well,' she said with a sour smile. 'Add it to your list.'

I reversed the bulldozer back into its garage, pocketed the keys, closed the heavy wooden door which didn't have a lock, just a hasp fastened with a six-inch nail on a string, and walked round to the front of the house. Amy had parked the Jeep there and was returning the bottle of Scotch as an excuse to check up on Arthur.

Dan the Man was walking down the drive towards the road, white jacket over his shoulder, sunglasses on against the still bright evening sun, Panama hat at a jaunty angle. The rest of the crew were on site by the skelly, all eight of them. All of them except the missing Joss.

And Fifi.

'Arthur's in the library and he's not coming out.'

Amy was sitting on the staircase, still holding the Scotch bottle.

'Come upstairs into the office,' I said, 'we have to talk.'

On the landing, under the portrait of Octavia Scrivenour-Swallow-Rivero, I pulled her close and asked her quietly if the shotgun was in the library with him.

'We couldn't find it anywhere,' she whispered. 'You don't think he's likely to do anything stupid?'

I shook my head as reassuringly as I could and ushered her into the office, closing the door behind us.

'Have you seen Fifi today?'

'No,' Amy said after a moment's thought. 'No, I haven't, now you come to mention it. You think she and Joss have gone off somewhere?'

'I have no idea. Ben would have said, wouldn't he? It's just that it is very unusual for a digger to be able to resist having a look when somebody finds a skelly.'

'She's definitely an archaeologist,' said Amy frowning, 'she told me she was. Said she'd met Ben at university in her last year.'

'In Dublin?'

'Yes, why? Is that important?'

'I shouldn't think so. But Ben hasn't said anything today, has he? About Fifi not being around?'

'Not a thing. She does disappear quite a bit, though, doesn't she?'

'Especially when I'm around,' I observed. 'It's like she's been avoiding me.'

'Don't get paranoid, dearest. I think you two would get on. You're really quite alike in many ways.'

'Spare me. Let's get Arthur sorted then we'll worry about the missing girls.'

And there were a few more things on my Amy agenda to come after that.

'What about the skelly? Shouldn't we tell the police or the coroner or somebody?'

'Not if Arthur has a Home Office licence, that means we can dig it up if it's in an obvious archaeological context, which it is. But the skelly is the key. Arthur's reaction to the news was fairly extreme, right?'

'Ballistic. He went mad. Couldn't wait to chuck us off site and take control.'

'What if a grave is what he's been looking for all these years?'

Amy pulled her chin in and furled her eyebrows.

'You mean he really thought it could be Boadicea's grave?'

'No. I never believed he thought that.'

As soon as I had seen how Arthur had excavated the skelly I knew he hadn't been looking for Boudica. However daft the idea, if it had been the Iceni queen's grave any decent digger would have concentrated on the lower half of the skelly, to expose the pelvis and prove the sex, then explored the area around the lower ribs and the lowest part of the grave cut where any grave goods would be – things buried with the body whether as part of a ritual such as a knife or a cup, or the remains of rotted clothing such as buckles and pins.

Arthur had concentrated on the skull, the neck and the shoulder bones and done it well, but he hadn't done it like a digger would have.

'Well, he's not really a digger, is he?' Amy had defended him. 'He's an amateur, probably never found a skelly before, didn't know not to start at the head end.'

'He was looking for something,' I said. 'Something specific.'

'What?'

I crooked a finger in her face, motioning her to come towards me. I opened the office door and jabbed my finger at the looming portrait of Octavia, then turned the finger on myself and pointed at my throat.

'Get outa here! You cannot be serious.'

'It makes as much sense as anything else around here. Did you really believe that story about Octavia wandering off to meet her GI boyfriend and getting caught in an air raid? An air raid on Ipswich in September 1944? I didn't buy that for a minute.'

'It would explain why there was no body.'

'Exactly, but I really don't think there were any air raids on Ipswich that late in the war.'

'We could check,' she said, 'on the Internet.'

She pointed to the PC on the other side of the office.

'Yeah, right, there'll be a website for air raid freaks.'

'Wouldn't surprise me.'

261

'Go on then, you go surfing. I'm going to look for those plans of Colchester Garrison.'

Amy turned on the computer and the screen and waited for the Windows program to kick in.

'What have they got to do with anything?' she asked over her shoulder, pulling up a chair to the PC desk.

'Nothing, I just want to make sure they haven't gone missing as well. Where has Gerald's painting gone?'

'What are you talking about?'

'The picture of the wheatfield that was on there the other night. It wasn't bad, actually.'

'That would have been a screensaver,' said Amy as if explaining to a child. 'Here we go: Settings, Control Panel, Display.'

She clicked away on the mouse as I began to sift through the pile of papers on the design board.

'This the one you meant?'

I turned my head. There on the screen was a smaller window version of the waving wheatfield.

'That's it. It's one of Gerald's paintings.'

'No it isn't, somebody's downloaded it from a website.'

I couldn't find the Colchester plans anywhere.

'I thought it had his initials in the corner, GS – Gerald Swallow.'

Maybe Arthur had put them away somewhere safe after I had lectured him the other night, but somehow I doubted it.

'Gerald Swallow my eye,' Amy was saying. 'It stands for Genetix Snowball. What the flying fuck is that?'

'How should I know? You're the one navigating the information highway. Found anything about air raids on Ipswich yet?'

'Give me a . . . Hey, Joss is back.'

She was straining up on her chair like a jockey in the saddle, looking out of the window. Coming up the drive was the Iceni Rescue van and following it was a Land Rover Defender.

'I'll see if she's OK, find out where she's been,' I volunteered.

'You do that,' she said bitterly. 'I'll keep working away.'

The door to the library remained closed. Arthur either hadn't heard the approaching vehicles or couldn't care less, so it was left to me to go to the front door as meeter and greeter and it was a job I suddenly lost interest in when the van pulled up and 'Jimbo' Scrivenour-Lindley stepped out rather than Joss.

His manners hadn't improved since the night we had met outside the pub.

'Where's Swallow, then?'

'He's busy,' I said. 'Can I help?'

The Defender rolled to a stop behind the van and a man I hadn't seen before climbed out of the passenger side. He wore rubber boots, jeans and a checked shirt, just as 'Jimbo' did and looked so much like him he must be the other brother. Staying put behind the wheel of the Defender was Hans Jankel.

'You an arkie, then, or just modelling for the Army and Navy Stores?'

I thought that was a bit rich coming from a fashion victim like him.

'I'm the dig supervisor,' I said. 'What are you doing with our van?'

'Hear that, Rob?' James said to his brother. 'He's asking what *we've* been doing. Got a nerve, ain't he?'

Robert, who looked to be the elder brother, came closer so he could put his face into mine.

'We've been pulling *your* van out of one of *our* fields, that's what we've been doing. And we'd like to know what it was doing there, on *our* land.'

'Where was this?'

'Six fields over, other side of the road.'

'Was there an accident?'

'There will be if I find the bloody driver,' James chipped in.

'No sign of an accident,' said Robert. 'You don't drive

fifty yards off the road into a field of rape seed by accident. I'll be sending Mr Swallow a bill.'

'When did you find it?'

The question threw them.

''Bout an hour ago,' said Robert, suddenly wary. 'Why?'

'Did Murray Hooper spot it from his spy plane?' I chanced.

'Is that any of your business?'

James made a move towards me and Robert grabbed his arm to restrain him.

'It is his business, James,' said Robert. 'He should know that we're watching him and his scruffy, druggy friends, watching them all the time.'

James grinned in my face.

'Yeah, roight.'

The Suffolk accent somehow didn't go with the air of hillbilly menace he was trying to project.

'Just keep off our crops, right?' Robert said with a farewell finger stabbing at my chest.

He tugged James's arm and they strode over to the Defender, which Jankel was already starting up.

'Thanks for bringing back our van,' I yelled after them. 'Any sign of the driver when you found it?'

Without turning round, Robert said:

'No. Lucky for him there wasn't.'

They had left the keys in the Transit so I moved it round the corner of the house, parking it next to Armstrong behind The Studio. I dropped the keys into my left pants pocket where they jangled with the bulldozer keys as I walked. I was getting quite a collection.

The light was starting to go but I could still see a crowd of diggers working down on site, one of them – unmistakably Kali from the physique – heading back with a wheelbarrow. Jason was in the yard near the barn which housed the bulldozer. The door was open and from inside came the sound of the angle-grinder in action.

Jason ambled towards me, hands in pockets.

'We're almost done out there,' he said in his Irish twang. 'Just bringing the tools in and sharpening them up for another hard day's digging tomorrow.'

'We'll have to see about that,' I said. 'How's the skelly?'

'Ben's bagging it up and we're bringing it in. Thought we'd leave it in The Studio overnight.'

'Good idea. I gotta go.'

'Ah, sure you have,' he said with a smile and turned back towards the garage.

I smoked a cigarette walking slowly back to the house, trying to think and trying to forget that I was getting very, very hungry.

Amy was waiting for me at the front door to take the cigarette from me in exchange for two sheets of paper she'd printed off Arthur's computer.

'What's this?'

'Air raids on Ipswich in 1944. There's not only a website, there's a book and a whole Air Raid Museum in Ipswich.'

'Somebody's gone to the trouble . . .?'

'Oh yes,' she said, 'and you were wrong. There were air raids in 1944 – flying bombs. Doodlebugs. V1 rockets launched from German aircraft out over the North Sea. Some anorak has even listed their serial numbers and German codenames, but bottom line is there was a raid on Ipswich on 18th September. That was the date, wasn't it?'

I nodded and scanned the sheet until I found the reference.

At 2335 hours on 18th September 1944, a V1 flying bomb had landed on Halton Crescent, Ipswich, killing four people and injuring eight, destroying fourteen houses and damaging a further four hundred.

'It doesn't list the victims,' I said.

'What do you want? Blood? Octavia could have been one of them.'

'Yeah, *could*. Come on, let's go have this out with Arthur then find something to eat. I'm starving.'

'Any sign of your friend Joss?'

'No. That was our friendly farming neighbours, the Scrivenour-Lindleys. They found the van in the middle of one of their fields. No sign of a driver.'

'Maybe she was doing her Genetix Snowball thing.'

'Her *what*?'

Amy stared me out while she took a last draw on the cigarette, then crushed it beneath her boot.

'The screensaver with the wheatfield just like that one over there?' She waved her hand vaguely to her right but by now it was too dark to see the orchard at the end of the site, let alone the field beyond. 'Wherever. The screensaver was downloaded from the Genetix Snowball site. GS. I looked them up. The agro-terrorists as the newspapers call them. People who oppose genetic modification in plants. You know, breeding triffids which will take over the world and produce corn flakes which are clever enough to pour the milk on themselves. That sort of stuff. They sneak into fields and make crop circles to show up where the secret breeding trials are taking place. You must have heard of them. Where have you *been*?'

'How long have you known this?'

'Since about five minutes ago.'

'You might have told me earlier,' I said haughtily.

The door to the library wasn't locked. Arthur was sitting in a battered armchair staring at the darkening sky through the uncurtained window. He glanced up as we creaked across the uneven floorboards and he managed a weak smile.

'You've guessed, haven't you?' he said.

Amy was about to go all-innocent and say 'Guessed what?' but I cut her off.

'I think so, Arthur. You've been looking for Octavia, haven't you?'

He took a moment, then nodded his head as if in agreement and ran a hand over his face as if he were wiping away tears.

'For many, many years,' he said gently.

Amy shuffled to my side and we stood there like children sent to see the headmaster.

'I always suspected something, though of course I wasn't here when it happened. I knew Gerald was besotted with Octavia because – well, because I was too and I was hurt when they got married. In a way I was glad they didn't tell me until afterwards because I don't think I could have stood seeing . . . being there. I like to think Octavia went along with the secrecy because she didn't want to hurt my feelings.

'And I know how Gerald must have felt when Octavia became besotted with her American, Oscar. Oscar and Octavia. It has a quaintness about it. But you must understand that Octavia was not a tramp, as we used to say. If she had fallen for Oscar then Oscar must have been quite something. Must have been a decent chap. It would not have been something she did lightly, even though there was a war on and people let their emotions rule them.

'Perhaps Gerald let his emotions rule him. Perhaps he thought it came indecently close after their wedding. Perhaps he thought he had lost me as well as her. I don't know.'

His voice trailed off into memory. He stared at the bookshelves seeing only the past.

'Did she die in an air raid in Ipswich?' I asked softly.

'Oh no, Gerald killed her. I'm sure of that.'

He heaved himself out of the chair and stood up straight, almost at attention. If this was his court martial, he was going to have his say like an officer and a gentleman.

'After the war, Gerald's health – his mental health – went downhill rapidly. So much so the only thing I could do was stay here and look after him and encourage him in his painting, which was the only thing he seemed happy with. He never spoke of Octavia or what had happened but I began to piece things together. When he learned about her American friend Oscar, he came home on leave and confronted her.

'When asked to make a choice, she chose Oscar, said she would pack her things and move into Ipswich. Now I'm sorry if this sounds harsh, but I cannot put it any other way. I think my brother waited until it was clear that she was determined to leave. Perhaps she was walking down the driveway, who knows for sure? But when it was certain, absolutely certain, that she was going, he shot her. He shot her with an old service revolver that my father had in the house from his army days. He shot her and he buried her and the next day reported her missing. The V1 raid on Ipswich that night provided him with a perfect cover.'

'You can't know this for sure,' Amy said, 'unless he confessed to you.'

'He never confessed,' said Arthur, stiffening his back as if with pride. 'I put the pieces together over the forty-odd years we lived together. Think about that. Even married couples don't know each other – really *know* each other – after that length of time. But I knew my brother, and I knew Octavia.

'Gerald never touched that service revolver again. Literally, wouldn't touch it. I still have it somewhere, in a box, collecting dust. That was one pointer, one sign. There were others over the years. But his only admission was his death and for that I blame myself.'

'But he killed himself,' Amy pleaded, looking at me for support. 'You can't blame yourself for that.'

'I do, my dear, I do. You see it coincided with my new interest in archaeology and my plans to start digging for Iceni artefacts.'

'And Gerald thought you were looking for Octavia's body,' I said.

Arthur hung his head.

'Precisely. I broached the subject over lunch one day and he just walked out into the garden and shot himself, but I can honestly say that at the time, my only interest was in Boadicea. It was only when I realized the implications of Gerald's action – Gerald's guilt surfacing after all those years – that I was sure he must have killed her and buried her here at Woolpack House.'

'You started in the house, didn't you?' I said and he nodded. 'You took up the floor and it never got put back properly. Then what? Did the archaeology became a front for you?'

'In a way, yes, it was a veil of respectability. Good God, I was an ex-magistrate not Burke or Hare.'

'And you set up Iceni Rescue to get yourself a Home Office licence to excavate bodies?'

'Yes. I had almost given up hope. My feeble efforts over the years resulted in nothing, then the Lottery win came and I could pay off my debts and have one last sweep of the grounds.'

He snorted in self-mockery.

'And when we do find a grave I behave like a total ass. The expression, I believe, is that I "lost it" this afternoon. I will have to apologize to everyone, if they can look me in the eye without laughing.'

Amy moved to him, putting a hand on his shoulder.

'Arthur, you have nothing to feel guilty about,' she said slowly and clearly.

'Ah, but I do, my dear, I do.'

'What? You haven't done anything wrong.'

'Yes I have, my dear, but you couldn't possibly know what it was.'

I cleared my throat to remind them I was still there.

'Was it you who wrote to Gerald telling him about Octavia's affair?'

There was an awful silence while they both looked at me and I shuffled from one foot to the other trying not to make the floorboards creak.

'You have a very perceptive young man there, my dear,' said Arthur, squeezing Amy's arm. 'He's mighty quick on the uptake.'

Oh no he wasn't.

He was far, far too slow.

Chapter Fourteen

Root Disturbance

Amy gave Arthur a hug and they stayed like that for a good two minutes. I expected them both to crack up and burst into tears. Then Amy patted him on the shoulders, pecked him on the cheek and stepped out of his arms.

'Is there anything to eat in the house or shall we go down the pub? I'm bloody starving.'

'Mrs Hawksbee will have left me a casserole,' Arthur announced cheerfully.

'Pub,' Amy and I said together.

'Nonsense, wouldn't hear of it. Let me see what's what in the kitchen.'

He bustled out, happy to be doing something.

'We still have to talk,' I said to Amy.

'About the house? Is it about the house?'

'That too, but you have to show me that Genetix Snowball site.'

'Why?'

'To see if it mentions Dublin.'

'Dublin? As in Ireland?'

'Yes. Ben met Fifi in Dublin.'

'So fucking what?'

'Fifi's been avoiding me.'

'Maybe the Irish have sense. She did look a bit Irish. She's got your mother's red hair.'

'That's what I was afraid of. We have to find her. And Joss.'

'Is she missing? I mean, I know Joss is, but is Fifi? Nobody's said she is.'

'Quite. And nobody's asked if Joss is back, even though the van is.'

Jason and Kali at least had seen me drive the van round the back, yet no one had asked about Joss.

'I'll just pop out back, see how they're getting on.'

'You want me to keep an eye on Arthur?'

'You could try and find the decent wine we brought the other night, but otherwise I think he'll be OK. Whilst you're here, dig out that Bible and look up Revelations chapter 2, verse 20.'

'More fan mail?'

'I doubt it.'

I cut through the kitchen to get outside and there was Arthur loading a large metal dish into the oven.

'Be warmed through in about fifteen minutes,' he said, wiping his hands on a tea towel. 'How about a drink while we wait?'

'Excellent idea. I'm just going out to see how the diggers are getting on,' I said.

'Surely they're all in now it's dark?' said Arthur, peering out of the window.

'Most likely.'

I had my hand on the kitchen door knob when he said:

'Fitzroy?'

'Yes?'

'I'm glad somebody knows. I'm glad *you* know.'

'Know what, Arthur?'

I winked at him and he smiled.

'By the way, who told you to call me Fitzroy?' I asked.

'Fifi did, I think. Yes, it was Fifi.'

'Thought so.'

Beyond The Stables and the Mobile Thrones block, there was nothing but darkness. I checked The Stables first and though the lights were on, nobody was home, not a soul. There was no one in the toilet block either, but as I emerged I spotted Ben coming out of The Studio.

'Where is everybody?'

'The skelly's in here, all bagged and labelled. Do you have a particular specialist in mind you want to send it to?'

He hadn't made eye contact with me and hadn't stopped walking towards The Stables.

'Ben, where is everybody?'

'I think they might have gone to the pub,' he said, still moving away, not looking.

'Ben! Where's Fifi?'

He didn't say anything to that, just marched straight into The Stables and clumped down the corridor.

I should have grabbed him and shaken it out of him, but he was too big, too fit, too young.

I ran back through the kitchen. Arthur was pouring wine into three glasses, saying 'I'll bring them through' but saying it to my back.

I collided with Amy half-way across the hall. She had steamed out of the library holding the Bible open in one hand.

'That does it,' she fumed, 'that just fucking-a does it. You know what this last message says? Listen: *To the angel at . . .* somewhere or other . . . yada, yada . . . here we are . . . *Yet I have this against you: you tolerate that Jezebel, the woman who claims to be a prophetess, who by her teaching lures my servants into fornication . . .* Well, it's clear as day, isn't it? She means me.'

'She?'

'It's bloody Fifi, isn't it? She's seen me with Ben and thinks I'm into his trousers.'

'Riiiiight,' I said slowly, trying to keep up.

'When did you get the message?'

'Hours ago,' I said, not knowing why she was asking but not prepared to argue when she was in this mood.

'Give me your phone.'

I handed it over and she began to search the archive.

'Just hope the bitch has turned her phone back on, I'll give her . . .'

Arthur was suddenly standing there with a tray of wine glasses. He could have been the butler, so smooth was his approach work.

'I'm not interrupting anything, am I?' he said politely.

'A small domestic matter,' I said, helping myself to a glass as Amy punched the call button and slapped the phone to her ear.

'I'll teach the little cow . . . It's ringing.'

And it was.

'Come on, bitch, answer.'

I reached out and gently pushed the phone away from Amy's ear.

'What?' she snapped.

God, she was beautiful when she went into avenger mode, standing there, one leg at seventy degrees to the other, in those shorts and pink socks, tapping her boot impatiently.

'Listen,' I said.

A phone rang, and again. Somewhere in the house. Somewhere above us.

'She's in the attic!' Amy and I said together.

Arthur pulled on the rope and the extending ladder slid down as the loft access slid back, neither making a rattle or a hum. She had oiled all the moving parts. Clever girl.

'Fifi? Are you really up there?' Arthur shouted up into the black square.

There was no reply, but I thought I heard a faint thumping noise as somebody moved position.

'I'm coming up there, Fifi!' He put one foot on the metal ladder. 'The light switch is at the top on the right,' he said to us.

Amy jabbed me with her elbow and hissed, 'You go.'

'It's his attic,' I hissed back.

I couldn't have stopped him if I'd tried. He took each step firmly, steadying the ladder with his weight, reaching a hand up to flick the light on. The square in the ceiling lit up for a moment, then he was up and half-way through, the light forming a halo around his backside.

'Oh Fifi, what have you done?'

Then he was up there and we heard boards creaking under his weight and his muffled voice and then a higher, female voice.

We stood at the foot of the ladder for about ten seconds before Amy punched me on the arm and I took a deep breath and started to climb until my head poked through the access hole.

The attic was much larger than I had imagined. There was flooring nailed between the beams to give a surface and plenty of height to allow standing over a fair area before the roof sloped into the gables. A single naked light bulb hung from the main roof beam, illuminating tea-chests, travelling trunks, boxes and bags, rolls of carpet, even a plastic Christmas tree still bedecked with plastic holly and fading, dusty tinsel.

Arthur was kneeling on the boards tugging at the knots in what looked like a rope clothes line. The rope bound Joss's hands then ran down to her feet which were also tied. Her mouth was covered by criss-cross strips of masking tape and her eyes were wide and furious. She still wore her baseball cap backwards.

'You are going to have to answer for this, young lady,' Arthur was saying. But he wasn't talking to Joss, he was talking to the other person up there.

The young red-haired female who was holding a large black revolver in both hands. Not only holding it, but pointing it.

At me.

'Do put that down, my dear,' Arthur was saying chattily. 'If I remember correctly, the Webley & Scott Mark VI weighs about two-and-a-half pounds. That's rather heavy. It's not a ladies' weapon at all.'

It stayed pointed at my head.

'Hello, Finnoula,' I said.

'Hello, Fitzroy,' she said.

274

'You're not going to use that.'

'Why not?'

Typical. She always had to argue.

'It's not loaded. I can see from here. The little chambers in the cylinder where the bullets go, they're empty. I'm told they work so much better with bullets.'

She left it for a beat for the sake of appearances, then shrugged her shoulders and tossed the gun on to a pile of folded blankets, raising a slow motion cloud of dust particles. Then she strode towards me as if to plant one of her trainers on my head.

'Get out of the way,' she ordered, 'and let me down. I'm dying for a pee.'

I scrambled down the ladder to the landing.

Amy was glaring at me.

'*Finnoula?*'

Six . . . seven . . . eight . . . nine . . .

'*I didn't know you had a sister!*'

. . . Ten.

I should have known. I mean how many twenty-two-year-old redheads who looked just like my mother, who had done archaeology as part of a combined degree course in Dublin and who would rather live in an attic than meet me, were there?

'Joss is probably bursting as well,' said Finnoula as she disappeared into the bathroom down the corridor. Then she turned in the doorway even as she was unbuttoning her jeans. 'Oh, hi, Amy. Love the pink socks. Nice touch.'

Amy weighed that one up for a nano-second to see whether it was a compliment or not.

'Just what is going on?' she demanded.

'You did know I had a sister,' I said in a vain attempt to claim the moral high ground. 'We mentioned it at my mother's party.'

Joss's legs appeared on the ladder and she shook her feet to get the circulation back. Amy and I grabbed an arm each to help her down the last few steps. We held on to her as she massaged her wrists. The skin around her mouth was pink where she'd ripped the masking tape off, but she managed a smile. Then suddenly the smile froze and she began to blush.

'She's your sister?' she said, panic in her eyes.

''Fraid so,' I said.

'Oh – my – God,' she said slowly. 'I've got to pee.'

She pulled herself free from us and shot down the corridor as a toilet flushed on cue and Finnoula had to press herself into the wall to let her pass.

Amy's eyes were on full automatic, firing tracers.

'I don't know what she meant by that,' I said defensively.

'She meant they'd been talking girlie talk while they were up there playing Anne Frank.'

'It's called the Stockholm Syndrome, isn't it?' Finnoula said cheerfully. 'Where a hostage strikes up a relationship with their captor and tells them all their fantasies and dirty thoughts?'

Arthur climbed down the ladder to join us in what was now a rather uncomfortable huddle on the landing.

'Would there be a drink in this house?' Finnoula asked.

Arthur opened another bottle of wine and put the Scotch on the kitchen table as well. It was shaping up to be a party and the casserole in the oven was smelling faintly appetizing, though that could have been the onset effects of malnutrition. As he was pouring wine, he leaned into me and asked if he could see a 'family resemblance' and I said – again – that she was my younger sister and he said that must be nice.

'Did Mother send you to keep an eye on me?' Finnoula opened.

'Not in so many words, but I suspect so. Did she know you were here?'

'Oh yes. Big mistake on my part, calling to say hello like that. From now on it's Christmas cards only.'

'She was probably worried about you,' Amy offered.

'Bollix to that,' she said, laying on the Irish accent, 'she was worried I'd do something to upset her boyfriend's godfather.' She smiled sweetly at Arthur. 'As if I would.'

'Just who were you planning to upset, Fi?' I asked.

We had all called her 'Fi' as a kid and 'Fifi' wasn't so far away. I should have twigged earlier.

'The forces of global poisoning, that's who,' she said cheerfully.

'You mean the local farmers?'

'Well, them indirectly, I suppose, but really their pay-masters.'

'I'm afraid you're losing me, Fifi dear,' said Arthur. 'What has this to do with archaeology?'

'Absolutely nothing, I'm afraid. It's just that Woolpack House is in the right place at the right time.'

'For what?' he struggled.

'For cover,' I said. 'Finnoula is a follower of Genetix Snowball. They go round the country disrupting genetic-ally modified crop growing. But it's getting tricky these days. Farmers can get an injunction against harassment –' I shot a glance at Amy but she didn't respond – 'and the National Farmers Union want protesting near a farm classed as stalking. Personally I think they should include texting in the Protection from Harassment Act.'

For the first time, Finnoula looked faintly embarrassed.

'Ah, yes, sorry, Fitz . . . Amy. Sorry about Armstrong's tyre too. That was supposed to be, like, a hint. The text messages . . . they . . . Oh hell, I was *bored* up there in that bloody roof. I thought you'd assume it was somebody you'd upset in London.'

'Me? Upset people?'

'I'm still not clear, Fifi dear . . .' Arthur started.

Joss lowered her wine glass and raised her voice.

'Excuse me, but as I'm the one who's been tied up, rolled around and *starved* for the last God knows how long, can

I just say that I am totally pissed off with everything and I'm going home tomorrow to leave you lot to it.'

That got our attention.

'Why were you in the attic, Joss?' Arthur asked politely.

'Because they kidnapped me.'

'Who did?'

'They all did!' she shouted. 'Even bloody Ben, who I thought knew better, was in on it.'

'He's not one of us,' said Finnoula, 'not really.'

'Not one of what?' Arthur reached for the Scotch.

'Your cell,' Amy said and now we all looked at her. 'I read it on the website. Genetix Snowball works on a series of cells of eight, none having direct contact with any others except through cut-out points, so they can't betray other cells.'

'Rory, Jude, Kali, Gregory, Shona, Jason, Cornell . . .' I counted, '. . . and you, Fi. That's eight.'

'Jason and Cornell were late replacements for the two Dans who went on the piss and got into a fight with the local farmers. Talk about drawing attention to yourself, bloody amateurs!' Finnoula raised her eyebrows as if saying 'You just can't get the staff, can you?'

'Ben just came along for the archaeology,' she went on. 'And me, I suppose.'

'So you are diggers?'

I had to give it to Arthur, he didn't let go easily.

'We've all dug before,' said Fi. 'It is a good cover as my darling big brother pointed out.'

'You were in charge of hiring people when they responded to the advert, weren't you?' I remembered somebody telling me that.

'Yes. It was a way of making sure our people got in here. We only needed two weeks, then we could drift away and I'd replace everybody with proper diggers. I didn't count on you and Amy turning up and Joss was already here as project manager when we arrived.'

'So why was she in the attic? Why were you in the attic?'

Good old Arthur.

'*She* was there to avoid *him*,' Joss said in his face, pointing at Finnoula then at me. '*I* was there because I followed them when they went on their raid last night and when I asked just what the fuck they thought they were doing, they jumped me.'

'Stress, sister, stress,' murmured Finnoula.

'And somebody drove the van away and dumped it?' I said to her.

'Ben did. Make it look like Joss had gone off in it.'

'Which is why no one was too worried when the van came back without you. Except me,' I added hastily.

'Raid on what? Fifi? Anyone?'

'I'm sorry, Arthur, sweetie, I should have said.' Finnoula went over to him and put an arm round his neck, which he seemed to enjoy.

'You just had the darned bad luck to start up a dig right next door to a field of genetically modified wheat where they're testing a new terminator gene. They've kept it very quiet – all the trial locations are supposed to be top secret – but we found out and my little team volunteered to come here as diggers and collect some samples as proof. They're not supposed to be using terminators because they make the seeds sterile. Apart from the damage they could do to the local plantlife, if they sell them to the Third World, a terminator doesn't allow people to collect their own seed. They have to go back to the company and buy more.

'Naturally, they keep quiet about things like this and they would have got away with it . . .'

'*If it hadn't been for those pesky archaeologists!*' I finished for her.

'Yeah! Scooby Doo!' Finnoula laughed.

Amy said, 'I see where she gets it now.'

'I've read about this genetically modified stuff,' said Arthur, shaking his head. 'They call it Frankenstein food, don't they? I never thought the Scrivenour-Lindleys would stoop so low.'

'Actually,' said Finnoula, 'they might not know about

the terminator. The company probably didn't tell them, just hired them to grow a GM crop.'

'What's the company?' I asked her.

'GGR – Global Genetic Resources. Calls itself a "life science repository". It's based in Rome. That smoothy Jankel, he works for them in Security.'

'He's got a plane photographing the fields, looking for signs that the crop has been disturbed.'

'We know, we're careful. We only go out at night and we don't get caught.'

'I caught you,' said Joss sulkily. 'And, by the way, I'm bloody hungry.'

'Casserole!' Arthur jumped up. 'I'll get plates.'

Amy made a beeline for me.

'I'm going to have a shower and then you're taking me out for a meal. I don't care where as long as it's expensive.'

I opened the kitchen door for her. Finnoula made to follow her.

'I knew it was unloaded,' she said out of the corner of her mouth.

'Sure you did.'

'Ah well, better round up the troops,' she said.

'Are they where I think they are?'

'Yup. We decided to bring the harvest forward this year. They'll be out there now, bringing in the sheaves.'

In fact they only brought in seeds, wheat kernels, in sandwich-size Tupperware tubs. Apart from the fact that they were armed only with hygienic, microwave-proof plastic kitchenware, they looked quite fearsome.

Ex-army clothing is, of course, *de rigueur* anyway for an after-dark commando raid on a wheatfield but they'd augmented their normal digging gear with black or brown woolly hats or balaclavas and gloves. Kali had even drawn parallel lines on her cheeks and forehead with two fingers dipped in boot polish, but then she'd probably have done that if she was going clubbing. They all carried torches with gaffer tape reducing the beams to the width of a pencil.

They hesitated on the edge of the site when they saw me and Amy there, but Finnoula gave a low whistle and waved them in.

'Any problems?' she asked Kali, the first to enter the courtyard.

Kali eyed us suspiciously until Finnoula nodded that we were now on the same side, or at least not on opposite ones.

'No problems, no surprises tonight. They won't know we've been and I reckon we timed it dead right. They'll be harvesting themselves within two or three days,' Kali said with a military precision Arthur would have been proud of.

'How's Joss taking things?' Jude asked. Her camouflage hat had a woolly bobble on top which rather detracted from the SAS image she'd been striving for.

'Grumpily, but she'll be fine,' said Fi. 'Come on, let's have your contributions.'

She had brought a large plastic box from the fridge in the kitchen and now she took the lid off and placed it at her feet. Kali and Jude opened their smaller tubs and poured the contents in.

'What do you plan to do with it?' I asked.

'We have a friendly lab which will analyse it then we'll go to the newspapers and prove that GGR is testing terminator genes when they shouldn't be and we'll put their DNA sequences and structures on the Internet so their competitors can copy them and their patents will be worth shit.'

'Won't that help the competition develop their own GM wheat in other countries?'

She thought about it.

'Maybe we won't do that bit.'

Amy muttered something about 'students' and said she was going to get a towel and have her shower and I'd better have thought of somewhere to eat by the time she got back. As she went into The Stables, Ben came out, hands in pockets, looking sheepish.

'Are you OK, love?' he asked tentatively.

'I'm fine,' said Finnoula. 'Big brother here turned out to be a pussy cat in the end. By the way, Fitzroy, what are *you* doing here?'

'Looking out for Arthur. Looking out for you. I'm not sure any more.'

Ben stared at Fi and then at me and then back at Fi.

'I didn't know you had a brother!'

'I'm a woman of mystery,' she said, giving him a kiss. 'How are we doing?'

Jason, Cornell, Gregory and Rory had all delivered their contributions to Finnoula's life science bran tub. Shona was the last, walking towards us peeling off her balaclava and almost removing her glasses in the process.

'What now?' Ben asked Fi and I suspected it was time for me to move away quietly and leave them to it.

'Get all the tools and things put away, so it looks like we've packed up for the night. Kill the lights, make like we're going to bed, then we slip away into the night. We can't afford to be caught with this stuff. We'd be done for theft, trespass and criminal damage for starters.'

Ben looked around and then began to pick up spades and mattocks and hoes which the diggers had dropped when Arthur had thrown them off the site that afternoon and began to stack them in a wheelbarrow.

'Can I come with you?' Ben asked and I began to roll a cigarette, pretending I wasn't there.

'Best not, love. Thanks, Shona, that's it.'

Shona had emptied her tub into Finnoula's collecting bin. Suddenly she leaned forward and embraced Fi.

'We've done it,' she said, her voice muffled because her head was in my sister's chest.

Finnoula eased her away.

'Time to get packed, Shona, so we can make a clean getaway.'

Shona glowed with pleasure.

'Anything you say, boss.'

282

'Er . . . this getaway,' I said, 'will be in what exactly?'

It stumped her hardly at all.

'We can use the van now it's back,' she said happily.

'You think Joss is going to drive you?'

'I can drive.'

'You've lost your licence,' said Ben, sensing a second chance.

'I've lost *one* of my licences,' she said slyly.

'So you're adding car theft to the Wanted poster?' I said, lighting my roll-up.

'Hmm,' she said, taking the cigarette from my lips and drawing on it.

'Tell you what,' I said in a rush of family loyalty. 'Take the van to whichever station you're going to, leave it in the car park and give me a ring tomorrow morning to tell me where it is. Amy and I will come and collect it. You have my number, don't you?'

'Brill, ace, banging plan,' she said, totally missing my final sarcasm. 'See, I knew something would turn up.'

'Something has.'

It was Jason who spoke. I hadn't paid him much mind since he'd emptied his box of Frankenstein seeds, only vaguely aware that he and Cornell had drifted off somewhere. I realized now that they had gone into the barn where the bulldozer was, as the light was on in there, and not The Stables.

Jason was carrying two rucksacks, one over each shoulder.

Cornell was standing beside him pointing something at us.

I thought back to when I'd seen Jason standing outside the barn early and the sound of an angle-grinder coming from inside.

Cornell had been busy in there, sawing the barrels off Arthur's shotgun.

Damn. I knew there was something I'd forgotten.

'We'll be taking that,' Jason said. 'Put the lid on, Fifi, we wouldn't want our samples to be contaminated, would we?'

'Go screw yourself, shitbag.'

I wondered just how much our father had spent on her education. It wasn't the language I was worried about, it was the why-you-should-be-frightened-of-guns lesson she seemed to have missed.

'Give it to him,' I said.

'What the hell do you think you're doing?' said Ben, stepping deliberately in front of Finnoula.

A noble gesture, but a dumb one. When faced with a sawn-off shotgun, don't bunch up. I took a step backwards.

'What's going on?'

'Hey?'

'Jason . . .?'

Finnoula's commando troop flocked around her. Idiots.

'You all shut the fuck up and move away from the box!' Cornell shouted, waving the shotgun in a small circle. It was more than I had heard him say all week.

'We just want the box,' said Jason, managing a nervous smile. 'Then we'll be out of here and you can do what you want.'

Finnoula pushed Ben out of her way so she could face them down.

'Just what the hell are you doing? Selling us out?'

Jason pretended to think about this.

'Yes, that's right. That's exactly what we're doing.'

'Why?' she asked stupidly, but it gave me the chance to step back another pace nearer to the tool shed, which was nice and solid and made of thick metal.

'For the money, Fifi, for the money.' Jason leered at her. I didn't think that was a good move on his part. 'Some of us have student loans to pay off, you know.'

'Some of us have drug dealers to pay off,' laughed Cornell.

'But you're with us, in our cell,' squeaked Jude.

'Fucking mercenaries,' spat Kali. Really spitting as she said it.

'That's the only true thing to come out of your ugly mouth all week,' said Jason, dodging out of her line of fire and moving towards the box.

Finnoula bent her knees and put her arms round the box. The others shuffled around her in support, making an easy target.

'For God's sake let him have it,' I said loudly.

Too loudly. Cornell swung the gun at me, tucking the butt into his right hip, his feet apart.

'Shut your fucking hole as well,' he snarled.

'Hey, I was trying to help you guys,' I said, keeping eye contact with him.

'Well, don't.'

'I told her to give the damned thing to you, stupid.'

'Don't call me stupid,' he shouted.

'Stay out of this, Fitzroy, it's our fight,' said Finnoula, her arms closing around the box. 'We're committed.'

'You're also unarmed and this low-life has a shotgun and he's unhinged enough to use it.'

'Shut up!'

At least it got Cornell looking at me again. I wanted that, I really did. Because behind him I could see – and he couldn't – that Amy was stepping out of the the Stables door and moving towards a wheelbarrow full of tools.

'Easy, guys,' I said, still holding Cornell's eyes, 'I'm on your side in this. That shit means nothing to me. Take it and go. Be rich, be happy.'

'We'll take the plans as well,' said Jason.

'What plans?'

'Now who's stupid?' Cornell laughed.

'The plans of the army garrison. I'm sure I can find a buyer for them.'

Cornell nudged his partner.

'Hell, we could even sell them back to the army!'

'I don't know where they are,' I said. I was being honest, but somehow I just knew they wouldn't believe me.

'Then you'd better remember, Mister Supervisor.'

Cornell levelled the gun at my stomach.

'You're not going to use that,' I said.

'You sure about that?' he grinned.

Amy brought the mattock up between his legs, the flat blade appearing at the crotch of his jeans like some bizarre metal codpiece. The shotgun slipped from his hands and his whole body, now seemingly devoid of air, began to deflate and fold in on itself in slow motion.

'Pretty sure,' I said.

Jason did a double take, not sure what to do, not sure what was happening, his hands still holding the straps of the rucksacks he carried on each shoulder.

Kali stepped up to the crumpled Cornell and swung a perfect right cross over him, smack into Jason's nose.

'Sisters! Respect!' yelled Finnoula.

What to do with a pair of traitors? Suggestions ranged from calling the police (dismissed as silly) to giving them a good kicking. While we were thinking it over, Kali actually did put the boot in a couple of times.

Jason moaned and rolled around on the ground clutching his nose, which was pumping blood. Cornell just lay there, eyes wide, mouth working like a goldfish but nothing coming out. He didn't feel a thing as Kali stomped him.

'That shotgun could have gone off, you know,' I said to Amy.

'You worry too much,' she said, turning to high-five Finnoula.

It was me who had to come up with a plan, of course, and it was me who had to reassure Arthur that everything was just fine and dandy when he appeared at the kitchen door saying, 'Is everything all right out here?'

I got Ben and Gregory to drag Cornell into the tool shed and told Jason to crawl in after him. Amy weighed the mattock in her hands and Kali took a step towards him and that seemed to convince him. When they were inside I locked the metal doors, leaving them in the pitch darkness.

'Now what, bro?' Finnoula said cockily. 'We leave them there while we disappear?'

'No, we find out who they're working for and how they planned to get away from here. They have no transport. Maybe somebody was coming to pick them up.'

'Good thinking, Batman. How do we get them to talk?'

'Easy.'

I took the mattock from Amy and swung it against the side of the tool shed. The metallic *clang* was loud enough to hurt the ears and we were on the outside. I was hoping that the reverberations inside were worse.

The diggers caught on quickly, each of them grabbing a mattock or a spade or using the handle of a hoe and joining in the impromptu rhythm session. I stood back from the fray, letting Kali and the boys enjoy themselves. Even Shona joined in.

'Where *are* the garrison plans, Fi?'

'Behind that horrible painting at the top of the stairs,' she shouted through cupped hands over the racket. 'Nobody ever looks at that.'

I let them play for five minutes, then called them off and opened the tool shed door. Jason was curled in the foetal position, his hands over his ears. His nose was a mess and still bleeding.

'Quiz time, Jason,' I said, then repeated it, shouting so he could hear. He looked as if he'd been in a blender. In a way, he had.

'Answer a few questions and I'll drive you out of here, understand?'

He nodded warily. Then he saw Kali standing at my shoulder and he nodded more enthusiastically. There was no point in asking Cornell anything but at least I saw his eyes move occasionally, so he was probably agreeing with what Jason told us.

When the two Dans, members of Finnoula's original cell recruited from among student archaeologists, had decided to leave Woolpack after their run-in with the local Young

Farmers' Club, the GGR corporation planted Jason and Cornell as a pair of ringers.

Double-ringers as it turned out, for they had been approached by Hans Jankel who had a nice little money-making scheme in which they could join. Let the GS commando steal the modified wheat and take the blame, then take it off them and sell it to an opposition multinational genetic research company. Finnoula's mob were hardly likely to go to the police, were they?

The garrison plans had been a bit of late improvisation – mostly Cornell's idea (and he was in no state to deny this), to boost their ill-gotten gains. They had no real plan as to how they would sell them or to whom, it just seemed too good an opportunity to pass up.

And for a getaway, Jankel would be waiting down the road for them. Waiting right now.

'Get them out of there, but keep an eye on them,' I said. 'If they move, hit 'em.'

Ben took a step forward, flexing his muscles.

'I was talking to Kali,' I said.

I gave Amy the keys to Armstrong and asked her to get him started.

'Where are you going?'

'Just got to get something from the kitchen.'

I almost tripped over the shotgun, still lying where Cornell had dropped it. None of the GS commandos had wanted to touch it.

I picked it up to take it back to Arthur but I couldn't resist breaking it open. Two brass-ends of cartridges peeped out at me.

I allowed myself a shudder.

They all gave me funny looks as I walked back from the kitchen carrying a plastic food box rattling with grain, but nobody said anything.

'I'll be back shortly,' I said to Finnoula. 'You can start packing.'

'You're giving them it?' Shona said, deadpan.

'As long as you have it, you can be nicked. And so can Arthur. Anybody got a problem with that?'

No one had.

'Right then. Get those two in the back of my cab.'

There was no shortage of volunteers for that.

'Do you want a hand with them?' Kali asked me.

'I reckon you've knocked the fight out of them.'

She almost smiled.

They all looked on gloomily as I got into Armstrong and pulled away, Jason and Cornell slumped across the back seat, their rucksacks thrown in on top of them, the plastic box of seeds balanced on Cornell's chest.

I couldn't see but I knew that of all of them, it was little Jude who would be smiling. In fact she would be beside herself because she had a secret I'd made her promise not to divulge until I'd gone.

But I had thought it only polite to apologize to her for stealing her tub of muesli from the fridge in the kitchen.

Chapter Fifteen

Dump Deposit

Jankel's Land Rover was about a mile down the road towards Hadleigh, just where Jason had said it would be, tucked into the hedgerow so as not to block the road, lights off.

I didn't worry about blocking the road. I pulled up alongside but slightly in front of the Defender and left the engine running as I got out and walked round to the nearside passenger door. I had already pulled Cornell out on to the road, dragged his rucksack on top of him and was heaving at Jason's arm, making him slide across the seat, before Jankel opened his door and showed himself.

'These are yours, I think,' I said. 'And these.'

I tossed him the box of muesli which in the moonlight through opaque plastic would have fooled any geneticist.

'What's the deal?' he asked, cool as you like.

Jason popped out of the door, clutching a bloody handkerchief to his nose. He took one step and tripped over Cornell, pitching forward and cracking his head on the Land Rover's bumper. He decided to stay lying down and concentrate on his groaning.

'Get rid of those two for a start, they've been trying to go freelance on you. Then get rid of yourself. Stay away from here and leave Arthur Swallow alone. The diggers will be gone by tomorrow.'

'They're not diggers,' he said, 'they are terrorists.'

'And you're a crook. But so am I, so you get what you

can for that box, like you planned, and I'll take a third. I think that's fair, don't you?'

He weighed up his options. It didn't take long.

'How will I get the money to you?'

'Send it cash, care of the pub, The Chequers. Just mark it "Angel". I'll tell them to expect a parcel. If nothing turns up within a month, I'm going to start sending nasty e-mails to GGR in Rome.'

He nodded twice and I slammed the back door and walked round to get back behind Armstrong's wheel.

If he actually did get anything for half a kilo of stale muesli then I would seriously fear for the future of genetic science, but I'd spend it.

It was gone eleven o'clock. Amy's idea of an expensive candlelit supper was a non-starter out here in the wilds of Suffolk. You can take the girl out of the West End, but you can't . . .

I would have settled for an all-night Greasy Spoon – there was bound to be one somewhere on the A12 – but at the moment, my stomach would have slit my throat for a Marmite sandwich. It had been a long day.

It wasn't over.

As I neared Woolpack House, a pair of headlights came down the road slowly from the direction of the village and turned into the driveway. I slowed and watched the beams bounce up and down as it headed straight for the house.

I hadn't seen the numberplate, but I had seen the car side on as it turned and I recognized the make and model instantly.

My stomach forgot it was empty and concentrated on producing acid.

Amy was going to get her red BMW back before I'd managed to tell her it had been stolen by her secret stalker. And I knew how much she hated surprises.

There was no way I could get to the house before the BMW

291

without Armstrong suddenly developing a hover capability, and turning up in the BMW's wake was not an attractive option as I had no idea what I would be barging in on. So as my conscience was (fairly) clear on the matter, I adopted the only decent and secure course of action open to me. I would park Armstrong just off the road by the drive entrance, then leg it over the gardens, using the long beds of rose bushes – the only bit of the garden which hadn't been terminated by archaeology – as cover, until I could spy out the situation.

After all, my stomach reasoned, Amy had had plenty of opportunities to tell me about her stalker. Maybe she had even suspected he was capable of burglary. That would fit in with her odd behaviour when we got back from Romanhoe and she wouldn't get out of the car, making me go in the house first. Typical. There could have been a homicidal maniac waiting inside. There could be one at Woolpack House right now.

And this was all because Amy hadn't been open and honest about things. All the secrets, all the deceptions, all the white lies – they're what will get you in the end. Arthur and his quest for Octavia's body, Finnoula and her gang posing as archaeologists, Jason and Cornell posing as members of Finnoula's commando cell, Jankel posing as a gamekeeper while he was busy poaching. Sebastian, the former supervisor, lying to the police in return for a home entertainment centre bigger than his home. Even Rupert Tyrell, posing as the concerned godson, was probably only wanting reassurance that the garrison plans hadn't fallen into enemy hands. And my mother – well, I just didn't know where to begin.

I was the only one who had been straight arrow all the way. Well, maybe Joss. I couldn't think of anything against her. And Dan the Man, although he might have been lying and secretly did respect older women. No, scrub that one.

I stayed to the left of the driveway, keeping low and running fast until I made the edge of the flanking rose bed. The bushes were thick and thorny and seven or eight feet high, which meant while no one up at the house could see me, I couldn't see the house.

I got down on my stomach and using elbows and toe-caps I crawled towards the drive and saw that the BMW had been parked head-on up against the front door, its headlights and interior light on, the driver's door open. The door to Woolpack House was open and I could see into the empty hall. From my angle of vision I could even make out the lower half of Octavia's portrait on the landing.

But that was all I could see, so I shuffled around and tried the other side of the rose bushes, which gave me a view of the left-hand side of the house and the silhouettes of the outbuildings which showed up against the outside lights on The Stables and The Studio. The place seemed deserted so I began to crawl down the length of the rose bed to get closer to the action.

I shouldn't have bothered because the action came to me.

Out of the shadows between The Studio and the Mobile Thrones block, somebody was moving. Moving towards me.

At first I thought it was somebody walking a dog because one indistinct shape turned into one and a half indistinct shapes, one about half the size of the other. I froze, realized how stupid I looked lying on the lawn like that, and so did an over-flamboyant commando roll side-ways into the rose bed, forgetting entirely that these roses must have been growing there long before anyone thought of genetic modification and they boasted a formidable array of spiky thorns.

By the time my eyes had stopped watering, the ghostlike figure coming out of the shadows had turned into a scene from *Night of the Living Dead*.

The initial figure now had a whole gaggle of zombies walking almost as if they had to keep a set distance behind him and they were all moving painfully slowly. They were talking, though all I could make out at first was a low collective muttering. But then, you don't expect sparkling chat from a plague of zombies.

I picked out Arthur's voice first.

'Now I am sure we can come to some mutual agreement here, before this situation gets totally out of hand . . .'

There were other voices raised in support of him – I made out Finnoula's for sure, Ben's and maybe Jude's – but I was hearing the noise not the words because the leading figure, the figure they were talking to, had come into focus.

It was a man and why he had appeared so odd when I had first seen him was because he was walking *backwards*, backing off towards the front of the house, and what I had thought was a dog walking at his side wasn't a dog at all, it was Amy. On her knees.

In fact she was stumbling, trying to keep her balance whilst crouched.

The reason she was in that position was that the man had all the hair at the back of her head bunched into his left hand and he was pulling her down and backwards. It was a grip which is not only painful, but remarkably incapacitating. She couldn't keep her feet under her, she couldn't stop moving and could only move in a crouched position. If he was strong enough, she couldn't even turn into him and try and resist. He seemed strong enough.

In fact he seemed quite happy with his slow, steady progress round the corner of the house. He wasn't worried about Amy's constant stream of invective as she used her hands to claw at his hold on her hair. Neither did he seem at all concerned about the pack of zombies coming out of the shadows at him, which seemed to consist of the entire crew. Arthur was there at the front and so was Finnoula and I spotted tall Gregory and the burly, rolling gait of Kali.

If it had been me, making Amy go somewhere she didn't want to would be a bad dream. Having Kali dogging my footsteps while I was trying to do it, would have been a nightmare.

But the shadowy man took it all in his stride. No doubt

his confidence was boosted by the fact that he held a large, shiny automatic pistol in his right hand and it certainly seemed to be doing the business keeping the angry mob at bay.

He was round the corner of the house now, crunching the gravel with each careful pace he took backwards. He was perhaps forty feet away from me.

I clearly saw Amy drop even further down on her haunches to try and loosen his grip, then turn and swing a fist at him. Before it could connect, he jerked her hair back, up and then down and she howled in pain, stumbled and landed on her knees. The man holding her didn't let up, he just kept pulling her back, her knees scraping along the gravel until she got her feet under her.

There was a collective groan of outrage from the following crowd who had also rounded the corner, still five yards away and not daring to get any closer.

'You scum!' I heard Kali yell.

'Let her go! You're hurting her!' A higher, female voice, Jude or Shona.

'Keep back!' the man shouted.

It was the first thing I had heard him say and it was only as he walked into the light from one of the windows that I saw him at all clearly. All that did was confirm that it was the guy I had seen lurking around Amy's office. It didn't seem to help. He still had Amy by the scruff of the neck and he had a gun.

I rolled from my right on to my left side to keep him in view, and almost yelled out in pain as all the keys in my cargo pocket jammed into my leg.

'What is it you want, my man?'

There was Arthur, fearless and right at the front. The nearest one to the gun.

'I want her, and I'm taking her.'

His voice had a faint northern twang and it was steady and businesslike. I wasn't sure that was a good sign, but at least he hadn't shot anyone yet.

'I don't think she wants to go with you, dear boy.'

I don't know about the psycho with the gun, but I think I could have shot Arthur for that fatuous observation.

'Just keep your distance and nobody will get hurt,' the psycho was saying. 'If anybody follows us, somebody will, that's a given.'

He was level with the top edge of the rose bed now and out of my line of vision. Arthur and the rest of the gang were level with me but none of them had so much as glanced down the garden. It was time I did something. It was getting quite uncomfortable lying there.

I began to roll to my left, away from the rose bed, away from Amy and her captor and their audience, away from the house.

After half a dozen revolutions I stopped to check my bearings and I distinctly heard someone say 'Angel'. I froze and held my breath.

It seemed as if the crowd in front of the house were doing the same.

'I said which one of you is Angel?'

It was the psycho with the gun, his voice loud and clear now I was away from the muffling effect of the rose bushes.

'I'm Angel,' came the answer.

It was Finnoula.

I couldn't resist waiting to hear if they would all step forward one after the other shouting 'I'm Angel' and 'No, I'm Angel', but they didn't.

'Don't take the piss! Where is he?'

'He's not here!' Amy screamed.

I couldn't see her but it was certainly her and her cry was followed by an audible dull *thwack* and then another scream and another from one of the other females and then a groan from the collective mass.

I started rolling again until I was in line with the back of The Studio. Without pausing to worry about being seen, I got to my feet and ran for it, staying as low as I could. I was banking on Arthur and Finnoula and company blocking me until I was round the side of the house and once I was running between Armstrong and the Iceni Rescue van, I knew I had made it.

If I had a plan at all it was based on a simple sort of logic.

When is the only sensible time to go up a man with an automatic pistol? When you're inside a tank.

And I had the keys to a tank in my trouser pocket.

They heard me coming, they must have. They could probably hear me in Essex. yet they didn't seem to have moved.

As I rounded the corner and the 'dozer's tracks began to grind up the gravel drive, I switched the headlights on and caught them all like rabbits. I could clearly see Ben staring open-mouthed, Rory grabbing for Jude's hand, Gregory grinning inanely, finding it amusing, and Kali, her fists clenched, mouthing 'What the fuck . . .?'

I was big, metal, painted bright yellow and weighed eighteen tons and I was moving straight towards them making one hell of a noise. Why didn't they move?

They did, suddenly and all at once but in different directions, like a school of fish disturbed by a shark.

I saw Finnoula grab Arthur and press him against the wall of the house. Ben did the same. Rory dragged Jude towards the bulldozer and to my left, the others scattered over the lawn.

Which left the psycho with the gun still dragging the stumbling Amy backwards. I could see blood pouring from her knees and realized that for the first time I could see her tormentor's face.

Except I couldn't, because his face was shrouded by his upraised arm as he sighted along the barrel of the pistol.

I saw the flash but heard nothing. The hole in the top left of the cab's glass windscreen seemed to have appeared there by magic.

I slid out of the driver's seat into a crouch on the floor of the cab, opening the door so that I could jump if I had to, and worked the right-hand joystick which made the blade of the 'dozer rise up, forming an armoured shield.

I heard two loud clangs as bullets bounced off the blade. With the lights on I would be disorientating him and the blade cut down the amount of target he had to aim at. The fact that I was bearing down on him at fifteen miles an hour might also have put him off a bit.

I straightened up and risked a look over the blade. He didn't shoot me because he was trying to get to the BMW and if he hadn't been pulling Amy with him he would have made it and got away before my home-made Panzer could have covered the distance.

Amy was brilliant. She sat down. Just let her legs go and dropped on her dainty arse. Psycho had two options: drag her to the car or leave her.

He left her, taking a parting swipe at her with the barrel of the automatic which she managed to deflect from her head to her shoulder by rolling sideways. Then the gun-man was aiming back up at me and there was another flash but no sound and then he ran frighteningly fast towards the BMW, leaping on to the bonnet and over the other side and diving in through the open driver's door.

I hit the decelerator pedal and held open the cab door to yell at Amy to get out of the way. She couldn't possibly have heard me but she had worked that one out for herself and was rolling clear.

The BMW, dammit, started first time and if he had just stuck it in reverse and punched it he could have shot down the drive and outpaced me. But he didn't. Having made the fatal mistake of not parking facing his quickest exit, he decided to reverse and turn.

I pulled on the joystick, took my foot off the decelerator and swung the 'dozer thirty degrees to the right and lowered the blade. The BMW reversed, spewing gravel up against the side of the cab I was so close now. Then he dropped it into first gear and the wheels spun and got traction and he swung the wheel in a right turn towards the drive.

In the time it took him to reverse I had cut across the

rose bed and had passed him on the diagonal, ripped-up bushes piling over the blade and on to the engine. I made the driveway just as he did.

A few more seconds either way and he would have beaten me or had time to brake but as it was he had to swerve: I wasn't going to. And the only way he could go was to his left into the other large rose bed, the mirror image of the one I had just managed to trash.

The rose thicket acted as a crash barrier and the rear end of the BMW bounced off it, the car losing that vital bit of grip which slowed it just enough for the blade of the 'dozer to catch it almost perfectly square on. In the cab I didn't feel a thing and from that split second onwards it was really just a question of keeping going until I got bored.

The lip of the bulldozer blade lifted the offside of the BMW clear off the ground and probably crushed the driver's side in the process. With two wheels spinning against nothing, it was only going one way – sideways – as I ploughed it across the rose bed and it gradually rose up until it was on its side as if the driver had attempted to do a wheelie that had never really been on the cards.

I kept pushing it, knowing that the driver was going nowhere. His door was buckled into the frame and his passenger door was pressed into the Suffolk soil. When I saw that the engine had given out, I pumped the pedal and slowed down, then clicked the joystick button for reverse and eased back a yard or two.

The BMW rocked gently on its side, whole rose bushes piled up against it as if it was some sort of bizarre garden feature which the roses had been trained over. There was also a fair amount of topsoil swept up against it. In fact the reason the engine had cut out was probably that the exhaust was blocked.

I turned off the 'dozer's engine and for the first time for ages I could hear something other than the throb-throb of a diesel thump. I leaned out of the cab door and looked back towards the house. There was a ghastly dark road-way where the bulldozer had ploughed a diagonal stripe from one rose bed to the other. Ah well, I thought to myself, Arthur would have got round to it sooner or later.

Jumping down from the cab I landed unsteadily as a touch of shock began to set in. The diggers had it worse. They were all petrified back at the house, not really believing what I had done to a car worth all their salaries combined for about six months. I wondered if they knew it was Amy's and whether that would make them feel any better.

When they saw me they started to bolt forward, breaking out of their reverie, but I held up a hand, signalling them to stay back, and pointed to the BMW on its side, one wheel spinning quietly, indicating that I wanted to check it out.

'Wait!' a voice croaked.

It was Amy, limping down the dirt highway I had just created, both hands clutching her left knee. Blood was seeping through her fingers and she was liberally smeared with dirt all over.

'I need to see as well,' she said.

I pulled her right arm round my neck to support her, my fingers slipping on hers which were wet with blood. I put my left arm around her waist and as she leaned into me I could see large dark swellings on her cheekbone and right temple.

'Are you sure about this?' I said softly and she nodded and began to shuffle forward.

I helped her as far as the blade of the bulldozer and made her lean on it as I approached the upended front of the BMW, hands on the radiator grille, and poked my head round to look along the bonnet and in through the now vertical windscreen.

There was no sign of the driver and I took another two cautious steps in order to get a better view of the car's interior, pulling away large branches of rose bush, their thorns screeching down the paintwork like chalk on a blackboard. If the driver had suddenly appeared sitting bolt upright, like they do in horror films, I was ready to dive to the side. I wasn't sure Amy had paid the extra for a bullet-proof windscreen and our psycho friend still had a gun in there with him. He might not be able to get out, but a bullet could.

I actually had to get close enough to wipe dirt off the windscreen with the sleeve of my shirt before I could see inside. The driver was scrunched up head first against the passenger door, his feet still in the well of the driver's seat. I couldn't see his head but I could make out a faint movement around the torso which suggested he was still breathing. That was good enough for me.

'He's alive,' I told Amy, waving at the others again to stay back, 'but unconscious and upside down. I'm pretty sure he can't get out. How airtight is a BMW?'

She didn't even smile, just hooked her arm around my neck again and I helped her limp over to the car so she could peer in and see for herself. She didn't have to see who it was, just make sure he was out of it.

'So that's Keith Flowers?' I said.

I don't know what reaction I had expected but I got none at all. Just silence. In fact the whole place had gone quiet, just the gentle *tick-tick* as the one wheel left spinning began to slow down.

'Amy,' I said as gently as I could, 'who the fuck is Keith Flowers?'

She removed her hand from her knee and wiped off muck and blood on the hip of her shorts.

'My husband,' she said casually as she was doing it.

There was a rustling in the rose bushes snarled up against the rear of the BMW, but Amy didn't notice it, waiting for me to speak.

When I did, I said:

'Come out, Finnoula.'

My sister stepped nonchalantly out from behind the boot of the car, hands in the pockets of her jeans.

'Bad time?' she asked.

We ignored her and she moved uneasily from one foot to the other then sniffed the air loudly.

'I think the fuel tank's ruptured. That's petrol I can smell,' she said.

Finnoula was right. The smell of petrol vapour was quite definite and getting stronger.

'My *ex*-husband,' said Amy suddenly, nodding to herself like it was a fact she had suddenly remembered and was glad she had.

Then she sniffed the air herself and seemed to come to a decision.

'Anybody got a cigarette?' she asked.

They all rushed to help us as we walked back towards the house, Amy hopping along with one arm round my neck, the other round Finnoula's.

'What . . . ?'

'Is he . . .?'

'Who is he?'

I waved away all questions until Arthur pushed his way – ever so politely – to the front of the queue.

'Wonderful tactical improvisation there, my dear boy. Must tell Rupert about this. You could teach him a trick or two. Now what can I do to help?'

'Got a first aid kit?'

'State of the art, de luxe version, top model,' he said. 'I *think* it's in the kitchen.'

'If you wouldn't mind getting it – and a pair of tweezers.'

I was thinking of the gravel embedded in Amy's knee.

'Don't know about that, old boy. Not much call . . .'

'I've got some,' Joss volunteered. 'And I'll get the first aid kit.'

'Is there anything else I can do?'

'Yes, there is, Arthur,' I said with as much gravitas as I could muster given the weight of Amy leaning on me. 'I want you to call everybody together in the library so we can finally solve this case.'

That shut them up. Amy and Finnoula turned their heads towards me.

'What?' they both said at once.

'I've always wanted to say that,' I said.

Amy was the only one not standing – sitting on one chair with her feet up on another while Joss splashed antiseptic and dabbed at her knees with a lint pad before going to work with the tweezers. Jude had thoughfully fetched a packet of frozen peas to hold against what was developing into a black eye. It was, I supposed, the vegetarian equivalent of slapping a raw steak on it.

It hadn't been a clever idea to get everyone into the library. There was hardly room to move with us all in there and certainly not enough room for me to stride about the place doing my Great Detective bit. So I climbed on to the one remaining chair to address the masses.

'Ladies and gentlemen, I have called you all together in order to get to the truth of tonight's baffling and potentially –'

'Get on with it,' yelled Finnoula.

At least I had their attention.

'In a few minutes I'm going to ask Arthur to call the police and an ambulance for our friend out there in the garden. If any of you are wondering, he's not dead, just shaken up a bit. Actually, shaken up quite a lot.'

'That might not be a good idea, Fitzroy,' said Arthur seriously. 'I have had several altercations with the local constabulary and I suspect they have me on their list of crank callers. It might be some time before I can persuade them to turn out.'

'I'm relying on that,' I said. 'Now for your information, the man outside is called Keith Flowers. He's Amy's ex-husband and as you will have gathered, he had a few personal issues with her which need not go into here. There will be a time and a place for that, I'm sure.' But Amy avoided my pointed glance in her direction. 'You've all seen that the man is obviously unstable, and he's just come out of prison.'

'What for?' Trust Kali to be the only one interested.

'I don't know but I'm sure he was guilty,' I said.

'Aggravated assault,' said Amy quietly.

'There you are then . . .'

'Robbery with violence,' she added.

'And robbery,' I said.

'Threat to kill . . . and fraud,' she continued.

'Bloody hell,' somebody said. They were all interested now, staring transfixed at Amy, their mouths open like goldfish.

Before she could go on, I said:

'So I take it Keith Flowers doesn't get anyone's sympathy vote. Good, because we're going to turn him in and I suspect that tonight's little escapade will not go down terribly well with his probation officer and he'll be back in the jug again pretty quick.

'We just need a few people to tell the cops the truth, and by that, of course, I mean the truth I'm going to tell them. I take it there are some of you who would probably prefer not to speak to the police at all?'

'You got that right, bro,' said Finnoula.

'Thought as much. As I don't think it will matter a toss whether Keith Flowers threatened five of us or ten of us, anyone who has an elsewhere to go to should go now. Finnoula, you drive and do as we planned. Leave the van somewhere and I'll pick it up.'

'That's a banging plan, brother o'mine. I'm outa here. Who's with me?'

'It might be easier to sort out who doesn't mind staying,' I said.

'Well, I'm your star witness,' Arthur said with a smile. 'I used to be a magistrate. I couldn't possibly tell an untruth. I'm staying at your side, Fitzroy.'

'You live here, Arthur,' I pointed out. 'Who else?'

Ben raised a hand, studiously looking anywhere but at Finnoula.

'I'll hang about.'

Joss broke off from wrapping a bandage around Amy's leg.

'I'll stay, if I've still got a job here.'

'Of course you have,' said Arthur. 'But I've a feeling we might have to recruit a few more diggers.'

'I might have a few contacts to help you there,' I said. 'Anyone else?'

There was a shuffling of feet and a roomful of people studying the floorboards all of a sudden.

'Very well, five will have to do. Just as well ex-magistrates count double.' They laughed at that, mostly in relief. 'The rest of you, get out of here quick.'

'That was really cool, man . . .'

'Fair play to you, Angel.'

'Top man.'

'Excellent result all round . . .'

They all wanted to punch me lightly on the shoulder or hug me, in some cases both.

I couldn't stop one hug – Kali's – which took the breath out of me.

'The owner of that car's going to fucking kill you,' she said as she released me.

'Don't I know it,' I said.

'How about a round of applause to show –' Jude started.

'No, forget that, you've got to go,' I shouted over the hubbub, climbing back up on to my chair. 'There is one thing I'd like to know, though, sort of a survey. We'll do it on a show of hands, but you've got to tell the truth.

'Which of you are here *primarily* for the archaeology? Now be honest.'

Joss put her hand up and so did Arthur, then he caught my glance and slowly lowered it.

'OK. Now which of you are here *primarily* because of Genetix Snowball? Be honest.'

Hands up from Finnoula, Jude, Rory, Shona, Kali and Gregory.

'Fair enough.'

I caught Finnoula's eye and held it. She'd got off very lightly so far.

'And who was here primarily to shag my sister?'

Everyone looked at Ben who put his hand in the air again, this time blushing furiously.

It took almost half a minute before they realized that Shona's hand had gone up too.

Chapter Sixteen

Post-ex

Arthur rang for the emergency services – all of them, or as many as they could spare – as the unit's Transit van disappeared down the driveway. Despite his misgivings, the police did arrive first and impressively quickly but the two uniformed constables didn't actually do anything except take off their caps and scratch their heads at the sight of an expensive new car on its side, half buried in a ploughed-up rose bed by moonlight.

Two paramedics in an ambulance then appeared, again with commendable promptitude as Arthur put it. I suspected they had some Nazi hospital manager making them work to unrealistic target response times, so they were used to driving at illegal speeds.

They certainly seemed to know what they were doing and after a quick assessment of the situation decided they could get Keith Flowers out of the BMW without troubling the fire brigade, who were on their way. Then they noticed the pungent smell of petrol and decided not to call off the en route fire engine just in case.

One of the medics, the woman, asked if we had moved the still inert form of Keith Flowers and I was tempted to say not since I hit him with a bulldozer but I kept quiet and nobody pointed out that we hadn't been near him at all for over half an hour. The paramedic said that was probably best as we might have damaged something permanently. If Amy had had her way we'd have gone for an impromptu cremation, let alone permanent damage.

From the back of the ambulance they produced a tungsten-tipped hammer shaped rather like a mountaineer's ice-pick. You see them on trains, in locked glass-fronted boxes with a notice saying that in the event of an accident you can use it to smash the carriage window. (What they don't do is give you a hammer to smash the glass to get at the hammer.) Before one of them could swing it at the BMW's windscreen I reminded them that there was a gun inside the car.

The two policemen took an automatic step backwards. The paramedics just shrugged their shoulders and said they'd had worse things than guns pointed at them on a Saturday night down at Ipswich docks when the pubs turned out.

When they pulled Keith Flowers out through where the windscreen used to be, he was still alive and apart from being unconscious, cut about the face and maybe having a broken wrist, remarkably unscathed.

One of the coppers crawled into the car and retrieved a shiny automatic from the floor well on the passenger side, using a pencil through the trigger guard to fish it out, and he landed it by dropping it into a plastic evidence bag.

A fire engine arrived and two firemen sprayed foam over the ground around the BMW just in case the petrol caught before it evaporated. The ambulance left with one of the uniformed cops inside after we pointed out that the victim of this bizarre midnight gardening accident was a known villain only one month out of a seven-year stay at the pleasure of Her Majesty.

Then two detectives turned up in an unmarked car and decided to hold off calling out the scene of crime team until the morning, but insisted on taking statements. We did that in the kitchen while I made Marmite sandwiches for everyone and even Amy agreed they were the finest she had ever tasted.

The first fingertips of dawn were in the sky when we were allowed to go to bed.

Amy was asleep almost as soon as I zipped her into her

sleeping bag. As I turned the light out I noticed she was smiling.

'The police have been and gone. Said you could remove the vehicles, so they did. Looks like there was a bit of a goings-on here last night.'

'You could be right there, Mrs Hawksbee,' I said.

I was nursing my third mug of coffee, having eaten everything I could find in the kitchen, and wandering around the garden.

It was nearly noon and I was the only one up and about, apart from Mrs Hawksbee, who was standing in the doorway of Woolpack House shouting at my back as I walked down the track I had created with the bulldozer. I had decided to let Arthur tell her as much as she needed to know, so when she had come sniffing round the kitchen dropping hints about no diggers on site and no Dan the Man and how unlike Arthur it was to sleep in this late, I had picked up my mug and gone for a stroll. If nothing else, moving the bulldozer would keep me out of her way for a while.

'And whoever tore up them roses ought to be ashamed of themselves,' she yelled after me. 'That's criminal that is. Them roses have been growing there for sixty years near as anything. It was my father planted those beds for Mr Gerald, just after the war and they've been there ever since.'

The scene of crime people – the SOCOs – had pulled most of the foliage off the BMW and I could see where they had sprinkled fingerprint powder over the steering wheel and dashboard. Other than that they didn't seem to have done much, but why should they? There was a car on its side with a bulldozer-blade shaped dent running along most of its bodywork. A few yards away, there was a bulldozer. Fairly elementary, I would have thought.

As I walked back towards the house between the caterpillar track marks, I wondered whether now was a good time to report the BMW stolen to West Hampstead police station. I supposed I ought to otherwise the insurance company might play hard to get, though this particular insurance claim was going to be a humdinger however we phrased it.

That was, honestly, all that was on my mind. It was a beautiful morning, shaping up to be the first really hot day of the year and I had caffeine zinging around my system. I felt good enough to roll the first cigarette of the day.

I stopped walking, got out a paper and my tobacco, put my head down and concentrated.

And that was when I saw it.

Or rather – *her*.

Joss was coming out of the Mobile Thrones block wearing a very long and very damp T-shirt with a picture of a wolf howling at the moon and a towel round her wet hair, though I hardly had time to notice.

I told her to get Arthur up and out on to the front lawn and to make sure Mrs Hawksbee was in the kitchen making something. And to bring a trowel.

Ben was almost dressed when I stormed into his room. I told him to find a tarpaulin or a sheet or something and to bring a trowel pronto. Then I grabbed my trusty trowel and the metal detector and left Amy snoring from the depths of her sleeping bag.

I couldn't claim to have stripped the topsoil deliberately like that, after all, I was intent on ramming a BMW when I had done it and the stripping was patchy to say the least and further torn up and confused by the roots of the rose bushes. But by accident I had uncovered – in fact I had driven right over – a patch of redeposited natural which looked suspiciously like a grave cut.

All I had to say to Ben was: 'What do you think?'

'It could be a grave,' he said, dropping to his knees and setting to with his trowel to clear away loose topsoil, roots and twigs in an attempt to define the edges.

I switched on the detector, dispensing with the headphones and relying on the speaker, and swept the area.

I got a single, strong, continuous signal about two feet from where Ben was cleaning. He looked up in surprise.

'That's the skull end,' I said.

Most people would have said, 'How on earth do you know?' or 'Pull the other one,' but Ben, being a real archaeologist, looked up to get his bearings and decide which way was north.

'It's roughly east-west then, so . . . Christian? Medieval?'

'More recent than that,' I said, starting to trowel carefully at the spot where the detector had bleeped.

Joss broke into a sprint over the last few yards, once she had realized what we were doing, drawing her trowel like a pistol. She said nothing, just went into a crouch and began to scratch the earth.

Arthur followed at a brisk walk, still buttoning his shirt cuffs. When he was standing over us he said:

'Here? In the rose bed?'

'Who had them planted, Arthur?' I said, not looking up, concentrating on what I was doing.

'Of course,' he said with a sigh. 'I've been walking past here for fifty-five years wondering when these bloody roses would die. Didn't realize they lived so long.'

He came and stood over me.

'What do you intend . . . what are . . .?'

'I'm just making sure,' I said, 'and then it's up to you.'

'You're not going to *disturb* her, are you?'

'As little as possible.'

He was silent for a while, then he leaned over so he could whisper.

'The body . . . will it be . . . I mean will you still be able to see . . .?'

'It will be a skeleton, Arthur. After all this time, it will be just bones.'

I think he was relieved.

Twice more I checked the signal on the detector and

continued to dig gently, just a small patch no more than four inches square. If Ben and Joss were wondering what the hell I was doing, they didn't say anything.

After five minutes or perhaps an hour, I really didn't notice, I found what I was looking for and all three of them sensed it and gathered round me.

Very gently, using the point of the trowel, I uncovered a short length of fine metal chain. I hooked the trowel point under it and carefully levered it up. A longer length of chain appeared and I raised the trowel until it was clear of the earth. It wouldn't come any more than about six inches, still anchored to something which I wasn't ready to disturb.

I took the chain between forefinger and thumb and held it taut, then followed it with the trowel in an arc back to the soil. The trowel hit something small but solid and I inserted the point and prised it up as carefully as a stamp collector steaming off a Penny Black.

It was metal, two inches long and a fraction over an inch wide and it was attached to the chain. It was also covered in dirt.

I used my thumb to try and clean it and instantly felt the raised lettering which had been die-punched from the back.

It was an American army dog-tag and I knew whose name would be on it.

I drove into Hadleigh that afternoon, found a supermarket and bought enough food to keep a small army going for a couple of days.

We had considered long and hard what to do about Octavia's grave. In more ways than one we had only scratched the surface, but the consensus – once we had told Joss and Ben the background – was that we would move her after dark. If the police came back to check a statement or anything, it would look a bit suspicious if we were out there digging. Putting a tarpaulin over the site would only draw attention to it as well. Even Mrs

Hawksbee might notice that. So I reversed the bulldozer – carefully – back on its tracks until it straddled what we had identified as the grave cut.

Amy insisted on getting up and Joss changed the bandage on her knee. She then spent an hour in front of a mirror with her make-up kit and suddenly she didn't have a black eye any more.

Mrs Hawksbee was avoided, misled and distracted until it was time for her to leave. I wasn't sure what she had done all day except make us a casserole for the evening. I drove her home to the village just to make sure she was off the premises and when I got back it was to find the casserole pot outside the kitchen door and Amy and Joss making toast to go with pâté and pressing crushed peppercorns and garlic into large T-bone steaks. It was something I thought I would never see. An archaeological site with no vegetarians. The carnivores had won.

I had bought wine as well but no one was in a mood to drink. We were, after all, planning on going grave-robbing later.

'I wonder if Oscar Rivero is still alive,' said Amy.

We had just demolished two cheesecakes between the five of us, sitting round the kitchen table. Ben and Joss were getting on very well together. So it was true: absence does make the heart grow fonder – and forgetful.

'Do you know,' said Arthur thoughtfully, 'I never met the man. Never will, I suppose, but I think I would have liked to. I suppose a psychologist would say I was trying to *be* him, buying a Jeep like he had. At my age, too!'

'Was that why you bought it?' Joss asked him.

'Good God no. Always wanted one of my own ever since I saw one during the war. Never had a train set, you see and I think a man's entitled to one toy.'

'As long as it's mechanical,' said Amy.

We all laughed at that. Some of us more nervously than others.

'There must be a way of finding out if he's still alive,' said Ben. 'The Americans are very good about that sort of thing. They look after their soldiers.'

'There's bound to be a website,' I said. 'There is for everything else.'

'Mind if I look?' Amy asked.

'Feel free,' said Arthur.

When Amy had limped upstairs to the computer, Arthur said:

'What are we to do about the digging? We have no diggers.'

Then he made a fist and lightly punched himself on the side of the head.

'What am I saying? The Woolpack House site is a joke. Iceni Rescue Archaeology – and yes, I will change the name now you've mentioned it, Fitzroy – is a joke. Who am I kidding? There's nothing here.'

'Yes there is,' said Joss, reaching out and taking his hand.

'You've got medieval pits and ditches and a skelly . . .' said Ben, then went on rapidly: '. . .which is probably Saxon. It might not be late Iron Age Iceni but it's stuff. You've got *stuff*.'

'That's a technical term, by the way,' I said and it got smiles all round.

'But I can't expect Fitzroy and Amy to hang around here and I have to say I am now slightly wary of hiring diggers I don't know.'

'Let me make a couple of calls,' I said, rolling a cigarette, 'try a few names from when I was on the circuit. See if anyone is free.'

'I'd be grateful, Fitzroy. I know I can trust your judgement.'

That was a relief. He'd already forgotten my sister's little commando unit and the fact that I'd brought a psycho gunman to his doorstep.

Amy reappeared in the kitchen doorway.

'There is a website,' she said. 'It's NARA – their National Archives and Records Administration. It can tell you if your great-grandfather fought in the Civil War but it gets complicated for World War II. Bottom line is you have to write – write, they won't take e-mails – to the Military

Personnel Records branch in St Louis. They warn you it could take ages unless it's something to do with a legal claim or a pension, something like that.'

'Well, thank you for looking, my dear, it was kind of you,' said Arthur.

I put my almost perfect roll-up (I was getting good at them) in my mouth and fired up my Zippo. Clicking the lid shut I continued to stare at the lighter and tried to remember where I had put a certain beer mat.

'I might know a quicker way,' I said.

Sergeant Virginia Richmond, USMC – and it really was her name – said that sort of information was probably classified, finding it was a waste of military resources and why didn't I go through the Information Officer at the Embassy? Because he doesn't drink in The Guinea, I said.

She called me back three hours later.

Oscar B. Rivero had won several medals in the Battle of the Bulge in late 1944, taken a battlefield commission and gone on to win even more medals in Korea. He had married twice, had a total of seven children and twelve grandchildren. He had been arrested for possession of cannabis at the age of sixty-one and for being drunk and disorderly at a veterans' reunion at the age of sixty-eight. He was alive, lived in Atlantic City and on his tax returns gave his occupation as 'Professional Gambler'.

My kinda guy.

We did what we had to for Octavia – and Arthur – when it was dark, but with as much care and dignity as we could.

Amy helped, even though kneeling on one of the 'prayer mats' was painful for her, and we gently packed what we could find into an old-fashioned travelling trunk Arthur had lined with a clean sheet.

Joss and Ben would know as well as I did that we might

not have got all of her, working by Armstrong's headlights as we were, but we did our best. None of us mentioned the fact there were no traces of clothing or any material around the skeleton. The only thing she had worn when Gerald buried her was Oscar's dog tag.

Arthur's plan was to wait until the gardens had been cleared and replanted and then he would find 'a spot for her' privately and with due dignity. Until then he would keep her safe somewhere and none of us argued with him.

Of course he could have reported the find, gone through the motions and Octavia would have been reinterred with official ceremony. But then Arthur would have had to explain things he wanted buried deeper than her.

I had insisted on lifting the skull as delicately as I could and placing it in the trunk.

I didn't want anyone else to see the small hole in the centre of the back of it. Nor did I want anyone to feel or hear the small piece of lead rattling inside it.

Later – much later – I looked up the fact that the Webley & Scott Mark VI service revolver fired a .455 calibre bullet.

Such a small, insignificant piece of lead in the scale of things.

Amy and I were packed and ready to leave. We had slept late again and had both had two showers to clean off the dirt of the previous night's work.

Arthur had treated us to lunch at The Chequers where we had said goodbye to Ray and Stephen (with promises to visit them again or else – or else they would visit us). Ben and Joss had remained on site, keen to 're-evaluate' the archaeology. I thought this could be the start of a beautiful friendship, but Amy said I watched too many old movies.

I had Armstrong at the front of Woolpack House and we were saying our final goodbyes when we heard the deep-throated roar of a motorbike turning into the drive.

Actually it was a bike and side-car, the bike an old Norton in immaculate condition. The rider of the bike, in leathers and a black visored helmet, and his passenger in the side-car, who was wearing a leather flying helmet and World War I if not II airman's goggles, both stared at the BMW still lying on its side as they passed it.

Then the bike combo was throttling back and pulling up on the gravel next to Armstrong.

The rider killed the engine and unstraddled himself, flipping up his visor and unzipping his leather jacket and taking it off to reveal a torn black T-shirt and incredibly muscular arms covered in tattoos of Native American chiefs. He had a Cavalier's beard and moustache and an earring from which dangled a black feather. His passenger stood up in the side-car and peeled off an ankle-length leather coat and then his helmet and goggles to reveal a completely bald head. He had a barrel chest and no neck and was built like a bullet.

The bald one flung his arms up in the air and yelled:

'Angel – you rang – we answered the call.'

I think at that point Arthur was trying to remember where his shotgun was.

The rider walked up to us, stiff-legged, rolling a cigarette in one hand.

'Yo, Angel,' he said casually. 'Where's this dig then?'

'Arthur,' I said, 'meet Richard and Tony. The two best diggers in the country. Taught me everything I know. Richard is structures, pottery, cremations and skellies. Tony is the best ditch man there is, bar none. Give him a mattock and point him in the right direction, then stand back. They'll do you proud. Trust me.'

'If you say so, Fitzroy,' he said, only half convinced.

'*Fitzroy*?' shrieked Tony, still standing in the side-car. 'Gawd, that's a *wanker's* name, innit?'

'Forgive my friend,' Richard said, bowing slightly to Amy. 'He has this problem: he's an idiot and not used to being in the company of ladies.'

'He's not in the company of one as far as I can see,' said Amy with a grin.

Richard did a double take.

'Is this Amy?' he asked me.

'That's Amy,' I said.

He elbowed me in the ribs and it hurt.

'Fair play, Angel, fair play.'

We were on the A12 heading south towards London and home.

From the back of Armstrong, Amy spoke for the first time in twenty miles.

'Go on, then.'

'Go on what?' I said over my shoulder through the partition.

'Say it.'

'Say what?'

'What you've been dying to say for the last two days.'

'Don't know what you mean.'

'Yes you do.'

I left it a few more minutes.

'Go on, you know you want to,' she said.

I stayed silent.

'You'll feel better once you've said it.'

I glanced in the rear-view mirror, then the wing mirrors, just to check there was nothing too close to cause an accident if I swerved.

'*I didn't know you had a husband!*' I yelled as loud as I could.

Boy, did that feel good.

Chapter Headings

1. Base Line – the line from which all recording measurements are taken, the base from which everything else is judged to scale on a dig.
2. Definition of Edges – the clarity of the edge of a cut or layer within a feature to determine whether a man-made feature or a natural condition and therefore a dubious judgement call.
3. Primary Fill – the first, usually naturally laid-down, deposit in a feature.
4. Surveying – the detailed assessment of a site or situation leading to a plan of activity.
5. Diggers – a.k.a. site assistants, excavators, field archaeologists, contract archaeologists, trowel fodder, grunts, proles, arkies, hobbits, gnome people, Time Teamers, students, etc. Those who nobly shift the dirt.
6. Field Walking – the preamble to many excavations; walking over and observing closely any physical evidence turned up naturally by man or weather.
7. Trial Trenching – the opening of initial exploratory trenches to determine whether further investigation is required.
8. Bench Mark – the establishment of a fixed level against which all other highs and lows are measured.
9. Machine Watching – following the progress of mechanical diggers stripping back topsoil to uncover hidden features.
10. Grave Fill – the material which goes to make up the contents of a grave other than a body.
11. Worm Action – the action of worms.

12. Cut – where man (or animal or plant) has gone deep enough to disturb the natural sub-soil.
13. Skelly – invariably used to mean a human, articulated skeleton where the body was buried before the flesh had decomposed.
14. Root Disturbance – the action of plant life intent on confusing the archaeological profile.
15. Dump Deposit – a deposit or fill clearly and deliberately placed in a cut by man.
16. Post-ex – the analysis of all the archaeological evidence found on a site after excavation is complete with a view to writing a report sometime in the following ten years.